Firedancer

Masters of the Elements
Book One

I0617820

S. A. Bolich

Also from B Cubed Press

Alternative Truths

More Alternative Truths: Tales From the Resistance

After the Orange: Ruin and Recovery

Alternative Theologies: Parables for a Modern World Alternative Truths III: Endgame,

Digging Up My Bones,

by Gwyndyn T. Alexander

Coming Soon

Alternative Apocalypse

Tales of The Space Force

Alternative Bedtime Stories for Progressive Parents

Windrider, Book Two of The Masters of the Elements

By S. A. Bolich

Firedancer

Masters of the Elements: Book One

Cover Design
Sara Codair

Published by

B Cubed Press
Kiona, WA

B-Cubed Press
Benton City, WA
© 2011 by S. A. Bolich.
© 2018 by B Cubed Press.
All rights reserved.
Published by B-Cubed Press
Benton City, WA
www.bcubedpress.com
Editor: Phyllis Irene Radford.
Cover art: Sara Codair
Printed in the United States of America
Print 13: 978-0-9989634-7-1
E Book 978-1-949476-02-6

Table of Contents

One
The Ancient

This fire was malicious.

Jetta felt it the instant she stepped through the door of the flaming houseplace she had once known so well. Heat blasted the naked skin of her arms and legs; smoke stung her nose. Startled, she took a step sideways, and shied again from hot grit crunching under her bare feet. She stopped just inside the door, heedless of the flames running up the lintel beside her, reaching hungrily for the carved ceiling. Her legs, her strong Dancer's legs, suddenly felt like grass bent before a storm wind. Shuddery cold swept through her, for all that the hot breath of the fire was in her face, a reek of charred wood and scorched stone that swept her straight back to a damp spring night laden with screams and the smell of destruction.

I can't. Not this time. Not again.

Fire exploded from the wall on her left. Jetta spun toward it and instantly shied back from the sight of white stone crawling with flame, paling rapidly from sullen red to eager gold. Here was no tame hearth fire escaped from its bondage to take vengeance on its captors. Only the deep fire, the heartfire of the world, the Old Man himself, could eat stone.

The Ancient was coming.

Fear struck her like a raptor, draining her strength as if great claws had pierced all her veins and bled her life away. She retreated a step, shaken so badly that for an instant even her training deserted her. All she saw was fire writhing in febrile, hungry curtains. *Like last time.* Reaching for her. *Like last time.* Out of control. *Like last time.*

She stumbled back, flinching from flame curling hot fingers over her toes, and turned blindly for the door. Two steps, and she would be free of this fire, any fire, forever.

A scream reached her, high and frightened, piercing the laughing roar of the fire like a thin-bladed knife. She jumped, and all around her fire leaped back. Jetta spun back towards the fire, instinct greater than fear rooted her in place. The fire retreated, uncertain now.

Shame drove through Jetta's fear. She took a step—forward, not back. Fire fled on the right. On the left it feinted, a licking yellow coil as long as her arm reaching for her face. She jerked her right hand up, palm out, in imperious demand. The fire recoiled. The smothering heat suddenly lessened as though winter had breathed on the flames. Jetta laughed and stepped into the Dance.

Bare feet ground soot and ash underfoot, the flagstones cool now against her soles. She shoved off from her right foot into a leap and spin, completely over a knee-high flame trying to sustain itself on bits of a charred chair. Her fear spun away with the turn; Jetta landed on smooth-polished stone and twirled on one foot, arms raised, exulting in the sudden cool rush of power that swirled through her. The Earth Mother's strength flowed through the pale stones to feed her dance, to give her mastery over fire. All at once the air tasted of damp earth and the green density of living forest.

She stamped an infant flame into non-existence, the smoke of its death curling impotently around her legs. Step, step, turn, shoving more smoke out of her way, her arms stretching now toward the ceiling in mocking imitation of the enemy. Her legs circled outward now in a demanding arc, drawing a line flame could not cross.

Step, turn.

Step again. Her feet grinding flame underfoot, forward into the teeth of avid death. Fire leaped and roared around her, licking eagerly into the air that was its goal, its life, its escape from its prison in the earth. Flame squeezed through the joints of the stone floor and walls and raced eagerly toward exposed lintels and furniture. Jetta raised one bare arm, her dusky gold skin glistening in the uneven light, and shoved her palm toward the threatened ceiling. Smoke parted before her gesture; the fire that had been crawling into the ornately carved woods recoiled.

Step, turn, step.

Another scream, fainter. Jetta faltered. She was not here just to fight the fire. She hesitated. Heat suddenly blasted her; bitter smoke and ash on her tongue as the sustaining cocoon began to shred around her. Malicious fire.

Memories of death, and pain, and screams, and another fire that too had laughed, a deep coughing roar as it consumed.

I am master!

Training and a lifetime's conditioning shoved down the memories, forced phantom pain from body. Jetta clapped her hands and pirouetted in place, willing the barriers of the Dance around her. Fighting rebellious quivers of fear, she looked closer at the flames running over the pallid stone. This was still only surface fire, pale and hot, but not yet the white heartfire that no water could quench.

She heard no hissing pop of collapsing rock as flame consumed the air in the porous windstone. This fire was malicious, yes, but as yet it was only a forerunner of The Ancient Fire that lived in the deepest core of the earth; it was not the foe that the Fire Clans had hunted since time began. The yellow of these flames was well diluted with the base red that spoke of uncertainty. This fire had not learned—yet—how to fully use its malice.

Jetta closed her eyes, drawing reassurance from the quicksilver feel of the Dance shimmering like a cool mist along her skin. It all but lifted her from the littered floor to defy the fire eye to eye where it roared over her head. She moved, a quick step and a turn into the heart of it. Time now was precious, before the fire learned to call its terrible parent. Now, while she, a Third Rank master, could still hold it alone, now while the Dance ran in her like a flood, the only flood that could tame heartfire.

She aimed for the door across the room, knowing where the screams had come from. She knew that door. She had run the halls of this place since childhood.

She leaped a small flame chewing at the floor, spurning the blackening spot to plant both feet on solid stone beyond. Flame spat at her; belatedly she remembered the meaning of the positions her body shaped without thought. She made a barrier of one leg stretched behind her, toe touching the littered floor, threatening the flames behind her even as she bent her arms into the open crescents that would trap flame into a tight, contained circle in front of her. The fire retreated instead, fleeing toward the walls.

Jetta smiled grimly and straightened. Ruddy light reflected dully off the leather hip guard and breast piece that were her only garments and played along skin turned a deeper gold by the light, catching red gleams from the silver promise bracelet around her right wrist. Heat scorched up around her but did not touch her any more than the light burned her. Smoke coiled around her, chains that did not know—yet—how to trap and bind a Firedancer. It breathed jets of flame toward her, but she spun away into the heart of it, fearless now, caught into the most ancient rhythm of her people. The Dance pounded in her blood, driving out heat and fear, smoke and memory, quelling her awareness of malice and binding the infant hostility of this fire to her will.

She stepped into the third movement, sweeping almost to one knee, hands at face level and touching at the wrists, fingers spread to form a bowl. With supreme arrogance Jetta filled it with fire torn from a licking tongue of flame that tried to curl over her head. She gazed through a shimmering crimson ball at its parent. The fire shied back in confusion. Jetta, cool as river water now, launched herself up and flung her hands wide, dispersing the flame to sparks. Flames sank and scattered, leaving a clear path to the door.

Another step and leap, and she was across the great room and into the corridor beyond. She did not hesitate and reached for the door of the nursery where old Minna had cuffed and applauded the stray brats roaming here as impartially as she had her own grandson, Kori.

Jetta shoved the hot wood of the door aside with the heel of her hand. Smoke and flame curled out of her way, exposing a small boy standing rigid in the center of a tiny clear space, short legs spread, guarding a smaller figure yet. Nekka, his sister, who cowered and sobbed in abject fear.

Her screams, not his. Nekka would never make a Dancer, but Tekkorin—there was a different matter. He had the gift, right enough, and the fire had not yet taken his nerve.

Minna would approve this child.

The boy's gaze found her through the smoke, childish blue and wide with fear in a small, grimy face. Relief flooded his expression, but he did not lower his arms from their half-instinctive, half-trained barrier stance.

"Good, Tekko!" Jetta called. "Stay as you are. This fire is mine."

With deliberate speed she danced, turn and turn again in a widening circle around the children. The girl, her screams silenced, now watched, a blackened tear streaked and sweating face, still showing her terror. Tekkorin's skin was as dry as Jetta's, though he was gasping from heat as much as effort. Jetta felt neither heat nor the acrid bite of smoke.

The Dance sustained her, a weapon forged over eons to balance the hunger of The Ancient: Dancer against flame, builder against destroyer, order against chaos.

With each step the flames withdrew, and everywhere her foot touched the fire died for an arm's length around. She began to sway, feet planted solidly on stone perilously warm underfoot. Straining outward to the farthest extent of her arms, she shoved the fire farther and farther from the children.

With the flames in retreat she followed. Stamping each foot down, the shock jolted power through every nerve, building and building until she felt as though it must flash out and consume fire and house and all. Jetta held onto it, building the shell of protection around the children, forcing the fire back. She moved on instinct and memory of this room, her head thrown back to eye the ceiling, spinning at every third step to prevent a bold rush. In one round of the room the fire sank to half the height of the walls; in another the space was clear, dark where it had been full of burning light.

"Tekko, come!" Jetta called, her mind stretching beyond the wall to the fire in the hall, which was trying to launch a new assault.

Without a word Tekkorin snatched the girl up by one arm. She came, stumbling but determined now that the way to the door was clear. Jetta leaped into the doorway. Fire had reclaimed the path she had forged to this spot, surprising her. Flame was rarely so bold, to claim a Dancer's footsteps. But then she heard the roar, a deep vibration more felt than a sound in the ears, underlying the sharp crackle of the flames running up the walls. Laughter.

"Jetta!" It came out a frightened wail, terror from Tekkorin at last. Truly the gift ran deep in him if he could sense the coming of The Ancient at his age.

Flames ran together in the center of the room, rearing up higher than her head. Jetta hesitated, seeing a *hysth* forming beyond the swirl of black smoke and the strange thickening of the air lent by the Dance. In a moment it would be living flame, able to understand its own malice—and do something with it. She brought her hands up, clenching her fists to pull the flames into an impotent knot, but the *hysth* was faster. It turned from hot red to pale gold in a breath, shading to white at its heart, working itself to form a doorway for the lurking The Ancient. Everywhere, stone groaned under the heat and began to hiss and crumble as the proud and perilous windstone gave up its air. A section of ceiling fell from the far corner near the door, priceless carvings shattering apart into a chaos of blackened wood. Anger exploded through Jetta, seeing something she loved taken forever by a thing without soul.

She leaped recklessly into the center of the great room, spinning as she went. She brought her hands up in the warding gesture of the Third Rank master's Dance in a full circle before she landed lightly astride a small flame racing for the safety of the *hysth*. But the *hysth* refused the smaller red flame and fled before her, leaving its younger brother to die in a curl of smoke. The deep roar changed to a thin crackle, its malice transmuting abruptly to fear. The *hysth* wavered, faded from pale gold to red, and lost its nerve. It retreated into the porous stone walls, dying to sparks and then to nothingness as Jetta's dance drove it back to its spawning ground. Abruptly the room was filled with smoke and nothing more, heavy amid an acrid stink of scorched stone and blackened wood.

"Tekko, the door!"

Tekkorin grabbed the girl and ran for the front door, where hands snatched them through into clean air and sunlight and safety. Slowly Jetta let her dance wind down, stepping lightly between holes in the floor. With bare feet and palms held flat as a barrier, she drove the fire deep into the ground where it always slept, waiting for carelessness, for a lapse in the watchfulness of the folk who lived in the air it craved.

Finally, deep in her bones, she sensed victory, a lessening of the quivering, fizzing sense of fire in proximity. This upstart youngster was beaten, licking its wounds in some deep crevice far below her, hiding from The Ancient, which would not welcome this setback. Another skirmish in a long, long war was over.

Abruptly the weariness hit her, the inevitable aftermath of the Dance. Jetta stopped in the middle of the littered, blackened great room, drooping like a wilted flower. Dimly she heard a shout and pounding footsteps. A hard-muscled arm slid around her waist and bore her up, and then sunlight touched her face along with a cool breeze clean of fire stink.

Kori, she thought, but that wasn't right; Kori was dead. Suddenly her arm hurt, and her leg; raw red pain licked like the very fire deep into her body. Jetta screamed and fought the hands trying to soothe her. She wrenched free, overbalanced, and crashed to the hard-packed dirt of the square in a graceless sprawl, setting off a sudden alarmed babble over her head.

She scuttled backward, seeing nothing but flame. Strong fingers seized her chin, halting the frantic thrashing of her head. "Jetta! Stop it! You are out and safe! Jetta ak'Kal! Stop it!"

The voice penetrated, ringing along familiar pathways. Jetta froze, looking up into a pair of intense dark eyes. Eyes as hard as containment stone. "Farahk ak'Kal," she gasped.

He released her. "Is your mind your own, ak'Kal?"

Shakily she nodded, and sat up, drawing her knees into an instinctive barrier. Farahk's eyes narrowed. Jetta caught herself huddling and surged to her feet, shaking off the memory of pain and loss still tender after a year.

Faces framed in charcoal-colored hair, bodies in the deep reds and yellows of the Fire Clans, surrounded her. She looked at her neighbors, villagers she had known all her life, and bit her lip, groping after the professional calm a Third Rank master should never lose. They crowded back, breaking the circle of concern drawn tight around her. Farahk stood up more slowly, hard muscles rippling in the late afternoon sunlight. It jolted Jetta to see him dressed in the brief leather hip guard of a Dancer with its protective flaps guarding buttocks and groin, his legs and upper body bare of anything the fire might snatch. His flowing black hair, like hers, was braided up tight and bound with a thong at the nape of his neck. Wide dark eyes met hers. Jetta stared, first in realization, and then embarrassment. Hot color flooded her face.

He waved impatiently at the gawking villagers. "It's done here. The fire's out, thanks to Jetta ak'Kal. Go and see what can be salvaged. Take Nekka to her parents and see to Tekkorin."

People scattered without objection. Quite apart from being a Fifth Rank master, Farahk seldom brooked being questioned. Hands brushed Jetta's shoulder in passing: silent thanks, appreciation, and then they were gone, and she stood alone with Farahk in an awkward silence.

"So," he said.

Stubbornly she looked away. Firin's house oozed acrid-smelling smoke from the fire-shattered windows facing the square; the roof of the great room bore a gaping hole, but the majority of the sprawling hall stood untouched, its opalescent walls gleaming in the golden light. The rest of Firehome still dreamed in the sun, a scatter of arrogant white stone and wooden roofs crowning a hill shaped like flame itself. The vulnerable trees of the forest formed a scantly-tamed green circle a hundred paces from the nearest walls, far enough away that The Ancient could not use them against the village. At the far end of the valley the sun hovered low over the hills, turning the river and the high falls pouring over the Guardian Ridge to silver. Tall hills hemmed the wide green bowl, dreaming in quiet peace, lush and verdant like no other place in ten leagues, for here fire walked with caution, and rarely. This was Firehome Vale, clan home to the Fire Clans. Every third person here was a Dancer.

Farahk's hand touched her shoulder. "Jetta."

The hard edge had gone from his voice. She turned, caught in spite of herself. Their eyes met, alike in the liquid blackness of mastery, as their faces bore traces of common ancestry in the wide set of the eyes, the winged dark eyebrows, the narrow nose and flat, hard lines of cheek and jaw. She saw compassion in his face, and flushed, caught all sideways.

"So, you are not as well healed as you thought," he said quietly.

Jetta looked up, her pride caught. "I did what was needed! The fire is driven deep, and Firin's house is still standing. And the children live."

"Indeed. You did well."

"But still you were set to come in after." Bitterness edged her voice.

"Were it needed, yes. Should the children have died for your pride?"

"How long have you had someone standing my watch behind my back?"

"You have not been cleared by the Circle again to work alone. Surely you knew that."

"I—" But she had known; she had just refused to think about it, as so much else of this past year was forbidden territory. Of course her credentials were useless; no one trusted a Firedancer who had failed her task. One dead village to her credit was enough.

Jetta stared at the ground, absently rubbing her left arm. He caught her hand, raising it when she snatched her head up, startled. Farahk only looked at her, still holding her wrist quietly. Jetta flushed again and wrenched away.

He ran a light finger down the unmarked golden skin of her arm. "It healed well."

"Dancers always heal well. And the Water Clan healers are adept. No scars."

"No scars *outside.*"

She met his eyes. "I am ak'Kal of the Third Rank! I'm not afraid!"

"Yes, you are." His voice was so matter-of-fact it quenched her anger as though he had danced it away. "You conquered it today. What of next time? What will happen when you meet with The Ancient itself? You came out screaming, ak'Kal. The fire has touched your flesh. Did it also eat your nerve?"

Her chin came up. "The Ancient has no hold on me. This fire was malicious, but it gained no victory."

His eyebrow lifted like a bird rising. "So? Then you did better than well, daughter of my sister."

She drew a deep breath, steadying as he let formality go at last. "It was a young fire, not The Ancient—but it tried to call the Old Man. It tried."

"Why does that surprise you? Any fire will try if you let it."

"Here in the heart of Firehome Vale?" She stared. "Since when would it dare?"

"Since when would it dare rise here to begin with?"

Jetta blinked. Since when, indeed? Suddenly uncertain, she stood, squirming like a First Ranker, while those eyes that had seen more fire than half the other Dancers in all the clans studied her face.

"You have great talent, Jetta," he said finally, startling her, for it was not what she had expected. "Since you were a child it has been expected that you would rise to Fifth Rank, perhaps even to the Circle. I have never seen a Dancer so aware of how a fire will run, of where it sleeps, of its mood when it bursts from the deep. Because of you, Setham Village was fire-clear for full five years. That is a thing unheard of."

"And now Setham Village lies in ashes because of me."

"No. You know why Setham died."

She looked away, her vision blurring with the easy tears of the past year. "Kori," she whispered.

"Kori didn't cause the fire any more than he caused his own death." Farahk's voice was gentle, but inexorable. Jetta flinched. She did not want to hear this, could not bear to think of that time. But Farahk's hand was on her chin again, forcing her head up. Finally she met his eyes, furiously blinking her vision clear.

He dropped his hand, a reluctant smile catching up one side of his mouth. "Your courage is intact. Find whatever path will lead you past Kori, and you will yet stand in the Circle."

"Lead past Kori?" Jetta echoed incredulously. "And should I forget him, my lifemate, my second self, who died because I failed?"

"Did I say forget? But he's dead, of his own mistake, and if you dwell on that mistake it will take you, too. Or, you will never dance fire again, and then how many will die who might have lived had Jetta ak'Kal had the will and the courage to dance for them?"

Jetta spun away, staring into the sun sinking over the falls. "I will not fail my duty," she said through her teeth.

Silence behind her. She waited, hating his trick of outwaiting opposition, but it worked nonetheless. She turned to find him still watching her with neither anger nor compassion in his face. He was master now, and she apprentice.

"Annam Vale has requested a Dancer," he said evenly. "You will go tomorrow."

Her mind raced, *No! No, ak'Kal! Not yet!'* "You think that wise?" she asked. Her hand stole against her will to the comforting smoothness of the promise clasp on her wrist.

"You object to backing on your watch, and yet refuse an assignment elsewhere? Make up your mind, *ak'Kal*."

Jetta jerked upright. "Flame has attacked Firehome itself! How can I leave?"

"And are there no other masters in Firehome, with more years of facing the Old Man than Jetta ak'Kal has been alive?"

That silenced her. Even now she could hear First Rank apprentices chanting the histories in the sprawling teaching house where she had learned the Dance. Firehome had no need of her to keep The Ancient at bay. Maybe it was only because *she* was on watch that the Old Man's spawn had dared to raise its head.

She looked away from Farahk's gaze. Setham Village lay like an accusing ghost behind her eyelids, a specter of ashes and tumbled walls and screams. Maybe if she stayed, it would be Firehome itself someday. And maybe if she left, it would be Annam.

"If you are fit to be a Dancer, if you are not broken, do this. Now is the time to find out, Jetta ak'Kal."

She forced herself to meet Farahk's eyes again. "I can dance," she said through stiff lips.

"Then you go."

Go with Circle sanction, or just go. That was in his voice, the thing that happened to Dancers who lost their nerve. Go to the wastelands where fire could find no foothold and make what life she might. When fire rooted in a human heart, it was too dangerous to stay. She looked down that road of bleak wandering, a magnet for The Ancient, welcome nowhere, and swallowed hard.

"Yes, Farahk ak'Kal," she said thickly. "Is that all?"

"No. Settak goes with you."

"Setti? You're sending Setti?" Inside she both warmed and chilled at the same time. Settak, or Setti as he had been to her ever since childhood was like a brother to her. A bumbling and barely competent brother to who took nothing seriously. "But he's only a journeyman, and Second Rank. He isn't qualified—"

"To take your place if you fail?"

"Old Man Fire! That's not what I—"

"But it's what you were thinking. There's no danger of you failing here, in your home, with a village full of Dancers to catch what you do not. In your heart you know that."

"I didn't know! I didn't know you were there, so why should I have feared failing?"

"Then why does Firin's house have a great hole in its roof? How is it that flame got such a hold there, if Jetta ak'Kal did not hesitate?"

"It was already well alight when I came, ak'Kal."

He frowned and looked down his nose at her. "So?"

"Yes!"

A little silence stretched. Her anger trickled into uneasiness as still Farahk said nothing. Abruptly he raised his eyes as if some inner debate had ended. "All the more reason for you to go, then," he said cryptically. "Settak is competent enough in the Dance, and he is driven. Annam lies in the heart of the containment quarries. The risk is small."

Which brought the bright blood rushing to her face again, in humiliation this time. "Then why send us at all?"

He watched her unblinkingly through a long moment that cooled her anger and hatched a small worm of doubt in her guts. Something was not right about Annam Vale, and the danger was greater than he pretended. "Uncle?"

He drew a quick breath and let it out in a sigh. "Annam is full of Windriders, sister-daughter. Think on that, if Old Man Fire indeed comes calling."

Farahk dropped a hand onto her shoulder, a quick, hard squeeze of reassurance, and walked away with the floating, arrogant step of the very top Dancers. She watched him go, hardly seeing him for the swirl of fear and excitement and doubt squeezing her insides into knots. She felt like a First Ranker again, facing the fire for the first time.

Windriders! Old Man Fire, what was she supposed to do with a village full of Windriders?

Two
The Circle's Blessing

Fire. Always, it seemed, she dreamed of fire.

Jetta lay shivering in the dim pearl light of dawn, shaking off the lingering effect of still another nightmare. Even the fine-woven blankets felt like needles against her skin. She threw them off, in frustration, knowing it was imagination and not the weave of the blankets. Knowing that her arm and leg were healed. But she remembered the pain. The pain of the rasp of blankets on scorched skin went hand in hand with the nightmare of fire rising around her, out of control, a living barrier between her and safety, with Kori lost somewhere beyond it.

She curled into a ball against the chill morning air. Grief caught her breath into a quiet sob; she rammed her fist against her mouth, fearful of her parents hearing it in their room beside hers.

That was humiliation in itself; to be back abed in her parents' house after seven years a ranked Firedancer, earning her own way. But there had been nowhere else to go after—when she had left the healers' care in Rrillis Farhold. A Water Clan, safe in its stone-free floating village and with precious little use for a Firedancer.

No land-bound village would take her without sanction from the Circle; no one risked life and home on a Dancer without clan credentials, and hers had been revoked the instant Kori died.

No matter the fault was not hers.

What mattered was that she had nearly died by fire, and that was a thing to remove the confidence of anyone not gifted with fire talent. And that was what the Circle questioned.

The morning chill began to penetrate her bare skin, as heat seldom did. Shivering, she got up and began to dress in stout woolen breeches and leather boots, a flowing silken shirt in the flame yellow of her rank, and last of all the master's badge. She stared at it in her hand for a moment, the three flames cast in silver shot through with gold, laid against a red oval background. So proud she had been to be the youngest Third Rank master ever, so happy the day she had received this badge from the Circle. Kori had swept her up and swung her in circles until she was dizzy, his face alight with pride and laughter, not in the least envious that she had passed him. So much laughter that day, all of Setham Village caught up in the elevation of their own Firedancer, so proud to claim her as their own.

I wonder, would they claim me now? She shoved the pin viciously through the cloth at her shoulder. All they knew burned to ash, and them left to start all over again. *Aye, I was an asset to them, no doubt of it.*

"Jetta? Ah, you're up. Here, let me help."

Jetta's mother came through the door, her unbound hair flowing around her ankles, all but hiding her blue skirts. Jetta gave it an envious look; her own hung barely to the middle of her back and might never grow that long again since the fire had touched it. Kirana's hair, still black as containment stone, draped her in a living curtain of night. Jetta watched her sweep it back with a practiced motion of one hand and wondered what her mother had been like as a Dancer, before choosing to give five children to the Dance. She was graceful and slim, even now. That hair, a Dancer's defiant beauty, proved that fire had never claimed victory over her.

Unlike me, Jetta mourned, acutely aware that every Dancer she met would know of her defeat.

Kirana watched her out of steady dark eyes, looking so much like her brother Farahk that Jetta flushed and looked away in sudden stupid guilt.

"Dreams?" Kirana asked, still her mother.

"No more than usual," Jetta muttered. "I must pack—"

"Already done," her mother said serenely. Jetta turned a frown her way. Kirana laughed. "*Farahk* already told us you were going."

Jetta's face flamed hotter. Kirana sobered and laid a mother's hand along Jetta's cheek. "It's an assignment, Jetta, not exile. Setti is so excited he is all but halfway there in spirit."

Jetta's mouth pulled down. "Setti is a child."

"He's the same age as you. But *he* remembers wonder."

Jetta wrenched away. "See if he thinks the same after half a year walking patrol."

Kirana folded her arms and said nothing. *Just like Farahk,* Jetta thought rebelliously, squirming under that steady gaze. *Who taught them that, anyway?* She caught herself raking her hair forward over her face, hiding behind its dark veil. Instantly she shoved it back and said, "I didn't ask for Annam Vale."

"No. They asked for you."

"By name?" That startled her.

"No."

Disappointment took Jetta, so hard and so fast that it astonished her with its depth. Once, villages *had* asked for her by name and tried to lure her from Setham with honors and promises. But Kori had kept her head on straight, Kori who asked her earnestly if they could do better in a fine house in Fornay than next door to the best baker in two provinces, whose life they had saved.

Tears came unexpectedly. "Ah, Jetta," Kirana said, reaching to enfold her daughter in arms that felt, to Jetta, more smothering than loving. "They asked for a Dancer, is all. Few know you are no longer under contract to Setham. Some believe you're dead."

"Better so," Jetta said bitterly.

Kirana stepped back, sympathy fleeing her face. "If you *must* feel sorry for yourself, then Annam is where you belong."

Jetta gasped, wounded from a direction she had not expected. "Mother!"

"Over a year now I have watched you grieve, Jetta." Her mother's face softened. "Kori was a fine man, and a son we were proud to claim, but he's gone, by no fault of yours. You take this guilt on your shoulders, but that is neither right nor healthy. Were the mistake yours it would be different, but—"

"That's right! Blame Kori for getting killed! Not the nit who let fire into his house—"

"No one invites fire," Kirana said tartly. "Fire is, and fire does. What use for Firedancers if anyone could predict what the Old Man will do, or put it out with a bucket? It hungers. We watch. That is our purpose, as the Water Clans throw back floods and the Windriders calm the storms. The Stone Clans delve, and without them none of us would live fire-free, so what right have you to your arrogance, Jetta ak'Kal?"

Ever so slightly she emphasized the *ak'Kal*. Words curdled in Jetta's mouth. Sullenly she swept up her red traveling cloak from its peg beside the door. "I'm journeying today. Best to begin."

"Jetta." Kirana caught her back as she started to storm past. Jetta flung her a hard look, daring her to keep her hand where it was. Kirana dared. Jetta drew a pinched breath and stood still, wanting wildly to be away, alone, on the road to Annam or anywhere else so long as there was no one to look at her or give her advice she did not want.

"Daughter." Kirana's tone softened, catching guilt into Jetta's throat. Her eyes blurred; she bit her lip, trying to channel away the stupid raw emotions still racking her. Kirana reached to stroke her shortened hair. "I know it's hard. We all loved Kori. But you can't stay indoors and grieve for him forever. Annam has real need—"

She broke off, biting her lip. Jetta turned her head to look at her. "Why? Farahk said it was built on containment stone. Fire can't eat containment stone."

She kept the part about the Windriders to herself, hoping to force more detail from her mother. Though she had given up the Dance long ago, Kirana had not given up her interest in it; she knew all there was to know about every village from here to the Great Water. If there was something queer in Annam Vale, she would surely know what it was.

Kirana reached up and started to plait her hair, sure sign that she was evading the question. Jetta stole Farahk's trick and simply waited in silence, until finally her mother spoke.

"The upper quarries are all but exhausted. Fire has surged there three times since midwinter. Stone barriers are no longer enough. The villagers are frightened that The Ancient will creep through the abandoned mines and root itself in the windstone beneath the village."

Jetta considered that thoughtfully. Black containment stone held fire helpless; white windstone served as its doorway. The Ancient traveled up veins of it, rising on a wave of heat that consumed the porous stone and fed on the air trapped within. Annam faced new dangers indeed, but no worse than what villages in less fortunate places endured as a matter of course.

"The Stone Clans should be more careful where they dig," she said coolly.

Kirana gave her a contemptuous look. "And you should remember where the stone from their diggings go." She turned away, abandoning the plait. "Come. Your father is waiting to break bread with you before you leave."

"Mother—" Ashamed, Jetta reached to stop her, catching a handful of ebony tresses. Kirana twisted a look over her shoulder, her face shadowed in a dark fall of hair. "I'm sorry," Jetta mumbled.

"You would do well to remember that all of the clans have skills that keep us alive. Firedancers aren't the only folk with purpose or talent."

She was gone out the door before Jetta could decide whether that was warning or threat. Jetta stared after her, uncertain now what she was traveling toward. A Second Rank journeyman for helpmeet, and The Ancient burrowing under a village with no experience of fire. Stone Clans that delved too deep in the name of protecting the rest of the world, and Windriders—Old Man Fire, Windriders. A village threatened with fire was the last place for folk who could summon the very thing The Ancient wanted most. Air. The lift of a Windrider child's hand could kill a Dancer with the unexpected fueling of a fire by the touch of an unexpected breeze.

Primitive terror twitched the hair on Jetta's neck; fire too made its own gales, that no Windrider could fully wrest from its control. *How are we to Dance with Windriders attracting every stray zephyr into the Old Man's maw, feeding the beast even as we're trying to kill it?*

Anger and fear took turns chasing themselves down her spine. She did not much care for Farahk's idea of humor.

She started to put her cloak on, and stopped as the black,

uneven ends of her woefully short hair brushed her arm. Hastily she reached up and knotted it on top of her head. Everyone in Firehome had grown accustomed to the sight, but she would not walk abroad with the evidence of her failure swinging loose for everyone to see.

With her neck prickling to the unaccustomed touch of the dawn chill, she caught up her cloak and went downstairs.

The kitchen smelled of fresh bread, frying meat, and the peppery scent of spicy tea. Her mother was bent over the hearth, where a captive fire burned sullenly in its black stone prison, lending its heat to the collection of pots bubbling over the flames. Her father, Vettahr, nodded at her entry.

The normally quiet kitchen's bliss was broken by the tall youth at the end of the table. Setti was all but bouncing in his seat with impatience to start. He leaped up when Jetta came through the inner door. He gathered her into a hug.

"Jetta! Finally!" he said, "I thought you were going to sleep the whole day away!"

His open, angular face, as guileless as when they were children, was lit from within with a child's excitement. She extracted herself and pushed him to arm's length. At least he was not setting out in Dance leathers like a First Rank hunting sparks; a sensible red shirt clung to his broad shoulders, belted over stout leather breeches and boots. Soot-colored hair swung free almost to his knees, thick and shining, rippling with his every movement. She swallowed envy, concentrating on his face, and blinked, taken aback by a vivid flash of blue eyes. Child indeed. Father Flame, how had he reached Second Rank with never a hint of fire to darken those eyes?

This is my partner? The traitor thought crowded into her head and would not leave. Ashamed, confused, she tried to rally to the friendship they had shared growing up. "Are you *still* the first one out of bed every morning? Father Flame, Setti, some of us need sleep!"

"You never were any fun in the morning. Wake up! This is exciting!"

"Exciting how? It's a long walk with a bunch of strangers at the end."

Setti rolled his eyes. "Feed her, Kirana ak'Kal. Maybe it will improve her temper."

"Doubtful." Kirana said. But she gave him a smile and handed Jetta a cup of steaming tea. "Drink," she said and without turning. "Setti, will you *stop* pacing? Sit and eat before you wear a hole in my floor."

"Sorry." Setti lowered his lean body onto a sturdy chair, his body still taut with anticipation.

Jetta sighed, watching him twiddling exuberantly with the plain double flame badge of his rank. After a moment he leaped up again, too restless to sit, and bent over an enormous pack beside the door. Jetta almost laughed; he was going to wilt in the first hour on the road. She met her father's grave dark eyes, and a look passed between them that touched a smile to his mouth before he turned courteously to Setti. Jetta slid into a seat, reaching for the hot bread on the platter beside her father.

"Are you sure you have everything?" Vettahr asked Setti, straight-faced. His eyes flitting to the bulging pack.

"Well, perhaps I should have brought that coil of rope after all. The road may not be good just now, with the snowmelt running. Do you think I should go get it?"

Earnest blue eyes lifted to Jetta's. "I think we will do fine," she said, and stuffed a piece of bread into her mouth before she laughed in his face. It seemed impossible that she and Setti were the same age; that they had entered the First Rank together twenty years ago. No one could doubt his enthusiasm, but the gift ran erratically in him, driving both him and the masters mad with his uneven grasp. Through sheer determination he had achieved Second Rank, though she still wondered how he could be so excited about a simple journey to another village.

But it is his first *journey,* she realized slowly. *His first assignment more than a couple of days' walk from his birthplace. His first chance to prove himself.* She remembered her own wild excitement when she had been assigned to Setham, and Kori's patience with her. Sadness touched her; determinedly she lifted her head and smiled at Setti.

"Perhaps we should go through our bundles and see what we forgot." She caught her father's wry wink and knew that half of Setti's pack would mysteriously disappear in the re-packing, while her own small bundle undoubtedly bulged with all the things her mother had included that Jetta no longer cared about. She had no doubt that a dress or three would show up when she unpacked in Annam, and sighed, knowing equally well there was no point fighting it. Dance leathers and good wovens were all she needed. Her mother's stubborn attempts to turn her back into a woman were pointless. She was a Firedancer, not a catch for some footloose Stone Delver.

Eventually only scraps remained on the plates. She could not face more tea, and Setti was about to explode with impatience. The sun stood well up in the clear sky, throwing long bars of light through the eastern windows. Firin's scorched house drew her eye. Her lips tightened.

"Will he replace the Fornay carvings, do you think?" she asked.

Setti stared, but Kirana said serenely, "I expect so. Firin's not one to have anything out of place for long."

"How did it start?"

Setti threw her a quick, startled look. "You don't know?"

Jetta's shoulders hunched. "I," she said and paused. "I was at the far end of the village when it began. I heard the alarm."

A small, awkward silence fell. Jetta's guts knotted. Setti looked troubled; her mother bent her head to let her hair fall across her face. Her father was examining his plate as if the pattern fascinated him. *Should I have felt the Old Man crawling up through the walls?* Jetta thought in helpless fury, but the simple answer was yes, she should. It was how she had kept Setham fire-free for so long, because she always *knew* when The Ancient was stirring, knew when fire began to creep up from its hiding places underground, daring to test the containment wall around the village, trying to root in the fields before anyone could see. Even as a tiny child she had run to watch, fascinated, until the masters realized, and began to follow Vettahr's youngest child on her seemingly random rounds. They had ambushed the Old Man time and again, until at last the fire lay sullenly quiescent in some underground hole. Firehome Vale had been free of flame for sixteen years. Until yesterday.

Why didn't I feel it? she wondered, chilled. It was a gift that had never failed her, so reliable that she and Kori had not shared other Dancers' exhausting and haunted sleep, turn and turn-about, on constant watch against the first tentative spurt of flame. They had slept soundly, and together, safe in the sure-fire sense that had awakened them on countless occasions in time to beat The Ancient to its chosen attack point. But yesterday she had felt nothing.

No wonder the Circle kept a second Dancer on her watch.

She thought of the doorway of Firin's hall, framed in fire. She had not hesitated until she was inside, nor even thought about the fact that the flames had so firm a hold. She had gone in, because it was in her blood to do so, because a lifetime's training had forced any other thought out of her head. But it had been years, she realized slowly, since she had been forced to brave a room so full of flame. Her gift had spared her that, all those years in Setham. The *hysths* she had fought in her life had been many but generally small. Until the night Kori died. Until that one, unforgettable fire, a wall of living flame between her and her love, the scattered *hysths* running, not from the Dance, but to join and meld into one huge *hysth* that had eaten everything.

She flinched from the memory. Her father, always her father, gestured her to him and she settled on the knee that she had sat on through many tearful sessions of her youth.

"You did well yesterday," he said, and set down his cup to pull her into a hug. "I expect Annam Vale is getting better than they deserve."

"And now," he scooted her off his lap as Jetta fought a sudden lump in her throat. "Shall we look at those packs?" He took Setti outside, snatching up Jetta's small bundle as he went. Jetta stood to help her mother clear the table.

"No, go on," Kirana said quietly, drawing her into a fierce hug. "Take care. Dance well."

"I-I'll try."

"You will do better than try. The gift is still there."

"But Firin's—"

"If you didn't feel the flame coming, it's because you did not want to. Think on that."

"Other Dancers have lost the gift."

Kirana drew back and looked at her. "Is that what you fear? Or what you hope?"

"*Mother!*"

Kirana smiled. "So you care a little, eh? You danced well

yesterday. Something remains. Whether all or part, only you can say, child."

Fear seized Jetta's throat. "The Circle will send me to Annam, not knowing if I can do the job? Mother, how is that fair?"

"Setti is with you, is he not?"

"He *can't* do what I do!"

"Neither can you, apparently. Go and find out, Jetta."

Anger flamed up, as fierce and hot as The Ancient itself. Jetta jerked upright; Kirana only looked at her, unmoved. "Go, daughter," she said. "Go with my love. Discover what is in you and learn to live with whatever you find."

Jetta drew a sharp breath. So even the Circle did not know how much of her gift Kori's death had taken from her. And yet they sent her to Annam, with only an erratically-gifted Second Rank journeyman to help. Suppose there was nothing left? Suppose even the Dance failed her? Jetta turned for the door.

"The trick to Windriders is to keep them in sight," Kirana said quietly behind her.

Jetta turned but Kirana had her back to the door and her hands full of crockery. Jetta knew the warning was all she would get, and perhaps more than anyone was authorized to say. Whatever test the Circle was imposing upon her by sending her to Annam, it was clearly about more than a Firedancer winning back her credentials. Much more.

The dawn breeze nibbled at her cheek when she stepped outside, cool with the damp chill of late spring and heady with the scent of the toa tree trailing pink streamers of flowers onto the corner of the house. Black fingers of shadow lay across the white dust of the dooryard, putting Jetta sharply in mind of the black pathways of Setham. She caught her breath and turned away, trying to breathe past the sudden tightness in her throat.

Her father looked up from jerking the straps tight on Setti's pack. It had dwindled to a manageable size. He looked up, his mouth acquiring a sad, thoughtful line, and then he winked at Setti. Jetta smiled at him, the ache subsiding into an upswelling of love that seemed to stretch her skin from inside. Of all the people in Firehome, only her father had never so much as asked her about that night, walking for hours with her in silence as she regained the strength in her leg. Their conspiracies ran deep, requiring no words.

It occurred to her that she was about to leave that unquestioning support behind. Once again she was setting out from Firehome, but this time there would be no Kori standing unflinching at her back, equal parts helpmeet and refuge. But this time she did not walk forth with all the world ahead of her and a reputation to make. Now she had one.

Jetta bit down hard on a sudden stab of anxiety and chagrin and reached for her own pack beside the door. Nerves already stretched, she jerked upright with a startled gasp when a clear, brassy note rang through the village and echoed away down the valley.

Setti looked equally taken aback, his blue eyes wide. Vettahr raised a black eyebrow at them both. "Did you think to go with no proper leave taking?"

"But—the Circle itself?" Setti looked torn between shy delight and outright terror.

Vettahr laughed. "Oh, come, lad. You've known all of them your whole life."

"But—they're the *Circle.*" Setti craned over his shoulder, but the solid bulk of the house blocked any view of the square. "They don't come out to wish journeymen farewell. Or even masters."

Maybe I'll finally get some information, Jetta thought, less than pleased with the prospect of facing the Circle of Elders on this morning of all. She just wanted to be gone.

She slung her pack over one shoulder, draped her red cloak over her right arm and turned toward Setti. "Best to get it over," she said sourly, stalking toward the corner of the house. At the edge of her vision she saw Vettahr turn to look at her, but she couldn't meet his eyes, plagued suddenly by a foul mood she had no wish to vent on her father. This was not his doing, and she had no desire to shame him further.

She heard Setti trailing her as she strode around the corner into the square. It took her aback to see the whole of Firehome gathered in a loose circle that silently parted for her and Setti. Heads turned toward her. A few of her kin smiled; one or two touched her shoulder as she passed. "Good journey, Jetta," someone murmured. Her nerves eased a little.

The sun threw long streamers of gold between the buildings, kissing color into the white stone and gilding the tops of distant trees. The glare off the great bronze summons bell in the center of the square all but blinded her. Jetta blinked away tears and dropped her gaze, and so came before the Circle showing a suitably humble demeanor.

"Jetta ak'Kal," a soft voice said. "Settak a'Kam. The blessings of the Beginning be on you."

She looked up. Awe touched her, wrenched unwilling from a frozen heart. The Circle so seldom gathered in public, even here in Firehome. They guided the clan and chose the masters and tracked The Ancient's incursions into every village in all the world, but one rarely saw them together. It impressed her despite her stubborn refusal to feel anything. They stood, not in a circle but in a line, seven dark-eyed masters clad in the white of hottest flame, embroidered in all the lesser colors of fire: red and yellow, orange and the dead black of the defeated enemy. The youngest had five fewer years than Farahk, but unlike Farahk, or Jetta herself, his eyes had no white left to them at all, as if The Ancient had burned them out in some deadly encounter long ago. Jetta stood still with difficulty under that obsidian gaze. At least, she thought he was looking at her. She could not see his eyes move.

Unexpectedly, Norlahk ak'Kal smiled. It lit his whole face, erasing even the haunting deadness of his eyes and lending them an illusion of youth. "I had not thought to see the day Jetta ak'Kal came to a summons bell with lowered eyes. What ails you, child?"

"Ak'Kal?" Jetta blurted.

Norlahk looked at Setti standing speechless at Jetta's shoulder. "Settak a'Kam. Do try to put your eyes back in your head. I daresay you'll need them before the day is out."

Setti fumbled for an answer as a ripple of laughter ran around the square. Jetta frowned; this was far from the parting chastisement she had expected. Norlahk stepped forward, startling her again; she had thought he was looking at Setti. He set his hands on her shoulders, a cage of hard fingers stilling any impulse to shrink from whatever came next.

His voice turned deep and solemn. "Jetta ak'Kal, Master

of the Third Rank of the Firedance, we send you forth."

Someone struck the bell. Jetta jumped and looked around at it shivering on its hook, its deep voice rolling away down the valley. Norlahk's hands tightened, forcing her to look back into that black and fire-eaten gaze.

The bell rang again, tolling announcement to the surrounding ridges, the flawless sky, the green mysteries of the forest and the silent rocks beneath, where lived The Ancient in its long frustration. Norlahk's voice followed its echoes.

"We send forth a master of the Dance, to Annam Vale where The Ancient enemy has dared to encroach on lands flame-free since the Beginning. We send with her a journeyman of the Second Rank, to learn from her and assist her in her struggle. Know this: The Ancient has grown bold since it defeated a master of the craft a year and more ago. It dares even the sanctity of Firehome, testing the defenses of this stronghold where it has never found root. Since mid-winter, three villages under our protection have suffered losses despite the presence of masters of the Dance. Now the fire explores new approaches, probes at old ones, attacks in ways not seen before.

"We, the Circle of the Fire Clans, have studied these incursions, but we cannot discern the pattern The Ancient is building. What lies at Annam, we cannot say, save that it will serve you ill to depend upon containment stone alone to keep The Ancient at bay. Be vigilant. Dance well. Report all incursions, however minor. Above all, show no fear."

That was aimed at me, Jetta thought bitterly, but Setti nodded. "To dance with fire is to leave fear at the door," he said, jolting Jetta from self-absorption back to a childhood spent on the Dance ground, learning the rhythms, the patterns, the unbreakable calm of a Dancer.

"To dance with fire is to leave fear at the door," she echoed, the words coming unbidden to her lips. The first and most ingrained creed of the Dance.

Norlahk nodded and stepped back. Somehow Jetta sensed that he was looking at her. His head tilted to one side. "Eyes so black so young," he murmured. "Truly you have the gift, Jetta ak'Kal. I was Fourth Rank before my eyes took on true black. You will do well at Annam."

"Master, I—" Jetta had no idea what she meant to say. The bell shivered again, driving vibrations deep into her bones. She jumped, felt Setti startle beside her. Norlahk's head tilted toward the sky, his infinite gaze leaving hers. The other six masters lifted their arms in the first posture of the Dance, palms together over their heads, mimicking the shape of flame. Instinctively Jetta let the cloak on her arm slide to the ground and raised hers in answer.

Norlahk twisted one palm upward. Flame whooshed from the ground beside Jetta. Without thought she shoved both hands toward it, fingers spread, extinguishing it before Setti could so much as blink childish blue eyes.

One by one in a rippling wave the ranked masters brought their arms down. Fire spurted at their feet, a line of crackling yellow flames racing to combine and grow strong.

Angrily Jetta nodded at Setti, half-insulted that the Circle should assign her to Annam and then test her on the morning of departure. Setti, wide-eyed, managed to subdue one end of the line. Jetta stamped her foot, driving the other flames into a confused huddle. She lifted one arm, intent on banishing them—and suddenly the fire flicked out, leaving only a thin spiral of smoke and a scatter of soot on the white stone of the square.

Norlahk turned his head, his unsettling gaze sweeping the line of masters.

"Not of our doing," Krailis ak'Kal said, third in line, Jetta's own blood kin.

"Settak?"

"No, ak'Kal!" He looked as confused as Jetta felt.

"Jetta?" Norlahk looked at her.

"No, ak'Kal." Foreboding swept through her, dousing her anger like a dump of snow from one of Firehome's slate roofs. "Not of my doing."

Norlahk folded his arms. "Then you see. Either The Ancient grows senile, or it grows clever. Either way, it will not act as you expect. I say again, be alert, be wary, Dance very, very well."

He stepped forward and kissed her forehead, then Setti's, and handed Jetta a letter to the elders of Annam stamped with the flame seal of the Fire Clans, the precious credentials lending her their approval. One by one the other masters gave them the parting kiss and followed Norlahk past the summons bell toward the tower at the far end of the village. White robes disappeared inside, and the door shut before the silence in the square broke into murmuring and subdued discussion. Jetta could detect an element of fear in their words. The Ancient had grown bold.

Setti turned to her, a smile twitching at the corner of his mouth. "Didn't I say this was going to be exciting?"
~~Setti~~

Three
The Journey

The road had become little more than a wide path as they climbed out of the lower lands. Soon they would leave even this path and take to the steep paths that followed the ridges and lead them to Annam Vale.

Perhaps sensing her mood, Setti remained silent as they walked the path that wound beneath the huge trees.

Jetta was grateful. She had not walked this way since she and Kori had almost strolled down it, their hair loose and free, the Ancient not yet such a personal fear.

They came to a group of fallen trees, the woods dark and damp. It had been a windstorm two seasons ago.

Kori and she had made love in those trees. Now darker, new undergrowth rising, but still the giant trees lay where they had fallen. A reminder. An unbidden sob pulled at her throat.

"Jetta?" Setti's voice startled her with its low, wary note of concern. "What's wrong?"

"Nothing."

"For a moment you looked—"

"I'm fine."

He reddened and lengthened his stride. Jetta caught his arm. "Setti, wait. I'm sorry. It's just..."

"You came this way with Kori?"

"Yes, but-"

"And I'm not Kori," he said, the bitterness she felt now tinged his voice.

Jetta caught a little hard breath. It had been bad enough leaving Firehome by the same road she and Kori had trod six years ago; to walk into a new village that would not even know Kori's name, as if he had never existed.

She dredged her voice out of the knot in her throat. "Oh, no, Setti—"

"It is okay," he said. "He was my friend. I miss him, too. I'm sorry. I shouldn't have spoken."

Jetta winced. "It's no tribute to Kori to think his friends wouldn't feel his absence, too."

He looked over his shoulder, his night-colored hair a cloak that gathered around him in the dim shelter of the fallen trees. His eyes looked brown in the slanting shadows, the most intense color she had ever seen in them. "I couldn't believe it," he said, "when the news came that Setham had burned, and Kori was dead, and you were in a Water Clan village for healing."

"The world is full of unbelievable things, a'Kam." She used the formal phrasing, naming him her student. A lesser Dancer.

He flushed. "As you say, ak'Kal," responding in turn with her title.

Her head jerked up. "Old Man Fire! I didn't mean to—"

"No, you're right. We're travel to Annam, and there we are not equals, nor were childhood playmates. Best we leave that behind. Best we establish that now."

"Setti!"

"Jetta," he laughed as only Setti could. "I will never make master even of the Second Rank. We both know it. The Circle would never have sent me if you weren't here. I'm grateful for the chance, however I got here. And now," he said, his face again becoming Setti's, "We have miles to go and despite your father's efforts, the pack is still heavy, the road will be long, but I will find joy in every step taken with you, my friend and sister, by my side"

For a moment his exuberance tried to return.

"You'll probably regret it before too long. I'm not good company anymore."

"Who said you were before?" He grinned and skipped out of reach, walking backward in front of her as she fought a smile and lost. "Ha! I knew Old Marra was wrong when she said you could sour milk."

"The old cow will talk of things not her business," said Jetta. Marra was the worst gossip and tale spreader in the village. "In fact, I would bet that Marra *has* talked, long and salaciously and about nothing else for a year, hasn't she?" She smiled a rueful smile and stepped forward again. "Yes, Jetta ak'Kal hiding in her parents' house, a whole village dead and no one talking about what happened? She was bound to invent something to fill the gap."

"Trust me, you don't want to know what she claimed." Setti's voice turned grim.

Jetta sighed. "I can imagine. Let's hear it."

"Jetta, really, leave it. You know what she's like. It's thirty years since she failed the Dance, and she's still bitter. I don't know why folk tolerate her."

"She's clan blood, and since the Old Man won't have her, she is no danger to anyone, unless she were to gore someone with her tongue."

Setti coughed and started to laugh. "You haven't changed, Jetta."

"I'm glad you think so," she said honestly, surprising a blush from him. She glanced up at the trail rising ahead. "Come on, let's hear it. If Marra is saying it, every trader from the Great Water to the Black Mountains will have repeated it by now, so I might as well be prepared."

Setti tugged absently at his knee-length hair, glanced at the black knot atop Jetta's head, and hastily let it go. "According to her, you and Kori were so busy making love one night that fire sprang full-grown into every house in Sctham Vale. Not just the village, mind you, but the Vale, and swept down and consumed everything while you shirked your duty."

Jetta spun around in the road, looking back to her home. "That old *hag!* How *dare—*"

Setti caught her back with a practiced grab left over from their childhood. "Didn't I say that you wouldn't want to know? Hold on! We can't go back just so you can strangle Marra."

Jetta pulled away and started on, half blind with angry tears. *It was* nothing *like that!* she wanted to screech to the uncaring sky, but bit it back. She could feel Setti's eyes on her; he must be burning to know the truth himself, but he just walked on beside her, demanding nothing.

From the corner of her eye she glimpsed his arms in motion, and stopped, taken aback. "What are you doing?"

His hands went on plaiting his own hair into a heavy rope down his back. Swiftly he curled the whole thing up and knotted it at his neck as though he were beginning a patrol. "If the Old Man leaps out at us, I'd just as soon be ready," he said without looking at her.

"How fast can you shed that shirt then?" she jeered, waving her hand at the baggy-sleeved trader shirt he favored over her own tight sleeves. His mouth quirked up, but he just shrugged and quickened his pace, leaving her with the back view of that neat Dancer's knot hiding his one bragging point.

Jetta's throat tightened. Even Kori would not have done that for her.

She blinked fiercely a couple of times, swallowed another knot in her throat, and strode after him into the shadows filling the Vale. A fine pair they were to impress a new village.

Four
Annam Vale

"Father Flame!" Setti stopped as he topped the towering ridge, staring.

Jetta's nerves coiled into knots. Already winded by what felt like a climb straight into the sky, she broke into a shambling run and panted up beside him, expecting a conflagration raging below. All she saw was a fair-sized village clinging to a steep ridge across the wide valley in front of them. She collapsed onto a black boulder in exasperation. For eight days Setti had greeted every new vista with the enthusiasm of a First Rank child chasing sparks, gawking at the shy, sinewy black furred neera of the heights that scampered freely across the rocks. Insisting that he stop to smell the snow-bitten highland air, so maddeningly naïve; she wanted to hit him. He was twenty-seven, not ten. They had lost half a day when he spied a cave from the trail. After two hours of sulking she had relented and freed him to explore. Exploration she could not trust him to do on his own, so she too had been dragged into exploring the small cracks in the face of the cliffs. There was naught to show for it but an abandoned den where the gnawed bones of small animals were left behind.

Now the journey neared its end. She gulped down a lungful of the crisp wind sweeping down from the ridge and eased her shoulders under her pack, all the while hunting whatever had caught his eye this time. Behind them, the world stretched away and away, green and rolling, sloping down to the Great Water far to the east. Ahead, the Black Mountains shouldered into the pale spring sky, stony ramparts stark against the blue, hiding in cloud in places. Snow still lay thick on the higher slopes but below, the streams raged with runoff and slender needle trees speared up green from the layered rock of the ridges. Up here where wind and stone fought an ancient war for standing space, the Delver Clans picked their careful way into the earth, hunting the inky containment stone that kept The Ancient prowling in frustration around the hearthplaces of folk with no skill to drive it away.

Setti turned his head to look at her. "It looks so vulnerable, so *unnatural.*" He flung out a hand toward the village that had to be Annam, the end of the road at last.

Jetta had to laugh. "That's what all villages look like that don't belong to Fire Clans."

"Black," Setti muttered. "I've never seen so much containment stone."

"Get used to it. That's what they do here, remember? That ridge sits over a whole warren of tunnels and mines."

Setti looked around at the outcrops of sable stone thrusting through the stunted trees struggling to take root on the heights. The tall, fat trees of the lowlands with their water-laden boles were absent here; these hardy dwarves looked like they had already spent time in the fire, their trunks gray and weathered, belying the delicate needles springing green from the branches. The highest ridge of all rose steeply above the one the village occupied, towering over Annam Vale, a bare black spine of the world, naked even of this tough growth. Indeed, it was a different world up here, the Stone Delvers' world. And the Windriders.

Jetta shivered. A brisk breeze smelling of needle trees and upland flowers rose from the bottom, chill with the coming of evening. Did it really warm to a Windrider's touch, or was that legend, like so much of the doings of that secretive clan? She had never met a Windrider. They were few, the most scattered of all the blooded clans. Some said it was because they had no hearth place, and so were forced to seek among ordinary folk for their mates, diluting the true Windrider blood. Jetta thought it more likely that their own lifestyle betrayed them. How did folk who followed the storms keep any sort of tradition, or hope to surround themselves with the simple joys of home and hearth? And why were they in Annam, of all places?

I suppose we're about to find out, she thought unhappily.

"Come on," she told Setti. "If we hurry we can make it down and back up again by dark."

He eyed the long hike down into the bottom and back up to the village. "How about we camp and arrive in the morning?"

"Coward," she said without rancor.

"To the bone." He grinned, but she knew he must be nervous. These people had no idea how he struggled for control of the Dance. They would expect him simply to do.

And me, too. Quite suddenly, his nerves caught her as well. She found her hand straying toward her hair in its half-truth of a knot atop her head, and jerked it away, clenching her fist. Torn between guilt and shame, she started down toward the stream washing the road at the bottom of the ridge, wishing she could go cloaked in her hair as she had arrived in Setham. Striding along with the black curtain of it whipping in the wind, the hair of a firedancer that had never known failure.

She studied the sprawl of houses nestled in a hollow of the ridge across the valley. The size of Annam dismayed her; there must be almost two hundred buildings, several streets, and a long tail of scattered houses dotted within the containment wall but outside the village proper. Twin silver forks of a stream split and tumbled around the town itself to north and south, running under a pair of bridges and out through a black containment wall so new the grass had not grown up around its toes to hide the dirt of its making. It looped unevenly around the whole place, a frail barrier against The Ancient, and none at all if frost heaved the deep, fire-laden heartstones into the strip of meadow within. The westering sun caught odd sparks from flecks of windstone embedded in the baser rock all over the hillside, but the houses themselves gleamed dull black in the slanting evening light, their stark outlines broken by gay blocks of flowers rioting in boxes at every window. After nearly a year amid the proud white gleam of Firehome's houses trumpeting their brazen challenge to The Ancient, this tight huddle of unrelieved ebon walls looked strange even to Jetta's eye. Here, she found not one rebel white house to catch the eye—or the attention of The Ancient.

A memory suppressed for a year struck her hard enough

to make her gasp. The houses that had burned the night Kori died had all been new ones, built of windstone in the happy complacency that had settled on Setham Village over five fire-free years under the watchful eye of their renowned Dancer. They had refused to import expensive containment stone for their houses. And paid for it with the ashes of their children.

The Ancient came where it knew it could. It's an opportunist. Isn't that what we were taught in First Rank? It's true. It could never have footed itself in a normal hearthplace so quickly. Kori would not have died had I said no. If I had denied them the windstone buildings.

They climbed down the steep trail in silence until they reached the stream. The water was cold and fresh.

Even the stones in the creek running merrily through the bottom of the Vale were black. Setti leaped from one to another across the shallow ford and turned on the far bank to wait for her. Jetta came more slowly, picking her way over boulders cooling their toes in the stream, their crowns slippery with moss. A thing of wonder, water, that could trap the living fire in heartstone until the rock cooled past lighting. But not The Ancient. Not even water could tame The Ancient. Only the Dance could curb the elemental fire, and that only if the Dancer kept her nerve.

I am master, Jetta told herself fiercely, but her nerves twitched at sight of the black sand sifting into new patterns on the stream bed with the uneven running of the water. Walking this Vale was like tramping through the remains of fire. She shivered and bumbled her last leap onto the far bank.

Setti caught her with a cheerful, "Whup! The light's going, but it's not that dim! Of course, you'd think Stone Delvers could lay a better trail, wouldn't you? This thing's about as smooth as Marra's tongue."

Jetta snorted, startled into laughter. Setti grinned, a faint gleam in the deepening gloom. "That's better. I'm sure we would inspire great confidence limping in with twisted ankles."

"Better than not arriving at all, strangers." The voice out of the dusk startled Jetta so badly she tripped again and would have fallen except for another of Setti's quick grabs. Both of them whirled to face the steep bank rising above the road.

"Who's there?" Setti demanded.

A snort of laughter blew over them like the deep rumbling of gas in one of The Ancient's lairs. "Firewatch. Who are you?"

Jetta drew herself up, still hunting for the owner of that voice amid the tangled weeds and brush atop the bank. "I am Firedancer Jetta ak'Kal of the Third Rank. This is Settak a'Kam of the Second Rank. We come at the request of Annam Village."

"Jetta ak'Kal!" The deep voice took on a tinge of surprised respect. "Here is an unexpected honor. If you would wait, I would be honored to join you and show you the way to the village inn."

"They've heard of you, Jetta!" Setti said in her ear, doubtless pleased and proud to accompany a master of proven reputation. Jetta groaned inwardly. He would not be so pleased when the village elders demanded to know why she was no longer under contract to Setham.

A low crash of brush bending, a crackle of breaking branches and a cascade of dirt from the bank announced the coming of whoever lurked atop the bank. "They're not too graceful above ground, are they?" Setti murmured, then stepped back involuntarily as the largest man Jetta had ever seen materialized out of the dusk. She gawked up at him, tilting her head back to see all the way up the enormous length of him. His breadth nearly matched his height. The width of his shoulders would have made two of Setti. He smelled of damp stone and new-turned earth, as though he had stepped straight from some deep, underground hiding place.

"Jetta ak'Kal." The Delver stooped to peer into her face, blinking round, fist-sized blue eyes that seemed lit from within. "Hmm. They said you were talented," he stood and smiled a mighty smile. "They forgot to say you were pretty. Such dark eyes!"

Jetta stared. The sun was well down behind the mountains, the night advancing fast. How could he possibly see what she looked like? He straightened to give Setti the same slow appraisal, concluding with a clap on the back that nearly sent him sprawling. The Stone Delver turned back to her, leaving Setti feebly trying to gather what was left of the air in his lungs.

"Rununn a'Kam," he announced, thumping a huge hand against his chest. "With your permission, I will guide you to the village."

"Permission? Of course. I would be honored."

"Then it will be all right if I leave my watch for an hour?"

"Watch? Ah. Firewatch, you said." Gamely Jetta grasped after a whole set of concepts and rules foreign to the governance of any village where she had ever been.

Rununn nodded, setting shaggy hair flopping around his face. For all his size, she realized that he was very young. "We have watchers posted all around the village, ak'Kal. Nowhere is safe these days. The fire comes at will, and we have only our eyes and our good strong voices to roust the village against it."

"With what?" Setti blurted and faded behind Jetta in confusion when both of them turned toward him in the gloom.

Rununn laughed, a sound like rock falling. "This is a Stone Clan village. Clap a trough carved from containment stone over flame, and it flees fast enough."

"Not very efficient," Setti said.

"Inventive," Jetta said tartly, picturing villagers stalking fire with stone. She shuddered and turned to Rununn. "And dangerous. I salute your folk for their courage. I saw no burn scars from across the ridge earlier. Delvers must be quick with their buckets."

"Assuredly, ak'Kal!" Pride rang in the journeyman's voice. "No fire has lived more than a few minutes. But—" His enthusiasm faded. "—We've been lucky as well as vigilant. And we grow tired, ak'Kal. It is hard, watching every moment, living in fear of seeing fire spring up behind you. The little ones cry at night in the dark, afraid The Ancient will rise in their beds."

"It's worse than I was told," Jetta murmured. She lifted her head briskly. "Come, a'Kam. Both of you. The night isn't getting any younger. Show us the way, Rununn."

"Assuredly, ak'Kal." Rununn lifted Jetta's pack neatly off her shoulders before she could snatch it back. "I'll carry this. A Third Rank master should not come to her place burdened like an apprentice."

Setti bristled, for it seemed like a rebuke, but Jetta touched him to silence. "Different clans, different ways," she reminded him softly, gratified to know that the Stone Delvers honored rank across clans. The Water Clans had scant regard for other talents, or perhaps it was only fire that failed to spark their awe. Things might be different if a Windrider found himself stranded among them. The huge, destructive storms from the sea that periodically scoured the coastal lands bare were half wind, half water. Generally it took both clans to deflect them. But fire never troubled the Water Clans' sleep.

The three of them tramped up the trail through an inky night that seemed to arrive faster here on the heights than in Firehome Vale. Perhaps the black ridges swallowed light, or maybe it was the proximity to the stars burning like small *hysths* overhead. They seemed very close up here, fixed and steady, staring at Jetta with hard little eyes. She swept one glance across that burning web and dropped her gaze, her skin prickling with sudden nerves. Walking this ridge toward a trusting village seemed suddenly very like approaching the Circle to dance her initiation into Second Rank. She felt like an apprentice again.

They came to the low stone wall circling the village and the southern bridge across the stream, that led into an open meadow with a row of long buildings on the right, hulking against the dimming sky. Another watcher stepped out of the darkness beside the bridge, a huge shadow silhouetted against the pearlescent riff of whitewater burbling away down the hill. Jetta and Setti both shied back a step but Rununn announced grandly, "I've brought them! Jetta ak'Kal and Settak a'Kam, all the way from Firehome Vale!"

Jetta peered up through the darkness, trying to make out a face in the black bulk above her, but all she could see were two huge lambent orbs far larger than stars. *Their eyes do glow in the dark,* she realized with a jolt of surprise, and then squirmed a bit in shame for knowing so little of this clan whose labors spared half the world from fire. In all of history, no Firedancer had been assigned to a Delver village. What need had there ever been?

A voice like a distant avalanche rumbled out of the night. "Welcome, Jetta ak'Kal, Settak a'Kam. Twice welcome to

Annam Vale. You are needed. The elders not on watch are gathered at the inn, Rununn. Take them there and return to your watch."

"Yes, ak'Kal," Rununn said.

Jetta, on the point of starting on, stopped and peered up again at those luminous eyes an arm's reach over her head.

"Ak'Kal? Is the Vale so hard-pressed that masters must stand watch in the dark?"

"All share the danger, so all share the labor," the master said mildly. "My name is Nuurn. I shall come later to the council."

"I look forward to seeing you there." Jetta moved past him onto the bridge. Setti's silence behind her told her exactly what he was thinking.

Why didn't the Circle tell us it was so bad?

The dusky solidity of the houses seemed to gather light and bury it. Jetta stumbled now and again on an uneven paving stone, longing for some friendly gleam to spill out from a window onto the night-shot cobbles. But the stars burned cold and dim overhead, and the houses stood shuttered tight against the menace lurking deep under their foundations. After Setti tripped and nearly fell, Rununn seemed to realize that the Firedancers did not share his keen night sight and slowed his long-legged stride.

"May I help?" he asked uncertainly, setting a huge hand under Jetta's elbow. "Ayesha keeps telling me that other folk don't see in the dark, but I seem unable to fasten it in my brain."

Jetta relaxed in the giant's grip and set her own hand on Setti's shoulder to steady him. "Ayesh?" she asked, her ear pricking to a name that had none of the deep, earth-colored tones of the Delver names.

"The Windrider quartered at our house," Rununn said casually.

Setti missed another stride and nearly took Jetta down with him. He stopped dead in the street, staring over her head at Rununn. "Windriders? Here?"

Belatedly it occurred to Jetta that in her brooding annoyance with Setti over the past eight days she had not shared what Farahk had told her about Annam being full of Windriders. Rununn turned his head, his cerulean eyes blinking in mild surprise. It looked to Jetta as though someone had shuttered the moons.

"Yes. Three winters now. They have taken lodging all over the Vale, since the inn was not large enough to hold them all."

"Father Flame!" Setti whispered. "Jetta?

"Don't worry about it," Jetta said tartly. "Rununn, is it far to the inn?"

"Eh? No, it is just there." His arm shot out, a black bar against the spangled sky, pointing at an anonymous building somewhat bigger than the rest, two doors farther down the street. Sadly Jetta missed the cheerful spill of light from Setham's merry travelers' rest, the music and the laughter that had shed its untroubled ambiance half the length of the main street. All gone now.

She lifted her chin and followed Rununn down the street and in at the door of Annam's inn. *The Stone Cup* said the sign swinging above the arch of the doorway, a quick glimpse caught as the door opened and light shot into the street as though attacking the night. A wave of warm air that smelled of burli brew and wood smoke, bread and roast meat and deep stone caverns rolled out with it. Setti coughed; Jetta, blinking, just had time to note that even the black, cleverly carved door of the place was stone before momentum carried her over the threshold into a sudden pool of silence within.

"The Firedancers!" Rununn announced to the room at large, sounding absurdly pleased with himself. "Jetta ak'Kal and Settak a'Kam. They passed my watch post just at dusk."

"And needed you to show them the way up the only road?" a deep voice said from somewhere by the hearth across the room. Jetta winced, but Rununn answered with dignity, "Of course. You must know Burrood, we are raised to honor ak'Kal?"

A deep rumble swelled in the room, vibrating the very stone under her feet. For a horrid instant Jetta thought that The Ancient was beating at the floor, until she recognized laughter, a sound like mountains falling. She looked around, squinting against the aureate glow of oil lamps burning in bright brass sconces along the walls. Stone Delvers jammed the room, most of them with their faces turned toward the hearth, laughing at the one Rununn had answered. It was a forest of broad backs clad in leather jerkins over green or gray shirts and jutting heads crowned with shaggy hair uniformly the deep black-brown of river dirt. She looked up at Rununn towering beside her and saw a round, unlined face the color of rich earth that she could not have spanned with both hands. Dark hair fizzed around his head, tumbling untidily to his shoulders. Rununn peered back at her in the same instant, and grinned, so untroubled that Jetta took heart.

"He got you, Burrood," a female voice said. Her focus clearly on the huge delver who sat scowling by the fire.

Jetta looked to the voice. The largest woman she had ever seen strode toward her, hands outstretched in welcome. She stood head and shoulders taller than Jetta and yet still lacked a head of Rununn's height.

"Father Flame!" Setti muttered behind her, taken aback. Jetta wanted to kick him. Still, the sheer size of these people unnerved her a bit. She could have hidden a Fire Clan family under the sweep of those green skirts.

"Be welcome to Annam, Jetta ak'Kal, Settak a'Kam," the woman said, swallowing Jetta's hand in both of hers. "I'm Urrana, keeper of this inn and head of the Circle of Annam Vale. You are most heartily welcome here."

Setti stiffened to respectful attention behind her. Jetta found herself peering up into huge, sky-blue eyes set in a lined brown face that bore an incongruously delicate beauty under its springing cap of curling brown hair. *Good bones,* Kirana would have said. Jetta found herself wondering what her mother would have made of an innkeeper as head of Firehome's Circle.

She fumbled in her belt pouch for the letter and proffered it into Urrana's huge hand. "Our credentials," she said, seeing the innkeeper's bemused look. "Thank you for your welcome. It gladdens us to find such warmth at the end of our journey."

"Such a tiny thing as you feels the chill, no doubt," a deep voice said disparagingly. She thought it was Burrood again, but couldn't be sure. Urrana threw a frowning glance over her shoulder.

"Talent chooses the vessel, not the vessel the talent," Urrana said pointedly, drawing another long avalanche of laughter. Jetta sensed undercurrents in the room, swirling at odds around herself and Setti, and wondered if Rununn had been mistaken in his assertion that all of Annam Vale looked forward to their coming.

Urrana smiled down at the Firedancers. "Come to the fire. Rununn, shut the door. Were you born under a stone?" Which drew still more laughter. Rununn flushed, a remarkable effect like the sun rising over the mountains, and took a step backward, one hand fumbling behind him for the door.

"I—um—must return to my watch. Jetta ak'Kal, welcome." He fled, pulling the heavy carved door closed behind him. Jetta gazed at it a little forlornly, feeling lost without his friendly bulk beside her.

Setti moved up to stand tight against her back, just as Kori would have done. Jetta, floundering in a sudden storm of gratitude and grief, almost missed it when Urrana moved away, threading a path through the heavy stone tables toward the hearth.

Stone, Jetta realized, belatedly taking a step to follow. Everything here seemed made of white or black stone: the tables, the chairs, the benches under the windows, even the plates and cups. And why not, if the only timber to be had was imported from the lowlands or confined to the stunted upland growth? Still, it seemed incredible that hands so huge could carve the delicate wreath wrapped around that cup there, or the smiling sun above the hearth, inset white in black. *How else pass the winter?* she guessed, and then they arrived at a long table set to one side of the hearth, where huge bodies slid obligingly aside to make room.

The benches stood waist high even on Setti. Jetta envisioned an awkward, undignified scramble to crawl up, only to sit with feet dangling like a child, and rebelled. "Urrana ak'Kal?" she asked, adding the title as a question, drawing every eye again. "Perhaps—"

Urrana turned. "I was master, but no more," she said, puzzling both Firedancers. "I am an innkeeper now. Urrana will do." She eyed Jetta's diminutive figure against the height of the bench and smoothly evicted a sprawling giant from a low-slung settle beside the hearth. "Get up, Burrood. Our guests have come far and the evening is chill. Let them sit where it's warm."

Burrood scowled but stood up, a hulking giant whose shaggy brown head nearly brushed the thick rafters. "Time I was gone home anyway," he said, and marched to the door without a glance at either Jetta or Setti. An awkward silence settled in his wake.

Setti shifted uneasily; Jetta stilled him with a quick hand on his wrist. Let the Delvers take the lead in courtesy. It was not for Dancers to apologize for their presence in a village threatened by fire.

Urrana picked up a poker the size of a small log and stirred up the fire snapping busily in its bed of containment stone. Abruptly she straightened and whirled to face them, the poker still in her hand. "Oh! Perhaps we should not have open flame here like this?"

Jetta laughed. "How else should we stay warm? It wouldn't dare leap out at *me*. And it does a Dancer's heart good to see her enemy dancing to another's tune, good Urrana."

Laughter bloomed in the inn again, erasing the chill of Burrood's departure. The innkeeper beamed. "Good! I never gave a thought to that. Will you sit now, Jetta ak'Kal? There is food warm in the kitchen, and burli in cups small enough to fit your hand. We have had much practice of late in making things to smaller scale."

Jetta sank gingerly onto the stone settle, prepared to find it unkind to her tired bones. It had no hard edges, only gently turned curves that seemed to enfold her as if the chair had been shaped for her alone. She watched Setti trying out the other end of the long seat and saw from the subdued amazement in his face that the same phenomenon had found him as well.

A sly chuckle rumbled through the room. She looked around into a sea of broad faces watching her, all huge sapphire eyes and masses of brown hair. The gleam of silver pins anchoring thick locks marked a few women scattered among the tables. Jetta smiled back, aware of a joke hovering. "Is this how you lure folk to stay the night, Urrana? I've never sat in such a comfortable chair."

Urrana's laugh soared above the deeper rumble of the men. Again, it sounded like mountains shifting, but the faces looked pleased. "These layabouts scarcely need encouragement to stay, ak'Kal."

A pair of youngsters, one girl, one boy, swept out of a door in the back of the room, their hands full of trays laden with plates and cups, pitchers and bowls giving up delicious aromas. They were neither of them past childhood, Jetta guessed, but either of them would have towered over her. They hurried through the crowd, their eyes flicking nervously from the trays to the Firedancers and back again, the pair of them clearly torn between curiosity and a healthy fear of dropping something. They were so alike that Jetta thought they must be brother and sister, both with the same underlying grace to their bones that marked Urrana. The innkeeper herself confirmed their ancestry as they came hurrying up.

"Mind that pitcher, Rinood! Would you dump the wine on the guest and feed the bread to the fire? Mururrn, it is customary to let the guest fill his own plate. How did children of mine turn out so brainless, eh?"

But her voice held no malice, and she reached to give the girl Rinood a hand as the heavy tray tilted, deftly snatching the pitcher sliding toward the fire. Jetta rescued the endangered bread and handed it to Setti, whose lips twitched madly as he took plates and cups from Mururrn's huge hands, which seemed unable to quite grasp anything so small. Chccsc, hot spiced meat that smelled wonderful, and sliced yellow noda roots rolled in what looked like crushed nuts all ended in stone serving dishes on the bench between Jetta and Setti; flanked by an array of cups and plates scaled to ordinary hands. Rinood and Mururrn stood back, trays empty, anxiously watching the Firedancers.

Jetta smiled at them. "Thank you. Well-served. The food looks wonderful."

Huge eyes blinked in unison, and then twin smiles lit their faces. "There," Urrana said, her voice more fond than chastising. "I told you the place would not burst into flame because they were in it. Get about your other duties now."

Setti, his mouth full of crusty warm bread, stopped chewing to stare. Jetta watched the children scamper away, an amazing sight with bodies so large, and looked up at Urrana in dismay.

"Were they truly afraid of us?"

Urrana waved a dismissive hand. "Like half the village, they are ignorant of strangers. They've seen only a few trader folk come for the containment stone, and the Windriders. Firedancers and Water Clans were tales to them. Strange tales, at that."

"But not now," Jetta said clearly.

Urrana sank onto a bench beside the fire. Jetta became aware that the room had taken on a listening hush as faces turned toward them. Eyes glowed queerly from the shadows at the far end, winking like stars seen through shifting leaves. Broad shoulders seemed to shuffle together into a solid wall between her and the door. She forced herself to keep on eating. Annam Vale had invited them. Surely there could be no menace here but from The Ancient.

Urrana threw a slow look around the room. A flick of an eyebrow brought one giant to his feet to stand beside the closed kitchen door; another barred the outer door to block any latecomers. A chill crept down Jetta's spine. It spread as Urrana turned her wide and troubled gaze on her.

"We are all masters here, Jetta ak'Kal, save for Settak a'Kam, and he must hear this. We would wait until a more civilized hour and allow you to rest before holding council, but you must know what you face before The Ancient takes a notion to strike again. We have no knowledge of fire's ways, and glad we are to see the pair of you this night."

Jetta reached steadily for one of the noda roots, wishing Setti would quit staring as though The Ancient loomed in front of him. The cold had congealed somewhere in her own mid-section. These people were terrified. Old Man Fire, what had the Circle sent them into?

"The Circle at Firehome said The Ancient has crept into the abandoned tunnels beneath Annam," she said, to break the hush. "Rununn said it's likely to spring up anywhere at any time, and that you've been chasing it with stone buckets. I commend your courage, masters. Please tell me—when did this start, and how is it that you came to call upon other clans to assist you?"

Thus, obliquely she asked for an explanation for the Windriders in the Vale, and the large chunk of the story the Circle had so thoughtfully left out.

Urrana sighed and fixed huge eyes on Jetta. "Mind, ak'Kal, there is no great secret here, but the danger is worse than the village knows, and so we are careful of who hears. Some believe stone business is for Stone Delvers alone, and they scorn help from outside. Burrood is only one. Many do not believe The Ancient could find a way to attack a village made all of containment stone."

"But surely if the danger is so great they must see it for themselves?" Setti blurted out.

"They have seen scattered incidents of fire quickly dealt with. They have not seen what three masters of this Circle have seen: The Ancient itself roaring in a long-disused tunnel in an abandoned mine."

Jetta felt as if someone had doused her in cold water. Setti sat equally frozen beside her, his hand suspended mid-reach for more bread. "Tell me," Jetta said, and marveled that her voice was so calm.

Urrana nodded, looking steadier than a few moments ago. "It started eight moons ago. Leaf fall in Annam is a strange time for The Ancient, I would have thought, with the snow already gathering on the heights. There are many abandoned workings down the length of the Vale. Some are depleted; others were given up as too dangerous long ago because the surrounding rock was unstable. Men died from stone falls and cave-ins, and so we moved to easier delving, but there were still rich veins of containment stone left behind. The mines we work are deep, ak'Kal, and delve deeper each year as the upper layers give up their stone. We thought to assess some of the old tunnels to see if there might be a way to work them again this year. So Errull, Rennuhr, and Nuurn went one day to the working at Wind Point on just such an errand. Nuurn."

Jetta jumped, recognizing the name and the deep voice that answered. She had not seen him come in from his watch by the bridge. "We three entered the tunnel," he said, "expecting to see blocked accesses and fallen ceilings, and those there were in plenty for the first few turnings. The accesses to the lower levels were still open, though, and we went down three levels without harm. But when we cleared the entrance to the shaft leading down to the fourth, we saw a glow and heard a roaring, deep, loud, and felt heat blasting up from below. The whole shaft was full of fire. Even as we watched, part of the wall below us crumbled into the flames and a section of the tunnel beyond us fell. We fled, I am not too proud to say."

"Wise," Jetta murmured. "But—if this was last autumn, why has The Ancient not traveled to the surface and burst onto the ridge itself?"

"We collapsed the upper levels," Nuurn said. "Two are filled with the remaining containment stone from depleted veins on the first and second levels. The last is filled with windstone and dirt, packed tight so no air can pass."

Jetta frowned. "That is extremely difficult, ak'Kal—"

"We had help," Urrana said simply.

"Ah," breathed Setti.

The same thought burst in Jetta's head. "Rununn says there are Windriders quartered in the village," she said delicately.

"Rununn seems to have said a great deal in such a short walk," a woman's voice said.

"Please don't blame him. He was most eager to make us welcome. And, as you say, there are no great secrets here, are there?"

An instant of frozen silence, and then came the laughter like mountains breaking. Setti blew out a long sigh of relief. *Why are we chasing sparks around the Dance ground?* Jetta thought, irritated with the whole game. A tunnel full of fire, the Old Man himself from the sound of it, inadequately smothered and left to rage and pick at his prison until he came roaring out in some other direction. Why had the Circle neglected to mention these details? Or had they known?

That thought settled her anger. She lifted her head to stare Urrana in the face. "What assistance might Windriders give in a crisis of fire, short of sealing the caves for you?" She pictured a wind howling into that tunnel, packing dirt and debris into every crevice and rift and crack, sealing the infinitesimal fissures that were all that fire needed to worm its way up from the depths. But her imagination skipped on without effort, picturing the same wind encountering a *hysth*, breathing life into a single tentacle of The Ancient. Fire flaring into a column, a wall, a mountain to rival those around this vale.

She shuddered and forced her mind back to Urrana's answer. The innkeeper's mouth quirked in an odd smile. "They're good folk, Windriders," she said. "Odd, until you grow used to their ways, but useful to have around. They keep the passes clear for us in winter and battle the storms that threaten to sweep us all into the valley. These mountains breed terrible winds, fit to scour the ridges bare. The Windriders call them gentle breezes, good training for them, who must stand and fight the great storms thrown up by the sea."

She chuckled. Setti and Jetta stared. "I see," Jetta managed. "And they're here. Now?"

"Yes. Is it a problem?"

Such staggering naiveté illustrated to Jetta more clearly than a hundred Circle warnings the real danger here in Annam Vale. These people knew *nothing* of fire.

"I suppose that remains to be seen, doesn't it?"

Beside her, Setti all but choked on his burli. Urrana gave him an uncertain glance, her vast eyebrows drawing into a slight frown. Jetta lifted her voice, wanting to kick Setti and not daring with every eye watching them.

"Ak'Kal, what you've told me makes disturbing hearing. The Ancient is cunning, and vicious, and takes ill to setbacks. If blocked in one direction, assuredly it will try again. Tomorrow I would like to see what was done at Wind Point and begin an assessment of the other abandoned tunnels. Have you been into any of those since discovering the fire in the first?"

"Yes," Nuurn said flatly. "They are fire-free."

"For now. I tell you, ak'Kal, if there is any way at all for The Ancient to advance into them, it will, soon or late. It will try hardest to come here, into the village itself—"

"It can't!" a chorus of voices declared. A single voice won out. A giant stood up, towering over the rest. Jetta made out a weathered face, ruddy in the lamplight, a great brown bush of a beard and a mane of dark hair cascading free onto broad shoulders. Huge, glowing eyes fixed on her, not angry, but adamant.

"It can't," he repeated, and then remembered his manners. "I am Errull ak'Kal, the master builder here. Though we never before felt the threat of fire ourselves, we design and test what others must build. Every house here is floored, walled, and roofed with containment stone. The Ancient would find nothing in which to root itself." He waved one huge hand around at the fireplace mantel, the stone benches and chairs, the crockery. "Pardon, Jetta ak'Kal, but stone is our business."

"As fire is mine, ak'Kal. Fire attacked even into Firehome Vale nine days gone. I fought it myself. It was malicious." And as mouths gaped and shoulders sagged in dismay, she added more gently, "The Ancient grows bolder, good folk. I've seen it attack an inhabited dwelling nestled among three others that weren't. It knows where life abides. It hates living things. It will attack here if we let it."

"How will you prevent it?" a harsher voice asked. Heads turned; Jetta saw frowns on many faces, Urrana's included. As Errull sank back into his chair, another master stood, this one shorter, but far broader through the shoulders, a massive barrel-shaped figure that looked as if it could stand against an avalanche. "I have heard of you, Jetta ak'Kal. Trader tales say the last village you guarded lies now in ashes."

"Enough, Nugurr!" Urrana snapped, but Jetta threw up a hand. The moment was here. Best to face it and get it over.

She lifted her head, letting a little silence stretch. Unwinking lambent eyes watched her like blue stars in the gloom. She turned to face Nugurr squarely, pleased when he shifted uneasily. Beside her Setti moved too, in protest, defense, she wasn't sure which. She touched his leg to silence him.

"I was assigned to Setham Village," she said clearly. "Five years and more my lifemate Kori and I lived there, and Setham was fire-free for all of it. Last spring—" Her voice wavered unexpectedly; fingering the silver promise bracelet on her wrist, she forced the lump out of her throat.

"Are you aware that spring is the worst season for fire, ak'Kal? Not the autumn when the grass crackles underfoot and the harvests lie in peril within the containment walls around the fields, but spring, when fire worms to the surface in heartstones heaved by the frost. Left unchecked, it will fight stubbornly for a foothold amidst torrential downpours and burgeoning greenery, race through veins of windstone and burn whole ridges to ash, until it meets some barrier it cannot cross, and rages in frustration until even the stone is consumed. Then the Fire Clans gather and the Windriders summon their power to turn back the storm winds that invariably spawn in the heart of flame." She gestured around at the village and the untouched green vale. "You have never seen such a thing here, ak'Kal, but in Setham Vale there were old scars on the hills, and we lived at a knife's edge every day, Kori and I, ever on alert."

She drew a long breath, aware of Setti frozen on the bench beside her, of eyes brightening and dimming as heads turned toward her or away to mutter to neighbors, breathy murmurs like the wind talking to itself.

"Last spring," she said, producing a silence deeper than wells, "The Ancient rose without warning and found a foothold in a house at the far end of the village. I had been ill all day and did not feel it come. Kori went to fight it alone. I woke to find half the village in flames, and Kori—" She faltered. "Kori was trapped in a house, trying to save some children. The Ancient—The Ancient was too strong for him. He was only a master of the Second Rank, taken by surprise when the fire turned on him. The house fell in. He died, and the children with him. I was injured trying to save him. The fire," she paused. "The fire took the village. I was taken by survivors to a Water Clan that healed me."

A long sigh muttered around the room. Setti bowed his head. Jetta wondered if he had heard the gaps in that story, but she could not—*would* not, rake open all those wounds and bleed for strangers. Urrana's face crinkled in sympathy, but Nugurr was unmoved.

"You haven't answered my question, ak'Kal. How will you prevent Setham's fate here? You're hardly more than a child."

"I am a master of the Third Rank! I am warned that The Ancient is loose, and I have a village full of children brave enough to chase fire with a bucket to work with. Will their parents assist, or stand dithering and wondering if their Firedancer is up to the task?"

The silence that time gathered so deep she could have drowned in it. Setti sat as though carved from stone, his eyes two huge blue pebbles that looked ready to fall out of his head. Urrana's face held no expression at all; not one of the assembled masters, man nor woman, so much as twitched a feathery eyebrow. Jetta would have laughed at the look on Nugurr's face if she hadn't been so tired and so angry and so aware that if she did, she might lose every scrap of goodwill in this place.

A woman's snort blasted into the silence. "Sit down, Nugurr. Since you don't know how to solve the problem, let us listen to someone who might."

Might, Jetta thought in dismay. But at least they seemed willing to listen, even if Nugurr had dented their trust.

Nugurr sank with grudging lack of haste onto his bench. Jetta looked around a sea of faces showing a new reserve in the way they regarded her, and cursed Nugurr ak'Kal for making her job twice as difficult. She itched to stand up but realized in time how futile a gesture that would be when everything in the room only underscored how small she must seem to them. She drew a deep breath and remembered tiny Minna. Kori's grandmother had been the greatest Dancer of her generation and managed to terrorize impudent children twice her size until her dying day. Jetta drew her legs demurely under her and sat up straighter on the bench.

Urrana stood up, breaking the frozen spell. "I thank you, ak'Kal," she said, taking authority back into her own hands. "We will meet again tomorrow to discuss these matters further. For now, you are guests under my roof, deserving of quiet rest. The rest of you, go. Save your questions for tomorrow."

She flapped a big hand toward the street door. Without protest even Nugurr stood up, ignoring both Firedancers. Jetta watched him make ponderously for the door, trailed by three or four other Delvers who crowded close around him, their voices a low rumble like the earth grumbling. They disappeared into the night, leaving Jetta wondering if the meeting would reconvene elsewhere to assemble new arguments for the morning.

"Well," Settak said breathily in her ear. "That was fun. I can hardly wait for breakfast."

"Ak'Kal, Urrana," she said after the room emptied. "I am the youngest Third Rank master to ever hold the badge. They did not give it to me. I earned it. If The Ancient wins here at Annam, neither Setti nor I will be alive to know it."

Five
Wind Point

They followed Urrana up a staircase with risers high enough to make them both stretch at each step and in at doorways looming half again Setti's height. Urrana spent a fair bit of time muttering apologies that all the rooms set aside for lowland traders were full. *Of Windriders, no doubt,* Jetta thought sourly, but she was too tired to care. Even the sight of a bed that threatened to engulf her like a child's toy tucked away in its box for safekeeping sparked only an intense longing for its soft embrace.

Alone in a room scaled for giants, Jetta dropped her pack beside the door and made for the makeshift steps of stone blocks leading up to that wondrous ocean of soft comforters and fluffy pillows. Setti's voice behind her startled her half out of her wits.

"Jetta?"

She spun around. "What are you doing here? Go to bed, Setti!"

Setti flushed and came farther into the room, his jaw setting with a stubbornness she recognized from long ago. His hair was unbound, hanging in silky disarray around him, as though he had started for bed and changed his mind. He shut the door and stood looking at her in a silence that crept up Jetta's nerves.

"Tell me the rest," he said quietly.

Jetta stiffened. "You know everything about Annam that I know. I'm sorry I forgot to tell you about the Windriders—"

"I don't care about them. Tell me what you didn't tell the Delvers. About Kori. About Setham. The Ancient is beating at the door here. Tell me how it defeated you, Jett"

Jetta quailed. "I—" She struggled with it; in a year she

had told only the Circle what happened that last night in Setham. But he needed to know. Deserved to know.

Nervously she reached up and jerked loose the thong binding her own hair, spilling it down in a friendly veil around her face. "We were asleep," she began jerkily, raking her fingers through the thick strands, putting them between Setti and herself. "It was late, half of the midwatch gone at least. We never stood midwatch, Kori and I, after the first year. I always knew when fire was coming in Setham. The veins of The Ancient run deep there, and it's a long way up to the surface. We always had time to rouse the villagers and meet it. That night, I didn't feel well, hadn't all day, so we both were abed early. I slept right through the first alarm. I still can't believe I never heard it, never felt the fire coming. I didn't feel Kori get up either. It was only when someone screamed outside the window that I woke and found him gone. The fire, it was in the house at the far end of the street, already soaring through the roof. So strong. It was malicious, the Old Man himself, and I never felt it coming."

She became aware of her own cowardice, flung her hair back and peered into Setti's white face. "I ran. We always slept in Dance leathers, so I was ready, but—I never saw a fire move so fast. It exploded into the next house before I reached the first. I didn't know where Kori was until I heard him scream. He was *inside* the first house, in the heart of it, with The Ancient all around him. The fire was dead white, and so hot, and I swear Setti, it was laughing, Setti. It was laughing." She closed her eyes, hearing again the deep, horrid gloating roar.

"The villagers tried to stop me from going in. Someone screamed it was no use, that Kori was dead. I wouldn't believe it. I went in. The fire was everywhere: overhead, in the floor, crawling up the walls, *melting* the floor, but it retreated from the Dance. A little. I didn't see at first that it was baiting me. I could still hear Kori screaming in an inner room. There were children with him. I didn't know it until later. And then I saw him trying to get out past a wall of *hysths*. He wasn't dancing. He—set"

Setti's head was bent, hidden by a curtain of night-colored hair, but the back of his hand gleamed wet in the lamplight. Jetta closed her eyes tight against a memory seared into her soul. "If he had danced, he would have had a chance, but he panicked. He was a master of the Second Rank and he panicked when the Old Man trapped him. As soon as he saw me he tried to break through to me, and that's when The Ancient sprang. The *hysths*—ah, Setti, the *hysths* all plunged together, just fell out of the ceiling and charged across the floor and up into a wall from floor to roof. I couldn't see him anymore, but I could hear him screaming!"

She drew a shuddering breath. "I tried, Setti. I tried to get to him, but the fire... Even the Dance couldn't stop it. Or I couldn't. I don't even remember dancing. I think I did. But the fire was laughing. That's what I remember. This deep, roaring laughter, and then a huge flash of flame rolling toward me. The villagers said it knocked me out the door. I don't remember. All I remember was when Kori stopped screaming."

Setti scrubbed at his face with his hair and looked up. "The Ancient ambushed you."

Jetta jerked away, refusing a notion that had gnawed at her for half a year. Legend said The Ancient had been penned in the deeps by the Earth Mother at the Beginning of all things to keep her angry firstborn from eating the world. It was *not* legend that the Old Man was malicious, hungry, an opportunistic killer. She knew in her nerve endings that The Ancient had a will and a purpose. But it had never seemed more than the cunning drive of instinct, like a hungry beast hunting for food. Could it truly be more than that?

"The Ancient doesn't think, Setti," she said, very low. "It couldn't—"

He caught her arm, halting her restless retreat. "Why did it pick that time, eh? Winter was dying. Snowmelt and rain—" He stopped under her scornful glance. Jetta saw him think about it, forced from Second Rank complaisance. Heartfire did not die in water but burned on until it either discovered it could not spread and retreated into the deep or died a stubborn and lingering death in cold stone. Enough snow, enough rain, might discourage it, but a river flooding through Setham would not have kept The Ancient from eating what it had already taken.

Setti frowned. "It makes no sense."

Jetta hesitated, with the worst of all jabbing her like a

hook in the guts. But this too, he should know, so that he might know things about the enemy the masters had never taught. She caught herself crossing her arms defensively across her stomach and forced them down to her sides, dropping her gaze from Setti's sudden, narrow look.

"It took me a while to understand. It wasn't until the healers told me why I was ill that day that I knew." She struggled a moment longer, and then finally said, very low, "I didn't know I was with child until after I had lost it. But The Ancient knew."

Setti gasped, his eyes the dark blue of deep water in a face gone the color of old ivory. *"Jetta-"* he began.

She turned away. "It's past and done. You needed to know. Now you do."

"But—how could The Ancient have known you were ill?"

"Because it came up without opposition. That's all it took. The Old Man is an opportunist, Setti, didn't you listen in class?"

Setti took a long stride and caught her shoulder, turning her to face him. "There's more to it than that." He shook his hair back, the lamplight making a golden mask of his face. "Jetta, it's never been proved that The Ancient is intelligent, only cunningly reactive, like a beast that learns to haunt hearths hunting scraps. If it knew you were with child—Old Man Fire, Jetta, it deliberately trapped Kori!"

"But it would have had no hold if Kori hadn't panicked. So says the Circle."

"Even masters die if The Ancient is too strong for them. Blaming Kori is no answer."

She looked at him, her face stiffening with the effort not to weep yet again. "And neither is speculating about it. It won't bring him back."

"Jetta!" His hands tightened, forcefulness so foreign to her memory of him that she looked up at him in frowning puzzlement. "Think about it. The Circle itself turned out to warn us. You saw those flames depart unbidden. If The Ancient is acting strangely now, could it be that what happened to Kori wasn't his fault? Maybe he did dance—and it didn't work."

She stared at him, her guts congealing into a ball of ice. "There's a happy thought."

He let her go and stood watching in silence as she rubbed thoughtfully at her arms, more to brush down the prickling hair than because his grip had hurt her. "Why wouldn't the Circle say so?" she muttered, more to herself than him. "They wouldn't send a Dancer into danger unawares, especially if the old patterns of the Dance have failed."

"You heard them. What if they don't know what new patterns will defeat it?"

She shivered. "Another happy thought. You're no fun at all, Setti."

He managed a laugh. "And to think that I thought it was an honor being assigned to a village at last."

A new and chilling thought occurred to Jetta, that she kept out of her face with difficulty. Why would the Circle send a half-capable journeyman and a fire-touched master to a village with no experience of flame to test The Ancient's grip there?

Because if we fail, they have lost nothing, she guessed. *We're expendable, Setti and I.*

Anger flamed through her, but she kept it off her face for Setti's sake. "Go to bed, Setti," she said, quietly enough not to sting. "I'm sorry I didn't tell you before. I—"

"Don't. I just needed to know what these children have been chasing around with stone cups." He shuddered. "Father Flame, they've nerve at least."

She managed a smile that felt stiff on her lips. "They've got you now. You won't fail them."

He gave her a long look. "*We* won't fail them, Jetta."

He released her and took himself out the door before she could summon any sort of answer, leaving Jetta with nerves jumping and no desire left to sleep. She lay wakeful in the clutch of the softest bed she had ever known, staring tight-jawed into the darkness, listening to the highland wind moaning under the eaves.

Why did they send us? Had the Circle not known? Surely they would not risk The Ancient bursting forth to rage unchecked down the length of the Black Mountains.

Those tunnels full of fire haunted her. The Delvers knew nothing of fire, had no concept of the danger in leaving The Ancient fretting behind a makeshift barrier of dirt. She pictured the Old Man patting at his prison with hands of fire, probing each cranny, each unevenness in the stone, searching restlessly for a way out, a way up, a path through the windstone that let it travel where it would underground. Any stone that could be heated was a pathway for The Ancient, and only the inert nature of containment stone could confine it indefinitely. Thrust blackstone into the heart of The Ancient's fury, and it would still be cold when The Ancient had been driven down again. But the tunnels and veins of containment stone were dwindling here, leaving long shafts full of air and shoring timbers that made splendid conduits for the Old Man's ambitions. Jetta shuddered, picturing the web of deserted tunnels that must run under Annam ridge, under the village itself and no telling how far down into the Vale.

"Old Man Fire," she whispered aloud, clenching the coverlets in both fists. "It would make Setham look like a harvest celebration."

The hostility of Burrood and Nugurr set her jaw clenching. *Rifts and factions in a village already in mortal danger!* she thought, shivering with anger and dismay. *Could there be anything more stupid than arguing about how to fight a thing they've none of them ever seen, with an expert sitting in front of them? While they wrangle, the whole village could burn down.* But pride had precious little sense, even less when fed by ignorance and isolation. The only outsiders most of these people had ever met were traders of no particular village or clan—and Windriders who claimed no home, no Vale; they were strangers everywhere, on common ground with no one. How much less could the Delvers understand a Firedancer, when the only times in history they had ever met were when The Ancient was raging loose and lives stood in mortal danger?

She squirmed deeper into the pillows. Her body felt like weights had attached themselves to her limbs, but her brain kept chasing untenable thoughts around inside her skull. Setham. Annam. A house in flames. A tunnel full of fire. Ash-black houses and snow. Water leaping merrily over black sand. Live heartstones trapped under stone buckets.

And me, she thought unhappily, remembering how she had hesitated at the door to Firin's house, with the fire heating her skin and the flames taunting her nerve. The last thing Annam needed was a Dancer known personally to Old Man Fire. It would always know how to find her now. Whispers from the Dance ground long ago breathed into her ear, shivery tales First Rankers told about Dancers who had been touched by fire and lost their nerve. Forever chased by the Old Man, fleeing its touch instead of standing to fight, bringing destruction on every place they settled.

No! Jetta turned restlessly onto her side. *I will* not *give the Old Man such a victory!*

Surely the Circle would not have sent her here if they thought she could truly bring harm to this place. But the thought curled into her bones like a spark nesting in damp leaves. Maybe dangerous. Maybe not.

Jetta gritted her teeth and refused the poison of *maybe*. She glared into the dark, forcing her mind back to the greater problem. The bedposts caught her eye, stretching up and up like needle trees, save that they, too, were made of stone, carved in fantasies of flowers never seen in the lowlands. She stared at the dark silhouette of the nearest etched against a wall painted a cool white to hide the dull blackstone. If Annam Vale stood on solid containment stone, how was it that fire could burst up at odd points in and around the village? Heartstones worked up with the frost or appeared when tremors shook the earth and cracked open deep rifts into the heart of The Ancient's territory. Occasionally a farmer turned one up and fled for his life when it burst into flame under his plow. The stones that contained The Ancient came literally from the world's heart and bore the living fire trapped there in the Beginning. How could they rise to the top of Annam ridge? Or had The Ancient found another path?

A tingling of fear crept up and down her arms. The Ancient had found its way into tunnels closed for decades, maybe centuries. How? Why now?

That thought kept her wakeful the rest of the night, jabbing her back to consciousness whenever she surrendered to the warm clutch of the comforters. She heard the household start to stir as the first light crept through the wide window, a glory of cool color creeping over the high ridge to the east. Blearily Jetta got up. Without thinking she pulled on her supple old black Dance leathers, worn shiny in places, and then stood shivering in the dawn chill, bemused and a little dismayed by how easily one slid back into old habits. For a year she had worn leathers only on those rare occasions when the firewatch fell to her; just being outside Firehome seemed to have erased the time as though she had never left Setham.

No, more than that. Burrood's disdain took her straight back to her first weeks in Setham, when she had fought the complacency of folk who had forgotten The Ancient's touch. *Must it always be a battle with the villagers as well as the Old Man?* she wondered, exasperated, but it was not the same. Not with Rununn's earnest, worried face in front of her. *He* believed in her, because he had no reason not to. Yet.

Jetta drew a steadying breath and stepped to the window, her bare feet objecting to the chill stone floor as they never would to the hottest sands. Beyond the glass, flowers in every shade of blue and purple nodded to the dawn breeze from a box hanging from the sill; enchanted, she threw open the tall panes and leaned out, careful not to fall out over the low sill. All of the enormous black-walled houses she could see wore similar collars of flowers under each window, red and purple, blue and white and brightest yellow, dangling high over any grab by the Old Man bursting from the ground. It bespoke a simple joy in beauty that touched her to the heart.

I could learn to like this place, she thought, sniffing eagerly at the clean upland scent of snow and pitch, flowers and dew-wet stone as the breeze swept in, stirring her loose hair back from her forehead. Despite its bite she let it play across her skin, rejoicing in air that held nothing of Setham's dust and cloying stickiness. Across Annam Vale, the narrow road wound up the ridge straight into the sun just peering over the tall needle trees atop the crest, framed in a flat band of clouds flaring in every color of fire. For an instant it looked like black flames licking at a window, shooting tongues of crimson and gold up to eat the sky. So beautiful it stirred an ache deep in Jetta's gut for the wonder of it. So deadly it made the hair creep on her arms.

You will not eat this place, Old Man.

The thought shot into her head and settled like a nesting bird, surprising her with its adamance. Restless images of tunnels full of fire below her feet drew claws of dread through her insides; deliberately she raised her hands over her head, wrists touching, hands cupped to cradle flame, and went up on her toes, her head up, her back hollowed to an uncomfortable degree. She closed her eyes, summoning balance, inner and outer. Her back tried to lock, protesting a ritual long neglected; Jetta forced herself to relax, straining to find the center that had once come so easily. Every morning in Setham had started this way, a deliberate reminder of the Third Rank badge she had earned, a brazen challenge to The Ancient. It shocked her to discover how difficult it had become.

If Setti could see me now. Oddly, the thought steadied her, stabbing through to some inner place of stubborn pride. Jetta gritted her teeth and held that first difficult control position of mastery as the sun crept over the ridge and explored her face with a bright finger. The space behind her eyelids turned the color of captive coals on a hearth: safe, tame. And suddenly her muscles, long locked in mute battle against the pull of Earth Mother, loosened, their energy flowing into harmony, pulling strength from the floor. The distant mutter of the tumbling stream seemed suddenly louder; the tangled scent of the flowers unlocked into myriad delicate fragrances she could taste.

A Dancer without harmony is a Dancer doomed to fail, Minna's tart voice said in her head, revenant of difficult days in First Rank. *Remember the Mother, and she will remember you.*

The Mother also remembers my name.

Jetta stood motionless, perfectly balanced, perfectly in control, perfectly connected to the source of all strength, even The Ancient's. And slowly, peace flowed in, too, welling up like a great, cool spring inside, proof against the searing malice of fire.

Smiling, she spun in place on one foot, feeling like a feather spinning on the breeze. Then she planted both feet flat on the stones and stretched, luxuriating in the feel of every muscle in her back flowing like the water outside, as supple as the Dance leathers she wore.

So then. One or two things remain.

How much? Slowly Jetta lifted her arms again into the shape of flame, still feeling that curious, effortless sense of buoyancy. After a moment she lifted her left knee to waist height, balancing on the ball of her right foot. The Fourth Rank position added levels of complexity she had never managed to master at Setham, but, wrapped in the Mother's embrace, nothing felt impossible. For one second she thought she had it, then her foot wobbled. Grimly Jetta steadied it. The muscles of her calf started to scream in protest. Without warning the sense of oneness vanished; the endless, flowing river of energy ebbed away with a suddenness that left her flailing wildly for balance. A breath from toppling she put her left foot down and opened her eyes, staring at the sun standing now a hand's breadth above the trees on the ridge.

And let that be a lesson in arrogance, she thought ruefully. She was *not* Fourth Rank, however many movements of that Dance she had learned to execute flawlessly.

Humbled, but calmer, the restless night conquered, she braided up her hair and drew a plain red linen shirt and stout woolen pants over the Dance leathers and pulled on her traveling boots. Almost as an afterthought she thrust her rank pin carelessly in at the shoulder and went down to the common room.

Setti already occupied the settle. They stared at each other a long moment, and then Setti laughed and waved her closer. "Don't you *ever* sleep?" Jetta demanded.

"I can't believe you're up before midday." He grinned and lifted a Delver-sized cup he could only hold with both hands. "I could learn to love this place. This is what they consider a wee wake-up drop in the morning."

"Burli?" She wrinkled her nose, disliking its sweetness, and then sniffed. "What is that?"

"I have no idea, but I want to wake up to it every morning."

He offered her a sip. Something dark and rich, tasting of spices she couldn't readily identify, swirled across her tongue and melted down her throat. "Old Man Fire!" she gasped and tried to steal the cup.

"Get your own!" Setti laughed and lifted his voice. "Mururrn! More of this in another cup!"

"Setti! Did Minna teach you no manners at all? Shouting at the innkeep's son like that."

Mururrn emerged from the kitchen, his broad face wearing an ear-to-ear smile. He held a cup to match Setti's in one big fist and a loaf of hot bread in the other. "Jetta ak'Kal," he said respectfully, offering her the cup. Jetta took it cautiously in both hands, expecting uncomfortable warmth against her palms, but the stone was cool.

"Thank you," she said, edging toward the low bench that had served so well last night. She slid a glance toward Setti. "Are we causing you extra work, Mururrn? If so, I apologize."

"Oh, no, ak'Kal! Some of the other guests were up an hour ago. The rest will be down soon. Please. Sit and enjoy the fire. The food will be ready soon."

He slipped back into the kitchen before Jetta could answer. "He's harder to pin down than a *hysth*," Setti said, tearing the hot loaf apart and happily stuffing his mouth. "Oh, this is wonderful stuff."

"It's just bread," Jetta mumbled, but it *was* good, full of unidentifiable crunchy things that gave it a wonderful lingering taste on the tongue. Like the Delvers themselves, in fact, who seemed to linger in the mind even when they weren't present.

The outer door opened. A smiling young giant entered, clad in brown leather belted with a silver chain. A Second Rank journeyman's badge gleamed on one shoulder, black with two mountains cast in silver, unadorned with any device in gold. It took Jetta an instant to identify Rununn. He looked different in the bright daylight spilling through the eastern windows than he had in the ruddy light last night: taller, if that were possible, and even younger. The expression on his round brown face, eager and full of anticipation, reminded her acutely of Setti.

He spread his hands respectfully at sight of her. "Jetta ak'Kal. Settak a'Kam. I am sent to guide you to Wind Point. Nuurn ak'Kal says he will meet us there to show you what you wished to see."

The doubts and worries of the long night resurfaced as nasty swirling sparks in Jetta's stomach. She kept her face serene. "Thank you. We'll enjoy the company."

Jetta watched, fascinated, as hot color turned Rununn's cheeks a richer brown. Setti took pity on him. "Will you eat with us?"

"I've already—"

The kitchen door opened. Mururrn staggered in under a huge tray bearing six times what Setti and Jetta together could put away in a whole day. Setti leaped up to help him with it. Rununn edged closer. "Is that some of Uranna ak— Uranna's spice bread? Thank you for your invitation, Jetta ak'Kal. I *will* join you, if Mururrn will bring me a plate?"

The boy's mouth turned down, but Setti winked at him. Mururrn brightened and scampered back to the kitchen. Rununn settled on a bench and took the plate Mururrn brought back, all but hovering as Setti and Jetta helped themselves to the bread and porridge and thin strips of grilled meat. Rununn went straight for the spice bread and broke off a huge chunk, sat back and chewed blissfully, one knee crossed over the other.

Jetta watched him, amused. "Urrana's a good cook."

"Oh, yes." A reverent look settled on Rununn's face. "She was wasted as a stonemaster."

"Why is she not ak'Kal anymore?" Setti asked, trying to balance a huge bowl in his lap and eat spice bread at the same time.

Rununn hesitated. "Well, it's no secret. Seven years ago Urrana's lifemate was killed in a stonefall in one of the lower tunnels. She blamed herself, because she had supervised the opening of that tunnel and the shoring of the roof. No one else blamed her. Sometimes tremors in the deep tunnels collapse whole sections. And Anuhr was one of the rare ones, a Balancer. He could always tell when a rock face was ready to fall, and he could stop the nervous shifting of dirt and stone long enough for the rest of us to shore it up. He even stopped a tremor once, like they say our ancestors used to do long ago. He was always to be found in the deepest sections. That day, three other Delvers were down there with him. He stayed to try and quell it. They got out. Anuhr didn't. Urrana took off her badge and opened the inn."

"Yet she is still head of the Circle."

"They wouldn't let her resign *that*. She's the only one who can keep the likes of Burrood and his cronies in line."

"Just threaten them with cutting off the spice bread," Setti said.

Rununn laughed. "That's closer than you think. She—"

Footsteps on the stairs turned all three heads that way. Rununn leaped to his feet; Jetta and Setti simply stared. A man of extraordinary looks stood there, nearly shoulder height to Rununn, but slim as a reed and so pale of skin it rivaled the snow on the peaks. Cobwebby hair spilled over his shoulders, framing eyes the clearest, deepest shade of blue Jetta had ever seen. He wore ordinary black leather boots and dark blue pants, but his shirt had been cut from some gauzy stuff that floated around him like cloud and swirled even to the slight movement of his breathing. Jetta squinted at it, trying to pin down its shade, but it seemed to mix colors as it moved, changing from pale blue to misty green to a motley of both from instant to instant.

How ridiculous. He'd go up like a torch if the Old Man came within arm's reach.

"Windrider," Setti breathed. "Father Flame, Jetta?"

Windrider. With a jolt Jetta realized she was staring and lowered her eyes. Instantly she raised them again, afraid he would think she was some gawky vale-bred just come out in the world. Her own confusion angered her; she watched him over her cup as he came down the stairs and into the common room.

"Rununn," he said with unruffled aplomb. His eyes swept over Jetta and Setti without interest. "I had heard the Firedancers had arrived."

Setti stood up. "I present Jetta ak'Kal of the Third Rank," he said, sweeping a hand toward her. "And I am Settak a'Kam of the Second Rank." His tone demanded equal courtesy.

The stranger showed no sign of taking the hint. He threw a glance at the kitchen door, sighed, and held out his hands to the fire, though it was hardly cold in the room.

"This is Wyth ak'Kal," Rununn spoke up, breaking a silence rapidly becoming awkward. "He leads the Windriders here in Annam."

"Ak'Kal," Jetta murmured, remembering Minna's lessons in dealing with cheeky inferiors. "I trust your business here has been successful?"

Languid blue eyes turned to her. "Not yet."

He returned his gaze to the fire. Setti looked ready to explode, Rununn alarmed. "Ak'Kal?" he said hesitantly. "May I bring you a chair?"

"You would do better to inform the kitchen they have a guest waiting," Wyth said without turning.

Jetta's eyes widened. Of all the arrogant—! She found her mouth open before she thought. "From what I've seen, the Stone Delvers seem to value self-sufficiency, ak'Kal."

The Windrider's odd shirt ruffled and fluttered like leaves on a gale for a few seconds. He turned his head, his eyes narrowed to chips of sky. "It is not for a master of Fourth Rank to scrounge for his breakfast like—" His eyes dropped to their assorted dishes scattered across the bench. "—lesser beings."

Setti laughed. "And yet I am fed." He guilelessly held out a crust of the bread to the scowling Windrider.

Rununn eased between Firedancers and Windrider, who had turned his back again. "Jetta ak'Kal, Nuurn ak'Kal awaits. Shall we go now while the day is bright? We are told clouds and rain will come this afternoon." By a Windrider, no doubt.

"Surely a Firedancer need not be troubled by a little storm," Wyth said languidly.

His hand moved. Flame whooshed up the chimney, hot and glaring bright. Setti shied back a step; Jetta whirled toward it in the first instinctive response of the Dance. Wyth laughed and dropped his hand.

"Fool!" Jetta hissed. She turned on her heel and stalked toward the front door past shocked Rununn and embarrassed Setti. Ignoring an affronted intake of breath from Wyth, she flung open the door and marched out into the street. And stopped, lacking any notion where Wind Point might be.

Behind her, the stone door slammed with a satisfying crash. "What a-a—" Setti couldn't find a word. Jetta glanced up into his flushed face, and some of her own temper cooled.

"No wonder my mother said to always keep a Windrider in front of you." She drew a shaky breath. "Old Man Fire, Rununn, are they all that bad?"

Rununn threw an apprehensive glance back over his shoulder. "Some of them. Come, ak'Kal. I don't care to explain to Urrana why we just woke up all the rest of her guests."

Jetta followed him up between the looming houses,

already regretting the loss of temper. For more reasons than one. It was cold out here in the glacier-fed wind and her cloak hung useless on a peg in her room. Beside her, Setti rubbed his arms and said hopefully to Rununn, "Is it far, Wind Point?"

"An hour's walk, no more."

Setti grimaced. Jetta swallowed an apology. Better to freeze for an hour or two than back down to that arrogant excuse for a clan master.

The hour's walk stretched to over two. Once again Rununn had forgotten the difference in the length of their legs, forced to shorten his ground-eating stride.

"The Ancient—isn't—going—anywhere," Jetta told him, halfway up the face of a sheer cliff where the path clung like a stray thread on a sleeve, ripe to be shaken off. Annam village, a scatter of obsidian blocks, lay far below to the right, overlooking the Vale that opened below to the north into a deep valley with the glint of the stream running crookedly at the bottom. Dark mouths of Delver mines yawned sporadically, gaping over meadows connected by the thin line of a narrow road.

Jetta peered up the narrow trail. "Rununn, you surely don't carry stone down this trail?"

He smiled at her over his shoulder. "We have, but the main access was farther down, until the earth shifted and blocked it."

More tremors. Jetta could hardly believe it, looking up at the great peaks thrusting snowy heads over the ridge above them, blocking the foot of the Vale where the river ended in a wide lake. Water cascaded down everywhere, shimmering over the flanks of the ridges from the mottled shoulders of the mountains. Black outcrops of containment stone jutted defiantly from thin scatters of trees and thrust sharp horns out of melting glaciers. Those glimpses of what kept this valley safe both disturbed and reassured her—and reminded her why they were here. For the first time since the Beginning, the stone here was not enough.

Why?

The unanswered question gave her mind something to fasten on besides the torture in her lungs and the ache in her legs. She puzzled over it until they finally topped out and stood panting in the cold wind shrieking up from the western side of the ridge.

"Wind Point," Rununn said, pointing straight into the teeth of it.

Setti made an unidentifiable sound deep in his throat. Jetta, shivering in the bite of a wind that smelled of glaciers, flinched from the sight of a wall of pale rock halfway down the ridge. An opening like a gaping black mouth faced west. The ridge ended just beyond it as if sliced with a knife, dropping away sheer below the mine into a narrow valley that climbed steeply to the first of the snow-capped peaks. Needle trees carpeted both ridge and valley, leaning into the frigid blast out of the west. Should The Ancient burn through its prison, then what? Her eye traced the vein of paler stone upward until it disappeared over the ridge. Twisted trees and tough mountain grass grew across the top, fuel for The Ancient's greed—with windstone above to carry the fire all the way up and over into Annam Vale itself.

Imagination fed her images of fire raining onto Annam's roofs in trails of smoke and curling flame. Unease warred with the peace discovered in the dawn. Jetta shivered again under a chill that had little to do with the snowfields above her. She hurried, head down into the bitter wind, longing for the shelter of the mine entrance.

Nuurn stepped into sight as they drew close, waiting with arms crossed and no expression on his broad face. Jetta looked up at him without apology. "Wind Point is aptly named, ak'Kal," she said. "Good morning to you, and might we go inside before we freeze?"

Nuurn's expression thawed. A grin parted his beard. "Lowlanders," he said indulgently, waving her past him through the entrance.

Jetta gawked up at the open door as she went by. Solid black stone, wider than six Delvers standing shoulder to shoulder, and twice as tall as Nuurn, it looked impossible to open or close without seven or eight full-grown Delvers to push and pull. But Nuurn set one hand to it as he went and shoved, a very little. It swung back clear to the dark wall behind it.

"How—" Setti gasped.

"Balance," Nuurn rumbled, looking pleased. "I have no

doubt even Jetta ak'Kal could handle this door by herself at need."

Let us hope the need never arises, Jetta thought. She disliked intensely the total blackness lurking in front of them and the way the light seemed to quiver and die a few steps from the entrance. She waited at the edge of the sunlight as Rununn picked up a Delver-sized lantern from a shelf by the entrance. A stone lantern, she noted, black and impervious to the fire it held. She stared at it, marveling at the skill which had carved it from a single lump of rock.

Rununn struck a spark onto the wick. Fire hissed up, captive and angry about it, licking vainly at the stolid walls of its prison. It settled after a few seconds, sullen but steady. Rich, warm light wrapped them around in a golden globe but failed to light the darkness more than a few steps around them on either side. The odd notion struck Jetta that the mine ate light, swallowing it down and giving nothing back.

Setti shivered. "You work all day in such blackness?"

"The working mines have lights every two arm spans," Nuurn said. "The deeps can be disconcerting even to those who are used to it. Follow, and be careful. The floor is uneven."

He led off into darkness that breathed out the dank, secret scent of cold, sunless stone, holding the lantern low to light a floor that seemed equal parts windstone and inky containment stone. The lantern flickered in stray drafts from the entrance but never threatened to go out. Jetta hoped its oil reservoir was as big as it looked. The thought of ending in the deep dark down one of these tunnels, with The Ancient lurking in the stone, made the hair on her neck creep. *But at least if The Ancient appears there'll be light on the way out.*

The thought did not comfort her.

"How far in does this go?" Setti was making a valiant effort to sound nonchalant, Jetta noted.

Nuurn looked over his shoulder. "The tunnel system, or this part of it?"

"Both," Jetta said, wondering how deep this network ran, and whether it intersected the pale rock at the entrance. And how close it came to Annam village.

"The blockage is just around this bend." Nuurn gestured with his free hand to where shadows wavered and slid out of their way a stone's toss ahead. A solid wall loomed on the right, a quick glimpse of faceted stone, then the shadows crept aside as they rounded the bend. There they confronted a mass of jumbled rock jammed floor to ceiling and tight against the rough-hewn walls on either side. The boulders gleamed black in the lantern light, with no hint of baser stone mixed into the pile. Jetta surveyed the barrier slowly, edging forward over fallen stones and crunchy debris until she stood at the very edge of it, peering down into the hollow spaces between the rocks.

"Packed tight, as you see," Nuurn said. He swung the lantern closer and poked a huge finger into a dusty space under a rock. "There. Feel that?"

Her skin crawling, for she disliked putting her hand where she could not see, Jetta ran her fingers down a rough-edged boulder until it encountered dirt. She tried poking her first finger into it, surprised when it yielded nothing to the determined scrape of her fingernail.

"No air trapped in that lot," Nuurn said with satisfaction. "Impressive sight, that, when the Windriders blew this mess all in together."

"Rocks and all?" Setti threw a startled glance at the jumble.

"Rocks and all," Nuurn said. A small smile lurking amidst his thick brown beard told Jetta he was rather enjoying their reaction. "We dumped a lot of it in loose and planted a big boulder in the center of the passage, then moved back. The Windriders stood around for a bit, seeming to do nothing, and then of a sudden the wind came up. *Stones and pebbles that was* a sight. The mountains fall on me if it didn't sort of swirl around outside the entrance for a moment or two, and then punch through here like a great fist, shoving the whole mass ahead of it. Kept it up for about as long as it would take to climb back up the ridge, and then it died away. We went in after the dust settled, and the place looked like this, all driven together and packed so solid you can't sink a pick in anywhere. I'd hate to have to clear this lot for any reason."

"How far do the tunnels extend beyond this? How deep into the ridge?" Jetta asked.

He turned to look at her, his smile fading. "There were seven levels, and The Ancient's up to the fourth. That would put it halfway down toward the village, if that's what you're asking."

"It is. And the windstone at the entrance? How far does that extend?"

Nuurn frowned. "What difference does that make?"

Setti caught his breath. "Ordinary stone! I never thought—"

Rununn edged closer. "Jetta ak'Kal? Is the stone a danger? These tunnels are all containment stone. How could—"

"Not all," Nuurn said harshly, his eyes on Jetta's. "These were never rich workings because they were so heavily veined with lesser stone. That's why they were abandoned when richer areas were found. We considered opening them only because the deep tunnels are becoming so difficult to work. But we always took both blackstone and windstone out of these workings together. More the latter than the former, I think. The sea folk pay well for windstone to use on their seawalls and jetties."

"I don't understand," Rununn said plaintively.

Setti turned, sure of himself for once. "Where windstone is, fire can live," he said, from the depths of First Rank teachings. "The Ancient lives in molten rock, deep in the world's heart. Heat finds its way up in lumps of heartstone, or creeps through veins of windstone until earth tremors or the wearing of rivers or the breakage of mountains exposes the stone to air. Then fire erupts to burn unchecked unless a Dancer tames it, or earth smothers it, or water cools it."

"But—if water is proof against The Ancient—"

Jetta turned, her voice harsher than she intended. "It's not. A heartstone buried in the sea may burst into flame years later when some unlucky fisherman snags it in his nets. It takes a *long* time for heartstone to cool to dead rock on its own. If it touches windstone, the heat transfers, crawling through the vein, consuming the air trapped in it and then the stone itself, until it finds open air. And ignites."

Rununn looked sick. "I didn't know, ak'Kal," he said humbly.

"It is our lore, not yours," she said, consciously smoothing her tone. But it rankled that folk could be so ignorant of a danger that threatened the rest of the world hourly.

She turned to Nuurn. "I've seen enough. I—"

Something brushed the hair up on her arms, her neck, ran a chill feather down her spine. "Jetta?" Setti turned. Impatiently she waved him silent.

The hissing lantern drew her eye. The flame burned steadily, unaffected by drafts this deep in the tunnel. It lit Nuurn's solemn face drawing slowly into a frown, Rununn's puzzlement, Setti's worry. Jetta felt like a fool. It was only this place and the talk of fire crawling, the knowledge The Ancient was here, somewhere under their feet—

The flame in the lantern soared into sudden, venomous life. Nuurn cried out in surprise and swung it away from him in a long arc of fire. Glowing droplets spattered onto the rocks. Instantly it exploded into myriad worms of yellow flame crawling over the scattered rubble of the blockage.

"RUN!" Jetta shrieked, snatching the lantern away from Nuurn with one hand, shoving Rununn with the other. It felt like pushing a mountain. He blinked down at her, his lucent eyes catching light from the fires and reflecting only bewilderment.

"Setti, take them!" Jetta yelled, and spun away to face the fire.

She was three steps into the Dance before they moved, Setti urging them in ever-less-polite tones to get out of her way. Heavy footsteps pounded away up the corridor; Setti yelped as he collided with something hard. The Delvers, their night vision aided by the fire, picked him up and fled, leaving Jetta alone facing a hundred infant flames.

Fear breathed down her spine but her feet were already moving in the Dance. Her hand thrust out, palm flat; fire died down the right side of the tunnel. The flames on the left raced together and flared up, bright, malevolent, desperate. Jetta turned on them, stumbling on the littered floor. *What is it eating?* some part of her mind wondered, shocked, for there was nothing but containment stone under those flames, only air above, and it could not live on air indefinitely. It needed fuel, and found it, in the spatter of hot oil flung from the lantern when Nuurn swung it away from contact with his body.

Flame soared up in a semicircle between her and the mine

entrance. Threads of white stone gleamed under its red eye, pointing the way up the tunnel toward freedom and the endless fodder in the forest beyond. Jetta stamped her booted foot, angry now, boiling with suppressed rage. That harnessed flame should dare act so! It defied all logic, all decency, all reason. She spun into the Dance in earnest, careless of the rocks, the uneven ground, the incipient *hysth.* She saw flame reflected dully from the stone, shining on her promise bracelet, reaching for the tail of her shirt, scrambling to combine and overpower her. Already the air felt thicker, the fire stealing what her lungs craved, mutually exclusive in need. She snatched in a breath that reeked of hot oil and smoke and sank to a crouch, muscles tensed to launch her high above reaching flame at need. Balanced, centered, the memory of harmony still green in every nerve, she thrust both hands out toward the fire, demanding its departure.

Nothing happened.

Jetta gaped. The myriad small flames began to flow together, growing, merging in defiance of The Ancient Imperative that should already have banished it.

She lowered her hands, shocked to stillness. And just that quickly, heat scorched into her face. Terror knifed into her brain. In that instant she knew what had made Kori hesitate and then fail. Surprise. Surprise had killed her love more surely than The Ancient. Fire was not supposed to act like this.

She stepped back, a wobbly retreat toward the rocks with smoke and heat coiling around her, rank in her nose, flushing her skin. The fire reached for the uneven black ceiling, a solid yellow wall turning white at its heart. Jetta saw the *hysth* forming from the younger flames; if it coalesced, its first thought would be to break the seal and let The Ancient loose.

Her training resurfaced at last. She danced a new pattern with the *hysth's* name at its heart. Rage bubbled and broke past the fear. "You will not—get—me—too!" she screamed as the shield of the Dance rose around her again, and advanced with reckless speed over the rubble, leaving dead ash where small flames had been struggling to find a foothold in the rocks.

For a breath, an eternity, a lifetime wrapped in a heartbeat, she danced with the flame itself. It crawled over her hands, twined in her fingers, dripped in liquid sparks to the inhospitable floor. It called to her, tempted her to come closer, dared her to wrap herself in living fire that reached with grasping fingers for the vulnerable cloth of her sleeves.

Setti's voice shouted "Jetta!" from beyond the wall of flame.

Reason returned with a rush. Jetta flung fire from her hands, beat out a spark worrying at her shirt, and clapped her hands sharply together. Beyond the fire, Setti was dancing as he had been taught, a pattern she already knew to be futile. But the *hysth* hesitated, caught between two Dancers, and in its hesitation, wrote its own death song. Jetta launched herself into a spinning leap, *through* the flames, landing lightly beside Setti. With a stamp of her foot, a clap of her hands, a last spin and derisive flick of her fingers, she banished the *hysth* into nothingness. It flickered, sank, and died to ash at her feet.

Darkness crashed down, enveloping them in sudden blindness.

A second trickled by. Two. Setti drew a ragged breath beside her. "Are you all right?" she demanded.

"Ye-yes. I—"

"That was brave. And stupid. What if it had turned on you?"

"What should I have done?" Setti turned toward her in the dark and stumbled on a protruding rock. "Ow! Left you to—ow!—burn like Kori?"

Jetta froze. Setti sucked in a sharp breath. "Jetta, I'm sorry. I didn't mean-"

"I know what you meant. Let's not stand here arguing in the dark like fools. Thank you. It was well done."

"You said it was stupid," he sulked.

"No stupider than jumping through a *hysth*. Come on. I want to think about this. Where are Nuurn and Rununn?"

"Here," Nuurn's voice said almost in her ear.

"Old Man Fire!" Jetta stumbled back and would have fallen if his huge hand had not clamped around her elbow. He steadied her without apparent effort, invisible in the absolute darkness save for the faint foxfire glow of his eyes shining an arm's length above her head.

"Come away, Jetta ak'Kal. I will lead you. I can see well enough even in this."

"I gladly follow."

She clung to his arm as he started toward the entrance. Behind them she heard Rununn guiding Setti, trying to point out boulders and pits in the rock floor. Setti fell over them anyway, eliciting a series of low yelps and moans. By the time the light trickling through the entrance grew strong enough to see the ground, it had become devastatingly funny to Jetta. She snorted when Setti tripped over a last outcrop, and then started to laugh, helplessly, from the belly, as she hadn't laughed in over a year. Nuurn stopped at the edge of the gray square of light falling through the mine entrance and turned to stare at her, his heavy face drawn into a disbelieving frown.

"Jetta ak'Kal? I see nothing funny."

"I'm sorry! I'm sorry!" She gasped in a whooping breath and turned to Setti, only to set off again at sight of him rubbing his hip with an aggrieved look on his face. Rununn looked crestfallen, his guidance clearly not a success. Jetta sat down on a boulder and howled.

Setti exchanged a helpless look with Nuurn and went down on his haunches beside her. "Jetta?" he asked tentatively, which only made her laugh harder. "Jetta! What is so funny? You could have died back there!"

She struggled to draw a breath to tell him how it sounded listening to him limping and complaining in the dark, but the words never came. Without warning the breath turned to a sob; her eyes filled, her lungs locked up, and she found herself weeping as madly, as uncontrollably, as she had been laughing.

"Jetta?" Dimly she heard Setti's voice over her head, felt a hand touch her shoulder. She wrenched away and huddled into herself, her arms wrapped tight around her empty womb. She thought she had cried all the tears that were in her this last year, but that was an inexhaustible well, she discovered now, with depths she had never guessed. She had grieved for Kori, but never for the other thing The Ancient had taken from her, not for the other innocent who had died that night, a life gone before it ever had a chance to know itself. Her child. Kori's child. A child who might have grown up merry and brave like Setti, who had probably run down that littered, dangerous corridor to her rescue and never stumbled once.

The might-have-beens fell upon her all at once and threatened to crush her under their weight.

Hands on her shoulders, shaking her, hard. Voices shouting, a jumble like a distant avalanche. Setti's piercing yell finally penetrated.

"JETTA!"

She wiped tears from her eyes and looked up, her belly as tight and aching as her throat. She whooped in a breath and promptly started to hiccup. Her sides hurt and she could see that Nuurn thought her mad. She knew that if she looked at Rununn she'd start in again.

"What was that all about?" Setti knelt in front of her, his hands resting on her shoulders, looking equally prepared to slap or hug. Jetta avoided his eyes, sober now, and excruciatingly embarrassed.

She tried to push his hands aside and stand up; he resisted, holding her down with effortless strength. "Let me up," she snarled. "I'm fine now."

"Is this reaction typical after dancing the Firedance?" Nuurn looked taken aback but willing to reserve judgment on things he knew nothing about.

Jetta could not lie into the face of such tolerance. "No," she muttered, her face heating. "No, it is not typical. I don't know what brought that on."

"Yes, you do," Setti said, his voice an octave deeper than its wont. She turned her head and found his eyes, looking a shade darker blue just now, staring steadily into hers.

"That was for Kori, and for flame knows what else, but I can guess," he said.

She looked away; he reached out and forced her head around so that she had to look at him. Nuurn and Rununn stood like rocks behind him, caught into the curious immobility of folk trapped in a private scene and wishing they were elsewhere. Setti ignored them, his eyes boring into Jetta's.

"The Circle sent you out before you were healed, Jetta ak'Kal," he said, with such formality that she stared. "I think that you have needed to get angry for a very long time, and couldn't, because it is not acceptable to get angry with the dead. But you got angry down there. I saw it. What you did—that was no part of the Dance. You saved yourself because you were angry, because you got past the fear when the fire changed on you. And Kori didn't."

She jerked away, affronted and suddenly furious again. "Don't drag him into this!"

"He's already here." Setti shoved her down again when she tried to stand, holding her against furious squirming. "He was a ghost in that tunnel, helpless and dead, and it was only the thought of ending up like him that got you mad enough to fight back. So, are you a Firedancer, Jetta, or a ghost like Kori? Have you shed enough tears?"

Her breath stopped on outrage. "How *dare*—"

"It's my life, too! I'd be dead if that had been me trapped on that side of the fire."

Which thought burned her anger to ash. She stared into those steady, no longer childish eyes, swallowed hard, and finally nodded. "Yes. You would be. As would I, I think, if you had not surprised the *hysth*."

"That certainly inspires confidence," Nuurn said dryly.

Three heads jerked toward him. "But—ak'Kal," Rununn protested. "They saved us—fought the fire, drove it deep—"

"Did they?" Nuurn asked mildly, looking down at Jetta from his great height.

She shoved off Setti's hands and rose. He did not resist her that time, setting a hand under her elbow to steady her as she wiped the last of the tears from her face and lifted her chin.

"That *hysth* is dead," she said. "It can't return. The fire rose from the lantern, not from the rocks, and that is what we must fear, Nuurn ak'Kal. The flame in your lantern had no connection to the fire behind that rockfall, and yet it answered The Ancient's call. Had there been a breath of a breeze down this shaft, we might all be dead. Setti was right. I needed to get angry. I've spent too much of the past year weeping and not enough in healing. I'm done with weeping now. It's time to think."

"About what?" Rununn asked, sounding afraid of the answer.

"About tunnels, and veins of stone, and open flame, and how to keep The Ancient from using them all to its own advantage."

Setti's eyes widened. She nodded at him curtly and brushed past him onto the chill and windy ridge beyond the mine entrance. And stopped.

A bone-pale man in a fluttery shirt stood there among the rocks, idly spinning wind between his hands.

Six
Sheshan

"Father Flame!" Setti blurted behind her. "Look at that!"

Jetta *was* looking, not quite believing what she saw. The Windrider was leaning against a huge boulder with one foot propped on a lesser stone, his shoulders braced comfortably against the rock behind him. His hands hovered at chest-height, his fingers moving in an intricate weave that never quite touched the fingers of the opposite hand. Between them, a trio of leaves spun and tumbled around and through each other in no pattern that Jetta could make out, accustomed though she was to the intricate patterns of the Dance. One leaf escaped the invisible globe between his fingers; the Windrider made a darting move of his right hand and the leaf fell back among the others, swirling and spinning ever faster until her eyes ached trying to follow a single pattern. A faint whuffing noise like the wind passing through needle branches caught Jetta's ear. It stopped abruptly when the Windrider looked up and saw them.

He dropped his hands. The leaves tumbled earthward, caught an updraft soaring out of the valley, and flew away, drifting up over his head to disappear into the rocks. Or perhaps it was the wind he had caught and now released that carried them away. It took Jetta an instant to realize that he had truly been spinning wind.

"Sheshan ak'Kal," Nuurn said, behind Jetta. "This is unexpected."

"Wyth said you would be here, Nuurn ak'Kal, and that it would be wise to come talk to you."

Suspicion flamed in Jetta's brain. What business had a Windrider among closed tunnels where fire lived? Why had the lantern flared so suddenly? Fed on a draft sent by this man?

"Why?" she demanded, before Nuurn could answer. "What wisdom is to be found in Firedancer business, Windrider?"

Sheshan reared upright. "And you are—?"

"Jetta ak'Kal of the Third Rank," she snapped. "Firedancer to Annam Vale."

"Ah." It came out so perfectly neutral that Jetta's cheeks flamed. He crossed his wrists, palms out, and gave her a graceful inclination of his head, his voice as bland as his tone. "Greetings from Sheshan ak'Kal, also of the Third Rank."

At least he did not outrank her. But Jetta's nerves still twitched from the close call in the tunnel, and she went back on the attack. "You haven't answered my question, ak'Kal. What wisdom does a Windrider seek here?"

Sky-colored eyes narrowed, regarding her steadily in a lengthening silence. Long bones, hair the color of spider silk, ridiculous fluttery shirt—he bore a striking resemblance to the rude Fourth Rank at the inn save that he was younger and not so willowy, and his lean face had an openness the other man's lacked. The bone-colored skin seemed unnatural to Jetta's eyes; he looked unhealthy, but there was nothing weak about his voice. It wrapped itself around her like the glacial wind.

"*That* is Windrider business, ak'Kal. I came to speak with you, Nuurn. If I might prevail upon a moment of your time? There is no need to detain these others."

"*These others* have an interest in whatever brings you here, ak'Kal." Jetta jabbed Setti in the ribs when he made an uneasy, protesting movement beside her. "I had to dance against fire just now in the tunnel. It acted strangely. Perhaps because there was a Windrider out here?"

"Jetta ak'Kal!" Nuurn protested. "Sheshan is a guest in Annam. Such an accusation is—"

"Typical," Sheshan said flatly. "Forgive, Nuurn ak'Kal. Fire and air are a volatile mix. I have no wish to ignite a conflagration here, in front of my hosts."

Jetta's head felt ready to explode with outrage. How dare he make her out the unmannered lout? But Rununn was looking at her, Setti too, and she could feel Nuurn's eyes at her back. *Temper, Jetta.* She could almost hear Kori saying it. The memory turned her anger to water. Sadness crashed through her again, quenching the flame of battle.

"Nuurn, forgive," she said dully. "Windrider, my apology. I'm tired. Old Man Fire has been up to his tricks, and I need time to think about them."

Setti threw her a sharp look, but Rununn all but sagged with relief. Sheshan only looked at her. His sapphire eyes— not childish at all, but sharply assessing—watched her without a waver or a blink. Unexpectedly he made her that graceful courtesy again: the crossed wrists, the little incline of the silver-pale head.

"Accept my forgiveness. I was unaware of your battle. Was it bad?"

"Yes," Setti said bluntly. "The flame leaped from Nuurn's lantern. Harnessed fire has never done that in my knowledge."

Pale eyebrows shot straight up. "Indeed? Is not fire the same anywhere?"

Jetta looked at him in wordless bafflement. "Your people surely have more knowledge of fire than that?" she asked, appalled. "The Windrider clans have fought beside the Fire Dancers. We've faced The Ancient together.

Sheshan gave a graceful shrug. "Can you read the message in a zephyr caressing your cheek, ak'Kal? Can you tell from the feel of it whether a wind will bring rain or drought?"

Her cheeks heated. "No. But if every hearth fire suddenly flared into a *hysth* as this lantern spawned, we would never eat cooked food again."

"Pardon, Jetta ak'Kal," Nuurn rumbled. "You spoke this word before. *Hysth.* I see that it has some significance to you, but all I saw was a wall of flame, brighter than most, but—"

"Fire is as fire is," Setti said harshly, stepping up to Jetta's shoulder to glare at Sheshan. First Rank knowledge, that, but to these people Jetta thought it would sound stranger than a trader's tale. "But know that what it *is* from moment to moment is not the same. There is the young fire, timid and yellow but dangerous, coming tentative from the rock, easily stamped out before it discovers its own power. There is red fire, sullen and spiteful, slower to die, perilous lurker in corners. There is the hot, quick fire that bursts from the heartstones—" Nuurn and Rununn both shuddered. "—and only containment stone or the Dance can halt that when it begins to advance."

"And not always then," Jetta said quietly. "The heartstones contain The Ancient, the heartfire, and to summon The Ancient is the goal of the *hysth*, the cunning fire that calls all its lesser brethren to challenge the power in the Dance. A *hysth* can be fought if the Dancer is quick and brave and strong enough of mind to force the fire to his will, but a Dancer who allows a *hysth* to form is halfway to defeat. *Hysths* are cunning, and they burn hot, but their purpose is not to run wild but to burrow and open a door for The Ancient, the white fire that lives in the deeps, craving the free air. I have seen it pour out as molten rock that explodes into the open, but more often it is white flame that lusts for the unlimited fuel of the wide sky and the forests and the fields. Its malice is unlimited, its hunger for destruction the reason that the Fire Clans dance, as we have danced since the Beginning of all things. The legends say we were born of fire to keep the Old Man from eating the world. But nothing in legend tells us how a spit of fire trapped in a lantern can call to The Ancient and form a *hysth*."

"You are not improving my morning, Jetta ak'Kal," Nuurn said dryly.

"How can the fire be alive?" Rununn whispered.

Setti gave him a quick glance. "It's not!" he said, too quickly.

Steady, Jetta thought. Of all the mysteries, that unresolved question must be held close, lest these inexperienced people panic.

"I have heard that Windriders attribute malice to the great storms and curse the Hag for her callous power," she said. "We too, find it easier to think that The Ancient is cunning and hostile than to believe such damage can be done by a mindless thing without even the capacity to hate."

Something flickered through Sheshan's face, agreement perhaps, or maybe a hint of those things every clan kept secret. He glanced into the tunnel. "I would swear by all the knowledge I have that nothing can creep beyond a wind-driven block. If—"

Wind gusted up out of the valley, cold and laden with rain. Drops splattered across Wind Point like needles of ice. Sheshan looked up at the gray clouds boiling overhead. Already swirling layers of mist and cloud hid the tops of the ebony peaks.

"It will be a miserable walk back to Annam, I fear. We can discuss this in the tunnel until it passes."

"No!" Jetta snapped before she thought and reddened when every eye turned to her. "I prefer the rain," she mumbled.

Sheshan gave her a curious look but said nothing. Setti looked unhappy at the prospect of trudging back over the ridge in the pouring rain but kept his place at Jetta's side. "As you wish," Nuurn said, and turned toward the mine entrance.

"Wait—" Jetta broke off in embarrassment when Nuurn set a hand to the huge door. Setti's arm went around her, a warm and reassuring weight that did nothing for her embarrassment, but she could not bring herself to shrug it off. She watched, shivering in the frigid wind, as Nuurn drew the door toward him with a light pull on the ornate handle. It thudded home with a gentle thump belying its enormous weight.

"How does it lock?" Sheshan sounded remarkably like Setti in his curiosity.

Rununn grinned. Pride in his craft fairly radiated off him. "Watch! Nuurn ak'Kal is the best of all the masters at this. When he seals a place, *nothing* passes."

"Rununn," Nuurn reproved him mildly. His back was to them, his hands flat on the carved stone above the handle. For a moment nothing happened, and then—

Jetta shook her head, her eye confused. Was the stone around the door moving? She couldn't tell if it was the walls or the door itself, but suddenly the small line of the crack around the door disappeared. The stone stretched seamlessly from side to side of the opening, a black bar against the paler rock of the cliff face, with only the heavy iron handle and the carved trees on its face to mark it from the native stone.

Sheshan exclaimed softly and stepped forward to run long pale fingers over the surface, digging delicately at the join. "Amazing. Even air could not pass this." Which seemed to be a compliment of the highest order, judging from the nod that accompanied it.

Jetta frowned. "If you could seal the tunnel this tightly, why bother with the rockfall?"

Nuurn turned around, looking suddenly weary. "This cannot be undone without shattering the door, Jetta ak'Kal. From this moment these mines are lost to us. They belong now to The Ancient."

Jetta stared from him to the door in numb silence. So. This too, was the price of failure. How long before other diggings were lost, depriving Annam Vale of all source of income? A crucial cog in the wheel of commerce gone, a village uprooted, others deprived of safe means to expand. Like ripples in water, The Ancient's encroachment into this place spread outward and touched the whole world. It seemed suddenly doubtful that the Old Man's incursion here was random.

Wrapped in that chilling thought, she did not notice Setti trying to turn her up the trail toward Annam until his exasperated voice in her ear said, "Jetta! Come on! If you want to freeze, you can do it without me."

She blinked back to Wind Point. The rain drummed down in earnest now, slanting needles one breath removed from ice. Setti bounced impatiently beside her, his dark hair already dripping, his breath smoking in the raw air. Nuurn and Rununn were looking at her; Sheshan leaned against the sealed door, watching Setti with indulgent amusement. He didn't appear in the least bit cold.

"Go on then," she told Setti irritably. "What are you waiting for?"

"You!" Setti turned away. "Rununn, lead off. Jetta's decided to join us."

She opened her mouth in hot protest and closed it again at sight of Sheshan laughing to himself by the door. She drew herself up and stalked up the trail after Nuurn, who seemed as impervious to the elements as Sheshan. This was probably a fine spring shower to him. The rain did not even penetrate that bush of brown hair springing over his head but ran off it like water from a shorebird's feathers. Jetta's already lay plastered to her skull, shedding cold drops with every shiver. She regretted more than ever the cloak tucked away safe in her room at the inn.

It seemed twice as far to the top of the ridge above Annam than it had coming down to the mouth of the mine. Jetta was panting and at least halfway warm from the exertion when they topped out for the second time that day and peered over. Annam Vale had vanished into a solid sea of slate-colored clouds moving in gentle eddies at their feet. The mountains around them hid their faces in the rain; only the wind shrieking up from the bottoms, rocking Jetta in dual blasts from either side, seemed unchanged from the morning.

"Why couldn't we have drawn an assignment by the sea?" Setti shouted miserably at her over the gusts.

"You would not like the great sea gales, Dancer," Sheshan shouted back. "This is just a fine breeze!"

Setti gawked at him incredulously. Jetta blinked rain off her eyelashes, staring at the Windrider standing with both arms spread wide to the conflicting winds, his head thrown back and his face upturned to the lashing rain. The shifting, layered stuff of his shirt, unaffected by the wet, rippled in the wind and shed the rain in steady rivulets. *Like a bird,* Jetta realized. That impractical-looking garment seemed suddenly the most useful of any on this ridge.

She shivered in a sudden blast and wrapped both arms around her own soaked and too-thin garb. "Come!" Nuurn called, his deep voice penetrating the winds without apparent effort. "Follow close, all of you. The trail can be treacherous in the wet."

He led off. Rununn waited, gesturing the others after them. "I will follow, ak'Kal," he told Jetta as she passed. "And make sure all arrive safely."

She went on by, following Setti, too cold to argue with what seemed splendid good sense. It was only after the trail dipped steeply and started down that she realized Sheshan walked directly behind her, not in front where she could keep an eye on him.

Acute anxiety crawled up her spine. *What* had brought him up to the mine? Sent by arrogant Wyth to spy on the doings of the Firedancers? What had he really been doing outside the entrance, playing with the wind like a child scattering sparks to amuse himself? Had a Third Rank master nothing better to do with his time?

A sharp gust out of the bottom rocked her, recalling her attention with a jolt. Quite suddenly the Windrider at her back seemed the least of her problems. She could see nothing on her left hand but swirling mist; on her right only sheer walls of stone weeping rain. The trail underfoot was nothing but bare rock running with wet, dropping at an angle that forced her to place each foot with care and test for traction before trusting her weight to it. She had never been put to such effort in simple walking; her legs already ached worse than on the climb up. The veil of mist on her left did nothing to erase her memory of the long, long drop to the valley floor. She had no illusions of a soft landing.

They stopped to rest on a steeply-angled switchback. Nuurn looked up at them, his eyes lingering longest on Jetta. "Halfway, Jetta ak'Kal," he said in rumbling encouragement. "You handle the trail like a Delver."

It annoyed her to be singled out, but she nodded gracious acknowledgment. "You're kind, ak'Kal. I feel more like a wet spark."

Nuurn grinned; behind her Sheshan laughed outright. "I think it would take more than this mist to quench your fire, Jetta ak'Kal."

Setti spun around in the trail so fast that his boot slipped on the slick rock. He staggered; both Nuurn and Jetta grabbed for him. He shook them off, glaring up at Sheshan. The depth of dislike in his face shocked Jetta to inner stillness. "I'll thank you to keep a civil tongue toward my master, ak'Kal!"

"Setti!" Appalled, Jetta slapped his shoulder to drag his gaze away from the Windrider. He looked at her with rain running rivulets down his face and dripping from stray wisps of hair, and his eyes looked almost master-black. He opened his mouth, shut it again, and turned away abruptly toward Nuurn.

"Shall we go, ak'Kal?" he said roughly. He took a step, forcing Nuurn to start on. Jetta blinked, staring bewildered at Setti's back. Old Man Fire, what ailed him?

She picked her slow way down the trail, frowning from more than the misery of rain in her face. Behind her, not a word from Sheshan. For that, at least, she was grateful. He had sense enough to wait on a quarrel until they were somewhere other than over a treacherous and fatal drop. She had thought Setti did, too. What had inspired him otherwise?

The several answers to that were equally troubling. Suspicion, perhaps, sparked by her own too-hasty attack on Sheshan at Wind Point. Setti was one to loyally carry a quarrel once he had picked a side. The need to prove himself, perhaps, the journeyman in this group of masters, save for Rununn, who was too young to spark jealousy by reason of rank. Plain maleness, perhaps, which needed to rank itself regardless of talent or craft skills.

She clicked her tongue impatiently, thinking about cross-clan feuds. *Grow up, Setti,* she thought, jolted still again into the realization that he did *not* have the experience to handle so potentially dangerous a quarrel, with folk of whom they knew next to nothing, endowed with skills anathema to their own. She thought of the leaves swirling between Sheshan's hands, trapped in a circle of wind, mentally substituted sparks for the leaves, and winced from the resulting conflagration. So effortlessly could things go to disaster, should Windrider and Firedancer arrive at cross-purposes.

She gritted her teeth, thinking of Wyth ak'Kal. *There* was a man unlikely to curb his tongue for the sake of diplomacy. Sheshan seemed more reasonable, but she remembered Rununn's answer when she asked if they were all as bad as Wyth. Perhaps Sheshan was in the minority. Happy thought.

Without warning her boot slipped on mud washed down over the rock. Her foot shot out from under her, throwing her backward in flailing disarray. Jetta clawed for a handhold on the cliff, her heart stuttering in panic, but the trail was wider here, the rough stone just out of reach. She felt herself falling over that endless drop, and bent every muscle honed through years of Dance training in a desperate attempt to twist herself in the other direction.

Something struck her on the downhill side, unyielding yet soft, shoving her hard toward the cliff. Jetta landed sprawling in the trail on her side, the breath exploding from her lungs in a gasping snort. Her head hit the stone hard enough to jolt tears from her eyes. She caught a dizzy glimpse of Sheshan, arms raised and crossed in a curious attitude, his eyes on the clouds, not on her.

Thanks for your concern, she thought disjointedly, and then Setti thumped to his knees beside her, his eyes enormous in a face bleached to pale, sickly tan.

"Jetta? Are you all right? Can you stand?"

"Yes. Give me a moment."

His hands ran down her arms and legs, checking for damage. "Are you hurt? Did you hit your head?"

"No," and then, "yes. I think."

She put up a hand to check; he beat her to it, running gentle fingers through her hair, lifting her head from the stone with his free hand. She winced as he found a knot at the back of her skull. His lips tightened.

"That's it. I'm carrying you the rest of the way."

"No, you're not! That's ridiculous!"

She struggled to sit up, but the clouds spun over her head in sickening fashion. She shut her eyes tight. "Just—wait," she gasped into Setti's anxious questions, trying to settle a stomach spinning to match the clouds.

"Ak'Kal, we cannot stay here." Nuurn's deep voice penetrated the jumble. "Settak a'Kam is right. Let us carry you the rest of the way. It's not far now."

"Then I—can make it," she said, determined not to arrive in the village like tainted freight. She made it to her feet past Setti's grab, grinning triumphantly into Nuurn's surprise. The next instant a rush of nausea almost sent her over the cliff. Hands, she didn't know whose, caught her back as she doubled over and lost whatever was left of breakfast.

"Enough arguing," Nuurn said behind her. Huge hands swung her up into arms like small trees. She found herself cradled against a broad, leather-clad chest with Nuurn's beard tickling her forehead. The sudden rush into the air left her dizzy again. She fought her stomach with closed eyes and willpower, deep breathing, and the practiced Dancer's count.

First step right, next back, third step left, fourth even. First turn right, Fire dies. Fifth step forward, no retreat.

"No retreat," she mumbled aloud.

She heard Nuurn say, "What?" but lost everything in the swinging movement of the Delver's long stride. The Dance filled her. Her blood pulsed in rhythm to the movement around her. The count filled her head, demanding, imperative, ageless. There was only the Dance!

Seven
Things Unspoken

Fire. Fire all around. Jetta spun in the Dance, tireless, floating, but it did no good. The Ancient rhythms were failing, powerless, and the fire laughed and roared closer. Sweat glistened on her arms, her legs, touched with heat that a Dancer should never feel, and panic touched her too. Fire, someone screaming, shouting her name. Kori. No, Setti. *Setti?*

"*Jetta!* Wake up!"

She woke, shuddering in terror. Setti was bending over her, his face wild, intent, his hands on her shoulders. "What?" she gasped, disoriented.

He drew back, easing the grip of his hands. "You were dreaming. The healer said the blow to the head might give you nightmares. She was right."

"What?" Jetta blinked up at him, still not understanding why he was there, bending over her while she slept. "The fire—"

"There's no fire," Setti said gently. "It was a dream."

"But—" It jolted back then. Wind Point, the lantern, the fire, the trail. The rain.

She turned her head toward the window. Night ruled beyond the closed panes and rain glimmered on the glass in nacreous trails, catching color from the light spilling out. A fire flickered sullenly on the hearth; beside the bed a delicate glass lamp threw a cheerful gilded glow into the room and up the white-washed wall. She was back in the Delver-sized bed at the inn, deliciously warm in the fuzzy ocean of comforters.

Hot blood scorched up her cheeks. "Nuurn carried me back to the village, didn't he?" She squirmed, thinking about a scandalous arrival in full view of all the people she was supposed to be protecting.

Setti ducked his head, fiddling with the blanket. "Yes."

Heat shot into Jetta's face. "And now the whole village thinks I'm useless, right?"

"No!" But he still would not meet her eyes. "Three different people have been at pains to assure me how dangerous the Wind Point trail is. Rununn says a Delver fell off and was killed there several years ago. It could have happened to anyone."

"Dancers aren't supposed to lose their balance!" She remembered vomiting over the edge of the cliff. "Father Flame," she muttered, her cheeks burning again. "How far from the village were we? Did I throw up on anyone?"

Setti threw his head back and laughed. "No. But there's an image I'll cherish. Too bad there wasn't a Windrider handy to receive the gift."

She caught an edge under the laughter and fought her way to a sitting position against the pillows. "Anyone in particular?"

He looked at her, his face turning fierce. "Take your pick. The inn's full of them, and one as hateful as the next. They thought it a great joke that the village Firedancer had to be carried back from her first tour of the place."

Jetta found herself grinding her teeth, and consciously relaxed her jaw. "Never mind. We'll watch them laugh when the Old Man bursts in on them some fine night. And speaking of nights, what time is it?"

"Not late. It wasn't a bad bump on the head. Urrana was more worried that you would catch your death of chill."

"Mmm, no." Jetta stretched luxuriantly under the mound of quilts, feeling decadently relaxed and warm. "What about you?"

"Urrana poured a pitcher's worth of that stuff from breakfast down my throat and I feel just fine. It's called noë, by the way."

"Noë." Jetta rolled it around on her tongue, listening to the nuances of it. "What an odd word."

Setti sighed. "A Windrider word. They brought the stuff with them. Now the Delvers trade for it with some obscure village far north of here I've never heard of."

"A place worth going, maybe. On your next assignment."

"Next assignment! We've barely begun this one!"

"True. But we nearly finished it this afternoon."

He dropped his eyes, the laughter fleeing his face. Firelight flushed the gold of his skin a richer shade, tinged with warm red hints like the promise of fire banked in coals. "Yes. I'm sorry if I misstepped. I didn't know what else to do. You needed help."

"Which a Third Rank master is not supposed to need." She leaned her head back against the pillows and looked at him somberly. "That fire wasn't right, Setti. I've never seen a man-lit fire act that way, like an old cart beast suddenly knocking the wagon to pieces. And it didn't answer the Dance. Not after the first few steps."

He stilled, his face white, set. "So all that I have struggled to learn all these years is useless?"

The deadness in his voice stabbed Jetta straight to the heart. "If it is, then it's useless to both of us. I refuse to accept that."

He looked at her, his now darkened blue eyes steady. "What if we're forced to accept it? Jetta, I danced to that fire this morning and had no effect on it whatsoever. It ignored me completely."

"No." She shook her head, regretting it when pain lanced through her skull.

"Jetta?" Setti leaned forward anxiously.

"I'm all right. Just—Setti, listen to me. You came back. That took more courage than I have. You distracted it, which is the only reason I'm here right now, I think. The Ancient is changing, learning how to counter the Dance. I don't know how that can be, but I believe it's so. Firedancers have always argued, generation after generation, whether The Ancient thinks or simply reacts. I think the debate is over."

He sat back, thin dark eyebrows drawing together in a thinking frown. "We would have a hard time convincing the Circle of that."

"Oh? The Circle itself demonstrated that *hysths* are acting erratically. The Ancient has chosen to attack Annam Vale, a place it has ignored for all of time, despite the fact that nothing has changed about it since time began except that the Delvers have gone deeper than they ever have. But they aren't encountering The Ancient down deep, but up high in the old mines, the ones layered with lesser stone. Why? Because the real mines are too deep below the surface, with only conduits lined with containment stone for The Ancient to travel. It needs the other to bring itself to the surface."

"That's not proof of sentience," Setti said, casting himself into the counter argument. "The Ancient has always traveled that way. A tremor killed Urrana's lifemate seven years ago. Perhaps it shook something loose underground, opening a crack that let The Ancient come up into territory it couldn't reach before."

Jetta considered it. "Possibly. But how did it know we were beside the rockfall this morning? How did it incite the lantern fire to do what it did?"

"You felt it coming, do you remember?" Setti said it almost casually. "Nuurn raised the lantern to look at you. If he hadn't, the fire would have caught his clothes for sure when it went up. He owes you his life. We all do."

Jetta tried to remember but had only a clear impression of a low roaring indistinguishable from the flaring hiss of the lamp—or the contained whoosh of the wind between Sheshan's hands on Wind Point. She frowned.

"What?" Setti asked.

"That Windrider. Sheshan. What was he doing up there? Was he outside the whole time, playing with his breeze, or did he call it from inside the tunnel?"

Setti's face hardened. "I asked him that. He laughed and said I should grow up."

Jetta winced, remembering how she had thought the same thing. "But I notice he didn't answer. What does Nuurn say?"

"I haven't seen Nuurn since he laid you here on the bed. Urrana ordered us all out. When I got downstairs he was gone."

"What about the rest of the elders?"

"There's mostly only Windriders downstairs." Setti grimaced. "They seem to have the same effect on Delvers they have on us. A desire to flee the vicinity."

"Then why are they still welcome in this village?" Jetta muttered. "There's a deal going on here no one is saying, Setti."

"Why wouldn't they tell us? Are they looking for the place

to go up in flames some fine night?" He threw up both hands in exasperation.

Jetta sighed. "No, nothing as drastic as that. But the Delvers aren't united on a course of action. Perhaps Burrood and his ilk are the ones wishing the Windriders to stay."

"What can *they* do? Against fire? Father Flame, Jetta, that's insane!"

"No more than sending us up here uninformed," she said darkly. "And that was our own kin."

He stared at her, dismayed. "I don't understand any of this."

"No more than I. But whatever you do, don't tell anyone that you think the Old Man is alive and plotting against Annam. Come on, help me up. I'm hungry."

He leaped up. "No, no. I'll get Urrana. She said to call when you woke up. Trust me, Jetta, you don't want to go downstairs."

She remembered the Windriders and was half tempted to go anyway just to prove their opinion of her wrong. But her head ached and the thought of bandying insults with Wyth did not appeal to her. Glumly she gave in.

"Go, then. Is there possibly any spice bread?"

He laughed and ducked out the door. Jetta leaned her sore head gingerly against the pillows and frowned at the harmless stone of the ceiling looming an impossible distance over her head. Containment stone painted to look like something else. What else in this village was not what it seemed?

Urrana came through the door with Rinood on her heels, both laden with trays. Rinood set hers down on the table beside the hearth; Urrana settled her own across Jetta's lap.

"There. No need for you to get up," she said over Jetta's protests. "If you want your head to stop aching sooner rather than later, you'll stay in bed and let the world keep a while."

Jetta settled, sniffing appreciatively. "I've never encountered such wonderful spices, Urrana. Do they grow here?"

She snorted. "The only spice that grows this high is bark off the teller trees, and little enough of that. These came from the lowlands with the Windriders."

"Teller trees?"

"You must have seen them on the way up. The ones that point in the direction away from the wind. They tell you which way the prevailing winds blow."

"Yes, I remember them. Very tough trees, I thought, to grow so high, in solid stone."

"Like Delvers." Urrana flicked a hand at Rinood. "Enough, child. If you polish that cup any more it will leak right through. Go and see if our guests need anything."

Rinood grimaced, caught herself, and hurried out the door. Urrana caught the look on Jetta's face. "Don't worry, ak'Kal. I'll rescue her before they get too nasty. But she's shy, poor thing, and needs a little toughening."

Jetta could think of better ways than throwing a child to the likes of Wyth but kept them on her tongue. "Are they all and always so—so full of themselves?"

The innkeeper settled her great bulk into a chair beside the bed. "Always, yes. All of them, no. The higher the rank, the worse they are. I must say it was a relief to see that a Third Rank Firedancer didn't put on the same airs. We didn't know what to expect."

Jetta blinked. That explained some of Burrood's attitude, anyway. "What gives them such a high opinion of themselves? The Delvers do equally dangerous work and create things that last." She touched the carved bedpost, the finely turned cup on the tray. "These things are useful. What does a Windrider leave behind but a bad taste in the mouth?"

Urrana chuckled. "Don't chart all of them on the same map. They have done us great service. They've opened our eyes to new things, like spices and new markets for our stone, and they have made us aware of the world beyond the Vale. In turn we teach them patience, I think. Some of them, anyway."

"Not Wyth ak'Kal, I'd wager," Jetta said sourly.

"Him, no. But he is a great one among their kind. Very skilled to match the arrogance. It was he who directed the winds that sealed Wind Point. Wyth, Ayesh, Thess, and Sheshan. Those four."

"Sheshan. He was at Wind Point."

"Yes, the young rogue. Probably flew up there, too."

"What?" Jetta jerked her attention from buttering a slice of hot, crusty bread. Not, unfortunately, spice bread.

Urrana cocked her head and filched a second piece for herself. "They do fly. At least, we think so. They turn up in too many odd places, with queer timing we can't explain otherwise. They won't say one way or the other."

"Why ever not?" Jetta was still trying to wrap her brain around the notion of a man riding the wind without wings.

Urrana shrugged. "Do you give away the secrets of the Firedance? No more than we tell all and sundry how to shape stone."

"What difference would it make? Knowing and doing are two entirely different things."

Urrana turned her head sharply. Heavy eyebrows twitched into a frown and she bit rather sharply into the bread in her hand. She chewed for a long moment in which Jetta wondered anxiously what she had said to insult her. Finally, the innkeeper swallowed and said, "That's wisdom. There are some in this village would do well to remember it."

She rose. "Rest, ak'Kal. I think that we will need you to *do* before much longer."

"Why do you say—"

But Urrana was already out the door, skirts swishing. Jetta stared at the closed door, trying to think past the ache in her head while the soup cooled and the fire snapped irritably in its captivity on the hearth.

How could such a small village contain so many unanswered questions?

The rain had stopped when Jetta woke in the morning. She did not care to press the knot on her skull too hard. but the headache had passed, save for a twinge or two when she turned her head too fast. Altogether the day looked far more promising than she would have wagered yesterday afternoon. She got up and tested herself against the iron control of the master's position, standing beside the bed where she could grab the bedpost at need. She managed Third Rank— barely—but the sweet connection to the power running in the earth failed her. Jetta sighed and hoped the Old Man would sleep today.

Someone had kindly washed her clothes, sparing her the necessity of dumping out her journey sack, which still sat fully packed in the corner. She gave it a thoughtful glance as she reached for the door handle on her way out. It spoke of impermanence. True, there had been little time to settle in, but it seemed to shout aloud her ambivalence toward this assignment. Nothing about it felt right or permanent. Not like Setham.

Her hand closed around the door handle and jerked it open. This wasn't Setham.

The common room was empty and one glance out the window told her why. The sun stood far above the mountains, smiling down on a village already going about its day. She wondered where Setti had got to, but forgot him when her stomach rumbled. Luscious smells drifted through the kitchen door; she marched over to it and shoved. And shoved again with muscle behind it when the stout, Delver-sized door ignored her.

It yielded, reluctantly, letting her into Urrana's domain of rich smells and heat and gleaming ranks of pots lining the walls. Jetta stopped, blinking in a dazzle of sunlight pouring through twin windows set either side of the fireplace across the room. The blackstone hearth was huge, twice her height and so deep she could have walked two paces into it. An odd device stood in the middle of it, stone growing like a thick obsidian spire from the floor, black and impervious to the fire at its feet. Iron arms sprouted at regular intervals up to several hands above Jetta's head, staggered in circles around and around. Pots hung from the end of each arm, some boiling, some simmering, the topmost probably lukewarm at such a distance from the fire. *Ingenious,* Jetta thought in admiration. No wonder service in this inn was so quick and the food seemed so endless.

"Ak'Kal!" a young and startled voice greeted her. She turned and found herself eye-to-chin with Mururrn stopped dead a pace away, his arms full of newly-washed crockery bound for the common room shelves. Hastily she stepped out of his way before he dropped the lot.

"Good morning," she said, seeing that he, like his sister, was shy. "Is your mother about?"

"N-no, ak'Kal. Please wait. I'm to serve you food."

He ducked his head and hurried past her. Jetta waited, admiring the well-ordered kitchen. Herbs hung in bunches from the rafters; barrels of flour and dried roots and fruit and salted meat stood under the windows. Gleaming stone bowls and deftly carved utensils sat on shelves or adorned the walls. Wooden spoons, she noted, slightly jolted. In the lowlands one saw only metal in any utensil destined to go near fire.

Mururrn came back, empty-handed and still shy, though he had been free enough yesterday with Setti. Jetta sighed, envying her journeyman's easy knack with people. Mururrn looked like he expected her to bite.

"Will you sit, ak'Kal?" He leaped to dust off an already spotless chair.

She hesitated, eyeing its height from the floor and the table it stood beside. She was tall enough not to end up shoveling the food directly from plate to mouth, but just barely. It would not be dignified at best. She spotted a low stool beside the fire and moved that way instead, disconcerting Mururrn.

"It's all right. This is more my size, you see."

His face cleared. "Of course! I'm so stupid!"

"Don't say that!" she said sharply. "Never say that about yourself."

He blinked huge blue eyes. She softened her tone. "Lack of experience does not qualify as stupidity, child. Don't rush to take on burdens you haven't earned."

"Yes, ak'Kal," he said humbly, but she was not sure he understood. She was not sure *she* understood what had brought that out so sharply. Maybe traveling with Setti. She remembered so clearly him saying the same sort of thing, bemoaning his inability to catch the basic rhythms of the Dance. How they had worked, she and Kori, hours every day after class, up on the hill above Firehome where no one could see, trying to teach him what he had been unable to grasp with the others of their rank watching and some, like the bully Rekkale jeering. They had sweated, all of them, but Setti got it in the end. The Dance was in him, or he would never have learned at all.

She frowned into the cup Mururrn set in front of her, thrown far back into times she had all but forgotten.

"Ak'Kal? Is something wrong with the cup?"

She jumped. "No! Please, continue. Whatever that is on the fire smells delicious."

He hurried to splash some into a bowl and set it in front

of her. Soup, thick and full of a lowland tuber Jetta loved. She breathed in the steam and smiled at Mururrn. "Delightful. If you can find me some noë to go with it I will be forever in your debt."

His eyes lit up. "For you, of course!"

He turned toward the inner wall and clambered up on the long table running the length of it, reaching for a small stone canister on a high shelf. He found a cup and spooned some dark stuff into the bottom, climbed down and carried it over to a pot steaming gently at mid-tier on the kettle-tree. He ladled hot water into the cup, sending the wonderful spicy smell of noë through the whole kitchen.

Jetta buried her nose in the steam when he set it triumphantly in her hands. "Oh, that's wonderful. Thank you."

He winked at her conspiratorially. "The traders are very late this year and we're getting short on it-"

"Your mother said she was out of it when *I* asked for it," a frigid voice said at the common room door.

Mururrn spun around, his eyes widening to huge blue saucers. "A-ak'K-kal." His voice failed, and he backed away from Wyth stalking into the kitchen.

Jetta set the cup down and stood up. Wyth was taller than Mururrn, though not much, more than a head taller than Jetta, but she refused him the advantage of his height, or to let him bully a child either. She stared up into his cold, pale face with her fists planted on her hips.

"A woman is entitled to choose what she serves in her own kitchen, ak'Kal. And to whom she serves it."

"Not when I'm paying for the service. Ak'Kal."

Jetta had never taken such an instant dislike to a voice in her life. Even Rekkale, the torment of her childhood, had never achieved that exact sneer that somehow relegated her to a lower form of life.

"I see that rank among Windriders does not come with manners. Ak'Kal."

Glacial blue eyes narrowed. He tried to stare her down, but Jetta stared back, chin well up, copying Minna's well-remembered stance. Oh, what she owed to that tiny old Dancer.

Wyth dismissed her with a flick of those gelid eyes and

tried it on Mururrn. "Noë. Now," he said flatly. "I'll take it by the main hearth."

He spun on his heel and started for the door. Mururrn threw Jetta a desperate look. "Please, ak'Kal," he pleaded to the Windrider's back. "I-I am not allowed."

Wyth turned around, his face a mask of sneering derision. "Not *allowed?* But you are allowed to serve Firedancers, is that right?"

"The—the village Firedancer is to have whatever she chooses," Mururrn said miserably. "The Circle said so."

Wyth's lips compressed into a tight, hateful line. "Did they. And after their Firedancer is brought back unconscious from her first foray outside these walls. Their confidence is touching. How is yours, eh, boy?"

He stalked closer and thrust a long finger into Mururrn's face. He shied backward, so close to the hearth fire that Jetta instinctively shoved him aside. "That's enough!" she flared at Wyth, stepping between him and Mururrn.

Wyth flicked his fingers toward the hearth. Air whooshed past Jetta, an almost palpable fist driving past her cheek, ruffling her hair in its wake. The fire gulped it down and spat upward with a chuffing roar, reaching almost as high as the mantle over her head.

The lower pots boiled instantly, spilling their contents onto the stones. Mururrn cried out in dismay, reaching unthinkingly to snatch the lowest pot out of danger. Jetta struck his arm aside and brought her hands together, shoving outward. Instantly the fire sank almost to coals.

Mururrn dissolved into tears. "The soup," he mourned, seeing the mess blackening in the sullen coals. "What will Mother say?"

"That you should have tended your guests better," Wyth said nastily.

He turned and shoved through the door to the common room, not without difficulty, Jetta rejoiced to see. The door stuck, just a little, so that his flat-palmed slap turned into a harder blow than intended and he exited shaking the blood back into his hand. Jetta hoped for broken fingers but retracted it in the next breath, because that would make him even more evil-tempered and likely strand him indoors where poor Mururrn would have to put up with him the day long.

She turned and found the boy on his knees trying to fan life back into the fire. Jetta touched his shoulder, drawing a white-faced, desperate look. "I must mend this—"

"You must let me help," she said gently. "You shovel up that mess and I'll tend the pots."

He stared for a dumb instant, wide-eyed. In a Delver that was wide indeed. She chuckled. "Not all foreign ak'Kal are like that one. Here."

She handed him the hearth shovel and turned him firmly to duty. While he cleaned the reeking mess off the stones she took care to stir all the pots, wiping the worst of the spillage from their gleaming sides. Then she told him to step back, extended a hand toward the dying fire, and clenched her fist sharply. The fire gasped into life again, leaping up out of the coals with renewed enthusiasm.

"Feed it a little wood to keep it happy," she told Mururrn. "There's no great harm done."

"*Thank* you, ak'Kal," he said fervently. "This is the first time Mother has ever left me in charge of the kitchen alone, and look what had to happen."

"Well, it wasn't your fault. Wyth has the manners of a cart beast."

Mururrn giggled. "Settak a'Kam called him a bag of wind."

Jetta bit the inside of her cheek hard to keep from laughing out loud. "Setti should know better than to criticize his betters," she said demurely, and then leaned close and whispered, "But if you ask me, he has the right of it."

Mururrn clapped both hands over his mouth to smother a laugh. "Tend your pots," Jetta said, swallowing the last of her lukewarm soup. "I've a mind to tour the village and see what there is to see. Do you know where Setti went?"

"He said he would patrol the village, ak'Kal, until you awoke."

Jetta faltered. Patrol. Setti was doing exactly what he should. "Thank you. Where are the other Windriders?"

Mururrn spread his hands. "Wherever the wind drives them, ak'Kal. They turn up in odd places. On roofs and up on the ridge, sitting on the containment wall or in the rocks above the falls north of the village. There's no knowing."

"I see. Well. It should be an interesting tour, then."

"That's not what Mother calls it."

Jetta hesitated, driven to gossip in pure desperate need of information. "Does your mother not like the Windriders?"

Mururrn lowered his voice. "Some of them, very much. Others are like Wyth ak'Kal. I don't think they respect any clan but their own, or many masters who aren't Windriders. Nuurn they like, and Huunall ak'Kal, and Burrood."

That last name surprised Jetta until she thought about it. If factions existed among the Delvers, doubtless the Windriders, having been here so long, had formed opinions as to the rightness of one side or other. Burrood must have his supporters, especially if he favored Windriders over Firedancers. From his attitude two nights ago she thought that a virtual certainty.

"Thank you. Best put the noë away now, eh?" She touched his thick shoulder and turned for the door as he leaped toward the abandoned canister.

She hesitated with a hand on the door to the common room. Not that way. She wasn't up to another fight with Wyth. Another door across the room led out the rear of the inn. Was it not her duty to learn the exits to every building in Annam? She sauntered past Mururrn clambering up to the high shelf, noë pot in hand, and out the tall door into the windy, sun-drenched morning.

The air smelled of rain-washed grass and melting snow. Jetta stopped, bemused by a scent that had already passed toward summer in Firehome Vale. But Annam lived much closer to the sky; spring came later here. She closed her eyes and dragged in a deep lungful of the brisk wind sweeping up out of the valley. For the first time a small excitement crept into her soul at being far from Firehome, in a place unbound with memories and authority and advice she did not want. Like Setham in the beginning. A place to start her life.

Again.

Her smile fled. Jetta opened her eyes and stared at the glorious sweep of sky over the deep green of ridges soaring up to the snow-locked peaks. Crowns of ice sparkled between the rise of black walls nearer at hand. Gorgeous. A place worth sharing. But. The ache of Kori's loss set a lump in her throat, for the life they had started together, and the end that had left her limping on alone.

Fiercely Jetta swallowed grief and moved off, following the

curve of the narrow street below the inn. Houses ran in a straggling line around the hillside, a disconnected sprawl that puzzled her at first, until she forced herself to concentrate and saw that the Delvers had set their houses where they would cause the least disturbance to the land that cradled them. They perched under outcrops or atop knolls that seemed to grow into houses in seamless transition, or stair-stepped down three levels to accommodate the fall of the land. Nowhere did she see a space that looked man-leveled and unnatural. Even the containment wall curled over the contours of the ground with hardly a level spot anywhere along its top. It curved outward around a few of the tough teller trees, enclosing them in its protective span rather than leaving them to the mercy of The Ancient. She smiled, liking the Delvers for that.

She crossed the footbridge that led to the foot of the Wind Point trail and followed the wall down around the village, across the meadow below and on into an area of big, low-slung buildings with no windows perched at the edge of the drop into the valley. A cart with a broken wheel stood beside the first, awaiting someone's attention; she wondered where the cart beasts were to pull it, having seen none in the village. She poked her head into each of the buildings and saw them filled with block after block of dusty black containment stone destined for the lowlands. The fifth one, however, held white stone, and she stopped to stare at it, disquieted. Harmless in itself, it made a grand target for The Ancient. Except—she knelt, and found the place floored with containment stone set so tightly she could not drive a fingernail between the paving blocks. She rose, feeling better.

"Do we meet with your approval, ak'Kal?" a rumbling basso behind her inquired.

She spun around. How did folk so big move so quietly?

The largest Delver she had seen yet stood in front of her, a mountain-sized silhouette blocking the sun. Jetta squinted up at him; hastily he stepped to one side with an apologetic grunt. "Sorry about that," he said, and sat down on the nearest stone block, which brought his nose almost level with hers. "You're a little bit of a thing, aren't you?"

"Big enough for the job," Jetta said coolly.

His booming laugh threatened to shatter the walls around

them. "Well said! Nuurn said you weren't one to back down. Glad to see it. I'm Huunall, by the way."

She sized him up in turn, this Delver the Windriders seemed to respect. Certainly he was big enough to impress. His green coat would have made a fine tent at a pinch, sheltering shoulders so wide he could not have fit through any door in Firehome without turning sideways. A great dark bush of a beard tumbled halfway to his belt, framing a weathered face that might have been carved from teller bark, it was so wrinkled. The startling blue eyes she had come to expect in Delvers lived in his face, too, but half obscured under the bushiest eyebrows she had ever seen. In the dark his eyes must look like the moons seen through trees.

An air of good humor sat on him like a mantle. The wrinkles looked like good ones, made from smiles instead of frowns. The curves of his face tended up instead of down, and he had Setti's direct stare that belied guile. But those eyes had seen ever so much more than Setti's and held a piercing quality Setti's would never own. Jetta found herself struggling to hold his gaze and stopped wondering why the Windriders had marked this man out.

"I'm honored to meet you, Huunall ak'Kal." She would have known his rank even without the master's badge gleaming at his shoulder. A gold miner's pick overlaid a whole series of silver mountains. She counted them and inclined her head in profound respect. One didn't meet a Fifth Rank master every day.

"Manners, too. What a nice change." Huunall beamed at her.

"Ak'Kal?" Worry touched her. "Has my journeyman offended you in some manner?"

"Settak? Haven't met him. Could do without some of the Windriders, though. Never mind. What brings you to the warehouses? Pretty dull stuff. Just stone and more stone."

"It's my duty to learn every building in the village, ak'Kal. Where they lie, what they're called, all their entrances and exits. If folk become trapped in them when fire rises, I must know how to find them, and how to get them out."

The laugh lines in his face sagged toward solemnity for a moment. "An unhappy thought. Nothing we've ever worried about. Until now. But you have, eh?"

She thought of Setham, the village in flames, people screaming. "Yes."

He eyed her keenly and stood up. "Well, we can't expect you to figure all that out on your own. Come on then. I'll show you."

"Uh—certainly. Thank you. Are you sure I'm not taking you from other concerns?"

He peered down at her with no smile on his face. "What greater concern can there be than the lives of this village, eh?"

She walked beside him into the brilliant sunlight again. "You believe that there is real danger, then? And that your Circle was right to send for Firedancers to come here where there was never need before?"

"You've been listening to Burrood. Fool."

Me? Or Burrood? she wondered, confused. Huunall snorted. "He never could see what was under his feet." His great rich laugh boomed out suddenly. "Reckon he'll have to look out now. It might be The Ancient."

He ushered her into the next storehouse. "One entrance. No exit. Should there be?"

She peered down its dim-lit, dusty length. "I've seen worse. How fast can your folk run?"

"As fast as the next man motivated by fear for his life, I imagine. But surely there's no danger. These are built on solid blackstone."

She tapped the floor with her heel, heard a reassuringly solid thunk. "I would think so," she agreed. "But take care nonetheless. The eaves are made of wood. Leave no trail leading within reach that the Old Man can follow."

"Such as?" He stopped to look at her, his vast face serious, intent.

"Such as weeds allowed to grow around the buildings that can touch any wood or windstone inside. I saw fire race down a road for a thousand paces once before it found the gate to a harvest field. It rooted itself in weeds the farmer had carelessly let grow around the gateposts, never dreaming so few dried and rattling plants could prove his downfall. And that was on a still day when the wind had no hand in spreading the flames."

Huunall puffed a great sigh that ruffled wisps of her hair

escaped from its knot atop her head. "I'll remember, ak'Kal," he said soberly. "What else?"

They toured the whole village together, poking around and between every building. Halfway along they met Setti and gathered him in, dressed in Dance leathers covering only his hips and shoulders and shivering in the nip of the spring breeze. Jetta forbore to ask him where his cloak was; she remembered being young and green at Setham, wandering the autumn nights clad only in leathers until Kori pointed out that it only took a second to rip a brooch pin free and let the cloak drop. Of course, that was after he'd practiced it for an hour himself.

She resolved to take Setti aside later. Wandering on with attentive Huunall who shortened his long strides to pace her, Jetta pointed out to them every potential avenue for The Ancient, every spot where fire could easily leap from one house to another, every nook where fire could bloom unseen from any window. Huunall looked thoughtful indeed when they ended in front of the inn after three intense hours.

"I never guessed," he said ruefully, "how lowland villages end in ashes, or how great a job it is keeping them from it."

"It will not happen here," Setti said fiercely.

"I know that." Huunall looked from one to the other of them, taking in Setti's passion and Jetta's reserve. "I think your Circle chose well. Twice welcome to Annam Vale."

Setti beamed. Jetta felt burdened by the Delver's confidence. He started to open the inn door; she stopped him with a hand on his arm. "Huunall ak'Kal, will you answer one more question?"

He turned. "Assuredly."

"Wait until you hear the question." She smiled to take the sting out of it, but he was warned, as she had intended, free to answer or not as he chose. "The Windriders, they won't make our jobs easier."

"And you want to know why they are here?"

"Yes."

Huunall drew a long breath and looked up at the ridge soaring toward the flawless sky. Jetta followed his gaze, noting how the distant teller trees bent to a stiff wind riding the tops. A gleam of light on an outcrop at the very point of the ridge caught her eye; she squinted and made out a tall, slim figure with pale hair catching fire from the sun, standing unmoved in the blast. Jetta shivered, chilled just watching.

Huunall dropped his great feathered gaze to hers. "Their reasons are their own. But they bring no harm to Annam Vale."

"No harm!" Setti squawked. "They could fan The Ancient to—"

Jetta waved him silent. "Do you trust them?" she asked Huunall, her eyes on that motionless watcher on the ridge.

Huunall shoved open the inn door with one broad hand. "Yes. This is *our* clan home, ak'Kal. We cherish it greatly."

He disappeared inside. Setti rounded on Jetta. "I didn't mean to offend. But Windriders in proximity to The Ancient—it's absurd!"

"Hush. They drive the great fires back on themselves, do they not? You've heard the tales. Farahk ak'Kal fought The Ancient at Ghesh in Meliam province beside Windriders."

"And barely lived to tell the tale!"

"I never heard that it was the fault of a Windrider." Jetta trailed Huunall inside, seething despite what she had told Setti. She remembered Wyth's casual, slighting gesture that brought flame roaring to greedy life in the arrogant certainty that he could dismiss it again just as easily. This village with no experience of fire trusted where they should not; the Circle had known it, and simply expected her to find a way around it.

Old Man Fire! she thought, furious. *Why did they send me?*

Eight
Fire in the Night

Huunall was standing beside the fireplace talking to Urrana when Jetta crossed the threshold. The innkeeper peered around him to see who had come in; she abandoned the conversation to hurry down the hall, hands outstretched, gray skirts billowing like sheets in a high wind. "Jetta ak'Kal! I'm glad to see you looking so well. Huunall says he has learned more this afternoon than in the last forty years combined. That is saying something."

Huunall winked at her behind Urrana's back. It upset Jetta's fine anger; she frowned without knowing it. Urrana's smile slipped. "Is something wrong?"

Jetta groped for manners. "No! I—just—"

"I fear I've upset her," Huunall rumbled.

Urrana rounded on him, heavy brows snapping together. "How?"

"We've been talking about our other guests," he said.

Urrana stopped short. "Oh." She turned slowly to Jetta and Setti, her broad face troubled. "Forgive, ak'Kal. You will have noticed that our Circle does not speak with one voice. It was a long and loud battle to get the majority to agree to send for Firedancers at all."

"But why?" Setti asked. "Do you ask a Firedancer to battle the sea? No more would you trust a Windrider to battle fire."

"But they have, have they not?" Huunall came down the hall, his tread all but soundless for all his vast bulk. "We've heard tales. Great battles against The Ancient. Windriders, Firedancers—sometimes the Sea Clans together."

"But it's very rare, ak'Kal," Jetta said. "And never within the bounds of village walls. When the forests burn and fire runs wild on the wind, aye, then the Windriders must help to tame the gale so we can Dance. That has happened, perhaps not often, but it has."

"Should have happened more often," Huunall said thoughtfully, watching her. "Should a whole village burn because the clans don't speak?"

Jetta's lips compressed. "At Setham I would have begged any help, ak'Kal. But there was none to be had."

"Then perhaps it's not so ill a thing to have them here," Urrana suggested shrewdly. "They do have their uses."

"Such as?" Setti challenged.

"Such as keeping the passes clear for the trader trains all winter. You'd not have noë in your cup of a morning but for them. There's been many a winter we've gone hungry by spring, but not since they came."

"Are they here all year then?" Jetta asked.

"Yes, three years now."

"And did you invite them three years ago? Why?"

"Stones and pebbles, no." Urrana laughed. "Ayesh wandered in one day, looking for a clean wind, he said, and climbed up to Wind Point and sat a whole day just breathing. Odd folk, Windriders. Then he wandered away again, and came back with a dozen more. To train, he said."

"To do what?" Setti wanted to know.

Urrana opened her mouth, but Huunall cut in. "To do what Windriders do. You're forgetting, Urrana. Last night. Decisions?"

Urrana frowned at him, then her face cleared. "Ah! Jetta ak'Kal, there's been no time up to now to show you where you will live. We've no suitable house for your use, I'm afraid, so you and Settak a'Kam will be quartered with Nuurn and his wife Anual. I hope that is suitable?"

"Of course," Jetta said politely, though she would rather stay at the inn. "We'll shift our things immediately."

"That would be best," Huunall said. "Nuurn is glad to have you. Fire seems to like his house. Three times since midwinter it's cropped up around the place. Once right at the front door like it wanted to come in."

Setti shifted restlessly. Jetta saw her own thought in his face. Nuurn had been holding the lantern yesterday when it went up. Indeed, the Old Man knew his name.

"One good thing about Nuurn's," Huunall said

conspiratorially, dropping his deep voice to as soft a whisper as he could manage. "No Windriders."

Jetta stared up at him. That wily old stone, talking about clan cooperation in one breath and separating potential combatants in the next. It pained her to yield the inn and Urrana's spice bread to Wyth, but she wasn't here to start a war. "I quite understand," she said demurely, and won Huunall's booming laugh.

"Thought you would. Get your things. I'll show you the way."

"I'll fetch them." Setti ran up the stairs, stretching long legs to take the risers without tripping. Urrana watched him go, shaking her head.

"He'll catch his death, dressed like that. What's wrong with this?" She fingered Jetta's practical linen sleeve.

"Burns too easily. Dance leathers leave nothing for The Ancient to catch and cling to."

"And nothing to the imagination, either," Urrana sniffed.

Jetta blinked. Lowland villages thought nothing of Dancers roaming their streets in leathers and nothing else. She had not considered that anyone would place modesty above survival. "A cloak would be welcome against the wind," she said carefully. "We can always shed it in an instant."

"Unless The Ancient finds it first," Huunall said. "Do as you must, ak'Kal. You are the master, we the apprentices."

Urrana's disapproval turned to a worried frown. "Yes. I must agree with that. Do what it takes to keep this village safe, Jetta ak'Kal. I'll see to it you are left alone to do so."

She gathered her skirts and marched toward the kitchen. "She must have been a formidable master," Jetta said appreciatively.

Huunall cocked an eye toward her. "Still is, ak'Kal. Still is. Doesn't take a master's badge to prove what you are."

"No," she murmured.

Setti appeared at the top of the stairs, his own pack slung over his back and Jetta's in his hand. "You travel light," Huunall said.

"Dancers need little but the Dance, ak'Kal." Jetta took her pack from Setti as he leaped down the last two stairs, landing with a jarring thud. Huunall reached over her shoulder and took it out of her hand.

"Light indeed," he said, swinging it casually from two fingers. "Come."

They turned to the right outside the door, uphill and no surprise to Jetta. That way lay Wind Point and the fire lurking in hungry frustration. Did one of The Ancient shafts run beneath Nuurn's house?

"Are there maps of the tunnels, ak'Kal?" she asked, stretching her legs to keep up with him. "All of them, the old workings and the new?"

"Nuurn said you'd be asking. Yes. Some haven't been pulled out of their cases in two hundred years. Errull's looking for them. What do you want to know?"

"How they run in relation to the village. How deep they go. Where the containment rock crosses windstone."

"Hmm." He thought about that, stumping heavily up the black-paved street. "Good questions. Puts a new face on things."

He did not elaborate. They walked the rest of the way in silence, up the winding street to the last house, built in the lee of a jutting cliff where the stream spilled over in an unbroken fall three times Huunall's height. The sound of the water thundering into its pool, normally a delight to Jetta, disturbed her now. It would make any alarm from the village that much harder to hear, but at least they were far from the inn and unpleasant chance encounters with Wyth.

Huunall lifted his hand to pound on the door but never got the chance. It flew open in his face, letting out a warm smell of baking and the smallest Delver Jetta had yet seen. She stood no taller than Setti, tiny next to massive Huunall, with an open face mapped in laugh lines that all pointed toward lively blue eyes that seemed to take up half her face. She barely came to Huunall's chest and had to tilt her head back to look up at him. Jetta warmed to her at once.

"You've finally brought them! Well past midday, I'll wager they're starving. Come in, come in. Wipe your feet, Huunall."

Setti ducked his head to cover a laugh. Jetta fought to keep a straight face as Huunall hastily scraped spring mud off his boots on a jutting paving stone. Jetta looked around to do the same but Nuurn's wife beckoned her inside with both hands.

"Come, come. Welcome to my house, Jetta ak'Kal. And

you too, a'Kam. I'm sorry, I've forgotten your name."

"Setti, ah—"

"Anual, child. No need to stand on ceremony." She ran a lambent blue eye up and down his lanky frame. "You must be half frozen. Come stand by the fire. Drop your pack there. You can take it upstairs later."

"I—uh—certainly." Setti dropped his pack by the door. Huunall set Jetta's beside it and edged backward, looking cowed.

"I'll just be on my way—"

"Oh, no, you great lump. You sit and have cake and noë like a civilized person. What do you mean, rushing off?"

"Noë?" Setti said hopefully. Even Huunall paused in his flight.

Anual beamed. "Ah. Urrana dug out some of her precious stock for you, eh? Good for her. Speaks well of you. Sit, sit! I'll be right back."

She bustled off through an inner door, leaving Jetta with a breathless feeling as if all the air in the room had gone with her. Huunall settled grumpily into a chair and gestured Jetta toward another. "Best sit. She'll not be happy until you do."

"She seems very friendly," Setti ventured.

"Oh, aye. Talk your ear to stone, she will. But good-hearted. Shame about her boy."

Jetta, hunting in vain for a chair that wouldn't leave her feet dangling in space above the floor, turned to look at him. "What happened?"

"Killed in a rockfall seven years gone. Anuhr was a good man. Good man."

"Urrana's lifemate was Nuurn's son?" Setti blurted.

"Rununn told you that story, I'd wager." Huunall drummed his fingers on the chair arm. "Just as well. Saves awkward questions."

"We had a thought," Jetta said slowly, "that the tremor then might have opened veins for The Ancient at Wind Point."

Huunall's impatient fingers stilled. Piercing blue eyes bored into her, and then turned distant with some internal thought process. "Hadn't considered that," he said slowly. "We—"

He broke off as Anual bustled back in with a tray groaning under a huge pitcher and a stack of cups, an enormous cake and myriad cookies the size of Jetta's two hands. The unmistakable aroma of noë wafted from the pitcher, setting Jetta's nose twitching.

"Ahhh," Setti said, taking the cup Anual poured for him. Jetta nursed her own between both hands because it was too big to hold in one and watched in amusement as Huunall tried to resist Anual's implacable hospitality. Jetta eyed cookies big enough to make a meal and hunted a graceful way to decline. Huunall caught her eye, raising his cup with a sardonic lift of one shaggy eyebrow. Jetta summoned her appetite and set her own cup down to take a cookie. Setti took two. Anual beamed.

"Thank you for opening your home to us," Jetta said, nibbling at the cookie. Like everything else in Annam, it offered foreign flavors and tantalizing bits of unidentifiable things that melted on the tongue and entirely defeated her willpower. She had a sudden vision of herself fitting one of Urrana's dresses by midsummer, fit only to fall on flame and smother it to death.

"These cookies are wonderful, Anual," Setti said with enthusiasm, reaching eagerly for the cake. He had managed to put away both the cookies and the noë, Jetta saw. Where? She was full on half a cookie, and there was still the cake.

"I like to cook," Anual said, still fussing with the tray.

Huunall seized his chance and stood up. "None better in the village. These young folk are fortunate in their lodging. I'll leave them to you. I've unfinished business up the hill."

"Mind you don't keep Nuurn until all hours," she said sharply.

"Circle business," Huunall said gently.

"Circle business! I've had all I can stand of Circle business of late, Huunall ak'Kal. You tell Nuurn we have guests and to come home and greet them."

"I'll tell him." Huunall winked at Jetta and escaped out the door, snatching a cookie on the way.

Anual stared after him. "That man! Slippery as a fish in the brook, but the best hand with stone in ten generations. Did he show you around the village, ak'Kal?"

Her tone changed so abruptly from flibberty stay-at-home to keen inquirer that Jetta stared. "Yes," she said, taking a closer look at this tiny terror. She saw what she had missed the first time: a rank badge at Anual's shoulder, almost obscured in the tumble of brown hair spilling from the green scarf around her head. Second Rank, but a master.

Anual noted the direction of her stare. "Aye, I've the right to say my say, and shouted down more than a few for the privilege of hosting you under my roof. Welcome to you both."

"Thank you. I hope it's not a burden."

"If you keep eating like a runtling bird I'll never even notice you're here." Anual cast a disparaging eye on the half-eaten cookie and smiled again. "But I expect a lass built like you isn't up to much of an appetite. Now. I'll take you to your rooms. I've found a bed small enough for you, Jetta ak'Kal, but you'll sleep in a Delver bed, young Setti."

"That's fine," he said quickly. "Lots of room to sprawl in."

They snatched up their packs and followed her up steps carved from stone like everything else in this village, its banister supported by carved children at play, the whole polished to gleaming alabaster. Jetta smiled at a stone child reaching to tweak the hair of another, marveling still again at the things Delvers could shape with those huge hands.

Her room was first along the upstairs corridor, through a whitewashed door opening into an airy room overlooking the valley. All of the furniture was her size, not just the bed.

"Children's stuff," Anual said, and withdrew rather abruptly to show Setti his room. Jetta looked at the scaled-down chair by the window overlooking the valley, the narrow, low bed, the chest at the foot and the table barren of any clutter such as collected in a room someone lived in, and realized with a sudden chill that this had been Anuhr's room. These things must have been his as a child.

She left unpacking her few things for later and explored the upper floor, poking her head in at every door. Six painfully neat bedrooms upstairs, all with a window, none of them with adjoining doors. A window at the end of the hall faced the waterfall. She glanced out as she went by, admiring the view, and turned back, setting the layout of the house in her head before running down the stairs to find Setti doing the same thing on the lower level.

He turned from examining the windows in the front room, and laughed when he saw her nose twitch under an assault of delightful smells. "The kitchen's that way. I warn you,

Anual will try to feed us again."

"Every assignment has its risks."

Setti grinned and shoved the kitchen door open for her.

Anual paused in her busy bustling around a table heaped with enough food to make Jetta groan. "All settled?"

"The room is very pleasant, thank you," Jetta said. "We usually go about learning all the houses inside and out. We've seen all your neighbors from the outside. Would anyone be at home now? Is there time before we eat?"

Anual tossed some sliced vegetables into a kettle. "Stones and pebbles, I can describe every house in the Vale and who lives there, too. What do you want to know?"

Setti and Jetta settled onto a window seat and pared noda roots and ground teller bark while the smells in the kitchen grew richer and the windows darkened as the sun slid down behind the ridge. The Firedancers knew every detail of every house on the upper side of the village, who lived there, the names of their children, and all the hottest gossip about all of them before a stamp at the door and a gruff "Where's the supper, woman?" heralded Nuurn's return.

"Keep that up and you can cook it yourself next time," Anual yelled back, but she shed her apron and scurried to the front door. Nuurn snatched her up and kissed her like a lovestruck boy before he spotted Jetta and Setti hovering in the kitchen doorway.

"Ah. You're here." He set his wife down, a flush creeping up out of his bush of a beard. Setti chuckled; Jetta turned away, envying them fiercely.

"Look forward, Jetta, not back," Setti said softly behind her.

"Mind your business."

She managed to get through supper, sitting in an oversized Delver chair with her feet dangling well clear of the floor, smiling and listening with half an ear to Anual and Nuurn eagerly discussing the merits of some promising new blackstone vein an avalanche had laid bare down by the lake. As soon as she dared she pushed her plate back, and smiled when Anual turned a disappointed face her way.

"It was wonderful, but I fear I can't eat as much as I'd like. A full belly slows the Dance."

"Logical," Nuurn said.

"If you'll excuse me?" Jetta slid down from a chair cushioned with three blankets folded to give her some height above her plate. "Setti patrolled all day. Now it's my turn."

"I'll come with you." Setti started to get up but she waved him back.

"No, go and rest. You can take the midwatch."

"Is this truly necessary, Jetta ak'Kal?" Anual looked troubled, Nuurn thoughtful.

"I hope not. But I would rather be sure." Jetta nodded to Setti and ran upstairs to shed her vulnerable shirt and pants.

Turning for the door again, movement against the wall startled her until she saw a polished silver mirror giving back her reflection. She paused, struck by how thin she looked, how very washed-out and frail compared to the big, earthy Delvers. No wonder they thought her not up to the job. Her Dance leathers, dyed the deep black of dead ash, the color of a Dancer's victory, looked stark against her skin, like smoke stains. Apprehension breathed a prickling chill onto her neck. For the first time she saw them as Annam villagers must see them—a ridiculously frail barrier against the monster in the deep.

Stop it. Jetta jerked open the door. Remembering Urrana and the cold wind outside, she caught up her cloak from the peg and ran down the stairs.

Bundled to the eyes, she stepped out the front door and stood on the black stone stoop letting her sight adjust to the night. The sky stretched clear and black overhead, studded with stars flung like a great net over the valley. On her right the stream thundered down the mountain in the fascinating, endless way of falling water, breaking to shimmering luminance against the rocks and sliding away in a pale ribbon. A brisk wind swooping down from the ridge in front of her swirled her cloak around her ankles and patted her cheek with cold fingers. Jetta shivered and started down the street, matching what her eyes saw with her tour this afternoon and Anual's detailed descriptions of what lay behind the shadowy walls.

Neither moon rode the sky, and darkness lay in the street like a fallen cloak, smothering all remembrance of daylight. Jetta stepped carefully down the uneven way, crisscrossing to every house, picking her way through mud studded with patches of burgeoning grass and humps of stone smoothed from the passage of many feet. She did not hurry, trying to set the village in her head, investigating outbuildings and detouring into the deeper shadows overlooked by no window, no door. She ran inquiring fingers over shutters, dismayed to find wood in many cases instead of carved stone. The eaves were uniformly wood as well, which she supposed could not be helped. She could not imagine how to lay a roof entirely of stone, or how to support it. At least the tiles were slate. But the eaves would funnel the Old Man with terrifying efficiency straight into the heart of these houses, for all their defiant walls.

End to end of the village she trekked, to the south bridge and back again, then down to the storehouses and a restless tour of the containment wall. The inn's shutters shed only slivers of light through the cracks but she could hear the deep rumble of voices, punctuated by occasional laughter, and guessed that the Windriders had not graced the common room tonight. Silently she went on by, rounded the next corner, and ran straight into Rununn.

"Oof!" Jetta all but bounced into the nearest wall.

"Ak'Kal! Stones and pebbles, are you all right?" Huge hands picked her up and steadied her on her feet. Rununn's glowing moon eyes peered into hers at a distance of a hand's length; he leaned down, looming over her like a tree bent double in the wind, anxiously trying to assess the damage.

"Perfectly, Rununn. Truly. I didn't see you. Sorry."

"Nor I you, ak'Kal. I should have been paying more attention. I am on firewatch."

"As am I. Shall we watch together?"

He straightened and looked over his shoulder. "This is my post tonight. Better than down by the river. Hunnood is by the bridge. A friend of mine. Would you like to meet him?"

"Yes." It surprised Jetta to find she meant it. Rununn was such an endearing creature she found herself looking forward to meeting more like him.

For once Rununn remembered to shorten his long stride to hers, pacing slowly beside her as they dropped down between the houses to the next street and turned right toward the bridge linking the road beyond the containment wall to the meadow.

"Hunnood is a Finder," he said, as if it should mean something to her. "I'm just a carver."

"*Just* a carver? Look around, a'Kam. I have never seen such beautiful work as you set carelessly all around your houses." She touched an ornate lintel as they went by to illustrate her point, and laughed at his confusion. "What is a Finder?"

"He can sense where containment stone lies, and which way the veins will run. He found a whole new vein down by the lake this afternoon."

With the help of a winter avalanche, Jetta thought, but didn't say it. They turned a corner and came in sight of the bridge, and suddenly heat flushed through her, warming even her chilled feet. Every nerve ending began to fizz and tingle and her gut cramped in a way all too familiar. She spun around, searching with narrowed eyes, but saw only darkness and stars, the solid walls of houses and the occasional lighted window.

"Jetta? Ak'Kal?" Rununn stopped dead beside her, bewildered. "What's wrong?"

"Fire comes," she said tersely. But where? Father Flame, where?

"My post!" Rununn yelped, and would have run, but Jetta stopped him.

"You could run straight into it! Follow!"

"But—how do you—"

She ignored him and started back up the street, running, her head swiveling from side to side. Fire was near; she could feel it coming, but for the first time in her life she had no direction, could not pinpoint the source of the danger. Panic sparked in her gut, setting her stomach churning and long tremors running through her limbs under the cloak.

The cloak. She stopped and threw it off in one violent motion, shivering in the ice-spawned chill of the spring night. The sense of fire all but overwhelmed her, beating at her brain in pounding waves. Memories of Setham swarmed up out of their cage; for a moment she could not see anything but fire rolling toward her, an inexorable wave with hunger at its heart. Jetta wavered, her skin crawling in anticipation of pain, her breath caught somewhere in her chest.

Control! old Minna's voice screamed at her through the confusion in her mind. *Control, Dancer! Would you have the Old Man win before you dance a single step?*

Jetta's chest unlocked. She whooped in a hard breath that tasted of night and snow and terror and said thickly, "Rununn, get back. Get away from here."

"But—"

There! A spark of light bloomed up the street, exploding instantly into flame. "Stay here!" she shouted at Rununn, and ran to confront it.

"Ak'Kal!" His forlorn voice followed her, and then she forgot him. The fire had found fuel, writhing into an exposed woodpile stacked beside someone's house. She shrieked a warning to whoever was inside and spun into the Dance.

A turn on the ball of her foot, grinding dirt into stone as her hands went up into the arch of mock flame over her head. A quick, difficult grasp after balance as her wrists came together. One heart-stopping instant of compressed eternity when the whole world seemed to stop—and then connection clicked inside like a lock into a hasp, unleashing flooding awareness of the power under her feet. It seared up through her like flame itself; Jetta cried something inarticulate in welcome and surrendered to the Dance, leaping lightly from stone to chill grass to drying mud in the bare spots. The mountain chill fled as her skin warmed, all but crackling with the raw energy of a summer storm, tasting of the sharp, bitter passage of lightning.

Fire swarmed up the stacked wood, a confusion of light and shadow writhing over the dull black walls hemming the alley. Smoke puffed into her face, an irritating wraith with evil intent. Jetta ignored it clinging to her face and arms with the persistence of a petulant child and hunted the ignition point. Sudden heat underfoot and a desperate flare of yellow flame warned her; she launched herself over it and stamped it to ruin with the imperious double step and clap of the fourth movement.

The fire in the woodpile refused to yield so easily, leaping up higher than her head. Jetta cursed the wind gusting around the corner of the house, fanning the flames upward every time she forced a small retreat. Lowlanders had the sense to build their towns in sheltered places and put up windbreaks, but not here, not on this wide-open hillside with only the spindly teller trees to object to its coming.

Vaguely she heard shouting, sensed people gathering behind her, but the Dance had her, mind and soul. Flame tried to leap over her head to root somewhere else; she caught it barehanded and flung it back, stamped on another sullen red worm and left it dead ash. She stalked the main fire with springing steps that felt scarcely bound to the earth, every muscle tensed to thrust her high if the fire flared underfoot. But only smoke and ash lay behind her, and the fire in front spun in on itself until it soared in a narrow column higher than the rooftrees of the houses flanking her. Blessedly the wind had shifted; without its interference she gained on the flames, forcing them to consume each other until only a stubborn pale core remained, looking for a way to spawn.

"Not this time," she told it through her teeth, and flung both arms wide, a defiant warding gesture that had no part in the Dance and every root in the frustration buried in her heart. The flame burst apart and died on the packed bare dirt between the houses.

Jetta froze, up on her toes with her arms still outstretched and the power of the Dance still pouring up from the very earth in heavy flood. Slowly she settled onto her heels, wary of some upstart spark, but even the wood was black and dead, the fire gone, the battle won. She lowered her arms. The fizzing energy cascaded out of her as though someone had opened her veins, leaving her trembling weary in the aftermath, and suddenly cold, so cold.

"Tear that pile apart!" a deep voice shouted. "Make sure it's dead."

"It is," Jetta said through chattering teeth, but huge forms moved past her anyway, big hands reaching for charred ends of wood. She stepped out of the way, exhausted and angry and that they did not trust her but equally relieved at their caution.

Cloth settled over her bare shoulders. Still at Dance pitch, she almost twitched it off until she saw what it was, and then gratefully clasped the warm folds of the Windrider's queer feathery garment around her.

She looked up and found Sheshan ak'Kal beside her, clad

only in breeches, his feet and upper body bare to the piercing wind.

"Thank you," she said stiffly, reaching up to give it back. He shook his head, his spider-silk hair flying.

"You have greater need than I. We do not feel the cold as you seem to. But the heat!" He turned his head to look at where the fire had fought its doomed battle. "How can you step so close to that inferno and not feel it?"

She hugged his shirt closer, astonished at how it held her body heat. "A gift of our craft, I suppose." A thought occurred. She turned her head to look at him squarely. "The wind died. Was that your doing?"

He made a small, deprecatory movement of his head. "I saw how it fed the fire. It was a small thing to do."

"It made a difference. Thank you."

She could think of nothing else to say, spared the necessity when Setti ran up and caught her shoulders. "Jetta! The word just now reached us. Are you all right?"

"Yes. Perfectly. Should I not be?"

She looked back at him in contained composure, tacitly reminding him where they were and who was listening. Setti looked around at the gaping villagers and drew himself up with a nod. "Of course, ak'Kal. How did it begin?"

The ritual question reminded her of her own duty. She walked over to the ignition point, scattering villagers who leaped aside when she pointed at the blackened hole in the dirt.

"Here." She turned toward a lantern suspended in a huge hand. "If you could bring the light?"

"And let the fire leap from the lantern again?" a deep voice behind her rumbled. "That would hardly be productive, Dancer."

Jetta turned, frowning. Burrood stepped out of the crowd and stalked up to tower over her, his heavy face set in a hostile frown. A breathless hush fell around them; Delvers froze to listen, their eyes glowing like a host of small moons.

"Burrood ak'Kal," Jetta said thinly, hiding clenched fists behind her. "There is no danger. The fire has fled. It will not return tonight."

"As it fled from Setham Village?" Burrood turned a sneering face to the watchers. "Pardon if I lack confidence in your word, ak'Kal. While you stand there shivering The Ancient may be probing elsewhere. It would seem that Sheshan ak'Kal is made of sterner stuff than the vaunted Firedancer we hired!"

Jetta shed the layered shirt in a single angry motion and took a half step to close the distance between them. She tilted her head back to glare up into the Delver's face, little caring if it made her look ridiculous. "And was it you who faced down the fire, ak'Kal? Was it you who braved the heat and the flames to keep it from spreading? Was it you who danced it to ash? Pardon, but I did not see you in the fire's glare just now, and I did not see you on the Dance ground in my youth spent acquiring the knowledge of how to fight it. Do you know the three great rules of fire, Burrood ak'Kal?"

Burrood peered at her as though the Old Man had sprung up in his face. Jetta raised her voice, slashing it like a knife through the listening hush. "The three great rules of fire are these. Show no fear. Allow no *hysth* to form. Retreat and die."

She advanced the scant inches separating them. Burrood retreated.

Someone in the crowd snorted. A rumble like a distant snow slide rose farther down the alley. Burrood's face turned the color of burning bark in the lantern light, twisting in fury as he belatedly realized he had made a fool of himself. He turned and plunged away, shouting names Jetta did not know. A handful of huge dark figures melted into the night with him, leaving a ring of glowing azure eyes watching her in expectant silence.

"It would seem you have recovered from the Wind Point trail, Dancer!" a cheerful voice called.

Jetta jerked around. "Jetta!" Setti warned breathlessly behind her. She froze, only then aware of friendly smiles and that the jibe seemed admiring, not pointed.

A brush of cloth on her shoulders startled her still again. Sheshan stood there, settling his shirt around her once more. Stiffly Jetta shook her head, stung by Burrood's implication of weakness, but the Windrider tightened his fingers, preventing her throwing it off.

He lifted his voice. "Will you show us the source of the fire, ak'Kal?"

Jetta glared, but fighting him would only make her look

a worse fool than Burrood. She turned toward the Delver holding the lantern, though she noted that he carried it well away from his body now as though it would bite.

The Old Man take Burrood.

Huunall arrived with Urrana behind him and Nuurn panting up with Anual. For all their long legs, Setti had easily outrun them, uneven streets and all. Huunall unceremoniously plucked the lantern from the villager's hand, heedless of the man's anxious gasp. He held it up to peer at Jetta.

"You are well, Jetta ak'Kal?"

"How not? Look here."

She pointed. Huunall angled the lantern to expose bare, scorched earth. Jetta knelt and dug gingerly into the heart of it, warm ash dusting her hands to the wrists. She plucked out a dull, gray lump of stone no bigger than her fist and held it up.

"Heartstone," she announced.

A collective gasp echoed back from the enclosing walls. "But—Annam is too high for heartstones to reach," a woman protested.

"Don't tell a Firedancer her trade," Jetta said coldly. "Look and learn. I've been told that tremors are felt here occasionally. Where tremors are, cracks in the heartstone deep under us can be. There are veins of windstone all through this valley. It takes only one intersecting with a heartstone to allow The Ancient a path to the surface. If some long-ago tremor cracked open a vein, The Ancient will never stop until it worms its way all the way up. There's no telling how long this stone has been on its way to the surface, or how many more have come with it. But as surely as earth freezes and frost pulls out in the spring, they will work to the surface eventually."

"The frost is gone out of the ground for the year," Huunall said. "How—"

"Did anyone drag a heavy load through here recently? This woodpile was high, and seemed barely touched. Was it just restocked?"

"Yes!" A Delver Jetta had not met thrust forward into the lantern light. "This is my house, Jetta ak'Kal. And yes, I pulled a stoneboat with a load of wood up here and stacked it last night."

"And churned up the mud in this spot, which thinned the layer of earth over this heartstone. They're *hot*, good folk. Hot as you cannot imagine until they burst into flame in front of your eyes. This one burned its way through the last handspan of dirt. All it took was an instant's exposure to the free air. You see the result."

Dismay muttered down the street. "Should we pave over all our grass then?" a mournful voice asked.

"No! That would be surrendering to The Ancient. This place is too beautiful to strip of its greenery. That is why Settak and I watch."

"As you watched at Setham?" a voice shouted from the darkness, touching off a rising babble from the crowd. Jetta watched the ground she had just won from Burrood eroding under their fears, and cursed him with every foul imprecation she could remember.

Urrana's voice lifted in a piercing bellow that rattled glass in windows and boomed back from the walls into a startled silence. "Enough! Go back to your homes and think about this. We hired Firedancers to teach us how to be safe. Listen then, and learn!"

The villagers trickled away, muttering and shaking their heads. Urrana waited until the street was empty before striding over to Jetta and seizing her hands. "You're freezing, ak'Kal. This was well done. Go and rest. You've earned it."

"Go, Jetta," Setti said. "It's time to change the watch anyway."

She looked up at the stars and saw that it was past the turn of the night, and she was suddenly exhausted. "All right."

She turned to go, remembered she still had Sheshan's shirt around her shoulders, and discovered him a silent spectator at her elbow. She offered him his shirt back. He waved it away.

"No, I'll see you home and take it back then."

Setti raised his head in protest. "A splendid idea," Urrana boomed over whatever he might have said. "Get her home and I'll scrounge a cup of noë for you when you get back."

"There's incentive," Sheshan murmured, flashing her a smile as white as his hair. "I'll hold you to it. Jetta ak'Kal, shall we go?"

His hand between her shoulder blades urged her away. She thought about her cloak lying discarded somewhere. "Where's Rununn?"

"Back on watch if he's wise," Urrana said. "Go, Dancer, before you fall down and must be carried home again."

That got her moving. Jetta set off up the street with Sheshan a silent shadow beside her, feeling Setti's furious gaze every step of the way.

She would rather, all in all, be dancing with the Old Man.

Nine
Wind and Fire

It seemed a remarkably long way to Nuurn's house. They passed no one in the streets; apparently when Urrana shouted, folk listened. Deeply annoyed, Jetta wished for someone, even Burrood, to step out and accost them, but the winding way belonged to her and the Windrider at her shoulder.

"It's kind of you to come," she said as they passed the inn. "But unnecessary. I'm all right."

Sheshan turned slightly, a tall shadow tipped with silver hair gleaming in the starlight. "You're exhausted. What if the fire returns?"

"Then I'll dance with it. And scream for Setti."

A chuckle drifted out of the darkness. "Wise. But he is only a journeyman, and I saw how the fire defied you, the master. Should I leave you to fight it alone?"

She stole a glance at him, but could not see more than a dim oval of a face. "What would you do?" she asked, curiosity getting the better of her.

"See that no wind reached it, at the least. We are not entirely fools about fire, you know."

"Did I say you were?"

"No." But it came out a clipped acknowledgment with bitterness buried at its heart.

"What's wrong?"

"Nothing." He thrust out an arm to point at the mountains rising at the north end of the valley. "Are they not magnificent? Have you seen such sights before?"

She looked up at the pale, jagged peaks occluding the stars, knife-edged ridges glistening where the thin light kissed the snow. Distant waterfalls sparkled faintly, a glimmer of motion in the night. "No," she admitted. "Annam is a beautiful place. Is that why you came here?"

He did not answer for so long that she thought he would not. "I'm sorry," she said. "I don't mean—"

"We came because the Delvers do not judge," he said in a rush. "Do you understand?"

She shook her head, at a loss. "No."

He started on. "It doesn't matter. Come."

Perversely she planted her heels. "No. What did you mean, they don't judge? What is there to judge?"

He turned to face her. A stray finger of light from a window down the street caught an expression half-defiant, half-weary on his face. "What stories run through the Fire clan villages about Windriders?" he asked obliquely. "What do they say of us where you come from, Jetta ak'Kal?"

She floundered for an instant, on the defensive and disliking it. "That Windriders have no clan home, no standing place. That they roam from village to village offering their services, and that they are few."

"We are few," he said tightly. "That's true enough."

"Why are you so angry?"

"Do I seem angry to you?" He started on. "I'm sorry. I'm not angry at you."

She was forced to follow. "Then with whom? Who judges you against your will?"

"No one. Everyone."

They are as strange as people say, Jetta thought, exasperated. A stray memory came to her; she blurted it out before the threads fully connected in her mind. "Ayesh told Urrana he came to Annam looking for a clean wind. He didn't mean the wind off the mountains, did he?"

"No." He stopped again, looking at her. "That was intuitive. What else does your intuition say?"

A stray gust blasted around a building, ruffling the restless layers of the shirt around her shoulders. She shivered. "That we'll freeze if we linger out here. Can you really not feel that?"

A smile touched his mouth. "That? That's just a balmy spring breeze."

"Balmy! And that gale the other day coming off Wind Point

was just a playful zephyr, I suppose."

"No." His voice deepened. "That was dangerous. It was a near thing when you fell."

"When I fe—" She remembered then, a glimpse of him with his face to the clouds, and something *pushing* her back onto the trail. "You caught me! I would have gone over the edge, but something pushed me back!"

"I thought it well not to take a chance."

"Then I owe you my life."

"Perhaps. I don't collect debts."

"Nevertheless." She started on, thoughtful now. "You're the first Windrider I've ever spoken to. Not counting Wyth."

White teeth flashed in the dark. "I heard about that. Wyth is unaccustomed to insolence."

"Insolence! That arrogant—"

"He is a Fourth Rank master. I would say he's entitled to his eccentricities."

"Is that what you call them?" Jetta asked sourly. "I can think of a better word."

He chuckled. "Several, no doubt. But he has great talent. I've learned much from him."

He stopped again. Jetta saw that they had reached Nuurn's door. The waterfall glittered and roared just ahead, spilling its torrent under the arched stone bridge and down the hill. Sheshan turned to look at it with the same curiously focused attention he seemed to give to everything. "A fascinating thing, water," he said. "Almost as fascinating as fire."

He returned his gaze to her. "Good night, Jetta ak'Kal. I am honored to have assisted you in my small way."

She took the Windrider shirt from around her shoulders and gave it back to him. "More than you know, ak'Kal. My thanks."

"And mine, for not allowing the house where I am quartered to burn down. It would have been most inconvenient."

He flashed her that gleaming smile and moved away into the night, a graceful shadow that seemed to skim rather than walk the stones underfoot. Jetta watched him until the chill began to penetrate her bare skin and she realized she was stupidly standing in the night wind when she could be sleeping in a warm bed. She fought the heavy door open and slipped inside.

By the stars it was very late. If Nuurn and Anual were upstairs and not engaged in some Circle argument at the inn, they must both be sound asleep. Silence ruled the house; from habit Jetta checked every hearth, but the fires slept secure behind screens of containment stone, banked down against the morning. Eventually she climbed the stairs, forcing her tired legs to each tall step, taking care lest she trip and wake the whole house. She fell into her bed still in her Dance leathers, and slept without dreaming until Setti pounded on her door well after dawn.

"Jetta! Do you plan to sleep all day?"

"Not anymore!" she yelled back, and drew the blankets over her head when he opened the door and stuck his head in.

"Get up. You'll miss breakfast."

"I don't care."

"There's a meeting at the inn in an hour. They want us to teach them how to minimize the risks from heartstone."

She pushed back the blanket and poked her head out. "In one day?"

"Probably. Come on."

She sat up, feeling frowzy and slow and none too clean. With reason. She wrinkled her nose over the Dance leathers she had not put off last night. At that moment all she wanted was a long soak in a hot bath. She looked over at Setti still leaning in the doorway, and saw that he didn't look much better. He too, had been up half the night.

"I felt it come last night," she said.

Setti jerked up straighter, his tired face regaining its animation. "Really? That's fine news!"

She waved a hand to quell his enthusiasm. "I couldn't tell *where*. I only knew it was near."

"Any warning at all is better than none. I felt nothing."

"Most Dancers don't," she reminded him sharply, lest he dive into the pool of self-pity as he used to. "So, it's watch and watch for us. Get used to being tired."

He shrugged. "At least we don't have to watch alone. The Delvers relayed the alarm so quickly I got there in time to see it die."

He must have half-killed himself running the length of the village that fast, over that ankle-twisting street. "A bellow like Urrana's is better than a bell," she said.

Setti grinned. "It was impressive, wasn't it?"

"It worked. Go. Tell Anual I'm on my way."

He vanished, shutting the door behind him. Jetta crawled out, looked in the polished silver mirror behind the door, and grimaced. Her coiled braid had come undone in the night and now spilled stray wisps of hair everywhere; soot smudged one cheek, her feet bore traces of dried mud and she reeked of smoke. Anual would be scandalized at the state of her sheets.

She washed the worst of it off in the basin, yanked a comb through her hair and bundled it back up. The window beckoned, full of sunshine and clean air innocent of smoke stink. Jetta resisted the urge to enter the control position and just stand there basking in the Mother's embrace. Remembering the sweet, pounding rush of it last night incited a fierce desire to wrap herself in it and let the Old Man do what he liked; thought of what waited at the inn told her she had no time for indulgence. She pulled on clean clothes and went downstairs.

Nuurn had already gone but breakfast still awaited her on the table: huge hot muffins and thick porridge with honey. Anual was kneading dough in the corner as Setti amiably devoured one of the muffins. Jetta climbed into her chair and let her feet dangle without a thought. She pleased Anual no end when she scooped up one of the muffins and ate half of it before coming up for air.

"That's better," the Delver woman said, beaming. "Dancing with fire seems to create appetites."

Setti reached for another muffin. Jetta picked up the miniature—by Delver standards—stone cup Anual set in front of her. "Your pardon, but let's hope it doesn't come to stimulate us every night."

Anual sighed. "A good wish. Tell me," she added slyly, "what did you think of young Sheshan?"

Setti became very busy buttering his muffin.

Jetta shrugged. "They're a strange lot, aren't they? He was better than Wyth, I'll give him that."

"Any of them are better than Wyth, child," Anual said tartly. "But Sheshan is better than most. There's a good heart in him, and he's excellent with the children."

"Oh?" Jetta, busy with the porridge, lifted an inquiring eyebrow.

"That girl of Urrana's is fair smitten with him, I can tell you, and the rest cling to him like filings to a lodestone. He shapes clouds for them to name and blows leaves around for them to chase. But he broods."

"I noticed." Jetta ignored a quick sideways glance from Setti. "He says the Windriders come here because the Delvers don't judge them."

Anual pounded the dough down with a bit more force than necessary. "He said that?"

"He did. What did he mean?"

The Delver woman went on kneading in silence for a moment. "You come from the lowlands. I daresay you've heard stories about Windriders."

"That they steal women when their own are scarce, and take any child born of a liaison between a Windrider and an outsider, leaving the mother bereft," Setti said flatly. "I've heard."

Anual concentrated on her dough. "And do they also say that the Windriders grow fewer every year? That the great storms on the seacoast three seasons past decimated the ranks of their masters, and that there are few left to train those remaining? Do they say that one in five Windrider children don't live to tame the winds? Do they say those things, Settak a'Kam?"

Setti's jaw dropped. Jetta, remembering how Sheshan had defended surly Wyth, how Ayesh had sought a clean wind, said quietly, "No wonder he enjoys the company of children."

Anual looked up then. "Even Wyth has his good points. Few though they are."

"I'll remember."

Jetta returned her attention to the porridge, thoughtful now, rethinking all those tales. Beside her, Setti sat in unwonted silence, picking his remaining muffin apart into tiny crumbs. Finally he said, "I'll meet you at the inn, Jetta," and left without another word.

Anual watched his stiff back disappear through the door. "Best watch him, Jetta ak'Kal. He is younger than his years."

"Yes, but he, too, has a good heart."

"But not the wisdom to know what to do with it."

Jetta frowned. "What—"

"Best get on to the meeting, ak'Kal," Anual said formally. "They'll be expecting you."

Thus dismissed, Jetta had no choice but to thank her for breakfast and go. She had taken no more than five steps past the front door when Sheshan turned up at her elbow.

She jumped, for he seemed to have stepped out of the air itself. "Where did you come from?"

"I like to sit atop the falls and watch the sun come up."

"It's two hours past sunrise," Jetta pointed out.

"It's a pretty place. And what else have I got to do?"

"I don't know. What else do Windriders do?"

He fell in beside her, matching his long-legged stride to hers. "Watch the clouds. Feel the wind. Breathe."

"Talking to you is like catching the breeze in your fingers."

"I can do that," he said gravely. "See?"

She glanced over and saw a bit of fluff spinning a tight circle between his spread hands. It brought all the hair up on her neck. "That's unnatural."

"And dismissing fire with a flick of the hand is not?"

He released the wind and snatched the fluff from the air, laid it across his hand and blew it at her, smiling. It brushed her cheek and tangled in her hair; Sheshan reached up and raked it out again.

"Such dark, dark hair," he said admiringly.

She pulled her head out of reach. "Is there no dark hair among your people?"

"Sometimes. But those folk never have much talent."

She gave him a startled, sideways glance. "Really?"

"Really."

She thought about that. Dancers were always dark of hair, golden of skin, different only in the shape of their bones. She eyed Sheshan's cloud-pale skin and spider-silk hair, and wondered if the irregular ways in which Windriders expanded their ranks had anything to do with the vagaries of their talent.

A happy shriek split the morning air. "Sheshan! Come and play with us!"

A trio of Delver children swarmed out from between two

houses, all flying brown hair and great blue eyes. Two girls and a boy grabbed Sheshan's hands and tried to pull him away up the street.

"Manners!" he reproved them. "Can you not see I'm with someone, and a master at that?"

The eldest girl noticed Jetta for the first time. "Oh!" Her brown cheeks darkened in embarrassment. "Jetta ak'Kal. Forgive. Mother says we must be respectful, or you'll set us on fire to make us mind."

"She said what?" Jetta stared, torn between anger and astonishment. All three took a step back.

Sheshan laughed. "Go, Giruun, before you find out if it's true. Dancers are not to be trifled with."

The three of them gave Jetta wide blue glances and ran off. Jetta rounded on Sheshan. "Why did you tell them that? What total nonsense! I don't want them to be afraid of me!"

"Do you want them underfoot while you work and get themselves burned for it?"

"I can protect them, thank you very much!"

He shrugged. "Why does it matter to you what they think?"

An acute pang shot through Jetta on a memory of hordes of Setham children following her on her rounds, trying to copy the intricate moves of the Dance when she and Kori practiced together. The little girls had coiled their hair atop their heads and the boys had made themselves crude Dancers' gear from twists of cloth, the tails flapping to every breeze. They had brought her sweets and cool drinks in the summer and hot pora on winter nights and beamed when she called them by name.

"It does." She lengthened her stride to leave him behind. To no avail; a flutter of pale blue announced his return to her elbow. She ignored it.

"Why are you angry?" Sheshan asked, low-voiced.

"You seek a place where you aren't judged. You shouldn't have to ask."

She heard a gasp, and then the inn door loomed in front of her, the sign above it swaying in the mountain wind that never seemed to stop. She pushed down on the latch and shoved the door open without looking at him again.

Jetta stopped short just inside, taken aback by the crowd

filling the common room. A sea of broad backs and dark hair confronted her, interspersed with not less than a dozen paler heads and feathery-garmented bodies. Jetta froze; so large a Circle was odd enough; now she had a double hand of Windriders to complicate the brew. Heads turned at her entrance; Setti, lounging by the kitchen door, leaped up and stared as Sheshan stepped in behind her.

Setti's face twisted into a mask of disbelief that slipped into disappointment and hurt. Sapphire eyes seemed to leap out of his head to impale hers before shifting accusingly to the Windrider at her back. Jetta recoiled, taken aback by the naked hostility behind his face. Easy-going Setti? Old Man Fire, what had Sheshan done to set him off?

Huunall's voice tore her attention away. He rose from a bench by the fireplace, where no flame burned this morning. The room was warm even without it; Jetta wondered if that were the reason for its absence, or if Urrana was taking no chances with wind and fire in the same room.

"I'm neither eldest nor youngest here," Huunall said, standing in front of the fireplace peering down at them all from under the tangled thicket of his eyebrows. His deep voice hushed the low hum of conversation and washed back to fill every corner of the room. "But I am the only Fifth Rank master in Annam, of whatever craft. Urrana wants an orderly meeting. Guess that means I'll run it. Burrood, you'll get a turn to speak. Until then, respect what everyone else has to say."

Burrood reared upright from a seat beside the window. "Why single me out?"

"Because yours is the loudest voice," Huunall grumped, drawing a laugh like a storm roaring down the mountainside. Burrood mumbled something and sat down, leaning over to whisper something in the ear of a Delver beside him.

"Jetta ak'Kal, will you join us?" Huunall extended a hand. Jetta picked her way through the crowd toward the hearth. She started to sit on the low bench, then deliberately chose one of the larger empty chairs, needing its height to see and be seen. It was only after she had settled herself with her feet tucked up to avoid making her look even smaller that she saw that Sheshan had gone to stand behind Wyth seated on the opposite side of the fireplace. He didn't look at her, but stood with arms folded, watching the crowd of Delvers, his face unreadable.

Setti arrived and took his place behind her. "What are you doing coming in with him?" he hissed in her ear.

She looked up at him incredulously. "What business is it of yours, a'Kam?"

His jaw dropped. *"Jetta—"*

Huunall said something. Jetta turned her shoulder to Setti and gave her attention to the big Delver, wondering what this meeting was really about. Certainly not to instruct the Delvers in how to avoid fire.

"Jetta ak'Kal. Wyth ak'Kal." Huunall gave them each a nod. "Thank you for attending. A good thing. We need to come to know each other. It's a dangerous time in Annam. We appreciate the unique talents here to meet it. The Windriders have done us great service, three years now. The Firedancers have wasted no time proving their worth."

A loud snort sounded from Burrood's direction. Huunall ignored it. "We've a common enemy. The Circle hopes—the majority anyway," he said clearly, "that Windrider and Firedancer will join with the Delvers to combine against it. The Ancient doesn't care what craft we are."

He let that sink in for a few seconds. "Wyth ak'Kal, you've been the guest of Annam Vale these three winters. Is it your intent to remain?"

"It is." Pale eyes flicked to Jetta. "If certain accommodations can be made."

Jetta's head came up. "What accommodations?"

Huunall jumped in. "Please, ak'Kal. We will hear the Windriders."

Setti blew a furious snort. Jetta set her jaw, wondering darkly what Wyth had on his insular, arrogant mind.

"The Windriders find the presence of Firedancers in this place disturbing." Wyth leaped straight to the attack. "We believe the incidence of fire will increase, not decrease, with their presence, with consequent increased danger to your folk. We advise that you send them away and continue to let the Windriders protect Annam Vale as they have done for three seasons now. It is still standing, is it not?"

"This is an accommodation?" Setti burst out.

"Hush!" Jetta snapped as a cold smile creased Wyth's

mouth. *If he's successful as a Windrider, it must be because he provokes the winds into doing something stupid*, she thought acidly.

Huunall sighed. "Not possible, Wyth ak'Kal. My regrets. Tell me true, had a Windrider been in the tunnel at Wind Point two days past, could he have conquered the fire that appeared?"

Wyth's smile vanished. "It rose to the presence of a Firedancer. The situation would not have come about had they not been there."

"But could you have vanquished it as did Jetta ak'Kal?"

"From what I hear, there was nothing so straightforward as vanquishing going on. It took her several minutes and the help of one of my folk to banish the fire last night. Something your people could have done alone by simply pulling the stack of firewood apart."

A murmur of agreement rumbled around the room. Jetta, dismayed, saw more than a few heads nodding. Setti quivered beside her like a branch over-laden with snow. She found her own jaw aching from gritting her teeth, and consciously relaxed it. Her nerves found it sweet relief when Huunall turned to her, his face an impassive mask.

"Jetta ak'Kal, what say you?"

"That Wyth ak'Kal was not present either time and knows as much of either instance as he does about fire."

Stunned silence descended on the common room. Scores of round Delver eyes blinked almost in unison, the only movement apart from a sudden agitated flutter of Windrider fabric at a dozen points around the room. Huunall opened his mouth, disappointment and reproof in his face. Jetta forestalled him, leaning forward to look Wyth in the eye. His supercilious smile froze on his lips; his clear, ice-chip eyes narrowed in sudden wariness.

"Let me tell you, ak'Kal—" she included every master in the room in that, "—what would have happened if you had attempted Wyth ak'Kal's method of dealing with fire. It started in the street beside—Wiruun's house, was it not?" That drew another murmur for her depth of knowledge gained in so short a time. "None of your firewatch posts had that particular spot in sight. Your posts are too few, too scattered, and the one roving watcher cannot be everywhere.

So had I not sensed the fire coming, it would have sparked to life unnoticed by any. Rununn was there with me. Call him in and ask him how quickly the fire migrated from heartstone surfacing in the street to the firewood a Delver's length away."

She threw a glance around the room. She had their attention now. "The fire found the wood and blazed instantly to Delver height and beyond. That put it within reach of the eaves. Had it rooted there, it would have run under the roof and into the house and down into whatever flammable things it could find. The sheets on the beds. The clothes on the inhabitants. The herbs in the kitchens." She paused, watching the images sink into their imaginations. Brown faces paled to the color of mud washed over windstone.

"By the time a passer-by, a neighbor, Wiruun or one of his family or the firewatch noticed the flames and began to fight back, the house would be alight. By the time they found non-flammable rods long enough to pull the fire away from anything that would burn, it would be too hot to venture inside. The flames would be seven times a Delver's height, sparks flying everywhere, seeking new territory. They would find it right next door, in the wooden eaves of the next house. In the wood stacked everywhere with no box of containment stone to shelter it. In the broken-down trader cart moldering beside a storehouse."

She saw the thoughtless habits of a fire-free lifetime pricking holes in their complacency. "And even if you correct all these things, ak'Kal, what will you do when a heartstone works up under your very feet? Smother it with a bucket? Roll it into the stream? If fire bursts from a layer of windstone in one of the mines, what will you do? Blow the entrance full of stone with miners still inside? Suck all the air out and spin it into a great ball like a child's toy?"

She did not look at Sheshan as she said it. Wyth looked as though he had eaten something poisonous. He opened his mouth once or twice, but a murmur from the Delvers turned his head toward the room in general. His cold gaze flicked over the faces, and his lips snapped into a tight, thin line. He sat back in his chair, arms crossed.

The Delvers swayed and fidgeted like flowers in a high wind, their agitated muttering thrumming to match the distant waterfall. "Well done!" Setti whispered gleefully in her ear, but Jetta was watching Huunall, whose craggy face had lost its humor. Almost—*almost*—she regretted striking back so hard, but they needed to hear it, needed to know what they faced.

Huunall turned to her. "What would you have us do, Jetta ak'Kal?"

She met his honest eyes, gritted her teeth, and compromised. "Trust us, Setti and I. Listen to us, and we will teach you how to protect yourselves. As to the Windriders, I confess that I was as disturbed as Wyth ak'Kal to learn they resided here. But a Windrider diverted the breeze for me last night and contributed in his way to the Dance. I cannot say that their presence here is a detriment to Annam Vale. I think there may be ways for us to work together."

The tight lines around Huunall's eyes eased. He turned to the Windriders. "Wyth?"

"I see disaster on that course, Huunall. I oppose this notion."

"Disappointing, ak'Kal," Huunall rumbled. "The Windriders have been our friends."

Wyth reared up out of his seat. "Will you throw us from Annam Vale?"

The room erupted in shouts and protests. Delvers shot to their feet, waving massive fists. A woman seated behind Burrood leaned forward and screamed something at him, poking a big finger into his shoulder at every word. Burrood ignored her, shouting something at Huunall lost in the general din. Urrana opened her mouth, but even her voice couldn't override the tumult. Finally she climbed up on a table and flung a tankard onto the stone floor.

It smashed in a shower of flying splinters that raked the nearest bystanders with sharp little needles of stone. Windriders and Delvers alike threw up their arms and ducked. The shouting died into gaping silence.

"Are you mad, woman?" someone roared, picking stone fragments out of his beard.

"No madder than the lot of you," Urrana said serenely, climbing down. "If any of you would actually listen to what Huunall has to say, my crockery wouldn't be made to suffer."

A gale of laughter swept the room. *They're as changeable*

as the weather, Jetta thought, and then surveyed the faces more closely. No. These were good people, steady as the stones of their mountains. They *wanted* to do right. Open-handed and open-hearted, they stood by their friends. For that she approved them greatly. But they wanted what they had always had: the peace of an unthreatened existence. Change frightened them, and she could not see how to overcome it save by frightening them with worse things.

Huunall turned to Wyth. "Ak'Kal," he rumbled. "You think so little of us? Would we tell friends to go? Turn you and your children out onto the roads?"

There are Windrider children here? Jetta thought in sudden, intense curiosity. She looked around as another thought struck her, but saw no fluttery skirts or female faces the color of frost.

Wyth's mouth turned down. His gaze flicked here and there, hunting support that did not seem forthcoming. Huunall pressed him gently. "Time to learn new things, Windrider. For all of us."

Wyth sat motionless a long moment. Beside him, another pale-haired master leaned over and said something in his ear. Wyth's mouth turned down, but he looked at Huunall and nodded. He settled sulkily into his chair, withdrawing from the proceedings.

Huunall nodded and lifted his voice. "We will hear Jetta ak'Kal's proposal."

What proposal? Jetta thought, startled, but she had begun, and now she had to finish. She stood up, because she could see necks craning in the back of the room in an attempt to see her.

"Ak'Kal," she said, suddenly nervous. The well-being of Annam Vale had just descended into her hands; to her would fall the sole blame if something went fatally wrong. Again. Those self-same hands turned clammy; she fought off a desperate urge to wipe them on her pants, swallowed a quiver threatening her voice, and looked into the great-eyed faces looking back at her with unblinking attention.

"My proposal is this. Setti and I will teach you and your children how to defend against fire. That is our basic duty as Firedancers, along with patrolling and fighting The Ancient whenever and wherever it appears. We will teach anyone who wishes to learn." Her gaze strayed over impassive Windrider faces and moved on. "We withhold no secrets. Our knowledge is yours. The Ancient cares not at all who or what it touches. Since the Beginning, the Fire Clans have fought it as the enemy of us all. It is our purpose."

She took a deep breath. "Setti and I are only two, and I see two areas of great danger: the village itself, and the mines. We cannot be in both places at once, especially if you open the new vein down the valley. You will have to post firewatch day and night in the places where we cannot be, and I ask the Windriders to assist. I have seen how their talents may help to deprive The Ancient of what it craves most, at least perhaps long enough for other means to defeat it."

"By spinning it into a ball like a child's toy?" Wyth asked, his face wooden.

She turned to face him. "If that is what it takes. I wouldn't recommend it. But wind can smother as well as feed. It can funnel as well as scatter. It may be that the Delver craft is about to add new lore to the building of mine shafts. Infant flame is stupid, easily trapped. Among us all—Delver, Windrider, Firedancer—perhaps we can build tunnels with firetraps where our combined talents can drive and defeat The Ancient even if no Dancer is present."

"Perhaps! Maybe!" Burrood's voice boomed over a spate of thoughtful murmurs. "Is that what we bought when we contracted with a fire clan? For us to do the work and *hope* that it *might* work?"

Intense dislike flashed through many faces. "Hush yourself, you great lump!" a woman's voice said clearly. Jetta blinked. When had Anual arrived?

A ripple of deep laughter vibrated the floor under her feet, but Burrood's hide seemed as impervious as the stone he delved. "Answer, Firedancer. Wyth ak'Kal is right. You've been here two days, and we have had two incidents of flame. Should we expect this as a daily occurrence from now on? The Ancient knows you're here. I say go, leave Annam fire-free."

"It was not fire-free before we came, or you would not have contracted us," Jetta pointed out. "I didn't put the heartstone under your streets. I didn't seal Wind Point. Is your mind sealed in containment stone, Burrood ak'Kal?"

Peals of laughter poured into the room that time, with Urrana's loudest. She stepped up beside Huunall, wiping tears of mirth from her eyes. "I say enough. Fools and quibbling aside, I like what I have heard today. Other places have learned to live with The Ancient lurking under their streets. So must we. If it means learning new things, so be it. If our tunnels are safer with new designs, is that so bad?"

A thoughtful hush greeted that. Jetta remembered Urrana's lifemate, dead in a collapsed tunnel, and saw the same memory striking home all around the room. Huunall nodded respect at Urrana and stood up, drawing all eyes.

"Are we agreed?"

"Yes!" The booming chorus overrode shouts of "No!" from Burrood's side of the room.

Huunall nodded. "Then I ask Nuurn, Errull, Urrana, Wiruun, and Windriders Wyth, Ayesh, Thess, and Sheshan to stay, along with Jetta ak'Kal and Settak a'Kam. Errull, did you find the charts?"

Errull stood up, forging toward the fireplace through the tide of outgoing Delvers, his arms loaded with rolled leather scrolls that looked like the village maps stored at Firehome. Urrana and Nuurn pulled a pair of tables together and set chairs around. As Errull dumped his load onto the nearest, Huunall turned and cocked an eyebrow at Wyth, who had not moved. Sheshan and the Windrider who had spoken to him earlier flanked him on his right. Another tall master stood on his left, much younger, with hair the color of withered autumn fields.

Wyth threw a hard look at Jetta, who kept her face impassive, her return glance neutral. Finally he stood up and came to the table, caught a chair and yanked it backward. The other three masters took their places behind him in silence.

Urrana turned toward the kitchen door. "Rinood! Noë and spice bread!" She turned a bland smile on the table at large. "That should sweeten things a bit."

The door closed on the last of the Delvers. Huunall settled into place at the head of the table and said, "Well, then, shall we begin?"

"May I know the names of everyone at this conference?"

Jetta asked politely.

"Eh? Oh, you're right. Nuurn you know. Wiruun—"

"My thanks for saving my home," the Delver said with a nod.

Huunall waited a beat for Wyth to introduce his own people, then smoothly did it himself when the Windrider just sat there with his mouth closed like a fishtrap. He named the Windriders left to right. "Sheshan ak'Kal of the Third Rank. Wyth ak'Kal of the Fourth. Ayesh ak'Kal of the Fourth Rank. Thess ak'Kal of the Second Rank."

That surprised her. She eyed Thess, whose eyes and hair were much darker than those of the rest of his kind, almost brown. He was the youngest of them, looking a little uncertain and lost. Were they so short on masters that a boy sat in council, or was his talent so great?

"Thank you," she said to Huunall. "Now then. Shall we begin with the charts?"

Ten
Accommodation

Four hours of poring over charts brought home to Jetta two things: the workings under Annam Vale were huge, and Wyth ak'Kal was the most unpleasant person she had ever met.

"What gives him the right to be so nasty?" she fumed to Setti, walking up to Nuurn's in the late afternoon between rows of houses looming tall and black on either hand like the mountains themselves. "This plan is ill-conceived," she mimicked, dropping her voice to a nasal sneer. "If he had said that one more time I would have thrown sparks at him, I swear."

Setti yawned hugely. "Can you imagine the panic if you had? I notice that none of the Windriders looked happy when Urrana relit the hearth fire."

"Think what he'd have been like *with*out the noë."

"A great sacrifice on Urrana's part, I'd say." Setti yawned again.

Jetta looked up at him. "I'll take first watch tonight. You need the sleep."

"I'm fine!" He stretched his eyes wide, succeeding only in looking like a child trying to stay awake.

Jetta snorted. "Orders, a'Kam. You *can* take them?"

Setti turned unexpectedly sullen. "Of course, ak'Kal."

"That was a joke, Setti. What's the matter with you?"

"Nothing. Half a day in a room with Wyth is enough to set anyone to sharpening knives."

Jetta eyed him. "I suppose. But I think we accomplished something anyway."

"Yes." Some of Setti's enthusiasm returned. "Huunall is brilliant. That firetrap he sketched—if it works we could use it even in the lowland villages—"

"Except that it takes a Windrider to make it work," she reminded him gently. "Try getting the Circle to authorize a Windrider stationed in every village alongside the resident Firedancer."

His face fell. "You're right. And I'm not sure myself I want to stand that close to a Windrider day and night." Setti's expression hardened suddenly. His gaze turned inward, contemplating something Jetta did not want to guess at.

"Ayesh isn't so bad," she said.

His head jerked. "No, he seemed almost like a real person. And Thess. Why do you suppose he sits in their Circle? He didn't contribute much."

"Urrana said he was one of those who helped seal Wind Point. He is a master despite his age. He must be skilled."

Setti frowned and walked on in silence, reflecting, no doubt, on the fact that he was still a journeyman of the Second Rank at several years older than Thess. Jetta touched his arm. "We should practice in the morning. I want to see how fire acts here when it is forced to come—if it obeys the Dance or not."

He threw her a startled look full of dismay. "What if it doesn't?"

"Then we make a new Dance, I suppose. One that it will obey."

"Easier said than done!" He stopped and faced her. "Jetta, I don't understand how The Ancient can overcome the patterns of the Dance. They were set in place at the Beginning. The Ancient was bound to them as we were in the making of the world. How can the bindings break?"

"Maybe they haven't. Maybe they've only changed, and we haven't learned the new pattern. Maybe an age of the world has passed, and it's The Ancient's turn to make the rules. I just don't know, Setti."

"So we set Delvers to patrol the mines and put Windriders underground to blow fire into places it cannot burn through, and teach children to smother flame with buckets. I want to strangle the Circle, each and every one."

Jetta walked in silence for a little. "I don't think they knew," she said eventually. "I need to send to them, tell them about the fire at Wind Point, and about last night. About the

Windriders. I think they are as baffled as we are."

"Then why send us alone? Why send *me?*" Honest bewilderment overrode his habitual self-denigration.

"You may be just what The Ancient doesn't expect."

Setti blew a disbelieving snort but Jetta stopped short, struck by the thought. "No one in the Fire Clans is more stubborn than you, Setti. You have beaten every prediction made about you. So who better to send to defy a recalcitrant Old Man to his face?"

That rocked him right back on his heels on the wind of a thought he had never considered. He walked in silence all the rest of the way to Nuurn's house and retired immediately to his room. Jetta wandered into the kitchen. Anual bent over a pot where the rising steam gave off the fragrant smells of unknown spices. She gave the mix one last stir then turned around with a smile for Jetta.

"Good meeting? I imagine it must have been with Huunall in charge. Easy-talking, that man, things seem to mind their manners around him. Did Urrana feed you? No? Well, we'll be eating in an hour. Perhaps you'd like a bath?"

Jetta stood up straighter. "Oh, yes!"

Anual dusted off her hands and led her through a door Jetta had not noticed in her prowls last night. She blinked at sight of a tiny sunken room lined and floored with gray stone. A wide trough in the middle cut completely from end to end and disappeared into the wall opposite. Water ran in an endless burbling race from its entrance through one wall to its disappearance out the other.

"Now you see why we built next to the waterfall," Anual said complacently. "Clean water year-round, and no need to haul it. Makes up for the walk to get here."

Jetta edged down to the lowest step and set her hand in the trough. She gasped and jerked it straight out again. Anual cackled at the look on her face as Jetta shook chill droplets off her hand.

"Patience, child." The Delver woman reached up and pulled on a rope beside the door. A gate dropped shut where the water exited. Instantly it began to spill out of the trough onto the floor, where it hissed and began to steam gently.

"Don't walk on the floor barefoot when there's no water," Anual warned her. "The stones are hollow and heated from the fireplace."

"What keeps them from cracking?" Jetta wondered.

"Delver secret, ak'Kal."

"Is that windstone?" Jetta saw only potential hazard, not convenience.

"Yes, and no. It began as ordinary stone. It isn't anymore. What a Delver shapes stays shaped, and no fire yet born has ever taken hold in that seal."

Jetta gave her a sharp look. "The stones are sealed against fire? Then why this?"

"Don't we seal the walls we build for lesser folk?" Anual shook her head. "It took three years to collect enough sap from teller trees to seal a room this size, and only Huunall and Nugurr in this Vale know what to do with it. All the Delvers in all the world, and all the teller trees, couldn't make enough of it to keep a single village anywhere safe from The Ancient."

"Oh." Jetta's excitement died as quickly as it had come. Just looking at that pale stone gave her a queasy feeling in her stomach. Still, containment stone transmitted no heat. What else could they have used but windstone?

The water rose rapidly over the second step. "By the time you get your things it will be warm enough," Anual said.

"How do you keep from flooding?"

"Close the upper gate, of course." Anual shook her head and went back to her stew.

Feeling stupid, Jetta went upstairs to collect a towel and soap and clean clothes. She thought to bring yesterday's things down and scrub them clean, but they were already neatly folded on the end of her freshly-made bed with, to her surprise, the red cloak she had dropped in the street last night. She sighed. Anual had been at the meeting this morning and still managed to accomplish all the household chores. Her efficiency made Jetta feel inadequate.

By the time she got back downstairs the water looked deep enough to swim in. Jetta eyed it with some trepidation. Swimming was not a skill Firedancers cultivated. She yanked the second rope to close the upper gate, relieved to see the water stop rising. When she knelt and put a hand in she discovered the water pleasantly warm. And about neck deep.

She hung her clothes on the pegs by the door and edged

down the steps. The floor was hot even against her Dancer's skin; she contented herself with sitting on the second step and scrubbing the remains of last night's fire out of hair and skin. The pool looked inviting, though. She remembered the children in the Water Clan village where she had been healed of her burns after Setham, paddling happily around the stilted huts ducking each other and diving like fish in noisy abandon. They had made it look so easy.

She jerked the rope to open the far gate and watched the water start to swirl away. A second later she closed it again, remembering Setti. Maybe he could soak out his bad mood and whatever ailed him. She pulled her clothes off the peg and dressed, and wandered back into the kitchen raking tangles out of her wet hair with her fingers.

"That was wonderful, Anual. I'll tell Setti."

Anual looked up from spicing a pot. "He's gone out."

"What?"

"Said he wanted a walk before we eat."

Jetta leaned one hip against a tall chair and picked thoughtfully at a snarl. "He told me he was tired. I thought he'd be resting."

"Young men," Anual said cheerfully. "All energy, no thought for tomorrow."

"Mm." Jetta didn't think that was it. She frowned into the hearth fire. Did he fear the plans they had set in motion today? She could understand that. Dancers on assignment were supposed to go forth with some certainty that their training would keep them safe, but the rules had all changed in Annam Vale. The Old Man was forcing them to make up new rules and test them as they went along, with dangerously unknown elements to skew the results. It left Setti, already uncertain of his abilities, dancing on windstone. He must feel as if at any moment it could burst into flame and consume him.

And all of us, she thought somberly.

"Would you peel those for me, child?" Anual asked.

Jetta jumped and turned her attention to a pile of rather withered-looking tubers. "How would I get a message to Firehome?" she asked. "I am bidden by my Circle to report the incidence of fire here. Does anyone come and go regularly who could carry a report for me?"

"To Firehome?" Anual did not look up. "There aren't twenty Delvers in all of Annam who've been over the ridge eastward, and none who've been to Firehome. The first caravan of the year is long overdue. They should be along soon. You can send it then."

Jetta peeled a tuber, frowning. "How did you send to contract with us?"

"You came through the crossroads at Baro, did you not? Anyone can hire couriers there."

"Would someone go down for us?"

Anual shrugged. "You can ask, but unless it's urgent, you'll not find many willing to take time away from the mines just now, when the stones must be readied and dressed to go with the drovers. Though if they don't get here soon with the cart beasts, we'll be setting apprentices to pack stone up from the mines. I expected better of Hylli Fargoer."

Jetta blinked, suddenly understanding the lack of livestock in the village. She had always thought the herds of loose cart beasts following the gaily painted wagons of the drover caravans were spare animals. She had not realized there might be places in the world so inhospitable they sent their beasts out for the winter and lived on the supplies brought over the passes.

Anual was still chattering on about the lateness of the traders. "Stones and pebbles, Hylli's always first up the pass, and long before this—" She looked up, suddenly fearful. "Do you suppose—?"

Jetta thought about fire running through an unprotected string of wagons and shuddered. "I hope not. Will you send someone to investigate? If so, I'll ask to send a message, but as yet I have nothing to say worth a special effort."

"Then we'll not fret about it." Anual looked up as the front door opened, and fairly ran to meet Nuurn coming in. Setti was with him, sparking a strange little jolt of relief in Jetta. He barely spoke at supper, however, and didn't resist her suggestion afterward that he try the bath.

Anual stuck a hand in to test the water and snatched it out, but for the opposite reason Jetta had. "It's hot!" she gasped, reaching for the rope to let some cold water in.

Setti stopped her. "Just right," he said with an odd smile, and went to collect his things.

"I guess it's true Firedancers don't feel heat," Anual said, awed.

From curiosity Jetta thrust her own hand in and winced from the sting of it. Not unbearable, no, but far hotter than she would have cared to sit in. She said nothing to Setti, just went up to change into Dance leathers. Let the fool boil himself, if that was what he needed to convince himself worthy to face fire.

Outside in the glacier-fed wind, she began to envy him the heat. Even through her cloak the air had teeth; she wondered if summer would bring evening temperatures above uncomfortably cool. At least there would be none of Setham's stuffy humidity and airless nights.

The Delvers had wasted no time implementing the plans arrived at in the afternoon, nor had the village folk been idle. Most of the uncovered woodpiles now sported temporary huts of unshaped blocks of containment stone, stacked into rough walls that would stop the Old Man's first mad rush. A new firewatch post had been established where the upper street met the lower below the inn. She greeted the Delver stationed there, a girl about Rununn's age, and turned toward the storehouses. There, too, the Delvers had been busy. Someone had raked the ground clean of last year's dead weeds and grass; the old cart had been removed; and another apprentice tramped in determined watchfulness up and down and in and out of the silent buildings.

"Good watch to you," Jetta greeted him, and went on with his fervent assurances in her ears.

From waterfall to bridge the village sprawled quiet and fire free, a collection of tall houses hulking black against the stars. She felt nothing, sensed nothing, and the night passed into the mid-watch without incident. Jetta turned back up the hill, intent on waking Setti for his watch and finding her own bed. Between one step and the next she found a tall shadow walking beside her across the meadow, silent as the stars overhead.

"Sheshan ak'Kal," she said, unsurprised.

"Jetta ak'Kal."

"Do you never sleep?"

"While others work on my behalf?"

She waved a hand around the sleeping village and its

watchful lookouts. "Then you will never sleep, Windrider. I, however, intend to."

"And waste such a beautiful night?"

"We had this conversation last night." She stalked on, making for the high street and the privacy of Nuurn's house.

"It is a good plan you conceived today," he said, changing the subject with the ease of a wind shifting direction. "Ayesh thinks it will work."

"And Wyth?"

"Wyth will do what must be done."

"That's good hearing." The waterfall came in sight, pounding down among its rocks. "Good night, ak'Kal."

Warm fingers closed around her wrist over the promise bracelet. "Must you go?"

She jerked her arm free, her left hand anxiously seeking the bracelet. Did he not know what it meant? Her voice sounded harsh in her own ears. "Why do you follow me?"

He turned his head toward the falls, presenting her with a profile of sculpted lines and pearled highlights. "You remind me of someone."

"Who?" She found she did not like that, somehow.

"Does it matter?" He looked down at her, his face turning to shadows again.

"I like to know who you're comparing me with." It made her angry for no reason she could put a name to.

He shrugged, a movement of broad shoulders that set the layers of his shirt fluttering. "Someone also wounded by life."

Jetta stepped back, all but flinging sparks in outrage. "How dare you! And what business is it of yours?"

He stilled, his head cocked. "Why are you angry? It's no secret that you lost your lifemate at your last assignment. It cannot have been through fault of yours, or your Circle would not have assigned you elsewhere. I grieve for your loss. It is no easy thing to lose a mate."

"Then can we stop talking about it?" Hot tears pricked Jetta's eyes; angrily she dashed them away and turned for Nuurn's door. "Kori is no concern of yours. I'll thank you to keep your tongue off his name!"

"I did not know his name," Sheshan said softly. "Good night, Jetta ak'Kal."

She fled inside, only just remembering not to slam the

door and wake the whole house. She leaned against the solid stone, fighting heaving sobs that closed her throat and twisted her stomach into a knot. She felt ambushed, violated, clawed by grief dredged up all unexpected. "He had no right," she choked. "He had no right. No right."

"Who?" Setti said sharply ahead of her in the dark. "What's happened?"

Jetta jerked upright, stilling the betraying impulse to wipe the tears from her face. Setti made only a deeper darkness in front of her, his face as hidden as she hoped hers was. "Nothing," she said, forcing it past the clog in her throat. "Go on watch. Everything's quiet. I sense nothing of the Old Man tonight."

He stepped closer. "Something happened. You're upset. Who was out there? That Windrider again? I'll teach him to bother you!"

He reached for the door latch; Jetta flung up both hands to stop him, encountering a hard-muscled arm that yielded nothing to her touch. "You will not! It's nothing."

"Nothing?" he said incredulously. "You were crying!"

"Over nothing that is Dancer business! Go on watch, a'Kam!"

"Jetta—" For a moment he sounded ready to argue, and then he stepped back and said stiffly, "As you say, ak'Kal. If you'll clear the doorway?"

Silently she stepped aside. "Setti."

He brushed past her out the door and vanished into the night, an instant's touch of warm skin and supple leather. No cloak. He was going to freeze.

She sighed and turned toward the stairs. First boiling water, then a frigid wind. Was he trying to kill himself?

Sleep eluded her until almost dawn.

~ ~ ~

She did not have time to investigate his mood come morning. She had barely found her center, poised blearily on the cold stone floor in front of her window, when Errull appeared at Nuurn's door, wanting Jetta's advice on how best to access the new vein down the valley without inviting

The Ancient into the digging. With profound regret Jetta abandoned the control exercise and the mindless peace inside the thrumming rush of the Mother's embrace, and answered Anual's knock at her door.

The morning turned into a long tramp down the road and across the burgeoning hillside above the tumbling little river, through meadows of flowers and scattered teller trees that gave way to thick stands of tall needle trees farther down. The air smelled of sun-warmed trees and the secret, watery scent of the river rushing down in a constant merry roar. She saw a pair of sinewy neera romping in the scattered black boulders of an ancient slide, shrill little alarm bells with their sensitivity to fire's coming and their loud chittering call. A shy, dappled roalt with three newborn fawns skittering at her heels fled from a huge raptor with iridescent green wings longer than Jetta's outstretched arms. It swooped down to investigate the eight Delvers tramping down-vale with her, all laden with picks and tools and timbers for opening and shoring an entrance to the new mine. Jetta watched the creature soar up and up until it made only a dot against the fluffy clouds high over the valley, wondering what it was like to spurn the earth like that and simply go where the wind chose.

She saw a Windrider's pale hair gleaming in the sun ahead of them before she made out a face. He was sitting quietly on a great rock when they broke out of the trees above the raw scar on the hillside where the winter's slide had torn the earth away. He looked up at them, a quiet-faced man of middle years. Her stomach unclenched from the knot it had formed the instant she spotted him. He was *not* Sheshan, nor Wyth, and she would have snapped at Setti for going around expecting unpleasantness. He gave the crossed-wrists Windrider greeting; she returned it, discovered his name was Heshah, and went to inspect the exposed veins of rock threading black and white fingers through the spill of dirt.

Errull caressed the darker stone on top with a possessive hand. "Good stuff, this. Deep vein. Little waste."

Jetta glanced across the valley. "What do you do with the excess rock?" She saw no sign of any great digging over there. The hillside looked untouched save for the scattered buildings of Annam village.

"Sell it. Use it for shoring. Plant gardens in it." Errull's dark eyes crinkled at her astonishment. "Lowland folk in the Barrens pay well for highland dirt. It goes down with the carts with the rest of the goods we sell."

"I didn't know," she said faintly.

"Here." Errull turned to point at the paler rock twisting up under the black containment stone. "This is the problem, if we understand you correctly?"

"Yes," she said, picking her way over the broken hillside for a closer look. Heshah came too, stopped a few feet away and stood listening. Jetta stooped to touch the pale windstone. "While I'm pleased that you've found an easier vein to work, Errull, it does present an opportunity for the Old Man to foot himself on both sides of the valley at once. And while the containment stone might cap the other and keep any fire from spreading upward, it can't keep fire from rising up from underneath and bursting out into the open air."

Errull puffed out his broad cheeks in a rueful sigh and tapped the windstone with his booted toe. "Likely these veins are twinned all the way through the ridge," he said. "It happens sometimes, like on Wind Point. You have to work them together. What that means for us is that only half the tunnel will be safe, ever. To get all the containment stone we'll have to delve straight in over this, and likely through it before we're done. A hundred feet on, the layers could be reversed, and the windstone could be on top. Either way, if you're right, The Ancient could run right up on top of us without warning."

"Yes. How will you shore this up?"

"Normally we'd use the windstone once we got the thing open and shored up." He gestured toward the heavy timbers they had brought down, which lay on the hillside, seats for the other Delvers waiting patiently to begin. Jetta saw at a glance that those massive beams had never come from teller trees but had surely been imported from the great forests of the south. They might be five hundred years old for all she knew. Perfectly dry, wonderful fuel. How had she missed them?

"I didn't see these when I walked the village?" She kept the accusation out of her voice, but it couldn't be denied.

"We have a storage yard away from the village on a bed of containment stone."

"Since we can't avoid the windstone, we may as well use it just like always," she said.

His face cleared. "That's what I hoped you'd say. Now, as to those firetraps. Heshah? Have you a notion on placement?"

Heshah gestured them back from the exposed veins. "With your permission?"

Mystified, Jetta watched with Errull as the Windrider turned to face the hillside directly. He stooped and pulled a few blades of grass, holding them between the long fingers of one hand. With the other he made a scooping gesture overhand. At the top of the arc, over his head, he opened his hand as though releasing something. An instant later a warm wind rushed up past Jetta, whipping her hair across her face and flattening the grass to the hillside.

Errull made an inarticulate noise beside her; she raked the hair out of her face with both hands and watched, fascinated, as Heshah released the blades of grass one by one into that steady torrent. He watched intently as they swirled and soared up over the rocks, then moved his free hand again. The wind reversed itself, rushing down from above as though a storm had risen over the ridge. Again he watched the blades of grass tumble in its grip, and finally turned to Errull.

The wind faltered and fell away to a gentle rising breeze out of the valley. Jetta found herself impressed against her will. She had watched Farahk and some of the other Fourth and Fifth Rank masters summon fire and play with it like that, but seldom so effortlessly. She took a closer look at Heshah's rank badge. Two wavy lines in silver on a blue background, with not a trace of gold. He was only a journeyman, and of the Second Rank at that.

Confused, she stepped up beside Errull to listen to the discussion. Heshah pointed to the right, where blades of grass lay in a forlorn scatter across the dull black stone. "There, in that hollow," he said, his voice sounding much like his name, soft and sibilant. "That is where the wind will drive The Ancient if called. Build your trap there."

Errull wheeled and waved one massive arm at the Delvers

lounging below. Instantly they leaped to snatch up tools and began to attack the hillside where he pointed. Errull moved in to help. Jetta found herself alone with the Windrider.

"Impressive," she said. "You have great skill."

"No. It took me longer than most to learn that."

"But you learned." It was like talking to Setti.

He shrugged. "It was but guiding the wind to do what it would do anyway. Mastery entails calling it out of its normal running and directing it where you would have it go."

"I see." And she did, for the Dance of a journeyman was not the same as the Dance of a master, and a Fourth Rank danced different steps than a Third Rank, and commanded more of a fire's running. *So what am I doing here?* she wondered still again.

The mine adit grew at an astonishing rate. Jetta sat on a sun-warmed boulder and watched; Heshah wandered aimlessly among the trees, occasionally cupping his hand up to the breeze as though catching it in his palm. In less than an hour the Delvers had a roughly squared hole excavated around the protruding rock veins, twice a Delver's height across and half again as high. They set the timbers in to keep the bank from crumbling around them, and then attacked the stone itself, cutting it into small blocks and setting them aside in straggling rows that were, Jetta realized, the first rough bedding stones of the road they intended to punch down to this spot.

"Aye," Errull said, following her gaze. "Tomorrow we will begin cutting the road bed. Stone's no good in the mine, and the carts need a way to haul it out."

Jetta mourned the untouched meadows and the playful neera disturbed from their home. But the world lived in containment stone, even the neera. Everyone had to share.

By late afternoon the entrance had progressed seven steps deep into the hillside and Errull was excited. The windstone thinned the farther in they went, leaving the tunnel almost solidly black. "Hunnood did well!" he exulted. "The boy said it was a rich find, and he was right. We may not need those traps after all."

"Build them anyway," Jetta advised. "Especially here at the entrance where you cannot avoid the windstone. Suppose The Ancient rose here, with all your folk inside? It doesn't bear thinking about."

Errull looked sick. "No. It doesn't."

He picked up one of the thin-bladed saws the Delvers used to mark the stone for cutting and walked over to the entrance. "Here?" he said over his shoulder. Heshah nodded. Quickly Errull etched the lines of a tall, narrow opening into the rough black wall and stepped back, surveying it grimly. "I hope that works," he muttered.

"It should," Jetta said.

"Then explain to them, who will have to build it," he said, and gathered his miners in to listen. Jetta, a little nonplused, for it had been Huunall's idea, walked over and turned to point at the pale windstone forming the opposite wall.

"If the Old Man comes, it will likely flare up here. The rock will have come in contact with heartstone deep below where we stand. The fire will travel up, seeking free air, until it reaches the end. The stone here will turn red and explode into fire, which will scatter in all directions, seeking fuel."

She looked at each solemn face in turn. "It is your job to see that it finds only what we wish it to find. Keep the ground in front of this face bare for twice your own height outward, save for a thin trench leading from here to here." She paced it off for them, this snare for the Old Man leading from the conduit of windstone to the as-yet-uncut door into the firetrap. "This you can fill with anything that will burn: oil, wood chips, old weeds and dead grass. Anything. The fire will follow it mindlessly, for young flame is blissfully stupid. It will run down the trench into the trap, and find only a well of containment stone at the end."

"But how, if the fire is still burning in the windstone—" a young Delver began. Jetta held up a hand, smiling.

"The windstone itself cannot sustain fire, only conduct it. It's porous, and crumbles to sand when crushed. It is full of tiny pockets of air, which is how the fire travels. The stone itself disintegrates fairly quickly, gives up its trapped air, and crumbles away. It seems to burn, but in truth the fire is consuming only air itself and simply shatters the soft stone. When the stone is gone it must find other fuel or die within a very few minutes. If a Windrider were to fan the fire even a little, it would consume both the stone and the fuel in the trench that much more quickly, and run even faster in hopes of finding more. It runs into the well and starves. The ignition point burns desperately for a few moments, but even with the heat behind, it cannot sustain itself."

"Dancer, forgive," another Delver said apologetically. "But what is to stop the whole wall of windstone from bursting into flame at once, or reigniting at point after point?"

She looked at all those earnest and frightened faces. "Huunall's design calls for breaks in the veins of windstone, places where you will cut completely through it and stake a trap at every break. If the vein is too thick, then the breaks will be lined with containment stone. Every length of exposed windstone must have its trench for the fire to follow into the nearest trap. It will take courage to stand and watch it, courage to blow air at a fire in hopes of killing it instead of feeding it. It is insane, and against every precept I was taught. But I think it will work."

"You think," an older man muttered.

"Life is full of risks, Delver."

"Risks you will not be standing here beside us to take."

"You think not?" she said, as Errull stirred angrily. "In this design the danger moves progressively deeper as we break the stone and stop any fire from moving to the surface. Should the traps fail, then I alone will have to dance with The Ancient at its strongest, there in the dark with no place to run."

She looked around at suddenly somber faces. "If the fire fails to die within the first minute or two, I want you to run, run for the entrance as you have never run in your lives. Stone is not worth your lives, no matter how rich the vein. Be wary of tremors. Check hourly for heat in any exposed vein. Look askance at any settling in the floors, for it may be that stone is melting somewhere and causing subsidence, in which case the Old Man is not far behind."

She had been thinking about Wind Point and The Ancient roaring in long-deserted tunnels, of tunnels collapsing as the walls melted in the heat from underneath, creating pocket after pocket of air to feed The Ancient's greed. She doubted very much if either the Windrider's seal or the Delvers' door had stopped all sources of air trickling into the mine. Wind Point was still burning, still dangerous.

"I'm not one to frighten for the sake of frightening," she

said. "Listen to one who has run toward fire from before the time she knew what it was. It is in my blood to know fire, as you know all the shapes and possibilities in stone. What I know tells me that even The Ancient cannot sustain itself if there is nothing to burn. We can starve it, we can hurry its death, we can fight it. What we do not do is let it root itself. There is a *lot* of stone in these hills for it to feed on."

"The deep mines are looking better," one of the younger Delvers muttered.

Errull laughed. "I thought you'd volunteered too fast, Doruun."

The boy grinned, abashed, and cocked a keen glance up at Jetta. "If you can Dance with the Old Man with nothing but a couple of bits of leather to protect you, I guess I can move a little stone out of the way."

She grinned at him, encouraged. It *did* sound like a mad plan, and one she hoped they would never have to test. For the Windriders it would be worse. One of them would be underground all day, every day, on constant guard at the deepest flashpoint, with no guarantees that The Ancient would not simply rise up through some impossibly deep vein and trap them all. Surely it was nothing envisioned in their lore: summoning wind underground.

Wyth must truly like it here. For indeed, accommodations were being made.

Eleven
Childhood's End

Jetta managed to avoid Sheshan for three days, mostly by dint of walking the other way at the first sight of feathery garments or pale hair. Setti was not as easy. Every meal, every change of watch she found him tight-lipped and uncommunicative. In despair she asked Anual what she thought ailed the man, and got only, "Let him work it out, ak'Kal. He will, in time."

"Work *what* out?" Jetta asked in annoyance, but Anual would not elaborate. Sadly, Jetta thought of the carefree boy who had walked the road to Annam with her. She couldn't find him in Setti's stormy face and wrathful eyes. His excitement over this assignment seemed transmuted to anger she could not fathom. Fear? She didn't think him the type to run from a fire he had not yet faced. Jealousy? Of what? Their friendship was rooted in a shared childhood, and whatever he thought about Sheshan haunting her heels he could just unthink. Insult? Perhaps it galled that the friend of his youth now gave him orders.

Thinking about it did not help her attempts to master the Fourth Rank control position. On the fourth morning, determined to force her body past its insistence that muscles could not do what she wanted them to do, she stood in the square of sunshine framed in her window and held onto that straining, impossible juxtaposition of arms and leg and head until quite suddenly a vision of Setti straining to hold the Second Rank master's form smashed through her uncertain concentration. She wobbled, tried to correct, and her right leg simply collapsed under her, spilling her hard to the floor. Jetta yelped and grabbed her elbow, her eyes watering from its sudden sharp contact with the unforgiving stone.

Ah, Setti. Quite suddenly she understood how he must have felt all these years trying to master even the simplest forms of the Dance. It shamed her that she had treated him like a fumbling stranger up at Wind Point when he had only wanted to help. He had once bloodied nasty Rekkale's nose for throwing live coals onto the training sands behind her as they all stood barefoot in Dance leathers, and then taunting her for the burns on her foot when she stepped on them. They'd been inseparable, she and Kori and Setti. Until she took Kori for lifemate and left Setti behind.

How hard was it for him, watching all of us who started out together leave on assignment while he barely stood apprentice in the Second Rank? The thought made her writhe. Cocooned in her own happiness, she had never once thought what it must have been like for Setti.

Grimly she got dressed and went looking for him. She found him in an empty storehouse, in leathers, sweating through the steps of the master's Dance for Second Rank.

Jetta stepped quickly into the shadows beside the doorway where he would not see her and watched, tight-lipped. Technically he had it right; the steps were precise, the movements fluid. But she doubted it would daunt the Old Man. A master should not sweat.

She shed her shoes and then, after consideration, breeches and shirt, and walked onto the swept stones, clad in linen approximations of Dance leathers. He blinked at sight of her and stopped, panting, his expression running through a rainbow of emotions from embarrassment to irritation and ending in wary watchfulness.

"What are you doing here?" While not actively hostile, his voice held no warmth either.

"I said we should practice. You've found a good place. Private. Non-flammable."

She smiled to show the joke, but he didn't return it. "You look to be expecting fire," he said.

"Because I intend to call it," Jetta said calmly.

He snorted and tapped the floor with one bare foot. "Out of containment stone?"

"No." She clenched her fist and closed her eyes, summoning the memory of fire, the essence of heat and light bred into her very bones.

"Jetta?"

She opened her fist and turned her hand palm down. Sparks dripped from her hand and burst into flame, falling like a comet trail to the dark paving stones underfoot. They curled and hissed and finally died, disappointed in the world they were born into.

"That's a Fourth Rank trick," Setti said flatly.

"I did study at Setham." Jetta looked at the pinpricks of ash underfoot, remembering how she had thrown herself into that study, yearning to be the youngest Fourth Rank ever, as she had been the youngest Third Rank master.

"Why do it now?" His angular face wore its carved-in-stone look, capping incipient hostility threatening to spill over like a boiling pot. She sensed pride at stake, and defused it in the next breath.

"Because I want to know which tricks still work. And which Dance patterns."

His head came up. "All right." He looked around. "There's nothing here to burn. They've done a good job following advice."

"I saw a lantern inside the door. That should do."

His eyebrow flickered up. "That was fun last time."

That sounded so much like the old Setti that Jetta laughed. "Here's our chance to get even."

She pulled the lantern down from its shelf, shook it and found it heavy with oil. Carefully she spilled a little in a small circle on the flat black paving stones in the center of the floor. With the lantern set well back out of the way, she looked at Setti. "Are you ready? I'll call the flame. You Dance. Stick to the patterns first. Improvise only if they don't work. We must see if all that we knew is changed."

He shook his head. "I'm not the one to determine that. My skill is erratic on the best of days—"

"Do your best. If things get out of hand, I'll back you up."

Steadfastly she set aside the memory of fire crawling up her arms, her legs, closed her mind to the sound of roaring laughter. This was here. This was now. But even so her nerves wound tight as she closed her eyes and summoned the enemy.

As the first sparks flowed from her hand she caught a glimpse of Setti's face, set, white, expecting disaster.

S. A. Bolich

"Concentrate!" she snarled at him. "You are defeated before you begin!"

Setti threw her a wild, startled look. The sparks landed in the oil. Fire flared up in a great gush of light and heat. Setti recoiled, but he was no coward, and the Dance ran in his blood. He stepped reflexively into the first movement, flowed easily into the second. The fourth brought him into balanced confrontation, and Jetta breathed a little easier to see the flames hesitate. The smallest ran greedily to snatch at scattered droplets of oil. Those flickered and died; the rest consolidated into a solid circle of yellow flame. Jetta saw it coalescing, trying to form a *hysth*, and almost called a warning, but Setti spun into the fifth form, both hands darting forward, palms out.

The circle broke, the flames retreating from directly in front of him. Jetta blew a sigh of relief, for that at least was as it should be. Setti's confidence returned as the fire bent to his will; he pushed it harder, driving it back in confusion. Jetta reached for the lantern and flung more oil onto the blaze, snatching the lantern back as the flames tried to form a blazing arc and follow the fuel back to its source. It spattered across the floor instead, a disconnected pattern that increased Setti's difficulties tenfold in an instant.

The oil, slow-burning, lent the fire hope. Setti, his face grim, intent, forced a path and advanced into the heart of the flames blazing stubbornly knee-high. Thus far it was an exercise on the training ground at Firehome, and Setti danced flawlessly, with fluidity vastly improved since she had last watched him work.

He clapped his hands sharply to drive the flames back on his right, but they did not retreat. The fire merely wavered, sank a trifle, and then scuttled sideways onto the damp and reeking patch where he had killed the first of the flames a moment before. Oil clung to the stones, a residue still potent. In an instant the circle re-formed and Setti stood surrounded by flame.

"Setti!"

Jetta leaped to the edge of the circle. Time slipped sideways. For an instant she stood in Setham, not Annam, looking at Kori, not Setti, surrounded by fire. She found herself stepping into the first movement, instinctively seeking connection through the dead containment stone underfoot, but Setti shouted hoarsely, "No!"

Jetta faltered. Setti shoved both hands at her in a wild warding gesture, pushing flame straight into her face. She leaped back, her first astonishment flaring to anger. Of all the stupid—

The fire thrown out of the circle by that ill-advised gesture splattered onto the floor, no longer united, no longer fierce, but a collection of red worms frantically hunting succor. Jetta stared at them, and then at Setti, whose astonishment lasted for one open-mouthed instant, and then he did it again, flinging the fire from him, breaking the circle once more. Jetta saw him try the standard second movement of Second Rank, a stamp and turn with left arm extended, right arm high, and watched the fire retreat. Setti flowed into the master's Dance he had been practicing earlier. The fire returned, the flames flowing together, soaring up, turning from infant amber to a pale, malevolent citrine. Heat poured into the storehouse, drawing sweat up on Jetta's arms.

Setti abandoned the Dance he had not yet the confidence to impose and retreated a step. The fire followed. Jetta sucked in a moaning breath and moved to intervene, but Setti spun completely around, poised lightly on the ball of one bare foot, and brought both hands together almost in the same gesture Sheshan had used to coil the wind.

The fire rushed together as though sucked up a chimney, massing into a column taller than Setti. A few stray flames flickered in abandoned pockets; without taking her eyes off Setti Jetta stamped them into curls of smoke. She ground her teeth, fighting the impulse to go to his aid, for this was no journeyman's task. This monster could turn to a *hysth* at any moment and turn the infant's native cunning into crafty protégée of The Ancient in a breath.

Setti hesitated. For a dreadful instant Jetta thought he would try the warding gesture again, which would scatter the flames but leave him to deal with all of them individually. She opened her mouth to cry warning, but he drew himself up, a dark silhouette against the column of fire, and reverted to the Dance. Jetta expected an imperious thrust of strong legs and a defiant leap into the fire's face; instead, Setti settled his weight on one leg, the other stretched in a long barrier line behind him, his skin glistening gold with the sweat of strain and fear. He turned his palms down, and Jetta caught her breath, seeing the tenth movement used on sinking fires that were nearly out, that should never work on flames so tall. Setti's arms corded with strain though they shoved at nothing but air, settling inexorably toward the stone floor.

Perhaps it was desperation. Perhaps it was Setti's stubborn will to succeed. Perhaps the fire had exhausted its fuel. It worked. Setti pushed his hands down and down, and the fire sank with them, protesting in snapping fury, spitting out raging jets reaching for the ceiling. But it sank, and it died, sputtering into sparks on the black paving stones.

Setti hit the floor on his knees, dragging in great shuddering breaths. Jetta ran to brace him up, hugging him close against long running tremors racking his body. "Well done, Dancer!" she said warmly in his ear, and kissed his forehead in an ecstasy of relief.

His arms came around her in a fierce, hard embrace. She tightened her own grip, remembering, only too well, the aftermath of a difficult Dance, the slow drainage of fear, the trembling need of human contact. Kori had always been there for her. Setti had no one—

Without warning his hand shifted, sliding upward to twine roughly in her bound hair. His face tilted up and he kissed her, a rough and ungentle joining of lips with more of desperation than affection in it. Shocked, Jetta tried to pull away but his hand behind her head trapped her in place, kneeling awkwardly in the circle of his arms.

She twisted her mouth away. "Setti!"

He released her, huddling head down, his arms wrapped tight around his body. He was still shuddering, the fine long muscles of his arms and back and legs quivering uncontrollably. Jetta, in a rare state of confusion, clenched both fists in front of her, torn between nurturing instinct and an appalling fear of what would happen if she touched him again.

"Setti?" she said, low-voiced. "Setti, look at me."

He ignored her and staggered to his feet to stand with his back to her, his head down, his shoulders hunched. Jetta's throat tightened in empathy, but she could not move to comfort him. Of all things, this she had not expected. Anual's vague hints suddenly crystallized into a pattern that made her cringe.

Stone sees more than I do. Her face turned hot; nervously she raked her hair out of its braid and hid behind the shield of it, peering sideways at his turned back. "I'm sorry, Setti. You surprised me, that's all. I didn't mean to hurt you."

He drew in a long slow breath and raised his head, but did not turn. "The fault is mine. There's no blame to you."

"Setti...."

He tilted his head back, staring at the shadowed black roof overhead. Light from the lantern tracked gold in a thin line down the cheek she could see. Jetta winced. He sucked in a ragged breath. "Don't. Let's just—talk about fire, shall we?"

"No! I want this out in the open. I can't live tiptoeing around it."

He sighed and slowly brought his gaze down. "It won't happen again. Let's move on."

"Setti," she said softly, resisting the urge to reach out and comfort him. "I'm sorry. It never occurred to me you had feelings like that."

He threw her a sullen glance from beneath lowered black eyebrows. "And shouldn't I? I've known you all my life. You were my friend from the time I remember having friends, and I loved you and Kori both for all that you did for me and all that we shared. You turned to Kori and I could live with that. But he's gone—and I still love you."

She winced from that bald declaration. "You are my dearest friend, Setti—"

His head jerked. "Kori was your friend! We were all friends! Why him and not me?"

Jetta felt sick. "I don't know," she said. She didn't need this. Not now. "I loved you both. I still do. But it's not the same."

He started to pace, his bare feet spurning the dead ash underfoot. "I couldn't match your talent. Kori could. I understood. Why would you want to harness yourself to someone you would always have to protect, to tutor, who could never match you? I worked so hard, and I could never match you. Or Kori."

Jetta raked her hair back and stared, taken utterly aback. Was that why he had so doggedly persisted in pursuit of the Dance, half-killing himself in those hours and hours on the ridge above Firehome? To make himself worthy of her? *Old Man Fire!*

"Setti—" She stepped forward, intercepting his pacing. He jerked away from her touch on his arm; she persisted, closing strong fingers around his wrist. "Do you think I ever cared who could and couldn't dance? *Rekkale* could dance!" She hoped to touch his humor, but he just stared at her. Desperation set her voice shaking; she could *not* lose him too.

"If we're fortunate, we find people whose company we want to keep all our lives. We don't make life mates of all of them; we can't. But we cherish them, and mourn their loss, and treasure their company just the same. If we are very fortunate, we know we can turn to them at any time, for any reason, and know they will be there. As you have always been. As I hope you always will be. I would mourn if you were not."

He would not look at her, but the set of his shoulders loosened. Finally he sighed. "Let it go, Jetta. A fool needs his pride. Let's talk about something else."

"Do you remember how Minna used to say the only fools were the ones who missed the flame under their noses? So what does that make me?"

He pulled away, but gently. "Discriminating." He turned and thrust a hand out toward the pattern of ash marring the paving stones. "What did you think of that?"

His voice was steady, the tone unforced. Jetta guessed that the worst of the storm had passed; he needed time to heal, which with him always meant carrying on as if nothing had happened and letting things settle in their own time.

She moved up beside him, careful to stay out of casual contact. "I think you did magnificently, a'Kam. Some of that was truly inspired."

"Some of that was truly desperate." The old self-deprecating smile twitched up one corner of his mouth, quickly gone. "I was terrified."

"Not so anyone noticed, least of all the fire. You vanquished it, Setti, with no help from me."

"But how, that's the mystery. It shouldn't have worked, what I did. I'm not even sure what I did. I just remember—I wanted it away from me. I wanted it to sink and die."

"And it did." Jetta knelt to examine the burn patterns, fingering the oily residue. She held her fingertips up to show him. "See? It still had fuel. It didn't just burn itself out. It was within a breath of forming a *hysth*, and you killed it. Well done. Oh, very well done."

Fleeting pride brushed his face, gone again in a frown. "We can't depend on the Dance, Jetta. What seemed to work was what I made up on the spot."

She stood up, brushing her hair back to look at him squarely. "The moves born of desperation, as you say. Of will. Of desire to defeat the enemy. That's the essence of the Dance, Setti, and always has been. It's what allows a journeyman to step up to mastery—or traps him in his rank forever."

She caught and held his unwilling gaze, letting the point sink home. He jerked away and said, "If desire is all it took, I would be Fifth Rank by now. The master's steps didn't work, but moves invented from nothing seemed to. I don't know about you, but that frightens me silly."

"Fear kills," Jetta said sharply. "Stand back. I'm going to try your moves and see if they work again."

"That's ridic—" Setti burst out, and stopped, reason conquering the reflexive self-denigration he had wound around himself like a second skin. "Yes. You're right. That is why you're a master, I imagine."

"Oh, stop it," Jetta said wearily. "Grow up, Setti. If you want to dance, then stop thinking about perfecting the placement of every finger and just do it."

She turned her back on him and picked up the lantern. The floor was already a mess; a little more wouldn't hurt it. With Setti standing in thunderous silence behind her, she poured a second circle, distant from the first to discourage any spread, and summoned flame once more.

The oil caught as eagerly as the first time. The flames soared higher than her head in an instant, taking Jetta aback. Tormented by a flashing memory of fire finding her skin, she fought an urge to simply step back and let it burn itself out on the unyielding stone of the floor. But Setti was watching, his stormy face clearing rapidly to worry. He had found a little confidence the hard way. It was not for her to destroy it.

She stamped a foot down, reaching for the solid feel of the earth under the stone. No soaring rush of power greeted her, but she felt it waiting, as unshakeable as the mountains. Reassured, Jetta swayed sideways into the graceful arc of the second movement of Third Rank, framing the flames in the circle of her arms. The fire ignored it. Experimenting, she moved through the first pattern, not really trying to impose her will, simply watching the flames, observing which forms made them hesitate. She caught a glimpse of Setti beyond the line of fire, shaking his head at her, his lips moving in unheard words she had no doubt were exhortations to kill it and be done. But the fire was not advancing, wary of a Dancer who neither hesitated nor retreated.

Jetta, tired of the old and spun away into the new. She repeated Setti's outward shove with both hands, gratified when it blew the fire in two. She *felt* something pass through her and out through her palms, as if her will had found physical form. Bemused, she did it again, and again, breaking the flames into smaller and smaller enclaves each battling to rejoin the others, struggling to survive long enough to form a *hysth.*

"No," she whispered, turning her hands palm down. The fire sank sullenly toward the floor, writhed and smoked and finally died, leaving only oily stains to mark its death.

"It worked," Setti gasped incredulously. "I can't believe it."

She flashed him a weary smile over her shoulder. "Believe, a'Kam. They may have to invent a new level of mastery just for you."

He gaped at her, decided she was joking, and shook his head, irritated. "I'll settle for knowing this will work every time."

Jetta shook her hair back, only then realizing that she had danced this whole time with it down for the fire to grab. She fought off a shudder. "It works on young fire. I, for one, am not keen on letting a fire burn long enough for it to summon The Ancient to test this on, are you?"

He blew an emphatic sigh and produced a weak chuckle. "Those are master's experiments, thank you, ak'Kal, and you are welcome to them."

Relief washed through Jetta. Perhaps she had not damaged their friendship beyond repair. Perhaps her innocent would come back to her. Perhaps he would forgive her, in time.

"Not today, but we *will* experiment." She transfixed him with an uncompromising stare. "And it won't matter whether you can force the fire to bend to the Dance as you know it. We'll be looking for something that works for you. And for me. If you are learning, a'Kam, I'll be unlearning."

He blinked and puffed out a slow, thoughtful breath. Jetta walked over and reclaimed her clothes, only then realizing how truly stupid her conduct of the past hour had been. Dance in linens and loose hair? Experiment with an oil-based fire that could gasp back to life on the fumes? Farahk would have sent her down to teach First Rank for a year until she remembered simple basics of safety.

"I'm a bad influence on you," she grumbled to Setti, pulling her shirt back on. Standing in the doorway in the westering gleam of the sun, he threw her a quick, sardonic look. She stopped dead with hot color flooding up her face.

"Father Flame—" Her voice scaled up suddenly. "Setti! Your eyes!"

He recoiled in alarm, his hands rising involuntarily toward his face. "They're fine. What—"

Jetta squealed in triumph and threw her arms around his neck. "They're darker! Setti, they're not blue anymore!"

He blinked stupidly, trying to take that in. Jetta, guessing his problem, hastily let him go, cursing the emotional coils trapping them both. The first dark tinge in a Dancer's eyes was an occasion; at Firehome they'd celebrate in his honor for acquiring living proof of a tangible victory over the enemy. Setti had finally left childhood behind, and here they stood, too awkwardly entangled to enjoy the moment.

A slow smile finally lit his face. "Go and look," she urged him. "I'll clean up here."

"Yes," he said, and was gone, running lightly back up to the village.

She doubted if the need to find a mirror was the only thing driving him away at such speed. "Father Flame," she muttered, and went to find a broom.

Twelve
Secrets

She left the storehouse as spotless as they had found it and trailed slowly homeward, jumping from rock to rock across the northern stream to wander along the containment wall. Enjoying the fresh smell of the grass after the oil stink in the storehouse, she clambered up through jutting black outcrops and a fragrant mass of spring flowers growing wild on the hillside. A few scattered houses stood here on the far northern edge of the village that she had not yet explored. Some had been abandoned for years, undesirable, Huunall had said, because the steep drop beyond the northern containment wall left them exposed to the fiercest blasts of the winter, which stubbornly blew roof tiles to pieces and drove snow through the finest cracks. The view was spectacular, but it came with a price.

She stepped up onto the containment wall to admire the whole sweep of mountains above Annam. Rank on rank of black capped with white, they speared into a sky slowly gathering colors out of the sinking sun. Snow blushed pink on the tops and high clouds curled like a necklace around the tallest, blooming a deep rose touched with gold. She lifted her face into the wind rushing up out of the valley, reveling in its freedom that seemed to call to her to come up with it and play. She closed her eyes and breathed deep of teller-scented air, again and again, rinsing the smell of dead ash from her lungs.

"Careful," a deep, amused voice said. "Or we will have to steal you away for a Windrider."

Jetta gasped and jerked around, swayed, and flailed for balance. Someone's startled exclamation accompanied a hand biting into her shoulder, yanking her roughly upright.

She looked down at the dizzy drop below her feet and jumped down on the safe side of the wall, twisting out of that long-fingered grip.

She rounded on the Windrider, certain it would be Sheshan, but it wasn't. Ayesh stood beside her, slowly lowering his hand to his side.

"Oh!" Jetta caught back the hot retort she had intended and said rather lamely, "You startled me, ak'Kal."

"Clearly." His alabaster face crinkled into a smile that took the sting out of both the words and his presence.

"Thank you," she muttered, feeling obligated, and annoyed by the need.

"I apologize for startling you. It's a very long way down."

"Even for you?" she challenged boldly. "They say Windriders can fly."

"Do they?" He parried her probe with maddening ease and lifted his face to the wind as she had done. "It is a clean wind here. There's nowhere else like it."

"No. I have begun to appreciate that."

That drew a keen glance from startling blue eyes. "Perhaps we are not so different then. I confess, I've never had the opportunity to speak to a Firedancer before."

"Nor I to Windriders before I came here. Not a good combination, I was taught."

He chuckled. "As was I. But I feel the world is changing. Old truths betray us. Perhaps we should make new ones."

She stilled, watching him. "What truths have betrayed you, ak'Kal?"

He looked out over the valley, his face troubled. "Do you not feel the change in the wind?" Then he caught himself and gave her a rueful smile. "No, of course you wouldn't. You have nothing to compare against, and fire lies in your bones, not air. We feel it, though, an undercurrent like—" He paused, looking for a word.

"Like things are not acting as they should," Jetta murmured.

His head turned sharply. "Do the Dancers feel it too, then? Is this incursion of The Ancient more than an opportunity created by some shifting in the earth beneath us?"

Jetta hesitated. Clan knowledge was for the clan, and

information carelessly given prone to start panics. But his grave, steady stare compelled her to truth, master to master. "I don't know. But it's true The Ancient has defied the Dance in recent times. It does not act as we expect. Dancers have died because of it."

"Your lifemate," he said quietly.

She looked away. "Yes. I think so. I don't know what the Circle thinks. But Kori was an experienced Dancer, a Second Rank master. I never knew him to panic. I don't know what happened exactly, but The Ancient was there when I arrived. Kori let the fire get out of control, allowed it to burn long enough for The Ancient to rise. I couldn't defeat it."

Which was more explanation than she had given the Delvers. Jetta wished the words back on her tongue, wondering what had possessed her to unburden herself to this stranger of another clan. But Ayesh only nodded and lifted his head to stare at the mountains burning with sunset over a Vale filled with shadows.

"Why did they send you?" he asked, not maliciously, his eyes still on the mountains.

"I don't know," she said honestly, though it burned on her tongue.

He turned and regarded her quietly. "I do."

A bitter snort escaped her before she could catch it back. "Then perhaps you could enlighten me, ak'Kal. I have no idea."

He smiled, a grave and courteous smile that did not lighten the intentness of his clear, sky-touched eyes. "You have a core of containment stone in you, Jetta ak'Kal. I think though you stood in the heart of fire The Ancient could never touch you so long as you kept your nerve."

"It touched me once," Jetta said bitterly.

"And yet you accepted assignment here, in the unknown. With Windriders." The smile widened and touched his eyes. "In a week's time you have defeated fire twice, shaken the Delver Circle to its roots, and drawn Windriders to fight fire alongside Firedancers. Underground. And *there* is a tale to set your Circle on its ear."

She laughed in spite of herself. She could picture without effort the consternation when that report found its way to Firehome. "They'll be scandalized," she admitted.

"Does it matter, if the effort is successful?"

She turned to survey the village sprawling below them, watching lights starting to wink in the windows and children racing home to supper. "No."

"The Windriders will back you, Jetta ak'Kal. Have no fear of that."

She couldn't resist it. "Even Wyth?"

His mouth quirked. "All masters deserve respect," he reproved her gently. "Even Wyth."

"You're right. But he is difficult to like."

"Nevertheless. What he says he will do, he will do."

She cocked her head curiously. "Did you come looking for me to tell me that?"

He turned toward the color flaming over the mountains, set one booted foot on the wall and leaned his elbows on his knee. "Me? I just came out to watch the sunset."

"Mm." Jetta believed that about as much as she believed in The Ancient's good will. "Good evening to you, ak'Kal."

"And to you. I think you will find the shortest path there." He pointed up between two crumbling houses toward a third set above the rest, stubbornly clinging to the hillside with its back to the wind. Light shone around the shutters, thrusting pale fingers through the cracks. Jetta squinted past it and made out the gleam of the waterfall farther on, silent with the wind blowing its uneven roar away from her.

"Thank you."

She left him sniffing the wind and hurried up the path. Deep shadow lay in the valley but here it was still light enough to see stones and hummocks that forced the path to twist a crooked way up the hill. Jetta picked her way upward, coming even with the highest house just as the door opened and spilled a bright bar of light across the hill. She stopped just short of crashing into a tall, thin woman carrying a bucket.

"Your pardon!" Jetta said hastily, and then her brain did a rapid readjustment. Here was no Delver. The bucket was one Jetta could have managed easily; the shirt bore a lowland pattern in purple and blue, tucked into breeches that emphasized slender bones, and the hair spilling to the woman's knees was black, not brown.

Jetta stepped back in confusion, trying for a better look

at this lowland woman living in an abandoned Delver cot. She made out a fine-featured face deeply lined around eyes and mouth, arms with the golden cast of the Fire Clans under a shawl woven in the greens and blues of the sea folk. Then the woman lifted her head, and Jetta gasped. Eyes as black as her own stared back at her in bitter amusement.

"What's the matter, girl? Did you think fire blood lived only in Firehome?"

"I—no. No. I—" Jetta found herself stammering in confusion, hot blood painting her cheeks. She drew herself up and looked down her nose at the taller woman, armoring herself in the hauteur of the Dance.

"I'm Jetta ak'Kal of the Third Rank. You are?"

The woman folded her arms, matching her arrogance for arrogance. "No one you can command, girl. I answer to no master anymore, and Old Man Fire is no concern of mine."

Jetta stared. The woman's thin lips pulled down in contempt. "'Ah,' she's thinking," the woman said bitterly. "'One of *those*. Failed the Dance, did she? Lost her gift? Ran away from The Ancient? Which, eh?'" Her chin lifted. "That is none of your concern. Go on wondering, girl, but stay clear of me, and I'll return the courtesy."

"But—"

Jetta found herself talking to empty air. The woman spun with all the grace of a Fourth Rank master and marched away up the hill, bucket swinging, shawl flapping in the stiff wind. Jetta stared after her, taken aback as much by the extravagant fringe on the shawl as by the woman's eyes. No Firedancer wore gauds of that sort for the Old Man to catch and turn to living death. If she needed proof that the stranger no longer practiced the Dance, there it was.

She glanced over her shoulder but Ayesh had gone. Why had he pointed her up here, to uncover a secret the whole village had kept from her? Why hadn't they told her a ruined Firedancer lived here? Did they not know what a danger they sheltered?

She started on up the hill, thinking to find the woman at the falls filling her bucket, but found only the creek smashing itself to froth on the rocks before it tumbled and splashed its way down the hill. Frowning, she trailed over the arch of the bridge and in at Nuurn's door.

"There you are," Anual said brightly as she came into the kitchen. "Setti is in the bath, fair bubbling over. He seems to have had a good day. Something about his eyes? I confess I didn't understand it."

"Oh—yes." Jetta fought to wrap her mind around Setti's triumph. "He danced fire this afternoon and found a new rhythm for the Dance. Look at his eyes when he comes out. They aren't blue anymore, but turning brown."

Anual paused in laying the table. "How can that be? Eyes are eyes."

Jetta smiled. "Not with us." She thought of the young Windrider Thess with his dark eyes, and added, "Nor with the Windriders, I think. We call our masters fire-touched, because their eyes turn blacker with each victory over the flame."

Anual looked at Jetta's eyes as if seeing them for the first time. "You have won many victories then, ak'Kal."

Not "child" this time, Jetta noted. "Yes," she said simply, and saw it sink home for perhaps the first time. Anual went on setting out the plates, her face thoughtful, her tongue unwontedly still. *She truly did think me a child,* Jetta thought, half insulted, half amused. *They have so little experience of us. They hired us on reputation, not from belief that we could truly solve their problem.* The knowledge sobered her.

Having a Firedancer who refused the Dance living next door could not have helped. Or could it. *Ayesh, you clever rogue, that's why you sent me up there. All masters deserve respect, indeed!*

"Anual, I just a met a woman up among the abandoned houses beyond the falls. A Firedancer."

Anual's busy hands stilled for an instant. "That is unfortunate. She wishes to be left alone. We respect that."

"Who is she? I don't know her. She must be of another Fire Clan."

"She cherishes her privacy, ak'Kal."

"I understand that, but don't you know the danger you shelter?"

Anual reared up, frowning. "That's unkind, Jetta ak'Kal, and unworthy. Because she can no longer dance—"

"That's not it! I'm not casting stones at her. We mourn

when a Dancer fails the Dance. She was a master. She must have been, with those eyes. Do you think I don't know how hard it would be to abandon the Dance? I'm astonished that she's here—that her clan let her leave."

"And why wouldn't they? Kettori has harmed no one—" Anual broke off and slammed a cup onto the table rather harder than necessary.

"Kettori!" Jetta murmured. "Old Man Fire. No wonder no one ever found her."

"You know her?" Anual peered at her suspiciously. "You said you didn't."

"I know *of* her. She's from a southern clan, and her skill in the Dance was very great. But something happened, no one ever learned what. She left her assigned village unprotected—just walked away one day without a word to anyone. The Old Man came. People died."

Anual stared. Jetta finished softly, "The Fire Clans searched for her. Wherever she went, fire followed. It is the way of Dancers who lose their nerve. The Old Man has learned their names. The greater the Dancer, the greater the likelihood that fire will find them. If they do not find the will to dance again, things burn. People die. *They* die, eventually. Almost always the Old Man finishes them."

Anual shuddered. *"No,* Jetta, not Kettori. She's been here since last summer, living quiet as a teller tree up there. I see now why she refuses a warmer house in the village. But there has been no fire because of her."

"Hasn't there?" Jetta said gently. "She comes, and by spring fire finds Annam Vale for the first time."

"I won't believe that!" Anual slammed her paring knife down onto the table. "Stones and pebbles, she came to a place of solid containment stone to live where Dancers freeze on a balmy night. There is no harm in her!"

"Harm in who?" Setti asked. He stood toweling his hair in the open door to the bath chamber, his eyes curious, and not, Jetta noted in relief, shadowed with other emotions.

"Kettori ak'Kal lives here," she said, earning a glare from Anual.

Setti froze with the towel drooping over his ears. "You're joking."

"No. I just met her." In deference to Anual she did not tell him where. "She's been here since last summer."

"Well, there's a well-kept secret. Any more like that lurking in the cupboards, Anual ak'Kal?"

Anual reared back in surprise. Jetta lifted an eyebrow. Something had changed in him; yesterday he would never have dared brook a master like that. She dared to hope it was a sign of confidence and not a result of his bitter disappointment this afternoon.

Setti climbed onto a chair, letting the towel drop around his shoulders. "This isn't good news," he said slowly. "I would warrant it's one reason Burrood has so little trust in us, isn't it?"

Anual leaned a hip against the table with a sigh. "Burrood is a fool. But aye, some look at Kettori and call her a coward, when there are Delvers who will not go near the lowest mines anymore. Every skill has breaking points, I'm thinking. Kettori found hers, and I have no blame for her. Nor should you," she finished sharply, pinning them both with the same stare.

"I don't," Jetta said, and meant it. "But it complicates things. Dancers like her are a lodestone for The Ancient, and no longer capable of defending against it."

"I'll worry when I see fire spring up around her," Anual said. "I ask you both to leave her alone. She's harmed no one here, and I will not see her burdens multiplied."

"What about ours?" Setti muttered, but Jetta was thinking about Kettori ak'Kal with little chills chasing the hair up on her arms. *It could have been me.*

There is a core of containment stone in you. Ayesh's voice came back to her, but it brought with it no comfort. *Does that make me tough, or just hard? How easily I hurt Setti today, without trying, without feeling. I never even considered what he had to give, just trampled on him. At least Kettori has enough feeling left to know what she's missing.*

"Excuse me," she said abruptly. "Setti, did you leave any hot water?"

"A whole stream full," he said with a grin, and then frowned, seeing her face. "Jetta?"

"I'm all over fire stink," she said. "Have I time before we eat, Anual?"

"If you hurry." Anual's eyes drifted shrewdly from Jetta's

face to Setti's. "I'll stop the gates. Go get your things."

Jetta abandoned the kitchen without a backward glance and hurried upstairs, tripping twice on the impossibly high steps. A cold knot lay in her belly, a tangle of emotions she most emphatically did not want to pull out and examine. Ayesh's comment, meant for a compliment, instead made her want to weep. Setti's silent gaze on her when she went back downstairs did not help in the least; guilt burned her, and regret, and confused memories of a lifetime's shared laughter and heartaches. At that moment she did not know where the line between friendship and love lay.

It took Anual's big hand rapping on the door to bring her out of the steaming water. She came reluctantly to the table, but Setti and Nuurn were both missing. Jetta wrung the last of the water in her hair into a towel and said, "Where are they?"

"Nuurn's gone to stare at charts of the mines with Huunall, and Setti is on patrol." She set a laden plate in front of Jetta. "He said to let you soak; it was his turn to take first watch."

Which was true, but she knew it was not the real reason he had removed himself from the house. She sighed. Anual chuckled. "He spoke up, didn't he?"

Jetta froze. "It's all over both your faces," Anual said. "And you refused him. I thought you would."

"That is the most— How—" Jetta floundered for words around outrage that everyone seemed to know her business.

"There's a ghost at your shoulder, Jetta ak'Kal," Anual said simply. "How is anyone to compete?"

"I don't want anyone else! Kori was my lifemate—" She found herself clutching the promise bracelet on her wrist like a lowland talisman against flame.

"No one expects you to forget him. But do you want to live like Kettori the rest of your life?"

The words hit Jetta so hard that she found it difficult just to breathe. She pushed her plate away and jumped down from the chair. "Thank you, ak'Kal, but I'm not hungry. I'll go and rest. I have the mid-watch later."

She escaped the kitchen, but Anual's voice trailed her up the stairs. "Ghosts make poor company, child."

They were back to "child." Jetta wanted to slam the big

door behind her but couldn't manage it. She flung herself on the bed instead, the child-sized Delver bed, and immediately got up again, dry-eyed and angry clear through. She flung on her leathers, snatched up her cloak, and stalked out. Anual's voice drifted out from the kitchen, lifted in a sprightly song Jetta did not recognize. Seething, Jetta let herself out the front door into the street, took two steps and stopped. She had no great desire to run into Setti and no idea where he might be. Nor was she keen to encounter Kettori again. After a moment she made for the top of the waterfall on the excuse that it offered a splendid view of most of the village. She could always say she was mounting firewatch.

She scrambled up through the rocks and settled on a boulder in the lee of an even larger stone, sheltered from the worst of the wind. The water tumbled over the drop practically at her feet, an endless, hypnotizing race that fascinated her with its constancy. Where did the water come from, and how could it keep going like that forever? It seemed to her that someday the water must simply stop, but it showed no mind to do so, tumbling down endlessly behind her and flowing over at her feet in ceaseless thunder. After a while the steady roar began to calm her frayed nerves. Too much, too fast—she felt buffeted from all sides, betrayed by Anual, under siege from Setti, distrusted by Burrood, despised by Wyth. She almost wished the Old Man would put in an appearance to give her something to fight, but the stars wheeled on their silent way and the lesser moon rose above the eastern hills, casting its silver light in undisturbed peace.

Gradually her anger cooled. She groped for its source to confront it and put it behind her, but it had none. Like the storm of tears up at Wind Point, it seemed the unraveling end of a knot she could not see, let alone pick apart. And like the Dance, the patterns of her life had changed without warning, and she did not know what new pattern to weave to reclaim control.

She looked down into the sibilant darkness of the valley and thought about how Kori would have hated it here. He had disliked heights and would not climb with her to the top of the cliff above Setham even on the most stifling of days when the only breeze lived up there. She smiled sadly, remembering. He would not have appreciated the sunset seen from the containment wall. He would not have appreciated the wind in his face.

Slow tears slipped down her cheeks. "Oh, my love," she whispered. "What we would have missed, living our whole lives in Setham Vale."

And they would have, she knew that now. She had wanted to explore other offers; Kori had been content with the bakery. She had studied passionately to earn Fourth Rank; Kori had been content with Second. Kori would have been happy lifelong in that village he knew by heart, with known challenges and established routine. And that, she knew now, was what had killed him. He had stopped stretching his limits, grown comfortable in his rank. The Ancient had surprised him, and challenged him, and finally overwhelmed him. Setti, frightened and full of self-doubt, had nevertheless done what Kori, a master, could not— changed the Dance mid-step and flung the challenge back in The Ancient's teeth.

It hurt. Buried truth worked up through her grief like heartstone worming toward the open air. For a moment Jetta could not breathe for the tightness in her throat, the hard band across her chest, squeezing out the air as truth tried to fight its way in. Her gut roiled as though fire were rising and she found herself shaking her head slowly, denying images of Kori sprawled lazily beside the stream in Setham, laughing at her sweating in the heat to master the Third Rank forms. *He was proud of me!* she wanted to scream over the water's roar.

Yes, he was, a smaller voice whispered. *But it doesn't change the fact that he didn't want to work that hard himself.*

She put her head down against her drawn-up knees, biting her lip hard, refusing more tears. *Fire is what fire is,* Minna's voice said wryly in her head. Jetta caught her breath, struck sideways by a double sense of betrayal. Hers, for thinking ill of her lifemate. And Minna's, *Kori's grandmother,* for ruthlessly inserting her unwanted wisdom into everything.

Ah, beloved. But the tears had gone, and the stars burned clear in her sight when she looked up again. Jetta drew in a long, slow breath, smelling grass and needle trees and wet stone. Ayesh's clean wind blew through her soul, shattering the chains of memory and guilt.

She sat there with the water pounding at her feet, washing clean the stones of Annam Vale, and watched the stars dance their secret dance into the west. Finally, with the crooked scatter of the Old Man's Finger directly overhead, she stirred and stood up. Her nether regions had lost all feeling from the chill of the stone and sitting so long but her mind no longer felt ready to explode. There remained Setti, and Burrood's distrust, and Wind Point, and Wyth, who was not going to like her next proposal at all. But somewhere in the wind and the steady murmur of the water she had found her center again. Those elements, as timeless as The Ancient, both flung themselves fearlessly into the unknown, and still there was always more water, always more wind. The Dance continued, even in new patterns.

She went in search of Setti, expecting him to be angry that it was past the start of mid-watch when she found him near the inn, but he said only, "I was going to let you sleep."

"Why? You're the one who re-patterned the Dance today. Aren't you tired?"

"No. I wanted to celebrate."

"We should have. I'm so sorry." And she was, genuinely contrite for ruining a special day.

"I did. Rununn smuggled me some noë and spice bread from the inn and he, Hunnood, and I had a party down by the bridge." His teeth shone faintly in the dark. "Delvers know how to party. The tankard he brought me was huge."

"I'm glad." They walked along together in companionable silence for a while, and then he said, rather abruptly, "Since you're up, I'm off to bed. All's quiet. Fire free."

"All right." She watched him walk away, biting her lip. *There* was a pattern that needed mending, but she had no notion how to start.

~ ~ ~

It seemed Setti's turn to avoid her. He was gone by dawn, down to the new mine, leaving Jetta alone at Huunall's mercy. He dragged her into the inn to chill her morning with a whole different series of charts dredged from an ancient pile, so old the parchment cracked when he rolled them out on one of the tables.

"See here," he said, running one massive forefinger down from Wind Point through the levels now filled with fire, down below the lowest level the miners had previously mentioned. "This shaft was begun and abandoned because of a rockfall, but look." He hauled out a different chart. "This is how the Finders of that time thought the veins ran. See the windstone branching? Here, and here past the fallen part." He traced it up, parallel to the original tunnels, to where it exited at the mouth of the mine. Jetta stared, chilled.

"So The Ancient can bypass the seals?"

"Yes. And here. More nasty news." He traced the other branch downward in a twisting path toward its terminus far down in the Vale, nearly opposite the new mine.

Jetta started. "That's the same vein!"

"Oh, yes. Whatever carved the valley broke it, is all. It may be that it runs deep under the river too, and this is all connected still."

"How can the Finders trace all that so far underground?" Jetta sought hope that died when Huunall said, "How do you know when fire is coming? The best of the Finders are never wrong. The woman who mapped this was the best we ever had. We're still opening shafts to veins she traced three hundred years ago."

Jetta stared at the chart with feathery chills of unease chasing themselves up and down her spine. "We may be worrying for nothing, you know. The Ancient has not broken out of Wind Point, nor has it appeared anywhere else. Perhaps it never will."

"Wishful thinking from a Firedancer? Not what I expected, ak'Kal."

"No," Jetta sighed. "I feel it coming, Huunall. Not now!" she added hastily, to take the sudden dismay off his face. "But it will come. I want to test the firetraps."

Which blithe announcement rocked him straight back in his chair. "How?"

"Mm." That part she was not looking forward to. "If Wyth will lend us a Windrider, I want to set fire in the stone at the new mine and see what happens."

"You're mad!"

"No, practical. If it doesn't work, why go to all the trouble of building more?"

He frowned at the table. "And if you lose control of the fire?"

"We'll have some scorched stone. It can't burn very far," she explained patiently. "Not with the containment stone layered above and all that dirt on the other side. When it's excavated down to bare rock, then I'll worry."

His worried face brightened. "Then the vein under the ridge is not so great a threat?"

How to explain? Even to her it sounded contradictory. "Yes and no," Jetta said. "The danger is greater in any tunnel where more of the windstone is exposed to air. But remember how The Ancient travels: up from underneath, pushing tremendous heat into the layers of rock above that consumes the trapped air and leaves only melted rubble behind. I can't generate that sort of fire, and anyway, any surface fire will be trying to spread into the free air, not downward into the rocks. Flame is not *that* stupid. If The Ancient gets into that vein from Wind Point, I believe it will run in both directions, seeking its freedom however it can. But it would be extremely difficult for fire to root in it from above."

"Hm." Huunall's chin sank onto his breast, his mouth a worried line.

"Ak'Kal, I will protect this village to the cost of my life. Have no doubts."

He jumped and turned great round eyes on her, his shaggy eyebrows twitching so that she wondered how he could see. "It's not your willingness or your ability I fear, Jetta ak'Kal." He laid a hand on the spread charts. "It's the magnitude of the problem."

To that she had no answer.

Huunall volunteered to speak to Wyth, an offer Jetta accepted with alacrity. Third-party diplomacy suited her just fine. She wandered out and up the street, thinking about windstone twining through the ridge beneath her feet. The only good news in those charts lay in the fact that the veins did not rise anywhere near the village itself, however uncomfortably close they came to the mines.

A high-pitched giggle, followed by an aggrieved shriek, turned her head. The waterfall sparkled just ahead, the end of the street if one discounted the ruins beyond. Quick movement caught her eye: a gaggle of children running and clambering over the rocks. Jetta hesitated, remembering her last encounter with the village children. She started to turn away toward the back door, and halted when something green and feathery brushed her face and a tall figure materialized at her shoulder.

"Jetta ak'Kal. A pleasure to see you again, after so long."

She forced a polite smile. "Sheshan ak'Kal. My duties have kept me very busy."

"I have no doubt."

Old Man Fire. The man was harder to prick than containment stone. Jetta tried to edge past him, but he blocked her without seeming to move. "The children of the village would like to meet you, Dancer. Mururrn reports good things of you. Will you come?"

She stopped, taken completely aback. His pale eyes, not quite blue, not quite gray, watched her steadily, his face maddeningly calm. But she saw a new tension in him, a certain set to his head that spoke of more than passing interest in her answer. Behind him, a horde of Delver children chattered and scampered where she had not encountered children this whole week. *The children cling to him like shavings to a lodestone,* Anual had said. And so he had brought them up here, to meet the fearsome Firedancer.

The tacit apology touched her to the heart. "All right." She walked beside him to meet the children.

They stopped their busy games when they saw who was coming. The older children stared at Jetta; the youngest, a toddler though her head came nearly to Jetta's waist, shrieked happily and threw herself at Sheshan, who caught her and swung her up, his face losing its gravity all at once. He laughed as he swung her around once and set her on her feet, firmly catching her hands to stop her pounding his leg while she demanded he do it again.

"This is Vinnual," he told Jetta, turning the little girl to face her. The child lost interest in being tossed in the air, staring solemnly at Jetta with one arm wrapped tight around Sheshan's leg.

Jetta stooped to meet her eye to eye. "I'm Jetta. I like your flower." She touched the bedraggled blue-petaled wildflower stuck haphazardly into a buttonhole of the girl's dress. "What is it called?"

"Skybell," an older girl said, a little scornfully. "Everybody knows that."

"Jetta doesn't," Sheshan said to them. "I don't think they have skybells in the lowlands, do they, Jetta ak'Kal?"

"Indeed they don't," she said. "But they have needle trees like yours, and those yellow flowers. What are they?"

"Soul's Ease," four or five of the children chorused. A boy tugged at her hand. "Do they have this one?"

He led her over to a tiny red thing growing at the base of the rocks, so delicate it looked as if would shatter under a breath. "No," Jetta said, bending down to see it more closely. "It's lovely. What is it?"

"Rockweed," came a general chorus. A girl tried to tug her in a different direction, elbowing the boy aside, but Sheshan said firmly, "Manners, remember? Let Jetta ak'Kal know your names, and then you may each run and find her a different flower, how is that?"

They thought that a splendid idea. Jetta's head spun under a barrage of names as rich and deep as the stone of the mountains, and then they all dashed off in hot competition to find her the best flowers. Even Vinnual toddled off, not quite understanding the game, but willing to stand and pick flowers in the sun. Jetta laughed, watching them climbing like neera among the rocks, vying with each other to find the prettiest flowers. They were so much bigger than the children she had known at Setham, and yet their laughter sounded the same.

A bright glimmer caught her eye, a shy movement in the rocks. "Wait," Sheshan murmured, when she went up on her toes to see what it was. A long moment trickled past, and then it came again, a flash of hair the color of ripe grain in a lowland field. Jetta caught her breath.

"Come out, Hannahth," Sheshan called quietly.

A pair of eyes the dusty brown of teller bark rose slowly over the rock, startling in a round childish face the color of new milk. Gold hair spilled in a glorious tangle down her back and over her shoulders, crowned with a straggling circlet of skybells someone had woven for her. She advanced shyly to Sheshan's outstretched hand and stood poised to flee, staring up at Jetta, shy as a roalt fawn.

A small grubby finger came up to point. "Fy'dance."

"Yes." Sheshan knelt beside her to straighten the flower crown. "Say hello to Jetta."

"'Lo."

Jetta smiled, enchanted. She went down on her heels to greet her properly, but Hannahth cowered behind Sheshan. He put his arm around her and gently pointed her toward the Delver children still hunting flowers on the hillside. "Would you like to find Jetta some skybells like yours?"

A speechless nod, a flash of great brown eyes, and Hannahth edged away, with many backward looks. Sheshan stood up, offering Jetta a hand up. She took it, craning to watch Hannahth's departure. The Windrider child did not walk so much as flit from place to place, as if the earth had no great hold on her.

"She's lovely," Jetta said softly.

"She is very precious. The only child of ours in this place."

She watched his eyes following the child's uneven progress through the rocks. "Yours?"

"No. I wish she were. She has no parents. They died soon after she was born."

"In the great storms three seasons ago," Jetta guessed.

He threw her a quick, sharp look. "Who told you that?"

"No one. Anual said there were many losses then. I'm sorry."

He moved away as though he could not keep his feet still, climbing up into the rocks above the waterfall. The children seemed to have forgotten them, lost in their game. Jetta hesitated, and then followed him up, settling on the same rock she had occupied last night. He stood at the edge of the water staring out toward the mountains.

"Children redeem our commitment to the world," he said after a long silence. "Without them I don't think that life would be bearable."

Jetta's throat tightened. "Sheshan-"

He whirled and caught her hand. "I'm sorry. I brought you here to make you laugh. The laugh of a child is balm for many wounds."

"Yes." The laughter of the sea folk children had been the first thing Jetta heard when she woke in that village, the thing she had clung to in the first hard realization of Kori's loss. In anger at first, for their blithe happiness when her world had shattered. Later, for the purity of their innocence, that managed to find joy in a world so monstrously unfair.

He lifted his voice over the roar of the falls. "Children! What have you found?"

Little heads turned. Hands snatched at treasures in the grass. The next instant they were all swarming up the rocks to stand ankle deep in the rushing water and present their finds to Jetta in a breathless tumble of words. She ended with a lapful of flowers of every color she knew and some she had not imagined.

"Well done!" Sheshan told them. "Now run and see what your mothers have for your lunch. It's past time, and they'll be blaming me if you don't make it home before it grows cold."

Chattering and shouting, the children leaped back down in a flood, racing each other until Jetta feared for their necks. She gasped to see small Hannahth climbing down at the very water's edge, but two of the Delver children caught her hands and swung her up, half carrying, half bouncing her down the slope in the way of children. They all disappeared down the street, leaving a queer silence behind.

"Thank you," Jetta said softly.

"It seemed the least I could do, after making them all afraid of you."

"I think I understand better since meeting Kettori."

He sat down on the boulder next to hers. "Ayesh said you had. I'm glad. It may be you can do something for her."

"Such as?" Jetta twisted her head to look up at him, but he had placed himself between her and the sun, making his face a black blur. *Deliberately?* she wondered. She never seemed able to read his expression when she needed to.

Long fingers plucked a few flowers out of her lap and began to twist them together. "I don't know. I've never seen anyone so wounded inside."

Jetta half rose. "Was *she* the one you—"

From that angle she could see his face. He looked startled. "No. Not her. Even in pain you don't pour your bitterness on others. At least not deliberately."

Don't I? Jetta thought glumly.

Sheshan finished the circlet of flowers and put it on her

head. "I hesitate to say this to a Firedancer, but yellow seems your color."

She laughed. "Where did you learn to braid flowers?"

He shrugged. "It's not a very good braid. I doubt it will last all the way down the hill."

"Hannahth's did."

"Beginner's luck."

Jetta smiled. "Her eyes are so dark. Unexpected. All of you except Thess have such pale eyes."

"Thess is young. His will change."

"I was right! Yours do change with mastery, like ours."

He laughed. "That explains Setti, then. It was a shock, seeing blue eyes in a man that young. It's—unnatural."

"Why?"

"Only the old Riders have such deep blue eyes. Among us it is a mark of mastery."

"As black eyes are among us."

He tilted his head to look at her. "Then yours are as unusual among your kind as his are among us."

"Because I haven't got white hair?"

He shrugged. "Few attain mastery before middle years among Windriders."

She caught a hint of condescension in his voice, and bridled. "You think dancing with Old Man Fire is less difficult than riding the wind?"

"I have no idea. I only know how difficult it is to bend the wind to my will."

"And yet you are a master, and not in middle years." He could not be much older than her twenty-seven.

"I had good teachers." He looked away, his reserve firmly back in place.

"Wyth?"

"Among others." He turned toward her again. "Don't let him ruffle you. He is touchy for good reasons. He lost both his lifemate and his son defending a village that did not even thank him afterward, or offer condolences for his loss. Instead they blamed him for their own loses. He is—very bitter."

"What sort of place would do that?" Jetta sat up straighter, outraged.

"Many more places than you think." Bitterness spilled

into Sheshan's voice. "The village where Wyth's family died was built on a plain beside a river, against Water Clan advice. One spring it began to rain and would not stop, and in panic the village council sent for a Windrider. Wyth answered, with his wife and his son, who was barely an apprentice. With the river rising too quickly to evacuate to higher ground, Wyth managed, alone, what it usually takes four or five Fourth Rank masters or better to attempt. He called the storm away for a very small and precious time that let the villagers get themselves out, but not their possessions. His strength failed at the last. The winds escaped him and destroyed the village. His wife and son were there, shepherding the last of the villagers to safety. They died, and some of the villagers too. The villagers said he did not do enough."

Such injustice all but turned Jetta's stomach. "There's a village that deserves to fend for itself from every element. Father Flame! I've never heard of such a thing in my life, and pray I will never encounter them."

"You are not a Windrider." Sheshan turned his face into the shadow again. "Firedancers have a more enviable reputation." He stood up suddenly, reaching a hand down to her. "Come. I see Setti coming, and I doubt he will be pleased to see us together."

Jetta twisted a glance over her shoulder, but all she saw was a tiny, indistinct figure far down the hill. "Long-sighted!" she muttered, and then, "What is there to see?"

"If you were Setti, what would you think, seeing us together?"

Jetta bounced to her feet. "There is nothing *to* think! Setti has no say over who I talk to or why."

"But peace is a desirable thing," Sheshan said. "And Anual will be expecting you."

"No, not really."

But his hand urged her down the rocks; she had to take a step or fall. He guided her to Nuurn's door and left her with a smile and a grave, "Give my greetings to Anual."

In the next breath he was gone, fading quickly around the house with that airy step that seemed to spurn the earth. Jetta, feeling oddly bereft, turned away inside.

Anual looked up when she came into the kitchen. "Best not let Setti see that on you," she said, and turned to stir a pot.

Jetta's hand flew to the flower crown. "Old Man Fire!" She snatched it off and would have tossed it into the fire, but Anual caught it.

"Here now, one should never spurn a gift. Bring you bad luck, it will, and besides, what harm have the flowers done you?" She settled it around a long-necked crock on a shelf and went back to minding her pots. "Yellow is your color, do you know?"

"So I've heard," Jetta grumped, and climbed the stairs to brush the pollen out of her hair. She had a strong urge to pack her journey sack and go, flee down the road out of Annam and leave Setti and Sheshan to the Old Man. Kettori was a master. Let her deal with it.

But a master was only a master who was willing to dance. Jetta leaned against the cool glass of her window and stared down the valley at the road, seeing the raw scar across the hillside where the Delvers had carved the beginnings of the branch down to the mine. Trusting in her to keep that mixed vein from exploding in their faces.

"Father Flame," she sighed, and went down to lunch.

Thirteen
Traps

Fire rose that night. Jetta jerked awake to a deep booming horn shivering the glass in the windows and Nuurn's voice shouting, "Fire, Jetta ak'Kal! Fire at the storehouses!"

She scrambled out of bed, throwing a harried look out the window. She could not see the fire over the break of the hill, but she saw a glow, the size of which turned her stomach to knots. She slept in Dance leathers as she had at Setham; she was halfway down the stairs before she recalled that this was how it had begun there on that last night of all. No warning.

How could I have not felt that? Maybe not all of the gift had returned after all.

Grief and anxiety wound together in her stomach. Ruthlessly she suppressed it and charged down the hill with Nuurn pounding along ahead of her. Clouds had rolled in since sunset; it was black as the inside of Wind Point between the houses, forcing Jetta to slow down on the uneven streets. Then a huge shadow loomed out of the night and Rununn said breathlessly, "Follow me, ak'Kal!"

His great hand caught hers and tugged; she followed, trusting his night vision as he wove around hummocks and ruts and jutting humps of rock. Her feet were wet and numb from the chill dew on the ankle-deep grass and her lungs felt ready to burst through her chest by the time they dashed over the slight rise and came to the first of the storehouses. Delvers with shovels, with buckets and picks, some half-dressed, others barefoot, milled around between her and the fire, determined to catch any spark.

"Let me through!" she shouted, pounding both fists on the first broad back. Rununn cleared a path with indelicate shoves of a broad shoulder and many a, "Pardon, master.

Please step aside," that would have set Jetta giggling at any other time. One Delver turned with a sharp, angry protest, planting himself in Rununn's path. Jetta almost shrieked at sight of Burrood.

"Remember yourself, a'Kam!" he snapped at Rununn.

"But—ak'Kal—" Rununn twisted an anxious look over his shoulder at Jetta, drawing Burrood's gaze after it. Contempt turned his mouth down.

Jetta, trapped amid a towering forest of giant Delver bodies, lost all diplomacy. "Move!" she screamed at him. "The fire—"

Burrood opened his mouth, but what he might have said, Jetta never found out. Rununn wrapped both strong young arms around the older Delver and simply lifted him out of the way, his face averted from Burrood's astonished outrage. Jetta darted through that convenient hole and halted, appalled.

Not one, but three separate fires burned on the road and in the spring grass on the uphill verge. Setti faced the largest, an inferno in the middle of the road roaring shoulder high with a yellow-white core. The other two were spinning threads into the damp and verdant grass, finding it tough going but racing to combine arms of knee-high reddish flame.

"Dancer, what do we do?" a panicked Delver shouted at her.

Jetta gathered her wits. "Clear a line around those two!" She pointed at the lesser fires, which would not spread quickly in that lush grass. "And stay back!"

She ran to join Setti. Outmatched, still he bravely stood his ground. He had kept this fire from spreading at least, confining it to an irregular circle twice Jetta's arm span. As she came up beside him he thrust his hands out in the move that had worked so well yesterday. The fire shied back but none of its flickering branches sank or died. Jetta saw the failure hit Setti like a blow to the gut and shouted at him, "Show no fear, Dancer! Take position on the other side!"

He turned his head and saw her. Relief washed into his face in a flood. He nodded and spun away, terrified but still game. Jetta stepped instinctively into the Dance, straight to the fifth movement.

No retreat.

The fire roared at her, malicious to its core. She felt its hostility as she had felt it at Firehome, at Setham. Heat blasted toward her and recoiled; she saw it withering the grass even where fire had not yet taken hold. Sweat glistened on Delver faces at the edge of the light. She set them from her mind, concentrating on the ground underfoot, reaching for the pulsing power under Earth Mother's skin. She planted both feet in the dying heat of ruined grass, uncomfortably warm for a terrifying, endless instant in which she could not feel the run of the fire even with it towering in front of her. And then it came, the sweet, staggering relief of the Dance connecting her. Connecting her to everything. Everything worth protecting.

The heat faded. The searing brightness dimmed as the air seemed to thicken into a shield around her. The acrid bite of smoke and scorched grass no longer afflicted her nose. Jetta scarcely noticed, for the center of the fire faded to palest yellow and then to white, and a *hysth* burned there, vanguard of The Ancient, defying the Dance, the Mother. Her. Jetta set her jaw and began to dance.

She abandoned the traditional forms. She already knew they would not work. Ruthlessly she shoved away the nagging conviction that such ferocity needed Fourth Rank mastery; she was not Fourth Rank. Third would have to do.

She wove together everything she knew, flowing spins into long stretches designed to block the fire's advance, every muscle thrumming with the power of the Dance. Without forethought she combined patterns drawn from Third Rank, from Fourth, even from First, a stamp and clap of the hands that drove an exploring trickle of flame to ash and a thin thread of smoke.

The *hysth* roared at her, divided itself and tried to advance on her flanks.

She stopped it with an improbable leap and twist that took her level with shocked Delver eyes for an instant. A stealthy spurt of flame caught her eye mid-turn; she touched down in a smoking clear patch and immediately stepped off again, landing squarely atop it. A moaning gasp rose from the Delvers, but the flame withered on the instant. Jetta spun away, driving flame ahead of her.

On the edge of her awareness danced Setti, brief glimpses

of random movements, out of step with her own, disconnected, though she saw that somehow he was keeping the fire from spreading on his side. He was not Kori; she could not expect his efforts to lock smoothly with hers, but still it distracted her on levels she sensed in tiny jolts to the smooth flow of the energy pouring through her.

And then she felt *It*, a malevolent intelligence, a driving need deep underground.

The Ancient.

The *hysth* lunged at her, breaking out of its circle to assault the ground at her feet, burning downward, striving to dump her into the arms of The Ancient. Dimly she heard Setti's frenzied *"Jetta!"* Panic shook her that he would make some ill-advised attempt to come to her aid.

She advanced, straight into the reaching arms of the *hysth*. A babble of Delver protests broke around her, lost as fire leaped high. She saw only the *hysth*, all blinding light and wavering flame; heard only the roaring voice of The Ancient mocking her. Close, so close. No time!

Jetta flung her arms wide, reaching into the flames on both sides. Fire curled over her sweat-glistening skin, dazzled her eyes, but still the Dance protected her. She felt only the cool flood pouring up from the Mother; smelled only the raw dampness of earth and stone, the mountain scent, the Delver scent, as she gathered her will and thrust the fire back. Deliberately she focused on her fingers, pointing them precisely toward each other to complete the circle of power, flat open palms facing the fire, forming a barrier she willed the flames not to cross. The *hysth* hesitated. Jetta thrust her hands apart, shoving fire back on both sides, and leaped, straight through the *hysth* to land beside Setti while the flames, split and confused, groped blindly to recombine and face her again.

"Now!" she shouted at Setti, and struck his near arm up. Dazed, he copied her movement, a beat behind, shoving at the divided *hysth*. Jetta went up on her right foot, reaching for mastery as though it were dawn in front of her window. Her arms arched high, wrists touching, capturing the fire's malice into the closed shape of flame itself. Clumsily Setti copied her, wobbling a little. The *hysth* wavered, roared, and began to sink. Jetta heard The Ancient's triumph change to fury in the crackle of the flames, and smiled grimly to herself. She sank to a crouch and thrust off from that rock-solid right foot, whirled in closer, and landed in the midst of hot, scorched earth and swirling smoke. The *hysth* shattered into scattered yellow flames racing to find new toeholds. Rununn, finding one almost underfoot, cried out and stamped a huge booted foot down on it. It disappeared into smoke.

The Delvers looked at each other and began to beat at the flames with shovels and boots, clapping stone buckets over them, dumping bags of black chips on confused yellow worms of fire. In seconds the glow vanished. Darkness reclaimed the road and the warehouses standing intact in a long, lumpish row.

Shaking with exhaustion, Jetta turned toward the verge and the two lesser fires. Only a charred spot in the grass remained, backed by twin heaps of dirt. Not safe, that, however it looked. She wobbled over to them and kicked the first mound away. It covered a bucket upended over what must be a small heartstone. Jetta looked at the other mound, guessed it disguised the same solution, and sat down on the near bucket, drawing a collective gasp.

"It's quite all right, so long as this bucket hasn't a hole in it," she said wearily.

Setti stumbled up to her and sank to his knees in the charred grass. "What you did," he breathed. "Jetta... I don't even *know* what you did."

"I stopped The Ancient," she said flatly, and then heard her own words under the sudden distressed babble around her. "We stopped The Ancient." She said it slowly, savoring words she could hardly believe.

"Jetta ak'Kal?" Rununn dropped to one knee in front of her, his huge eyes looking even bigger with anxiety. "Are you well?"

"Yes," she said. "Very well."

Very, *very* well. Here had been malicious fire, a *hysth* as cunning as any she had encountered at Setham, and behind it The Ancient. And she had won.

She threw back her head and laughed, turning Rununn's eyes to great astonished moons. "The Ancient is sulking. It has met Delvers, and been driven back, as doubtless it did not expect." She lifted her voice. "You have done well,

Annam!"

The sea of lambent eyes watching her in confusion blinked and dissolved into laughter and merry backslapping. Yellow light bloomed again, startling Jetta to her feet, but from lanterns this time, brought out to inspect the damage. She exchanged a rueful smile with Setti as the Delvers turned their fear into a celebration, gathering around the smears of ash where the fire had been, pointing and chattering like children. Jetta touched Rununn's arm and smiled up at him, who had defied a master to get her to where she needed to go. She thought his face would crack in delight; his smile was as vast as the Vale.

"You did well, a'Kam," she called over the noise. "There is a deal to be said for the direct approach!"

He ducked his head in shy confusion, so incongruous in a creature so huge that Jetta could not help laughing in sheer affection. His uncomplicated friendship felt like the rock of the Dance ground back home, impervious to all assault.

"Buckets and shovels!" a sharp voice cut through the babble. "The Ancient will return, Jetta ak'Kal. Will you stand there congratulating yourself and let these folk believe they can defeat it with buckets and shovels?"

Shocked silence swallowed the merriment. Heads turned; luminous eyes stared at Kettori standing at the edge of a lantern's spill of light, wrapped in her extravagant shawl and glaring at Jetta from eyes as black as pits in the wavering glow.

Anger burned Jetta's good mood to ash. What right had this bitter old ruin to douse these people's new-won confidence and splash doubt over their triumph?

"Kettori ak'Kal. Had Setti and I not been here, what else could they have fought it with save buckets and shovels?"

Kettori hunched the shawl closer around herself, the fringe fluttering clear to her ankles. "False confidence will kill them, and you. The Ancient has more tricks than a child. The likes of which you cannot possibly have even heard of, let alone fought. Cease your silly celebration and begin to ponder on its next coming, ak'Kal."

Her scathing glance included the Delvers. Jetta took a step forward, furious. "Then tell us, *ak'Kal*, from the depths of your wisdom, the tricks we do not know. Dance with us, Setti and I, and teach us what a great one of our kind used to know."

"I do not dance," Kettori said curtly.

"Then leave us to craft our own tricks in peace," Jetta said coldly. "If you will not help."

Kettori stood for a few seconds more, thin shoulders squared against the wind, the inadequate light stealing her expression into the shadows. Then without a word she turned and walked away, the shawl whipping its long strands around her like smoke. As she turned, Jetta saw that her blue-black hair was braided back from her face into a gleaming coil at the nape of her neck. Bare feet made no sound in the grass.

An incredulous suspicion overtook her. "Kettori!" she called, but the old Dancer disappeared into the night without a backward glance.

Jetta stared after her, suddenly cold, and weary beyond belief. She shivered, and found Setti's arm around her in an instant.

"She is old and bitter," he said, his voice raspy with anger. "Don't let her upset you. You did an incredible thing tonight, Jetta."

"She's right!" Burrood stamped up beside Nuurn, a huge shovel slanted across one broad shoulder. "Will it return, this thing we fought tonight? Where did it come from, and how are we supposed to fight it? *We* cannot leap untouched through fire."

"Well, at least you noticed that much," Setti said bitterly.

"Aye, I noticed!" Burrood turned his head to include the whole watching throng. "I noticed a journeyman Firedancer outmatched and hesitating, and I noticed a so-called master of the Dance playing with it like a lover—or a fool hoping to impress greater fools. Show me the danger! I think she called it herself!"

Glowing eyes blinked and dimmed, twinkling like stars in the nervous heat dance of the lowlands. Jetta gaped at him, stricken to incredulous silence.

Not Setti. He took a step, coming up on his toes though it put him no closer to standing eye to eye with Burrood. "Are you mad?" he cried. "Jetta could have died!"

"Was she so desperate, then, that she must leap into the arms of flame? Do Delvers run headlong under an avalanche to stop it? No! We are *not* such fools!"

What will it take to win their trust? Jetta watched the myriad little moons of their eyes looking anywhere but at her, and could not believe that even yet Burrood believed he could put things back the way they were by ridding Annam of Firedancers.

Setti drew an audible breath; Jetta caught his arm. She wanted to sleep. She wanted to hit Burrood. She wanted to find Kettori ak'Kal and claim back from her the warm feeling she had stolen. Instead she walked over to the center of the pattern of ash where the *hysth* had died, and prodded with a toe the biggest single heartstone she had ever seen.

"Even a Dancer cannot carry unquenched heartstone bare-handed, good folk. This is where it came from. I suggest you pave this stretch of road with containment stone. When the heartstone rises several at a time as it has done here, it's an indicator that a vein has worked its way up close to the surface. I've seen it elsewhere. There's no knowing how many have broken free and still lie buried here."

She set her bare foot on the one that had spawned such fury, drawing a gasp or two from the crowd. "This one is dead. Safe and cold. Take it and use it in a wall somewhere to remind yourselves that The Ancient can be defeated."

"With buckets and shovels?" someone shouted.

She turned and pointed at the other two ignition points. "Yes! Keep fire contained, and it cannot grow into a door for The Ancient. Be—not—afraid! *That* is the code of the Fire Clans! Where fear is, fire wins!"

It rang in the night, a clarion challenge. Jetta glared up at Burrood through a silence that seemed to still even the restless wind. Then Rununn's voice shouted, "Where fear is, fire wins!"

Another young voice picked it up, then a deeper bass that turned into a din to make the mountains sit up and wonder.

"Let Kettori stew on that!" Setti shouted in Jetta's ear, grinning like a madman.

But Jetta thought of the coiled hair, the bare feet, and wondered. Had she come to dance?

~ ~ ~

"Tell me true, Anual," she said, perched at the kitchen table after a few hours exhausted sleep and a soak in the bath chamber, which was rapidly become her favorite room in Nuurn's house. "How many think like Burrood? Is he truly a fool, or is it just Jetta ak'Kal, the Dancer who failed at Setham, that he cannot bring himself to trust?"

Anual sipped at a cup that smelled of lowland tea and avoided her eyes. "It could be the Circle erred in not making known the real danger below our feet," she said obliquely. "So many instances of fire since you've come, and all those whispers about Setham. Aye, some believe that a desperate master might reclaim her reputation by putting on a great show. None here know anything of the Dance, nor its limits. Nor yours."

Jetta bit down hard on a sharp retort. Rekkale, always proud and boastful, as well as a bully, used to egg his friends on to make the practice fires bigger so he could show off his prowess in damping them. Burrood, a Second Rank master well into his middle years, might cherish ugly resentments and bitter dreams.

"Only fools play with the Old Man," she said. "And I am sorry that any here think I have so little honor as to endanger the very village I am charged to protect for my own glory."

Anual lifted sharp blue eyes. "No one in this house believes that, ak'Kal. I saw you dance. I saw Setti's face when you leaped into the heart of fire. I saw yours when it retreated. I saw no triumph, only relief."

"Enough to fill a well," Jetta admitted.

Anual chuckled. "Patience, Jetta. Delvers are as slow to change as our mountains. I daresay Urrana had a few things to say to Burrood. I'll have Nuurn speak to him as well, if you like."

"No! No," she added more quietly when Anual's eyebrows shot up. "That would make it worse. I will be *patient.*"

Anual cackled and stood up. "Not too patient, Jetta ak'Kal. It tickles me to see you stirring new thoughts in old heads. Go and stir some more. I've work to do."

Jetta slid down from the chair, hardly noticing the drop anymore, and wandered down to the inn. For once it was not a solitary walk; children began to turn up in her wake, dancing and skipping and thrusting flowers and cookies and bright pebbles at her. She traded cookies for flowers and they all walked on content, arriving at the inn smelling like a meadow. And there stood Sheshan, leaning against the wall watching her progress with folded arms and a wry smile.

"I see you've found the path to their hearts," he said, rumpling the hair of a Delver boy busy stuffing the last of a huge cookie into his mouth.

"Go and play," Jetta bade them. The whole horde abandoned the pair of them to run away down the street, pouncing on harmless stones and burying them under fistfuls of thrown mud. Watching them, a slow chill worked its way down Jetta's spine.

"What's wrong?" Sheshan asked. "You seem somewhat of a hero this morning."

"Kettori was right about them getting hurt. Fearless is one thing. Ignorant is another."

"Then cure their ignorance," he said simply, and when she frowned up at him: "Teach them what they can safely do and what they cannot."

She sighed. "That may be the only way to keep from waking to an inferno, I think."

"I saw what you did last night. It was rather incredible."

"I didn't see you." Nor any other pale heads among the crowd, for that matter.

"It took but a glance to see that a Windrider in proximity would only make things worse. I was on the hill above with Wyth and Ayesh."

She looked up into his grave, steady gaze. "And what did you see?"

"Courage," he said succinctly, lifting a hand to touch her cheek. "Your eyes are darker this morning, did you know?"

Her hand lifted, as Setti's had done. "They're already black, there is no more to be done."

He studied her for a moment, so intent that she blushed and dropped her gaze. "The black seems to have spread a little," he said. "Is that possible?"

Jetta shivered, thinking of Norlahk's ebony gaze. "Yes. But few Dancers acquire that much black. It speaks of many encounters with The Ancient."

She reached up and tugged at the door latch, wanting suddenly to leave this conversation behind. Sheshan placed his pale hand above hers and pulled it open, standing back to let her into the inn ahead of him. Such innate courtesy pleased her even as it embarrassed her. What would people think, seeing them together all the time?

Rinood turned from dusting the mantle when they came in. Her face lit up at sight of Sheshan. "Ak'Kal!" And to Jetta, with less enthusiasm, "Jetta ak'Kal. I will fetch my mother." She vanished through the kitchen door.

Jetta nudged Sheshan. "Anual says she is quite smitten with you."

A blush on that frosted skin was an astonishing thing to watch. Jetta crowed with delight. "Be careful, Windrider! You'll have Urrana after you, and then where would you get noë?"

He shook his head and started to laugh, so that when Urrana came into the common room they were smiling together like children. She stopped, one heavy eyebrow shooting up in surprise. "Well, here is solidarity," she declared, planting huge fists on hips. "The Ancient had best watch itself."

Jetta stepped hastily away from Sheshan, fighting the hot color flooding her own face. "I came to ask about teaching the children," she said, though the thought had not occurred to her until Sheshan said it. "They see their elders throwing dirt on fire and expect to do the same. I would like to teach them—and anyone else who cares to come—when to throw dirt and when to run."

Urrana's shrewd glance slid to Sheshan, who gave her back a bland look. "A good idea," she said. "Especially the part about anyone who will listen. What will you need?"

"A place to gather. A little wood, perhaps. Somewhere fire cannot get out of control."

"From what I hear, it seems likely to do that anywhere," Urrana said, setting an anxious cramp in Jetta's gut until she added, "But I think our Firedancers can handle it."

Our Firedancers. So casual, and yet it returned some of the glow Burrood had stolen. Jetta flashed her a grateful smile.

"The patch between the stream and the containment wall

will do," Urrana said. "There's plenty of flammable scrap lying about. We'll see you get what you need. Begin in the morning?"

"Uh, yes," Jetta agreed, taken aback still again by the decisive speed with which the innkeeper got things done. "That will do."

"The little ones will be there. Go and enjoy a day of rest. You've earned it."

She bustled back into the kitchen, leaving an awkward silence behind. "Well," said Sheshan. "That sounds like a splendid idea to me."

"I should practice," Jetta said, panic threatening her. "The Dance. For tomorrow."

He just looked at her. "One doubts that you will be teaching the Dance to Delver children. And why practice a Dance that no longer works on your enemy?"

"How do you know that?" She gaped at him.

"I don't believe that any Dance of any rank calls for the Dancer to leap into the fire's embrace, does it?" His face turned somber, his pale gaze boring into her. "That astounded even Wyth. I—You frightened me profoundly."

"You don't think it was a fool's leap to impress the gullible?" Despite her resolve, bitterness leaked into her voice.

"No, Jetta ak'Kal. And neither does Wyth. Annam Vale is morc fortunatc than it knows." He held out his hand. "Come. If you won't rest, then let us do something practical."

"What?" She made no move to take his hand.

He lowered it again, seeming unperturbed. "Huunall told Wyth that you wish to test the firetraps. The first one at the new mine is finished. Shall we go and see if it works?"

Jetta hunted for an excuse to refuse. Yes, she wanted to know if the traps worked, but she had not envisioned working with Sheshan to find out. Nothing came to mind. She hid dismay and found a polite smile.

"Yes, of course."

It seemed a very long walk down the valley to the mine. Jetta tramped along in silence, wishing Wyth had seen fit to assign a different Rider to this task. Sheshan was altogether *too* accommodating, far too quick to turn up in her path. She found herself liking him, and didn't want to; she found herself hoping Setti would not wander down here, and could not convince herself it wouldn't matter. Setti would not see a Firedancer and a Windrider, a clearly ridiculous combination. He would see what Anual saw: a woman in the company of an available man. Worse, a woman who had refused *his* company.

This is impossible, she thought miserably.

Sheshan did not seem to mind her silence; he walked beside her with that floating stride, looking keenly at the trees and the flowers and smelling the wind. "Rain before long," he said once. Jetta glanced at the clouds overhead and quickened her stride.

"Remind me not to go walking with you," she said. "Every time I do it rains."

"I thought women liked rainwater in their hair," he said innocently.

"Hair, yes, soaking them to the bone, no."

"But you have fire in your bones to ward it off."

He had an answer for everything. She rolled her eyes and walked on. He laughed quietly, no doubt pleased with himself.

She hardly recognized the mine. The timber shoring had been replaced with containment stone carved from the hillside, and the shaft was already deep enough to need three lamps down its length. The firetrap had been hollowed out to the right of the entrance, just inside. A shallow trench lined with black stone ran across the mouth and on down the hill to end in a pool also lined with stone. With typical Delver efficiency they had made it into a drain to shunt excess rainfall away from the entrance. When the pool filled, they would have a pleasant place to sit and wash the dust from their faces.

She approved the arrangement, for the Old Man had nowhere to go in either direction. "But what will keep the bait from washing down the hill every time it rains?" she asked.

"Look again, ak'Kal," Errull said, well pleased with himself.

Jetta looked, and smiled in appreciation. The bottom of the trench across the mouth made a continuous run of windstone from the vein jutting into the trap. "Oh, that will work," she murmured, picturing it. Any fire that found its way to the free air would mindlessly continue to follow the line of windstone, straight to its death in the trap, whether or not the innocent-looking dead grass now almost obscuring that pale stone fed its greed or not.

A gust of wind laden with the smell of rain buffeted her from behind. "The wind has shifted," Errull said in dismay. "It's blowing across the hill. Wrong direction."

Sheshan moved up to stand beside Jetta. "We can't count on the wind favoring us. That is why there will always be a Windrider here when the mine goes deep enough to make a dash for the entrance a chancy thing."

"You could spend a fair portion of your life underground, Rider," Errull warned. "Never thought I'd see that day."

"Annam has made us welcome. Unless you wish us to leave, what else have we to do?"

"Welcome you are," Errull said fervently. "Dancer, shall we try this mad idea of Huunall's?"

The first spattering raindrops fall across Jetta's face and hands. "Yes. Before we get soaked."

"Better soaked than burned," Errull said cheerfully. "You lot, stand back!"

The Delvers obeyed with alacrity, crowding the hillside on either side of the entrance to watch. Jetta got a nod from Sheshan and stepped up to the twisting ribbon of pale rock winding down the left side of the mine shaft, protruding like a great tongue at the entrance. She laid a hand on it, warier now than a few days ago, but it lay cool under her touch, free of association with The Ancient. So far.

"I need a lantern. Or at least oil."

A murmur of disappointment ran through the Delvers; Jetta turned her head and grinned at them as she splashed the oil on the stone and gave the lantern back to the girl who had brought it. A gasp of astonishment rippled up when she closed her eyes and flung sparks at the stone.

Fire exploded seemingly from the rock itself, an impressive display that drew an awed mutter. Jetta stepped back, doing nothing to stop it following the oil drips earthward. "Give the word," Sheshan said tightly beside her.

She glanced at him. His shoulders looked as though he were bracing up a great weight and his face looked even paler than usual, his eyes locked on the fire. He held his hands poised in front of him in that spread-fingered readiness she had come to know. *Wind and fire,* she thought as the hair on her neck prickled up. *Of course he is terrified.*

The fire tried to crawl away across the hill, blown in streamers by the storm wind. "Now," Jetta said, tensing to do something if this didn't work.

Sheshan's hands came together and locked, forefingers pointing into the wind. Jetta watched the fire swirl and flicker and burn straight up for an instant as the wind fought Sheshan's pointing fingers shifting toward the mine. And then a great gust nearly blew her flat as the wind changed direction, blowing steadily up from the valley and straight into the trap.

The fire streamed madly sideways and dripped down into the trench. Instantly the dead grass caught, swirling up in greedy sparks. Jetta, alarmed, reached to snuff them out but Sheshan said, "No!" He stood like a teller tree, pointing in the direction he wished the wind to go, swaying now and again to a fiercer gust. Jetta saw his wisdom in waiting to see if this would truly work in every regard.

She chewed her lip, watching the fire race down the trench, consuming the grass in one great puff. Sparks swirled onto the bare dirt inside the mine, flickered and flared and then starved to death. The flame lucky enough to have found the grass raced on into the firetrap, soaring up the chimney, where nothing met it but cold black stone. Jetta expected Sheshan to drop his hands, but he let the wind blow its steady breath into the trap, swirling the dying fire around and around and refusing to let it back out.

The flames flickered, turned yellow, red, sank to glowing ash and then to nothing.

Sheshan released the wind. It spun into a whirlwind on the spot, whipping stray strands of Jetta's hair painfully across her face in the process of resuming its interrupted course. The storm swooped down from the head of the valley, driving the rain ahead of it, efficiently soaking every stray spark.

The Delvers ran for the shelter of the mine, Jetta and Sheshan with them. Standing soaked and dripping just inside with the rain pouring in a waterfall into the trench, Jetta looked up at him and said, deadpan, "This is the last time I go anywhere with you, Windrider."

He lifted both pale eyebrows. "This little drizzle bothers you? You have no appreciation for nature, Dancer."

Errull roared with laughter and clapped him on the back. "It worked! I tell you, the Old Man will get a surprise if he comes sniffing around here. Jetta ak'Kal, it was a good day when the Circle sent to Firehome Vale."

Jetta, embarrassed but pleased, almost missed the soft voice in her ear. "Indeed it was," Sheshan said, so close that his breath stirred her hair.

And Jetta couldn't even slap him with all those Delvers watching.

She pretended not to hear instead. When she looked at him again he was watching the rain, his gaze distant. Jetta dropped her eyes, puzzled. Changeable as the wind, were the Windriders, and about as predictable.

All the way up the hill after the rain passed he said not a word. At Nuurn's door he stopped her when she reached up for the latch. "I offended you. I'm sorry."

"No, you didn't!" Guilt had ridden Jetta all the way up the hill. What, after all, was wrong with being appreciated?

Clear blue eyes narrowed. "It seemed so."

"Then," she said, "we are both sorry. You did well, ak'Kal. You are very powerful."

"I was well motivated," he admitted. "Fire terrifies me."

"I saw that. But you didn't flinch."

"How could I, when I see you leap into the heart of it?" His mouth quirked oddly.

"I'm a Dancer! There's no comparison."

"But every need. I will see you tomorrow when you instruct the children." The quicksilver smile ran through his face. "Most fitting, I think."

Before she could answer he was gone, elusive as the wind itself.

"Infuriating man!"

Fourteen
Lessons

Jetta strolled down the street past the inn, clad again in Dance leathers. Yesterday's rain had blown on down to the lowlands; the sun smiled on Annam. Its warmth felt so good on her skin that she ignored the scandalized looks she got from a few Delvers. The only way to teach fire was to bring fire; with the Old Man acting as though it had never heard of the Dance, she would take no chances. She came in sight of the containment wall, and stopped, disappointed. Fifteen or twenty children waited in the meadow, but only a handful of adults, mostly people she knew. Burrood was not among them. Nor was Rununn, which gave Jetta an anxious pang. Was it duty that kept him away, or was he being punished for his uncouth temerity toward Burrood?

Setti spotted her and strode across the burgeoning grass to meet her with a flock of children at his heels. "Isn't it grand?" He beamed at her. "They're listening, finally!"

"Some, anyway." A glimmer of pale cloth caught her eye. "Oh, no," she blurted, seeing Wyth, Ayesh, Sheshan, and a handful of other Riders lounging against the containment wall or leaning against trees. "What are they doing here?"

Setti's excited smile faded. "Ayesh told Urrana they came to learn."

Urrana herself hurried up, green skirts billowing. "Jetta ak'Kal, we are ready to learn, as you see." She gestured toward a pile of buckets and firewood by the stream. "Show us what to do with those."

Jetta did not know whether to laugh or weep. Buckets against The Ancient! But she had seen the Delvers pursue fire with courage and determination, and in the end, was that not half a Dancer's advantage?

She drew a deep breath and walked down to stand among them. "Good morning. Huunall ak'Kal, Wyth ak'Kal. I'm honored."

Wyth gave her a stiff nod, but Huunall smiled. "I'm old to learn a new dance. Won't have it said I refused to try."

Wyth stiffened. Hastily Jetta said, "Would that all were as open-minded as those here, ak'Kal." She smiled around at the reserved faces waiting to judge whether Kettori or Jetta ak'Kal had the right of things. Father Flame! Where to start?

She looked at Setti waiting quietly to follow her lead, and found herself flung back all at once to the training ground long ago, when they had both waited for Minna or Norlahk or whoever the instructor was that day to begin. And thus she found her starting place.

"In the Beginning of all things," she said, and a sigh of recognition whispered across the meadow. Teaching tales began that way everywhere. Jetta sank cross-legged into the grass and began.

"Earth Mother had three children: Fire, Wind, and Water. Fire was eldest, restless and angry, forever rebelling against the Mother's restraints, cracking her again and again, until in desperation she summoned Water from the reaches of sky beyond Fire's control. Water fell and pooled into great oceans that cooled the barren stone where Fire lay. Raging, Fire retreated deep into the womb of Earth Mother and sulked. To coax him out again, she blew upon land and ocean, and Wind was born, who danced down into the deep cracks to entice Fire out to play. But Fire was jealous of his siblings, and tried to consume Wind, until Water poured forth over the land and filled every crevice, nearly killing him. Earth Mother, greatly afraid for her firstborn and missing the warmth of his touch, made Fire a hiding place, deep, deep in her womb where Water and Wind could not go. She made it of black stone that neither Wind nor Water could scour away, a barrier to keep Fire safe. Too late, she discovered that Fire had no power over it either, and he raged in his prison, safe, but denied the freedom aboveground.

"Wind and Water, fearful that Fire would break free, sneaked beneath Earth Mother's skirts to look for him, to make a seal of their own about his prison. Carefully, hiding from their mother's gaze, they crept down the long fingers of black stone she had made to mark the way to Fire's abode. But at the very brink of Fire's prison, Earth Mother caught them! Angry, she drove them back to the surface. Wind and Water fled, splitting themselves into fragments that sped upward in all directions, following the paths of dark stone. In their haste they left pieces of themselves behind, long trails that hardened under the Mother's angry breath to stone as white as foam on the sea, laden with Wind."

Delight flickered through the watching faces. Doubtless the Delvers had their own explanation for why blackstone and windstone, opposite in their properties, were so often found together, but Jetta saw that it tickled them to hear their own mysteries given a new face.

"Fire heard the commotion and raged so fiercely his prison cracked! Only a little crack, but enough. He found a white trail left by his sisters and pursued them, storming after with all the wrath of his jealousy and hatred hot in his heart. When he reached the surface, he snatched at Wind, daring even the sea, spitting flame that Water could not quench. Flame ran wild across land and sea, threatening to consume even Earth Mother.

"Horrified, the Mother gathered bits of stone and ash from land already blackened by the passage of flame. She breathed upon them, creating children born of Fire's touch: gold and black like fire and victory, and set them to battle Fire. And they danced a great Dance and drove their elder brother back into the deeps, but the crack in the prison remained, for they could not go so deep underground and live. And so Earth Mother made new children, great, stout-hearted giants to delve deep and find the path to Fire's abode, and there seal him in."

Heads popped up. Eyes went wide. Looking at Huunall's startled face, Jetta guessed that nothing in Delver lore included this purpose for their existence. She saw Wyth straighten from his indolent slouch against a tree, frowning. Why? It was only a tale.

Jetta put on a solemn face and looked at each wide-eyed child. "But the skirts of the Mother are vast. To this day the Delvers have not found the path to Fire's prison. Someday, perhaps, all the trails left by Wind and Water in their flight may have been tried, and consumed, by the Old Man. Until then, we must watch, and dance, and be ever vigilant, ever ready for Eldest, the Old Man, the most ancient of all beings save Great Mother herself, to strike again through the crack in its prison."

Wyth's cold voice cut through the sigh of appreciation that greeted the end of the tale. "I note that nowhere in Dancer lore is there a place for Windriders."

Jetta turned her head slowly, arranging her expression to what she hoped was neutral interest. "Then perhaps you would school us in Windrider lore, ak'Kal?"

Wyth looked down his long nose at her. Sheshan touched his arm, earning a frown that he ignored. Sheshan stepped past him, smiling at Jetta. "I would be delighted, ak'Kal."

Wyth folded his arms and leaned against his tree, surprising Jetta. He looked sour but made no objection, shifting her understanding of Windrider relationships. She had thought him an autocrat, firmly controlling what his folk did and did not do, but it seemed that was not the case. She looked at Ayesh, who winked at her.

Sheshan strolled down to stand beside her; Jetta stood up, feeling hopelessly outmatched down there at knee-level. He gave her a graceful nod and lifted both hands toward the sky.

"Wind grew up," he said, and clenched his fists. A breeze swooped down from nowhere, rippling the grass and snatching at the Delvers' hair. Jetta felt it tugging at her coiled braids, and for an instant a thrill of elemental fear shot through her. In the face of fire, such a wind could destroy her in a breath.

Without thinking she stepped away from him. Instantly the wind died. Sheshan turned to her, his hands quiet at his sides. "With Fire imprisoned, Wind grew bold. Earth Mother paid no attention, for she mourned her mistake in trapping her firstborn. Wind roamed unchecked, sometimes swooping out to sea and teasing Water into a rage. Then storms pounced upon the land, raking all before them as Water tried to force Wind to go away. But Wind was elusive, and finally Water called upon the Mother to help contain her troublesome sister.

"The Mother roused herself and looked out across the land, and saw the ravages wrought by Wind. She snatched down cloud from the sky and pulled it into man-shape, and breathed it to life. That first Windrider of all was named Heffesh, and he sang to Wind, calling her from her roaming. She came, and listened, and fell in love, and came docilely to his hand. Their children were few, but their mother loved them and protected them and always came when they called. Until one day, Water, jealous of the love between Heffesh and Wind, snatched him from the bank of a great river and bore him away. Wind, frantic, searched for him everywhere, but no trace did she find. Her grief turned her fierce. She raged across the sea, across the land, and no longer was she Wind, the gentle creature who cooled the baking earth and snatched rain from the sea to feed her children. The Hag was born, a fierce and terrible creature bent upon vengeance. She stalked abroad and brought ruin wherever she went, until at last her own children were forced to unite against her. They sought advice from Water, and the sea sang them a new song. They wove it into the call their mother had taught them, and so learned to tame her rages. But nevermore did Heffesh come to Wind, and no more children were born."

Sheshan's voice deepened, softened. "The children of Wind scattered in search of their father, hunting land and sea, high places and low. They seek him even now."

Without warning tears stung Jetta's eyes. It explained so much, if it were true. But it was only a tale. Wasn't it?

Sheshan held out his hand to her. Hesitantly Jetta took it and found it warm and solid in hers, no ephemeral ghost-thing made of tales and rumors. Sheshan raised their joined hands aloft. "See, people of Annam? Wind and Fire may occasionally come together without harm."

Jetta all but snatched her hand away, her cheeks burning. "Thank you, Rider. An enlightening tale."

Sheshan's smile faded. Gravely he inclined his head and stepped back. "As was yours, Jetta ak'Kal. Please—continue with the lesson."

He stepped around scowling Setti without a glance and made his unhurried way back to lean against the containment wall. He did not look at her or any of the Windriders, but seemed absorbed in watching the drift of clouds overhead. Jetta clenched her fists, trying to gather her scattered wits.

She became aware of myriad interested eyes, and found her voice from sheer desperation. "That—that is the first lesson taught to all Dancer children. Beware the white stone. Black is our bulwark, our friend. But black stone is not enough, so the next lesson is this. Settak a'Kam."

Setti jumped. He threw her a trapped glance; impatiently she gestured him up. This, even he had mastered without difficulty.

His jaw set in a tight line of concentration, Setti caught up a handful of tinder from a basket and flung it into the grass at his feet. Jetta watched the quick, intricate motion of his hand, the stamp of one foot just so, and remembered how Setti had been first of all her class to call the fire. The masters had thought him promising until it became clear he had far greater ability to call it than to put it out.

Fire spurted up from the dead stuff, drawing a gasp from the Delvers. A couple of Windriders edged back a step. "Look!" Jetta called. "What do you see?"

"A problem!" a deep voice called.

"Look closer! Describe the fire!"

A moment's blank silence, then Uranna said tentatively, "Uh—small, red, smoky."

"Setti."

Setti leaned down to blow on the flames, and leaped back when they scorched up with unexpected fury. Jetta managed not to jump, aware of eyes watching her every twitch, but it reminded her acutely of that moment in the square at Firehome when flame played its own game. It burned brighter now, trying to crawl away through the thick, ankle-deep grass in the meadow.

"Now what do you see?" she asked the Delvers.

A girl spoke up. "Yellow fire, ak'Kal, with red roots."

"Observe fire in all its forms, if you would live!" Jetta lifted her voice and watched them jump, moon eyes flickering as they turned to her. "Judge a fire by its color, its speed, how it runs, and how quickly it reaches for the sky. All fire longs for its sister Wind, but I have seen a Windrider turn the very air against it, and so I believe Earth Mother was wise. She created her children to form a balance, and if fire is greedy, still there are ways to thwart it."

She looked through the sullen smoke at Wyth and caught

him for the first time with his face unguarded, wearing a thoughtful, intent frown as he looked at the flames struggling in the damp grass to flare into something more, something rapacious and hurtful and mindless in its hunger. Just as the winds that had taken his family had not cared at all what they destroyed.

Jetta dropped her gaze before he saw her looking. "Observe!" she bade them all, and spent the next hour working in tandem with Setti to show them every face of fire save the *hysth*, teaching them how to read the wind to predict its run, how to spot flammable hazards in its path, how to use even the tiniest rolls in the ground to delay it and give the alarm time to summon help. Most of all she tried to pound home the difference between the small, groping infant flames that might yield to a thrown bucket, and fire that had already grown hopelessly out of containment, however small the flames looked from a Delver's great height. When she dismissed them at last, she gathered from the thoughtful looks and mutters that—perhaps—she had instilled a little caution into their enthusiasm.

"Well done, ak'Kal." Ayesh appeared at her shoulder, his eyes on the smudgy scars in the grass.

She looked up at his pale, calm face. "It was a start."

"Others will come, I think. You'll continue the lessons?"

"Of course. And if possible, I would like to borrow a Windrider now and again to practice, but somewhere safe. We must discover how best we might work together."

"A splendid idea. I'll speak to Wyth."

"Can he not speak to me himself?"

"Do you really want him to?" Ayesh smiled his enigmatic smile and wandered away.

"Wyth!" Setti muttered, stamping a bare foot into a very dead bit of ash. "Stone has more humor. 'Nowhere in Dancer lore is there a place for Windriders'," he mimicked savagely. "Maybe for good reason!"

"Stop it!" Jetta snapped. "We have to work with them—"

"Them? Or just one?" He walked off before she could summon an answer.

"Grow *up*, Setti!" she yelled, and regretted it when his back stiffened. He dropped into the stalking tread of an angry master and went on up the hill.

Disgusted, Jetta fought down her own anger and strode back to Nuurn's house to write a much-delayed report to the Circle at Firehome, to go with the first trader caravan when it came. If it came. She longed to ask them why they had sent a child to battle The Ancient, but refrained. It might be they would not automatically associate that reference with Setti.

Father Flame. When did life get so complicated?

Fifteen
The Caravan

Spring turned to summer, and still the caravans with their precious trade stocks did not come. Anual stopped baking cookies and Urrana began to speak of organizing an expedition to the lowlands to bring back flour and other staples running low throughout the village. Jetta fretted, her report unsent, and began to wonder about the ominous silence enveloping the world outside Annam Vale. The lessons continued, gradually drawing in more people, but still she felt their reserve, a silent expectation, of what, she could not guess. For her to drive the Old Man out altogether? For fire to burn down the whole village and prove Burrood right? It maddened her that there seemed no in-between.

Even The Ancient seemed in conspiracy against her. No more alarms rang in the night, no more flame leaped unbidden from the ground. Whispers began to run through Annam Vale that The Ancient had retreated, driven out by the Firedancers. Others spoke darkly of sealed doors at Wind Point and missing traders. The Circle voted down a proposal to thank the Firedancers and send them home, but Jetta saw worry in Urrana's eyes when she reported the results.

"Too close," she breathed in Jetta's ear. If it came up again, Jetta guessed that the Old Man might win after all.

Setti brooded. He never spoke of that day in the storehouse, but it hung between them in awkward moments when reaching hands touched inadvertently, in conversations that started with a gay "Do you remember—?" and ended in painful silence. She felt his eyes on her at dinner, at meetings with the elders, in sessions with the children. He had buried his feelings, not lost them, and she did not know how to talk to him anymore. But talk to him she must. She remembered the wrongness in their uncoordinated dance to tame the heartstones; they needed to practice together, to find rhythms born of old moves or new that did not accidentally counter each other, but Jetta shrank from the intimacy of practice, and Setti's newfound ability to disappear seemed designed to thwart the very notion. Nor did it help that Sheshan turned up at her elbow whenever she felt most jangled, offering silence and a soothing presence she began to miss when it was not there. She no longer questioned how he knew where to find her, or why he came. But he always left when Setti appeared, leaving more silences that she did not know how to fill.

Ten days before midsummer the first of the summer caravans came creaking over the pass at last and up the road to the village. Jetta, inspecting the new paving by the storehouses, turned toward the clear chime of bells and the slow snorting of cart beasts straining on the steep grade. She blinked at triple yokes of squat beasts the golden brown of harvest fields, their pendulous, fire-sensing beards swaying at every stride and their spiraling horns capped in the gold of many prosperous journeys. The longest tail of wagons she had ever seen wound down the hill, all long-bedded and high-wheeled, with swaying, gaudy covers or gaily painted boxes that served for home and shop alike. A mix of clean-shaven men and women, sporting the shoulder-length hair the drovers preferred, occupied the drivers' seats, all of them in baggy breeches and tight-sleeved shirts of every color imaginable. Barefoot children hopped down to join the Delver youngsters swarming among the wagons, shouting names and greetings and racing off to play.

"Not strangers," she said to Huunall, who had supervised setting the paving stones.

"Old friends. First in every year and last out. Used to race the snows before the Windriders came, making sure we had our winter supplies. Good folk. Well timed. The cupboards are nearly bare and the storehouses nearly full. They need clearing out."

Jetta walked with him to greet the driver of the first wagon, a lean, leather-faced man wearing the flat, brimmed hat and tall boots of every drover she had ever met. He flicked his lash over the broad backs of his team straining up the last steep incline, and caught sight of Huunall. His face split in a grin, then his jaw dropped at sight of Jetta's Dance leathers.

"Huunall!" He abandoned the team to jump down and take the Delver's hand. The cart beasts stopped to munch the grass beside the road, forcing the rest of the train to pull out around or stop on the grade. "Dancer." The drover looked her up and down, his expression torn between surprise and alarm. "Firedancers in *Annam?*" His tone echoed the consternation the villagers must have felt the first time fire bloomed in the Vale.

"And a fair day to you too, Hylli Fargoer," Huunall said mildly.

The drover flushed, but his eyes raked the storehouses and the new paving with keen assessment. "I can't say a loading surface without mud isn't welcome, old friend, but is it truly The Ancient that has inspired what we've not been able to wring from you these twenty seasons?"

Huunall chuckled. "See? Something good comes from most everything. A few problems, aye. Nothing Jetta ak'Kal cannot handle."

Fargoer's thin dark eyebrows shot straight up. "Jetta ak'Kal. Weren't you at Setham?"

Her chin lifted. "Yes."

His eyes narrowed but all he said was, "Delver business, I suppose. Don't know why I should have thought Annam immune, what with all the problems in the lowlands."

"Problems?" Jetta seized on that, hungry for news from the world outside the Vale.

He threw her a sharp look. "Surprised you haven't heard, being a Firedancer and all. Fire everywhere this spring. Lost a village away south a half moon ago and the Dancer too. We've spent weeks detouring around rumors of fire. A man's liable to find heartstones springing up under the team in the middle of the road. Seems better now that the frost is out of the ground, but I still hear tales of fire blooming where it's been quiet for the length of an old man's memory."

"Like Annam," Huunall rumbled.

Fargoer frowned. "And sorry I am to hear it. It was always pleasant to come to a place where you knew you wouldn't be bothered by such things."

"Just snow and wind like to blow you down the mountain." Huunall chuckled and pointed up the hill. "Pasture's same as always. You'll want to leave the third storehouse for last this year. Full of windstone," he explained at Fargoer's inquiring look.

"Hylli! Will you stand jawing all day while the teams break their hearts waiting on you?" A voice from somewhere in the caravan jolted Fargoer into a hasty turn toward his own wandering beasts. He prodded them on, not without another look at Jetta. She did not wait around to collect more of the same but walked on up the hill beside the stream, frowning over the news. She had close kin in villages scattered all up and down the eastern coast. Somewhere a Dancer had died, maybe more than one. The Ancient was growing bold everywhere.

A flicker of movement on her right caught her eye. Expecting Sheshan, she caught a glimpse instead of Kettori vanishing behind a boulder in a swirl of sea-colored fringe. Jetta had not laid eyes on the old master since that night by the storehouses. Yet her scorn had inspired a host of good consequences, and Jetta thought it only right that she know it.

She climbed up to where Kettori had vanished, hunting in vain among the rocks. The woman was more elusive then a neera. Jetta stopped and said clearly, "It may please you, ak'Kal, that I have taken your advice. The villagers know how to use their shovels and buckets to good effect now."

"And do they sleep with them as well?"

Kettori stepped from the rocks higher up and stared down at Jetta, her lined face as uncompromising as ever. "I have watched you struggling to teach them the difference between a spark and a *hysth*, girl. What good will it do them? You can't be everywhere, and what chance have they with their puny buckets when The Ancient arrives in their bedrooms, eh?"

Jetta's spirit of conciliation vanished. "At least they won't die of panic. They've learned to manage their fear. Are you so blinded by yours that you can't see the difference between caution and retreat?"

Kettori's head snapped back as if Jetta had slapped her. "What I fear you cannot imagine," she said coldly.

"Then enlighten me! What turned Kettori ak'Kal of the Fourth Rank from her duty and killed folk she was sworn to protect? What do you know of The Ancient that you will not tell me? You were a great Dancer—"

Kettori snorted. "The Mother's touch burns as well as blesses, girl. Would you dump all on me simply because I once mastered a few tricks you don't yet know?"

"Will you let these who sheltered you die for your pride?"

Kettori gave her a wild look and spun away, fringe flying. Jetta lunged after her. "Kettori! You were Fourth Rank! Teach me what I do—not—know!"

But Kettori had vanished amid the labyrinth of rock as thoroughly as wind itself. Cursing her own temper, Jetta climbed up to the top of the falls, hoping to catch a glimpse of her, but Kettori knew the rocks around her door far better than Jetta ever hoped to. She gave up and sat watching the caravan sort itself into camp in the high meadow north of the storehouses. Women dressed in stout trousers like the men rounded up children to collect wood and bring water from the stream, establishing housekeeping with speed that left Jetta shaking her head in admiration. These people lived their lives on the road, claiming no hearth, no clan, no standing place of their own, taking even their name from the beasts they drove. Not a life she would treasure.

Like Windriders. The thought disturbed her. It occurred to her that one day she might wake up and Annam would be empty of Windriders, gone to fulfill some other contract, or perhaps to find a different wind. If they left, Sheshan would go with them, and she found that she would miss him turning up behind her, and his companionable, undemanding silences.

Frowning, she got up and walked down to find the inn humming with deep Delver voices overlaid with the higher pitch of outland accents. She pushed open the door and threaded her way through a forest of broad backs and tables full of drovers and Delvers amiably swapping news. She had nearly reached the fireplace when Setti pushed his way through from the kitchen, dressed as she was in Dance leathers and holding a sealed scroll. She glanced into his white, set face, and instantly developed a cramp in her stomach.

"From Norlahk and the Circle," he said. "For you."

Jetta's heart all but stopped. It could only be bad news. Numbly she took the scroll from him and sank onto the settle by the hearth that had become theirs by unspoken consent. It took her a moment to nerve herself to slide a fingernail under the seal.

The first line relieved her fear; the second made her angry. She hissed and flung the scroll at Setti. Apprehensively he righted it and sat down beside her to read. "What do they *want?*" he flared, looking up to exchange glares with her.

"The Ancient wrapped and sealed and delivered, apparently. Have they all gone mad?"

She snatched back the scroll and read it again, more slowly, trying to fathom what insanity had beset the Circle.

From the Circle of the Fire Clans to Jetta ak'Kal. Events beyond Annam Vale have not touched any of your blood, nor those of Settak a'Kam. But we find your silence uninformative and against orders. Word from Annam Vale speaks of incursions by The Ancient, which you were sent to prevent, and to report if you could not. Since your death has not been reported to us, we assume your continued health and success in the Dance. You are ordered to report your progress in safeguarding Annam Vale, with particular emphasis upon how The Ancient was driven back after hysths *had formed. If it is true that flame attacked a master of the Dance as it did at Setham Vale, then it is your duty to report how it was defeated. We expect to hear from you by midsummer.*

Dance well, ak'Kal.

"Well, there's a wish unfulfilled," Jetta said, letting the scroll drop. "Short of flying to Firehome. How long has this been on the way?"

"News by caravan is seldom swift." Setti picked up the abandoned scroll. He read it again and looked up, frowning. "Who could have told them about the incursions here?"

"I've not seen anyone leave, but then, I don't know everyone yet. Perhaps someone had business in the lowlands." It puzzled her. She thought Anual or Urrana would have told her if someone was going, so that she might send word home.

"I think," Setti said slowly, "the Circle is looking for help. The drovers say there is fire springing up everywhere. A

Dancer's been killed, yet we've been successful. They must be desperate to know what works now and what doesn't."

Jetta took back the scroll and read it again, guilt overtaking her anger. The unknown Dancer might not have died if she had asked a Delver to take her report down to Baro. But on the other hand, what could she say? That she had invented a Dance and now could not remember what movements she had used, or in what order? How could she tell the Circle her solution had been to leap into the fire, and perhaps it was only surprise that had killed the *hysth?*

Scowling, she stared at the floor until Setti brought her back with a practical and difficult question. "What are you going to tell them?"

"They will be so thrilled when I tell them I've enlisted Windriders," she said crossly. "I don't know what to tell them, Setti. I'm making it up as I go along. How can I pass along wisdom when I don't have any?"

"You are the best Dancer I've ever seen," Setti said flatly. "Just tell them what happened and let them puzzle it out. They have to listen to you."

She snorted. "Why?"

"Because we're still alive."

Which stark fact burned the last of her bad temper to ash. "You're right. I just would like to know how they know all this."

Setti shrugged. "Maybe a Windrider flew over Firehome and dropped a message. They seem to turn up everywhere else."

He didn't quite look at Jetta as he said it.

"I haven't yet discovered if Windriders *can* fly," she said, after a pause a shade too long. "But I would like to see the Circle's faces if I sent a scroll that way."

He laughed, but it sounded a little hollow. *Oh, Setti. Stop breaking your heart over this. There is nothing between Sheshan and me.*

Nothing, she realized, except that she did not relish the thought of living forever in Annam Vale if he were not in it.

"I have first watch," she said abruptly, and stood up.

"Don't go! Mururrn is smuggling me out some noë. I'm sure he'll bring you some too."

"This village will be awash in noë now that the caravan's

come with fresh supplies. He won't have to smuggle it out anymore, so there will be other occasions."

"Will there?" he said bitterly, then shrugged. "Forget I said that. I just wish—"

"No more than I." For a moment it was true. She knew him as well as she had known Kori; they shared the same memories, laughed at the same things. Life with him would be cheerful, and comfortable, and safe from the unknown. But it would not be passionate. He deserved better.

He looked up in sudden eager hope that changed to a scowl when he saw the regret in her expression. "Go. Dance," he muttered, and picked up the scroll and pretended to read it again.

Jetta sighed and left to prowl darkening streets far more crowded than usual. Children lingered in the long summer twilight, racing about with drover brats at their heels, ignoring impatient shouts from meadow and village alike to come in to supper. Lanterns and cookfires winked in the meadow, disquieting her; she saw not golden sparks in the night but many more opportunities for the Old Man to come walking.

Still, the drovers lived their lives in the open, camping without Dancer protection the year round. She found their livestock safely penned against wandering accidents, the wagons parked far enough apart that no infant fire could leap the gaps. The young Delver on firewatch at the storehouses greeted her cheerfully, neither bored nor sleepy with the raw new paving under his boots to remind him to stay awake. By midwatch all the children were safe in bed, the camp quiet, the village dark. Jetta left the patrol to Setti and went to bed, but sleep eluded her. She stared at the dark square of window, half expecting the sudden, heart-stopping glow of fire painting the night. Which of her kin had died down there in the lowlands, and how? Had The Ancient ambushed that unknown Dancer as it had Kori? Had complacence killed another member of her clan?

Finally she slid out of bed, lit a lamp, and finished her lengthening report.

Fire has risen in Annam Vale three times since our arrival. No damage has yet been incurred beyond a wood stack and a hole in a road now paved with containment stone. I have faced The Ancient once, when three heartstones surfaced together, including one so large that Settak a'Kam had no chance of preventing it forming a hysth. It was through his experimentation earlier in practice that we defeated it. He discovered forms that are not now part of the Dance, which drove the fire back. These I applied, along with a combination of Third and Fourth rank movements. I cannot tell you what combination, for I do not know myself. I urge you to experiment, for The Ancient is outgrowing our present knowledge.

I have enlisted the twelve Windriders in this village to our aid. They seem to have sense enough to know when to call a wind and when to stay away when fire rises. They have been most helpful thus far.

I fear for Annam. Veins of windstone mapped under the village may prove a very great danger to more than Annam Vale. And I must report the presence of Kettori ak'Kal, whose arrival here last summer may have first attracted The Ancient's notice to this previously untouched place. She refuses the Dance, yet I could wish for her knowledge. If there is Fourth or Fifth rank lore related to stopping fire in stone, ak'Kal, I beg you to forward the scrolls.

Greetings to my kin, ten days before midsummer.

"That will set the sparks ablaze," she muttered. "If there are scrolls to send, it may at least gain us another Dancer."

She blew out the lamp and went back to bed, and dreamed of The Ancient raging behind the seals at Wind Point. In the curious way of dreams she stood both deep underground and on the ridge at once, able to see both the fire beating at the jumbled stone and a handful of pale figures waiting in the rocks beyond the sealed door. "No," she cried, or tried to, but the wind rushing from the valley snatched her voice away. She heard The Ancient roaring in triumph as the rockfall somehow melted into nothing, saw the flames leap up the tunnel and attack the Delver-carved door.

"No," she cried again, and started to run down the ridge. She saw the sealed door grow hot, the carvings sagging, running like water down the face of the stone. Then the door itself canted and fell, and The Ancient burst into the open air with a roar that shook stones from the mountains.

The wind rushed to meet it. Fire consumed it, flashing

out in a great fist that reached into the rocks and snatched the Windriders into its palm. In a breath they were gone, dissolving to ash in front of Jetta's horrified eyes.

"No!"

That time she managed sound. She woke sitting bolt upright in bed with her own scream still ringing in her ears.

Footsteps pounded down the passage. "Jetta? Are you all right?" Anual threw the door open and stood in a cloud of nightdress staring at her.

"I-I'm fine." But her teeth chattered and her stomach churned so badly she thought she would be sick. "A dream. Just a dream."

"You've seen enough for a few nightmares, I imagine." Anual waved behind her back at someone in the hall. Jetta heard a heavy tread moving away, and regretted disturbing Nuurn from his bed.

"Never worry about waking us," Anual said, reading her face. "We were up, even if just barely. Nuurn's off to cart his trinkets down to the trading. They always fetch a fair price."

Anual's tone belied the disparaging "trinkets." Jetta had seen Nuurn's carvings, his hobby of a winter night, scattered all through the house and on half the doorposts in town. Those big hands held a rare talent.

Anual cocked her head. "Are you sure you're all right? You were screaming."

"It was a dream," Jetta said, embarrassed. "That's all. I'm quite well now."

Anual's face spoke her opinion of that, but she only bustled around the room, reviving the banked fire, setting the stone washbasin on its shelf over the flames to warm, shaking non-existent dust from the curtains. "It's tradition to make a special effort for the trading," she said casually. "And that's a fetching dress in the wardrobe there. The one with the red stitching. Though yellow would be better," she added, with a sly grin over her shoulder.

"I need to be ready to dance," Jetta said. "Dresses aren't practical." Although her mother had managed to stuff three into her pack.

"But a certain Windrider's eyes would pop, seeing you in it."

Leaving that to burn in the air like live sparks, Anual

hustled out the door before Jetta could gather her wits for a scathing reply.

Seething, she got up and hunted in the wardrobe for a shirt and breeches. In vain. Somehow Anual had managed to make off with everything but the three dresses and a few underthings. Jetta, standing in Dance leathers that needed a good scrub, wanted to throw something, but nearly everything in the room was too heavy. She knew without asking that Anual would have everything she owned soaking by now; it would do her no good at all to force the issue.

She snapped a curse and dragged the dark green dress with the red stitching off its peg. It was the best of the three, her favorite back when she had cared about such things. She hauled it down to the bath chamber through a kitchen mysteriously empty, and soaked in the hot water until her fingers started to shrivel and she was forced to come out and face the day.

It felt odd to leave her hair loose, to feel heavy cloth swirling around her ankles. Jetta could not remember the last time. She did not want to go outside the house in it, or with her hair flowing around her shoulders, for all that it almost reached her waist now, no longer quite such a disgrace. This was not the Firedancer Jetta ak'Kal. This was a person she no longer knew how to be. But Anual had left her no choice.

Setti, trailing tiredly through the front door as she came out of the kitchen, stopped dead at sight of her. "Jetta!" He closed his gaping mouth with a snap and stared some more. "I-I haven't seen you dressed like that since you and Kori—" He stopped, biting his lip.

Since the day they had pledged for life. Jetta shook her head against memory and pain and raised a smile. "Anual's idea of proper attire for the trading," she said dryly.

"She was right. Hang on. Let me splash some of the grime off and I'll join you."

He leaped up the stairs before she could say no. Jetta tried to head him off as he dashed back down again, laden with his own best clothes, soap, and towels, but could not get a word in past his enthusiastic, "Wait there!"

So she waited, with her stomach winding into a knot that had nothing to do with the fact that she had missed breakfast. Setti's renewed enthusiasm for her company bespoke another confrontation she wholeheartedly did not want. He knew how she felt. Why did he push?

He came out of the bath dressed in the deep coal red of his rank, chased with gold around cuffs and collar. Broad-shouldered and handsome, she guessed he would turn many a head among the drover women if he would only look back. But his eyes saw only her, eyes an indeterminate shade of brown flecked with blue. No child's eyes anymore, and he was a long way past the feckless boy who had walked the road with her from Firehome. It touched her that he took care not to take her arm as they went out the door together, making no claim on her as they walked down the hill. Such a good man. Why couldn't she see him in Kori's place?

Why am I thinking of anyone *in Kori's place?* a voice wailed, deep in her mind. Shocked, she concentrated on keeping her skirts out of the way and could not think of a thing to say.

A whole flock of Delvers ambled gaily down toward the meadow ahead of them. It looked like the entire village descending at once on the drover camp, dressed in every shade of brown and green and gray gaily embroidered in the myriad colors of spring flowers. Some carried goods for trade; more went empty-handed, looking to carry things back, she guessed, or simply ready to wander and enjoy.

She saw a Windrider making his solitary way down the hill and tensed, but it was only Heshah, who greeted them politely and walked on. "What's the matter?" Setti asked.

"What should be the matter? Let's go see what they've brought to trade. Besides noë, that is. I think we can count on that."

He laughed. "If they haven't, they'll likely never trade in this Vale again."

Jetta smiled and walked on toward the first of the wagons with its goods laid out on the grass beside it, a collection of pots for which she had no use. The drover in charge greeted the Firedancers with civility but no warmth and spared them no second glance when they walked on.

"Doesn't waste much breath on non-customers, does he?" Setti muttered aside to Jetta.

"Sensible man." Jetta turned toward the next wagon,

drawn by a mouth-watering scent. "What is that spice you're using?" she asked a fair-haired woman tending an aromatic pot over a slow fire burning in a clever portable hearth. "I never smelled anything so delicious."

The woman turned, all smiles until her gaze dropped from the Delver height she had expected to Jetta's small bones. "Dancers," she said without enthusiasm. "The blessings of the day be with you."

Jetta blinked. "And with you. Is something wrong?"

"Wrong?" the woman echoed warily.

"We seem as welcome at your fire as the Old Man himself," Setti offered helpfully.

The woman straightened, brushing her hair back with a nervous flick of her hand. Her eyes strayed over the rank badge at Jetta's shoulder, widened a trifle, and darted toward Setti. "Your pardon, ak'Kal, a'Kam. You startled me, is all. I expected a Delver with a pocketful of change to spend."

"And here are we with scant need to cook," Jetta said, a little coolly. "I would spend coin on that spice for Anual, if you would tell me its name and its use."

"You're quartered with Anual?" The woman's face lightened. "Aye, she could put this to good use. Bura, it's called, and no stew should be without it. Would you care to try?"

Belatedly she remembered manners and ladled samples into wooden bowls, handed them to Jetta and Setti and watched them take cautious bites. The stiffness melted out of her face when Setti's eyes shot wide and Jetta's closed in bliss as the taste explored her mouth.

"Oh, that's good," Setti sighed, erasing the awkwardness of their meeting with unstudied enthusiasm. "Might there be more where that came from?"

"Setti! Will you devour all her samples and leave her with nothing to show?"

But the woman smiled shyly and took back Setti's bowl, ladled it full and thrust it back at him. "Ak'Kal?" she asked, her hand hovering over Jetta's bowl.

Jetta wavered. "Well I-"

The ladle erased her objections. They ate sitting on the wagon tongue, watching the camp fill with color and laughter. A tame neera slunk out from behind a wagon wheel and lifted its sinewy body onto its hind legs in hopeful appeal; the drover woman swatted it away without rancor. Setti offered it stew; it swarmed up onto his shoulder, startling him. Jetta laughed at the way it disappeared into his hair, peering at her from black eyes all but lost in shiny black fur. Setti, charmed, scratched its pointed muzzle until it hissed suddenly and darted away.

"What did I do?" he asked, fingering a scratch on his neck.

Jetta pointed at the cook fire where the neera licked greedily at a splash of stew dropped from the ladle. "They sense fire, remember?"

The drover woman looked around. "Slink's a right nuisance, but he's warned us about the Old Man more than once. Hylli won't travel without a neera or two along."

She turned away to haul out sturdy canisters of spices Jetta had never heard of to show a dozen Delver women, who nodded at the Firedancers and settled to hard bargaining after a scant sniff at the kettle. Jetta and Setti waited politely for a lull to give the empty bowls back, but business was brisk, and finally they set them on the tongue and moved on down the row. They found little on display of use, but it was fun to watch Delvers bargaining with drovers as if neither side had ever seen the other. Time after time it looked as if the negotiations might break down in anger, only to end with a laugh and fist touched lightly to fist in perfect amity. Jetta, accustomed to the more relaxed trading style of the lowlands, shook her head, watching Urrana arguing with a drover half her height over the price of flour.

"You disapprove of the wares, Firedancer?" a cold voice asked in her ear.

She spun around. "No, of course not. Why do you ask?"

A middle-aged drover stared back at her, twitching a display of threads and needles fussily into perfect alignment. "Wouldn't wish to offend a *Firedancer,*" he said with heavy emphasis. "Never know what might happen."

"Explain that!" Setti snapped.

The drover scowled. "Wouldn't want the Old Man in these fabrics, is all," he muttered, waving vaguely over his shoulder at the rainbow bolts piled in the wagon bed.

"The Old Man wouldn't waste its time," Setti said, and caught Jetta's arm. "Come on. There are more interesting things to see."

He marched her away, his back very straight. "Slow down!" she protested, stretching her legs to match his angry stride.

Setti stopped, frowning down at her. "Why does everyone in this caravan look at us as if we had insulted their mothers?"

"Not you. Me," Jetta said quietly. "Pay them no mind."

"I will!" he snarled. "They're an ignorant lot of rock-brains, and they've no call to treat you as if your very touch burns."

"But it does," Jetta mumbled, caught all sideways. Just so had the survivors of Setham treated her, and for cause.

"Jetta!"

She squared her shoulders against the pull of the green dress, that made her feel oddly more vulnerable rather than less. "It doesn't matter, Setti. Come on. Look, there's Nuurn."

She started past him, ignoring the set to his shoulders that told her he wanted to argue. For a horrid instant she thought he would not follow, and gulped down relief when she heard his footsteps behind her. The last thing she wanted was to treat the whole Vale to a public display of Firedancers squabbling like children.

Nuurn stood behind a trestle table showing some of his carvings to a hawk-faced drover trying in vain to disguise his interest. Jetta guessed that Nuurn would get the best of that trade, judging from the number of drover folk standing around wistfully fingering the delicate figures and fanciful flowers wrought in black and white stone.

"I hope Nuurn takes his last coin," Setti muttered, his jaw still set in an unforgiving line.

"If he does it will be because the piece is worth it," Jetta said coolly. "But I prefer these!"

She quickened her stride, sighting a dejected figure standing alone beside a blanket strewn with small bits of windstone polished so that they gleamed in the sun like the icecaps over the Vale. Rununn stood behind it, watching the activity at Nuurn's table with wistful eyes.

"Just a carver!" Jetta said scathingly, swooping down to snatch up a carved Dancer no longer than her hand, in Dance leathers and braided hair, up on one foot in the control movement of Third Rank. She shaded her eyes to peer up at Rununn.

"How do you know this position?"

He blushed the rich deep brown of good plains dirt. "I saw you at your window one morning as I was coming off firewatch," he mumbled. "The lines of arm and leg were so beautiful." He dropped his head. "Have I offended?"

"No! Oh, no," Jetta breathed. Setti took the little Dancer from her hand and held it up to the sun, marveling at the fine detail in the carved braid, the face that bore a strong resemblance to Jetta, the minute folds of the Dance leathers and flow of carved muscles.

Jetta swallowed hard, awed by the skill in those huge hands. "Rununn—it's wonderful. I cannot believe people are not fighting over these." She eyed the other small figures and thought she could put a name to every carved Delver caught in everyday tasks or laughing as they drank Urrana's burli, tiny carved tankards lifted in miniature fists.

Rununn blushed deeper. "Oh, no, ak'Kal. Folk want useful things like Nuurn ak'Kal's masterworks, that you can put into any house and have them seem to fit right in. What can anyone do with these? I carve these bits of foolery to keep my hands limber, no more." He sighed, a gust that ruffled Jetta's hair back from her shoulders. "I had hoped to make a bit of coin, is all, to buy better tools."

Setti eyed him shrewdly. "Better tools just to keep your hands limber?"

Rununn ducked his head. "There's no harm in wishing."

Jetta closed her hands gently around one of his huge fists. "Or in striving, a'Kam."

She did not look at Setti, but she felt him stiffen. He, who had fought harder for his rank than anyone she had ever met, could teach a stone stubbornness. Perhaps his inability to give up would shore up Rununn's sagging self-confidence if these two spent much time together.

An unpleasant thought trickled in on the heels of that hope. Setti was stubborn about a good many things. Was it even possible for him to give up on what he wanted?

Her hand brushed her hip, seeking an absent pouch. "Rununn, please save this for me. All my coins are up at Anual's—"

"That I won't, Jetta ak'Kal," he said, snatching the carved

Dancer from startled Setti. He presented it to her with a flourish. "You were the model, and I am honored you find it as beautiful as—" He broke off, blushing furiously.

Setti snorted a breathy laugh. Jetta refrained from swatting him and took the Dancer from Rununn, touched to the heart. "Mine is the honor, a'Kam. Thank you."

Rununn seemed so torn between pleasure and embarrassment that Jetta took pity on him and moved away to the next display, her fingers gently caressing the carving. She had never felt stone polished to such a flawless, pleasing smoothness under her fingers. The patience that had gone into it staggered her.

"Do you know that Burrood had him work a tenday in the new mine for laying hands on him the night of the *hysth?*" Setti asked tightly.

Jetta stopped dead, staring up at him in consternation. "No!" Suddenly she knew why Rununn had not come to so many of those early lessons. Anger flushed through her, as intense as the rising of flame. "That gape-mouthed *fool!* If Rununn hadn't shifted him we'd all have been dancing at The Ancient's whim—"

"What I hear, that's nothing new for Jetta ak'Kal."

The deep voice behind Jetta stopped them both in their tracks. Setti snatched in a breath laden with outrage and spun around; Jetta, shocked to inner stillness, caught his arm and turned more slowly.

"You have something to say, Hylli Fargoer?"

The caravan leader stared down at her, arms folded, his weathered face grim. "I knew folk in Setham. Went through there last spring. Not much left to see. But I heard plenty."

"And did you hear your gossip from the people of Setham, or on the road?" Setti flared. "Unless you were there, keep your opinions behind your teeth!"

"Setti—" Jetta tried to tug him away but Setti shook off her hand and planted himself in front of Fargoer with the same hard-faced determination he brought to the Dance.

"Stand aside, a'Kam," Fargoer said, undaunted. "My business is with Jetta ak'Kal."

"Nice that you remember her rank," Setti said through his teeth. "Too bad your memory is too short to recall respect for your betters!"

"Setti!" Jetta gasped, for this man, while no clan master, had earned respect on his own merits. Setti never even blinked.

Fargoer's head came up. "Does that include you, a'Kam?"

"Have respect for our Firedancers!" Rununn shoved his way through the crowd, his broad brown face flushed with anger. He stopped beside Jetta, such a solid bulwark in his gray festival tunic that she felt like a very small tree sheltered by a sun-kissed mountain. His loyalty warmed her to the core even as she wished he had stayed out of it.

Fargoer glared at them. "You don't speak for the Stone Clans, a'Kam," he said, dismissing Rununn with a flick of his eyes. And to Setti, "Nor you, whatever your name is."

Setti came up on his toes. "You—"

"Here now!" Nuurn pushed his way through the gathering crowd, bodily setting aside a drover who seemed disinclined to move. He stopped between Fargoer and Setti, frowning down at both of them. "Harsh words are poor fare for a trade fest."

"Tell it to this drover!" Setti snapped. "He accosted us, not the other way around."

"Setti, let it go," Jetta said.

Nuurn turned great blue eyes on her and said, "Better to draw out the poison now, Jetta ak'Kal, than let it fester in the dark."

She flushed as he turned to Fargoer. The drover tilted his head up to meet Nuurn's gaze, unrepentant. "Poison, is it? Will you take the side of a woman whose incompetence destroyed a whole village? Will you shelter her and risk the same here?"

"That is Delver business," Nuurn said mildly, but Fargoer would not be put off.

"*My* business, when I take my folk where I thought it was safe, only to discover it's not!"

A chill shot up Jetta's back. What world of dreams did this drover inhabit? He sounded like Burrood. "And where in the world is safe, Drover?" she asked clearly, drawing Fargoer's hostile gaze. "Have you never lost beasts to bad roads, never misjudged a river crossing, never had a child chase heedless after a neera and become lost? Do the perils of daily living never touch your caravan because Hylli

Fargoer leads it?"

The drover flushed. "I have never misjudged badly enough to bring them all to ruin at once, Dancer. And it is in my mind that staying in Annam past tomorrow would be just such a misjudgment."

Dismay muttered through the crowd. Drovers and Delvers looked equally taken aback. "Shortsighted of you, Drover. Will you flee any village where fire ever appeared? Then I pity your folk, for they will find precious few places to trade their goods."

"We will take our chances in villages with Dancers who know their trade!"

Setti's hand came up; Jetta caught his arm, staring levelly at Fargoer. "Then put floats under your wagons and go trade with the fishes at sea, for nowhere else will you be safe."

Nuurn gasped and turned to stare at her. Jetta looked down at the little Dancer still in her hand. Rununn still stood like a sheltering mountain behind her, in trust so complete it demanded an equal return. Jetta ran a gentle thumb over the perfect arch of the little carved arms, thinking of Setham, who had also trusted her. For a moment courage failed her. *What if I am wrong?*

But dead Dancers and ruined villages spoke of problems greater than Jetta ak'Kal's tarnished reputation. She raised her head. "Hear me!" she called, her voice ringing off the nearest storehouse. Setti drew a sharp breath; Jetta tightened her grip, knowing, as he did not, that truth picked its own season. She met Nuurn's troubled eyes.

Fargoer watched her warily, sensing momentum slipping from his hand but arrested by her tone. *Judge this time from knowledge, not ignorance,* she wished him, and raised her voice.

"There is more to the death of Setham village than you know. More than the Circle of the Fire Clans knows," she said, ignoring the muttering and Fargoer's angry frown. "No one knew it a year ago when my lifemate died in The Ancient's trap. I didn't. I nearly died in the same trap, and Setham fell to fire because no one knew what has now been proven, here in Annam and elsewhere. Firedancers have died this spring, as my lifemate died, because the Old Man is not acting as fire should, as fire has for all the ages since the Beginning. The Ancient has broken the rules of the Dance, and suddenly knowledge and courage are no longer enough."

Fargoer dropped his arms to his sides, his expression torn between consternation and disbelief. Nuurn reared upright; Huunall sighed and bowed his head. Jetta felt Setti's eyes on her, but would not turn and meet his incredulity.

"It's true, good people," she said quietly. "I wish it were not. The greatest Dancers in history could stand where I stand, and still Annam would not be safer than Setti and I have made it, for they, too, would have to do what we have done: create a new Dance from the broken pieces of the old. And how is that for reassurance?"

A second's dead silence, and then a low rumble of Delver laughter washed up against the stone walls of the storehouses. Fargoer threw a wild look around. "I see nothing funny! Nuurn, are you mad enough to believe this?"

Huunall stepped out of the crowd, gently elbowing aside a knot of white-faced trader women. "He may not be. I am. I saw Jetta ak'Kal face The Ancient. Saw her leap into fire. The Dance surely never taught her that. And I saw The Ancient retreat from such mad tactics. She said that courage is not enough. I say it is the only thing that will keep Annam from an unthinkable fate. I trust to the courage of Jetta ak'Kal. And to her judgment. I do not believe the Fireclans would have sent an incompetent to the place that delves the stone half the world depends upon."

Which simple truth sank home to Jetta for the first time. He may as well have lifted the mountains off her shoulders. Setti's jaw dropped. Rununn grinned like the sun coming up.

"I agree," Nuurn said.

"And I!" Urrana stepped out of the crowd, and where she walked folk gave way in respect. Faces turned thoughtful, eyes dropped, whispers muttered through the watchers like a low wind in the grass. The innkeeper smiled at Jetta as she turned to Fargoer, towering over the drover, her smile turning stormy.

"I thought Hylli Fargoer a cannier man than you've proven here, Drover," she said, matching him frown for frown. "Many's the year your folk and ours have traded to the benefit of both. What sparks this sudden lack of sense, hey?

Or have you been talking to some who were born without?"

Fargoer's gaze hooded. Urrana snorted. "I thought I spotted you drinking with Burrood last night. Only a fool leads a blind man along a cliff, Hylli. Should I ask who was leading whom?"

The drover flushed the color of young flame. "I have *seen* Setham, Urrana ak'Kal!"

"And I have seen a woman I could break apart between my hands stave off The Ancient. If it's true that the Old Man has broken the bindings, then what happened in Setham was no fault of Jetta ak'Kal's. No, nor of her lifemate that died, either. I trust the Dancers we were sent. Delver business, not drover. Are we agreed?"

Her eyes bored into Fargoer's, no longer kind and friendly moons, but disks of blue ice. The drover sniffed and fidgeted. "Delver business," he muttered.

"And you will stay the full week?" Huunall rumbled.

A hush fell in the meadow. Anxious drover faces turned to Hylli, for on his answer rode a sizeable share of their summer's profits. He looked around at his people, at Jetta, and last at a wrathful figure standing with arms crossed at the rear of the crowd. Fargoer met Burrood's eyes, and suddenly his head lifted and turned with a snap to Urrana.

"We stay. Better to take your goods out of the Vale and profit by them than let the Old Man have them for free."

"You—" Setti took a step toward him; Huunall's big hand caught him back.

"Prove him wrong, a'Kam," Huunall said into the furious look Setti turned on him, and to Fargoer, "Keep your suspicions if you will, Hylli, but keep them to yourself."

Fargoer's head snapped back as though Huunall had struck him. His mouth opened, pinched shut again, and then he stalked off through an avenue hastily opened for him by his own folk, leaving a miasma of dismay in his wake.

Jetta watched him go with dread prickling down her skin. *What did I just do?* An angry drover could spread disgruntled rumors from the mountains to the Great Water in half a year; if lowlanders cursed Jetta ak'Kal's name now, what would the Circle say if her word set the plains in a panic?

Quite suddenly she wanted to vomit.

Sixteen
Dancing With Truth

Urrana looked around at the crestfallen faces and drew herself up. "Madgi, have you any more of that spiced stew? I'll trade you the recipe for my spice bread for a winter's supply of whatever you put in it."

"Now there's a trade!" a Delver voice quipped.

Laughter broke the strained silence. The spice dealer Madgi scurried up, giggling in relief. Urrana turned away with her, the broad sweep of her skirts all but dusting the discord off the grass and away into the air for the wind to disperse. Delver and drover swirled together to resume their haggling. Huunall wandered off in the direction Fargoer had taken. The man who had been admiring Nuurn's carvings fairly dragged him away, his mask of indifference shattered in the need to bury the recent unpleasantness. Rununn touched Jetta's arm and hurried away toward his blanket that now had three people stooping over it.

"Old Man Fire," Setti breathed, and then caught a glimpse of Jetta's face. "Jetta! Are you all right?"

"Perfectly." Jetta's voice sounded strange even in her own ears.

"You don't look it. Are you worried about Fargoer? Don't. With Huunall behind you, what can he do?"

Unpleasant possibilities raced through Jetta's mind, but the thing was done. She might be misjudging Fargoer; panicked villagers and upheaval would not help his trade. She managed a smile and tucked her hand through Setti's arm. "Come on. I've a yen to look at hairpins. I lost all mine at Setham."

He looked at her hair falling in a blue-black flood over her shoulders. "Hairpins! Father Flame, Jetta, you just announced to the whole world a thing even the Circle doesn't know and now you want to buy hairpins?"

"Whether or not The Ancient burns the world to ash tomorrow, until then I would like to put my hair up occasionally with something more elegant than a scrap of leather."

His eyebrow shot up. Someone chuckled, very low, very soft. Jetta threw a startled look over her shoulder in time to see Sheshan disappearing into the crowd. She blinked, taken aback by the sight of him. The pale layered shirt had gone for a lowland tunic of shimmering sky-blue belted over a shirt the color of sea foam. The colors made him look like a creature of sky and water made somehow corporeal, and elegant beyond measure. The sense of loss at sight of his back moving away shocked her to inner stillness.

Setti's voice landed in her ear like a hot spark. "Are you in love with him?"

"What?" Jetta gawked up at him. "Father Flame, Setti! What could make your fire addled brain ask such a question!"

"You stare after him like a child after her first spark?"

Jetta froze, hunting an answer. "Because. . ." she shook her head. "You wouldn't understand."

"I understand a deal of things better than before I came to Annam, Jetta."

Jetta took in the darkening eyes, the unhappy set to his mouth. "Then you're luckier than I, journeyman of mine. I understand less, and what I've learned is mostly things I have no wish to know."

He looked away with such wretched misery in his face that her heart twisted inside her. "Oh, Setti! Please. We are friends, always we have been friends. Even if we cannot be more, never let us be less." She stopped and turned her face up to his. "We cannot be more. My heart is not free. Not for you, not for anyone. Can you understand? I need you. But by my side as a friend."

"Maybe it would be better," he said, very low, "if I ask the Circle to assign me elsewhere and send another Dancer here in my place."

She stared at him, stricken by the very notion. "I—no. Please don't."

"Why not?" He looked at her, his eyes haunted. "What good does it do anyone for me to remain here?"

"And who would there be to confuse The Ancient?"

Setti coughed, a strangled cross between a gasp and a grunt of pain. "Is that all I am to you? A jester to throw at the Old Man?"

"No! *No!*" The words tumbled out, a jumble of desperation and truth born of a thoughtless attempt at humor. She caught his wrist, filled with a driving need to make him see what had only now become clear to her. Sullenly he tried to pull away; she clamped her hand around his arm, digging her fingers ruthlessly into muscles that clenched to stone against her. "I mean that! Nuurn was right about the Circle. They sent me here because they wanted a young master to assess the Old Man's newest tricks, a master not so set in her ways that she would stand and stupidly fall when fire refused to act as it should. And they sent you, because you have what other journeymen do not—"

"A decided lack of talent," he said bitterly.

"A stubborn streak as wide as the sea!"

His head jerked and he stared down at her, his dark brows twitching tighter together. She forced him to listen, to hear what a lifetime of taunts had taught him to disbelieve. "Who else in all the Clans has worked harder to attain his rank? And who else would be so stubborn—or so desperate— as to invent a new Dance from pieces of the old to force mastery to fit his skill? Your mind is open. *That's* why you were chosen to come here where the Circle suspected old ways would prove useless. Because you could see past the end of your nose. Don't prove me wrong. Don't wrap yourself in your hurt and wound us both more than we already are."

"Jetta..." Remorse crept into his face. "I never wanted to hurt you."

"Nor I you."

She looked into his face and away, embarrassed. Abruptly they both became aware of folk passing to either side, leaving a respectful open space around the Firedancers but their eyes sliding sideways in wordless curiosity. Setti reddened; he drew himself up and gently out of her grip on his arm.

"I should go patrol."

She caught him back. "The whole village is out and about.

There will be ample warning should the Old Man dare to show his face. Walk with me. Will you leave me to enjoy the fest alone?"

His face turned to her, piteously confused. "Make up your mind, Jetta! Will you have me or no?"

She fought the urge to show her frustration in a sigh. "I will have you for a friend, now and for always. If more grows from it, then let it come in its own time. You cannot force anything else."

He stilled. Eyes still shot through with a misty hint of childish blue dropped to the battered silver promise bracelet on her wrist. Slowly he nodded.

"You're right. I'm sorry—"

"Apologize once more and I *will* send you home. Am I clear, a'Kam?"

A smile touched his mouth. "Yes, ak'Kal."

"Then let us walk. Folk are staring."

Hesitantly he offered her his arm again. She took it, forcing a smile onto her lips. "The spice bread sounds good after all. Shall we find some?"

"I thought you wanted to look at hairpins."

"Later. Food first. I need strength after that scene with Fargoer."

Setti's eyes darkened. "The man is a fool. And arrogant, and rude, to attack you so. He doesn't even know you!"

"Should we trouble ourselves over a fool?" she asked, with more complacence than she felt. "Here." She handed him the little Dancer. "Hold onto this for me, will you? I don't want to lose it."

He put it carefully away in his belt pouch. "Look. Folk are buying from Rununn. Look at him blush!"

Anual stepped around a wagon. "There you are!" she shouted. Heads turned. "I've been looking for you, Jetta. Dannal has some gorgeous cloth this year, and I've a mind to make you some clothes in keeping with your rank. Your work shirts would shame a First Rank apprentice."

Jetta stared. "But they're just for working, Anual. You don't have to—"

"My gift, Dancer, for keeping this village fire-free. Come now." Briskly she caught Jetta's other arm and towed them both away to the same wagon full of cloth bales whose owner had been so sullen. He was all smiles now, anxiously falling over himself to pull out a bolt of yellow cloth embroidered with tiny black leaves and vines.

"Ha!" Anual said triumphantly as Jetta's face lit up. "A woman's heart does beat under those Dance leathers. Stand aside, Setti, this is woman's business."

Setti laughed. "Then I'll leave you to it. Jetta, I'll find us that spice bread."

"Setti—"

"I'll be back." He smiled down at her and made off with a long loose stride that reminded her of her father when he danced. *He will make master yet,* she thought, jolted by the truth in it.

Anual's hand on her arm drew her back to the spill of bright cloth on the drover's table. She forgot Setti in a vain attempt to dissuade the Delver woman from adding two more bolts to the pile, one in red, one in clearest, heart-catching blue like an autumn sky. It reminded her of Sheshan; guilt froze her tongue for a critical instant, so that Anual seized on the silence and added it to the tally.

"Now folk will know our Dancer's rank just by looking at her," Anual said in deep satisfaction, gesturing for the drover to make his cuts and bundle up the lot.

Jetta stared. "Do you mean—"

Anual snorted. "Folk judge by appearances, ak'Kal. And there you were, trailing into the inn in dusty linens an apprentice would have scorned, half the height of a Delver child and half as willing. What were they to think?"

"Oh," Jetta said faintly, only now seeing through Delver eyes. "Unwilling?"

"Your heart was still raw, plain to see for those who looked," Anual said more gently. "Your Circle did us all a favor, sending you here, but it was not so obvious that first night. What was your mother thinking, sending you here in those rags?"

"She had no choice, as I recall," Jetta said ruefully. "I took out half of what she packed. But she had the last say." Her hand brushed the fine green dress and the heavy sweep of skirts.

Anual laughed. "A wise woman, your mother. Oh, this yellow will do you proud, child." She fingered a corner of it before it vanished into the stout linen wrapping cloth, smiling with such genuine pleasure that Jetta's misgivings vanished. She thought of Anual's son, her only child, born in a house built in hopes of many more and gone now forever, and realized that Anual would take great joy in the making.

"Thank you," she said, so warmly that Anual turned the color of the new-turned earth at the mine and hefted the package like a wall between them.

"Small repayment for keeping the whole place from burning down." She grinned around a corner of the course linen wrappings. "Why don't you go and see what Gadge has to offer? Third wagon down that way."

She nodded to her left. Jetta saw only another drover wagon surrounded by a crowd of Delvers who blocked her view of whatever was on offer there. "All right," she said, but Anual had vanished with the surprising silent grace inborn in Delvers.

Jetta shrugged and edged around the rear of the crowd until Rununn noticed her and elbowed her a path with scant regard for manners. "I sold all my carvings!" he whispered, so ecstatic that heads turned, grinning. Jetta walked in his wake, smiling to herself. Friends like Rununn made life so much easier. She ended up between him and Hunnood standing at the front with the child Hannahth perched on his shoulder, an ivory bird with a golden crown. She smiled at Jetta around the thumb in her mouth, clearly unafraid of heights. The journeymen towered on either side of Jetta like needle trees over a blade of grass; she smiled up at them, then instantly forgot them both as a flash of bright motion drew her eye to what had so enthralled the crowd.

Sheshan stood at one point of a triangle facing Ayesh and Wyth, the pair of them also decked in festival finery, deep forest green on Ayesh, silvery gray like the glint of distant streams on Wyth. A low table filled with a jumble of shiny balls and fanciful cubes of glass stood between them and the onlookers, with a drover leaning against a tall wagon wheel behind them, grinning in delight. The three Windriders seemed rooted in place, their hands held chest height, only their fingers moving. A score of the glass balls floated and spun in the open space between them, held aloft by nothing Jetta could see. They swirled and bobbed in a racing pattern so fast that she could barely follow any one of them with her eye. The sun caught fiery sparks from crystal facets and flung them in a scatter of colored light across the faces of the Windriders, the grass, the wagon, the table. Occasionally one of the balls seemed to slip, but never actually fell, snatched back by one or other of the Riders.

"What is happening?" Jetta murmured to Rununn.

He grinned. "Masters' game," he said in a whisper that carried like thunder. "Ayesh challenged the other two. Whoever lets one slip has to pay for the lot."

Jetta eyed the number of balls spinning in the triangle and reckoned it was going to be an expensive game. The drover looked unworried; likely he was pleased to have drawn such a crowd, and at any rate, he was out nothing even if they let the whole lot crash. The balls crept higher, from chest to shoulder height, to head height and on up, until the three Windriders were squinting into the sun riding high overhead.

"Now it gets interesting," Hunnood muttered.

Abruptly a small red ball spun out of control. "Not likely, Wyth!" Ayesh cried. The red globe shot skyward, only to stop as if snatched from the air by an unseen hand. Sheshan laughed, and three more spun out of the pattern, darting like bright birds toward Ayesh and Wyth. Two twirled into a tight dance scarcely a hand's breadth from Wyth's face; the third swooped gracefully back into the pattern and was lost in the dizzy swirl.

Without warning the whole pattern broke apart. Balls swooped and dove, escaping the tight little wind spinning the grass into a tangle at the Windriders' feet. The crowd gasped and then began to laugh, cheering the Riders on. Still as silent as the sky overhead, the masters strove to regain control against the determined efforts of the others. Jetta caught her breath as a globe grazed Sheshan's cheek before he spun it away. His face drew tight with concentration, but a smile lingered on his lips; he was actually enjoying this mad and dangerous game.

Ayesh swayed aside as two balls dove at his head and swooped around his ears like demented flutterbys. He flicked one of them toward Wyth, who never moved, but suddenly all the balls ceased their random darting and shot straight up. A collective gasp blew across the meadow and every head craned skyward, squinting in anxious search for the return of the globes. Ayesh and Sheshan looked too; a small smile creased Wyth's mouth.

And then the globes fell like rain, streaking down in a scatter of color and movement almost too fast to track. Ayesh yelped and flung his hands up as if spreading a net; Sheshan made a queer, sinking motion with one hand. The balls slowed as if suddenly falling through mud. They settled quite gently to the grass, all but one, that spun lazily up and settled into a spin in front of Ayesh at eye level, a gentle, wordless accuser.

Ayesh flung up his hands and started to laugh. Sheshan clasped his hands in front of him and inclined his head to Wyth. "Your victory, Master," he said, smiling.

And Wyth, grim Wyth, laughed and let the last ball settle gently to earth. A gust of wind, released from his control, kissed Jetta's cheek and lifted the hair from her forehead. "That should teach some here to challenge their betters," he said, sliding a sideways glance at Ayesh.

"You had to work at it, ak'Kal," Ayesh said with a grin.

"Not as hard as some here," Wyth said blandly, turning to the drover. "I'll have this one." The last globe shot up to his hand, blue with a tracing of gold in a random spiral across its surface.

"Take it, ak'Kal, to mark your victory," the drover said. "And a fine game."

"That it was." Wyth plucked the ball out of the air and strolled away.

Jetta stared after him, dumbfounded. The crowd swooped in to snatch up balls from the grass and thrust them at the drover, demanding prices. Windriders at play was a rare sight, it seemed, and the souvenirs to be cherished.

Jetta turned away, thinking about that laugh on Wyth's lips. Somewhere in the lowlands a village had stolen the Windrider's laughter, as indifferent as Hylli Fargoer to injustice. Suddenly her eyes prickled with tears for losses neither of them had been able to prevent.

"Jetta?"

Setti's voice startled her upright in a flurry of skirts. She almost tripped in her haste; his hand caught her, warm and solid under her elbow.

"Are you crying? What's happened?"

"Nothing! I looked up just now and got a face full of sun." That was truth, if not all of it.

He frowned down at her, his hands full of spice bread and two mugs that could only be full of noë, by the scent. "Has someone said something to you? Has Fargoer come back?"

"No, I think Huunall has him somewhere, pounding sense into him." Gaily she stood up and relieved him of one of the mugs, burying her face in its steaming depths with genuine gratitude. She let the first sip settle on her tongue and closed her eyes in bliss. "Oh, this is good. Thank you."

Slowly his face cleared. He set his own mug on the wagon seat and tore a huge chunk off the loaf of spice bread and handed it to her. "Urrana sent this. She said to eat up because there will be dancing later, and you'll need your strength."

He laughed at the look on her face. "Come now, a Dancer afraid to dance?"

"With the Old Man? No. With some stone-footed drover? Yes!"

"Then I'll have to save you from such a fate. For *I* know how to avoid stepping on a woman's toes." He made a grand gesture with one hand and put on a mincing smirk. "A Dancer has other duties than keeping the Old Man in his placc. A Danccr must sprcad good will as wcll as kccp his charge fire free, for without the cooperation of the village The Ancient will surely gain footing. Therefore you will dance with the headman's ungainly wife, and enjoy it, too!"

By the end Jetta was laughing, remembering Minna's ferocious lessons in Dancer duty. She set her mug down and raised both hands in the first position of the Dance. "And you, Jetta Vettahrsi, take that scowl off your face and bend your elbows!"

Setti collapsed onto the tongue of the wagon, his face alight with laughter and reminiscence. "She was a terror, wasn't she? I miss her still."

"So do I." Jetta smiled gently at the ground. Those had been magic days, the three of them running wild in the old stone house across from her own, she and Kori and Setti, until Minna would catch them and ruthlessly set them to another lesson in deportment. "Can you see her here, among these giants? If they had trouble accepting me, think how they would have greeted her."

"She would just have punched Burrood in the knee and got on with the job," Setti said, wringing a snort of laughter from Jetta. "You're a lot like her, you know."

"Me?" Jetta turned her head to stare. "I think not!"

"I think so." Setti laughed at her expression. "Minna never backed down from The Ancient in her life, nor from anyone lesser, either. Neither have you."

Her eyebrow shot up. "How could I back down from Burrood and let his stupidity ruin this whole village?"

Setti smiled a smug smile. "And *that* is why the Circle sent you."

She looked away. "And because they didn't want me moping around the Vale anymore."

"It worked, didn't it?" He shot her a quick, sideways glance. "It's good to see you smile, Jetta. It's been too long."

"Yes. It has."

His eyebrows shot up in amazement that drew a rueful chuckle from her. "Close your mouth, Setti. It's been a day for revelations, and I've come to a few conclusions."

"Such as?" he asked warily.

"Such as I can think of worse places to spend my life than Annam Vale, among these people."

He cocked his head quizzically. "You think the Circle won't recall us? I thought this was a temporary assign—" He caught his breath, a funny little catch of realization. With The Ancient running loose, Annam would never be fire-free again.

Somewhere close behind Jetta, a drum boomed, so loud they both spun around into the first movement of the Dance, hunting the source of that rolling thunder. Jetta stopped, flushing hot in embarrassment as a drover woman trilled the long, melodious cry that announced the end of trade. Pipes and a flute twined into a sprightly tune she knew. Around her the crowd started to swirl inward toward the sound of the drum. Jetta glimpsed a cleared space in the center of the wagons' circle, and looked up at Setti with a sly smile.

"Still want to dance, a'Kam?"

His face still wore that hard, uncompromising look. He

stared at the backs drifting away from them as though he wished them all in the lowlands, and then he looked down at her with a reckless grin. He caught her hand. "Why not? It's up to us to set a good example. Come on!"

Misgivings overtook Jetta; she did not know this mood in him. But he was already towing her across the meadow, grinning ear to ear. Folk made way for them, catching his smile and laughing back. Setti caught her other hand as they broke into the open space in front of the musicians, whirling her into a lowland dance brought to Firehome Vale by some returning Dancer long ago. Reflexively Jetta fell into its rhythm, her feet finding the steps unbidden, as she had danced with Setti and Kori when they were children. Setti's laugh infected her with joy. Almost, the years since childhood fell away, and they were only Setti and Jetta again, not journeyman and master, with nothing strained between them.

Three more couples whirled onto the dance ground, drovers all, the women for once in skirts of the rich rainbow colors that made them look like the flowers adorning Delver windows. Rununn appeared with a Delver girl in a blue dress stitched with yellow flowers, her face red with embarrassment that did not, Jetta noted, stop her from prancing as merrily as Rununn. The flute skirled up and up, the pipes spun the tune, and the drum set toes tapping all over the meadow before the dance ended in a crash from the drum. Setti snatched Jetta up by the waist and tossed her into the air, caught her again and spun her around in sheer excess of good spirits.

The onlookers cheered. Jetta flushed but Setti only grinned wider and flipped them an airy salute that drew a general laugh. The music started up again, drawing a rush of dancers. Setti reached for Jetta's hand but she laughingly fended him off.

"Oh, no! One of us has to be fit to dance with the Old Man if needed. Go spread some goodwill among the drover girls. Can't you feel their eyes all but burning you?"

His eyes widened. Jetta laughed and slipped away as he twisted a look over his shoulder. Three girls giggling near the musicians were watching him, so admiring that Jetta wondered how he really didn't feel scorched by them.

The sun hovered above Wind Point, setting shadows creeping together under the wagons. Clouds burned red and gold in the west. Torches came out, tame fire burning in safe globes of iron open only in the front so that flame could not leap onto the wagons and run mad. She eyed the nearest, no longer trusting the docility of harnessed flame, but it chewed contentedly on the oil in the base of the torch and showed no sign of running amok. She wandered among the wagons, listening to the music and laughter behind her, and felt decadently free.

"Jetta ak'Kal," a voice called. Jetta stiffened, thinking of Fargoer, but it was the cloth seller, beckoning conspiratorially with a broad grin. "For you," he said, handing her a jeweled hairpin with a head shaped like a flutterby, all rich greens and blues laced with gold. Jetta eyed it in pure delight.

"How did you know I was wanting hairpins?" she asked, fumbling for absent coins.

He waved her apology away. "I was told to give you this, ak'Kal. And fine it will look in your hair." His admiring eyes lifted to the shining black mass of it.

Jetta, harboring embarrassing suspicions about whose hand had sent the pin, blushed and found herself tongue-tied for one of the few times in her life. "I—thank you," she managed. "And to whoever sent the pin."

With a knowing wink the drover took it from her nerveless fingers, expertly twisted up a lock of her hair, and pinned it in place. "There," he said. "Now everyone will want one."

Jetta, her face burning, slid away, fighting a traitorous pleasure in being admired for something besides her skill at the Dance. *Mother would be pleased,* she thought wryly, so intent on escaping she failed to watch where she was going. Thus she managed to round a wagon and crash head-on into Wyth in the darkness beyond.

"Father Flame! Ak'Kal, your pardon. I didn't see you."

"Nor I you, obviously." A wintry smile touched his mouth, given color by the ruddy torches. "No harm done. Why aren't you enjoying the dancing?"

"I dance enough at other times. I would sooner watch."

He turned his head to look at hopeful traders still haggling with the diminished crowd in the circles of torchlight. "I suppose one should see new faces now and again," he said indifferently. "If only to remind one of the joys of familiar company."

"The Delvers are good people. I am glad of this assignment."

Pale eyes turned to hers. "And they are fortunate in their Dancer. Good evening." He went on by, leaving her gaping in his wake.

Jetta stared after him, almost doubting her ears. "Progress," she muttered, and suddenly felt like dancing again. She turned toward the music and the dancers now casting wild shadows in the flaring light. A drover appeared at her elbow, his smile half challenge, half invitation. Jetta lifted her chin and let him spin her away into the crowded space lit by captive flame. Another man claimed her after that, then Setti found her. Recklessly she gave him her hand, and they found in the music a new dance, one born of old patterns and new and founded on the great Dance that was the purpose of their lives. Jetta began it but Setti followed as though he could see into her mind, matching her so quickly it looked as though they had rehearsed. Step for step, flawless mirrors one for the other, they cleared the dance ground as other couples gave them room in growing awe. Something seemed to click into place; unlike the night of the heartstones, Setti's dance felt like an extension of hers, a partnership akin to what she had felt when she and Kori danced fire together. The music lifted her out of herself, cleared her head of worry and doubt, let her simply revel in the rhythms bred into her bones. Stamp and spin, a circle back to back, Setti's strong hands twirling her aloft and catching her as easily as Wyth had caught the glass ball. She smiled into his intent eyes and whirled away, laughing when he caught her back.

The music spiraled up and up and ended without warning, leaving her hand in hand with Setti, at full arm's stretch away from each other, each dependent on the other for balance. Out of breath, and slow to pull out of the music's spell, Jetta looked into his laughing face, and only then realized how great a fool she had been.

Trills and hoots and stomps of approval washed over them. Setti laughed and held Jetta's hand up, giving her the credit; Jetta blushed and swiped at him, drawing laughter and a flood of people onto the dance ground. She dragged Setti away since he would not let go of her hand, and stood in the cool darkness by a wagon watching another dance begin.

"That was fun," Setti said. "Like being home again."

"But we're not," Jetta said softly.

He leaned against the wagon, his eyes on the dancers. His face looked carved from fire, painted with torchlight, his eyes catching sparks. "We're good for each other, Jetta, you know we are. Could the Windrider have danced with you as I did?"

"No," she said. "But it means only that we know each other well, Setti. No more."

He shoved himself away from the wagon. "I need food," he muttered, and strode away into the darkness, his back so stiff Jetta wondered that he could move at all.

We will not dance like that again, she thought with a little pang of regret. Oh, why could she not love him as he wanted her to?

The music changed to a song she had last heard in Setham, a lively, swooping thing with a hundred verses. A drover began to sing, a passable tenor that nevertheless jarred against her ear. It should be a baritone, rich and true, answering the urging of every villager in Setham to sing a ballad Jetta had loved. She caught her breath on exquisite pain, realizing she could not remember the exact sound of Kori's voice.

The dancers blurred in her sight; she turned away, hardly seeing the broad Delver bodies that stepped aside for her. Darkness enfolded her, she slipped through the circle of wagons and out the other side, not aware where her feet took her until she found herself beside the waterfall, panting from the climb. Grimly she stared over the edge at the water smashing into the pool, and then gathered up the heavy skirts and sat down on her usual boulder. The stone chilled her rump even through the green cloth; Jetta refused to move. She sat there twisting the silver bracelet on her wrist around and around, staring over the lights and the music at the ridge hiding the long drop to the lowlands, and Setham Vale, and Kori's ashes.

She could not weep, though her throat ached with trying.

Nor could she quite grasp such injustice, that the mind could not retain the clarity of vision and sound that would keep her lifemate alive in the forefront of her mind, could not maintain the sharpness of grief that had kept his voice, his face, in front of her day and night for a year.

Jetta bowed her head, her eyes closed to try and force those images to come clear. But only bright edges came: the quick curve of a smile, the lift of a dark eyebrow. The whole eluded her like water running through her fingers, so unfair that a little whimper escaped her, lost in the rumble of water over the falls.

Does Wyth still feel this way? she wondered, cringing from the thought. A lowland village had burned his soul to ash. Three years, seven years, a hundred without laughter or joy. Jetta soared to her feet, disturbed to her bones—and there sat Sheshan behind her, silent as stone on his chosen rock. His eyes glinted pale in the clear light of the lesser moon rising over the road; he looked at her and then away, lending her privacy in that odd way of his.

"It was a good song," he said. "But hardly beautiful enough for tears."

It surprised a laugh from her that came out half a sob. "I wasn't crying."

"But you wanted to."

She gave him a sideways look, wondering how he always knew. "Yes." She sighed. "I don't seem to have any more tears."

"There comes a time when the mind decides to look forward and not back. It doesn't seem to matter what the heart thinks, once the mind chooses that road. We are carried along whether we will it or no."

For once the flooding moonlight caught his lean face in perfect alabaster clarity. Jetta had never seen quite that look on it before, of resignation and regret. *It is hard to lose a mate.* The words she had thought trite comfort suddenly hit her hard enough that she landed back on her boulder with a jarring thump. In confusion Jetta looked into the dark water catching moon sparkles in its ripples as it rushed past her feet. Eventually she found words around the odd tightness in her throat.

"And when in these past three years did yours start to

carry you forward?"

The rocks around them seemed no more still than he. Then he took in a deep breath that drew shimmering glints from the rich stuff of his tunic, and said, very low, "On the trail from Wind Point."

Jetta stared. "What?"

His mouth quirked. "I saw a woman there, bedraggled, soaking wet, her hair plastered to her skull like a crone's, vomiting over a cliff in the rain from dizziness and still refusing to be carried, and I thought, 'Why does she go on fighting?' And for the first time since that day on a cliff beside the sea, I found myself curious. It was such an odd feeling I found myself investigating it, encouraging it, actively seeking it. It made a welcome change from being numb. Now I find I can scarcely live without it."

The tears she had not been able to shed for Kori blurred Jetta's vision. "That day by the sea," she whispered. "What happened to her?"

Sheshan did not move his head or alter his position on the rock, but she sensed him hunching against pain, and waited quietly through a long silence. "She died. With many, many others. Even the sea folk do not remember such a storm as that. It flung itself at the shore like a great, malicious beast, savagely angry at anything that stood in its way. It tore at the land, raised up waves so tall they pounded the tops of cliffs a hundred fathoms above the sea and washed the rivers back impossible distances, threatening to scour the whole coast clean. We lost nearly our whole clan that day, but together with the Water Clans we turned back the storm, forced it to turn away from the land and back upon itself. We spread the winds thinner and thinner until they no longer had the power to do harm nor the will to come together and try again. But the damage was done. The storm had found the cave where the sea folk swore it could not come, the one that sheltered our old ones, our children, and those like Fythia who had stayed behind to protect them. We found it full of water, with their hair floating on the waves like pale seaweed..."

He broke off, looking inward at a memory as horrible as anything Jetta could set against it. Her hand flew to touch the flutterby hairpin. She caught her breath, wondering how he could even look at a woman's hair ever again.

"I never knew," she said, very low. "Even Anual never told me that."

"She teased us once about fleeing from our women. I fear Wyth was not kind, though he sought her pardon later. In a way it's true. All of us lost mates or sisters or mothers that day. None of us had the heart to go seeking another clan in hopes of finding those things again."

"So you came here, where you cannot smell the sea," Jetta guessed. "Ayesh's clean wind."

"Yes." He lifted his face and drew a long, slow breath. "I could spend a year just breathing."

Jetta drew her knees up and rested her chin on crossed arms. "Do you plan to stay in exile forever?"

"Exile?" His head turned. "There is need for us here."

"But no others of your kind. Your ranks are already few."

"So I should just go blithely find a mate?" For the first time since the night he first walked her home she heard anger in his voice. "Did you?"

"That's—" *Not fair*, she meant to say, but swallowed it. She too, had been hiding.

"No. But it would be a sad and dangerous thing, were there no more Windriders in the world."

"There are other clans. It was our misfortune, is all, that we were closest when the sea folk sent for help. It was our duty to answer, as it is yours to dance in Annam Vale."

"My duty took me out of myself. Where will yours take you?"

The moon chose that instant to go behind a cloud, frustrating Jetta because she could no longer see his face. Only his shoulders moved, a shrug that set his tunic shimmering. "Where the wind takes us. While Annam has need, here we will stay."

"And after?"

He turned his head, his eyes a pale gleam. "Can you say there will be an after? The Ancient has found Annam. Unless you propose to dig out every smallest pebble of windstone, there will always be danger of fire from now on. A lifetime commitment, it seems to me."

Jetta looked around at the mountains and the stars and breathed in the heady rush of flower-scented wind. "There are worse places," Sheshan said quietly.

"Yes." Jetta slid him a sideways look. "Thank you. For telling me about your clan. I understand many things now." She touched the hairpin. "And for this."

He stood up, looking down at her with his straight, strong profile silhouetted against the larger moon. "Things of grace belong together. I am glad you came to Annam Vale, Jetta ak'Kal. I find it—refreshing—to look forward instead of back. Good night."

He stepped down through the rocks as lightly as the night going on its way. Jetta watched his moon-kissed hair disappear around the first bend in the street, her fingers tracing the delicate outlines of the pin in her own. What had it cost him to buy it? Certainly far more than whatever its price in silver.

Below in the meadow, the dancers still stamped and whirled to music drowned in the voice of the waterfall. Jetta saw Setti's red-clad form whirling with them, partnered with a drover girl in a pale dress. Relieved that he had not come looking for her, she turned away, her own taste for merriment fled on a vision of drowned children. She picked her way through the rocks and slipped in at Nuurn's door. With a shade of regret she shed the green dress and the beautiful pin, braided her hair up and donned her mundane leathers. She knew she would not sleep. Might as well patrol.

Folk were starting to drift back up the hill. Jetta, clad in her cloak against the mountain chill, turned away from a gaggle of broad Delver forms coming up the street and doubled back over the bridge below the falls, cutting down across the hill to check the houses north of the stream. Overhead, the moons danced their silent, graceful dance, enfolding the night into their silver light. Intent on keeping her footing amid the confusing shadows among the rocks, she did not see Kettori until her voice dropped like icy rain out of the night.

"So you do remember your duty, Dancer. I had wondered, watching you and your journeyman prancing together. The Old Man would have relished eating the festival finery off the pair of you."

Jetta stopped, stung by a rebuke this fire-touched old hag had no right to make. "It is no business of yours, Kettori ak'Kal."

The old Dancer stepped out of the night, a shadow wrapped in the fringed shawl. "This is my home now. Should it burn to the ground it would assuredly be my business."

"You have the skill to stop it." Jetta strained to see her face, but Kettori had managed like always to wrap herself in mystery, a faceless shadow in the night.

"I dance no more," Kettori said shortly.

"And why is that?" Jetta stepped closer, suddenly minded to be as offensive as Kettori. "What drove you from the Dance, ak'Kal? Why did one of the greatest Dancers of her generation flee and leave her village to burn?"

Kettori drew back. "That is my affair and none of yours."

"Isn't it? You live in the village *I* am charged to protect. Is it coincidence that half a year after your coming fire appeared here for the first time? Does the Old Man know your name, Dancer?"

Kettori drew an audible breath. Jetta waited through an endless silence. The music from the dance ground drifted across the meadow, full of life and acute reminders of the precious things she was sworn to defend. She saw Kettori's head turn toward it, and knew she felt it too, the responsibility that never quite went away, no matter how far a Dancer ran.

"I didn't bring the fire," Kettori said finally, very low. Jetta started; she had expected no answer at all. She compressed her lips against questions, for having started, the old master went on, her voice a breathy whisper. "I came because I—I knew that fire must rise here eventually."

"What?" It escaped Jetta's lips before she could stop it. She cursed herself, fearing it would drive Kettori away, but the dark head turned toward her, a faint movement against the moon-hazed stars.

"This place, the only fire-free place in all the world. Where else would the Old Man fret and gnaw and probe with restless fingers, eternally seeking a way in? Long have I studied the ways of flame, Jetta ak'Kal, the ways outside the bounds of the Dance—where it attacked most diligently, where it was defeated most easily, where it would not come. I saw a pattern, one that disturbed me. I studied it longer, hoping I was wrong. But I was not wrong, for everywhere I predicted that fire would come, it came, even in the places where it had never been strong. Especially in the places it had never been strong. And always those places had felt tremors in the earth, sometimes years before the Old Man appeared. Always."

"So when you heard of the earthshakes here seven years ago?"

"I knew it was only a matter of time." Nervously Kettori twitched the shawl closer around her shoulders.

"I still don't understand. Why come here, after what happened in your own village?"

Kettori's voice snapped out of the darkness. "And what did happen, girl? Do you know? Have you heard that tale?"

"That Kettori ak'Kal abandoned her post? That fire then claimed the whole village? I've heard it. I could scarce believe it, but I heard it."

"It happened." The cold voice shattered around her like glass. "I fled from my vows. I fled from my charge. I fled the Dance. I fled because I knew that fire would come to my village, and that go or stay, I could make no difference there. I fled because I have met The Ancient face to face, and it *knew—my—name!*"

Jetta gaped. The night still hid Kettori's face. Only her voice seemed to hang in the darkness, the words twisting their way into Jetta's heart. "There is a saying, Kettori," she said carefully. "The Ancient is not intelligent—"

"Is it not?" Kettori's hand shot out of the shawl and clamped onto Jetta's shoulder with force enough to make her gasp. "I heard it! I heard it speak my name!"

She's mad, Jetta thought breathlessly. *Step carefully.*

"And that's why you left?" It pleased her that her voice neither shook nor sounded odd to her ears, though her guts were twisting. Kettori's fingernails felt like claws in her shoulder.

"I left in hopes it would follow me," Kettori said bleakly. "It didn't. It took the village instead."

"And so you came here, to the place you thought it might come next?" Jetta could not keep the incredulity from her voice. Kettori's hand left her shoulder as though burned.

"You are a child! You could not understand."

"Then help me to understand, ak'Kal! *Nothing* in Annam is as I was taught. All I know is that the Old Man is acting strangely, and nothing seems to work as it should and a Fourth Rank Dancer will not help me out of simple duty to her own kind. I need what you know and there you stand, pretending none of this is your affair."

Kettori snorted. "Third Rank, Fourth Rank—why strain yourself trying to achieve Fourth Rank mastery if nothing works? Bring your head back. There's mastery. For all the good it will do you."

Jetta caught her breath. Was that genuine advice, or just another bitter taunt? "Why come to Annam when you *will not help?*" she all but screamed in frustration.

But she was talking to the night. Kettori's silhouette became a glimpse of a shadow among the rocks higher up, and then there was only the moon-shot night.

"Father Flame!" Jetta snapped bitterly. "What was that about?"

But only the music and the wind answered.

Seventeen
Choices

Restless and angry, Jetta prowled the village, avoiding returning revelers. Visions of fire and a voice whispering her name from the heart of flame walked with her. She caught herself flinching from every glimpse of torchlight in the meadow, and cursed Kettori for planting images in her mind she could not readily shake.

Eventually the torches went out and the dancers fell into bed in the dark ring of wagons. Jetta wandered through them on her rounds, thinking of Hylli Fargoer in one of them, sleepless, perhaps, waiting for Jetta ak'Kal to fail her duty once again. His scorn burned her, all the worse because it was not baseless. Setham had died, and Annam still could, and *flame find Kettori*, why would she not simply lend a hand, or at the least tell what she knew? Why such maddening secrecy, when clearly she wanted someone to know what she knew?

Spare me from ever putting my own pride first, Jetta thought crossly, stalking on toward the storehouses. Her bare feet trod the warm dust of the dance circle, where the grass had been ground to bare dirt by the whirl and stomp of exuberant feet. And then guilt struck her, for she had put herself first for a year, cowering in Firehome, too ashamed even to venture out and talk to old friends like Setti. *And I did not even walk away and abandon Setham, but nearly died trying to save it.*

The truth did not comfort her. Two villages had died, and now Dancers were falling to tricks no one could predict. Why? She stopped at the end of the row of storehouses, frowning at the eastern ridge above the new mine. Dawn fingered the treetops up there, a hint of gray, a smear of light rivaling the moons fading in the west. Tomorrow the drovers would begin loading their wagons for the long trip back down the mountains. With them would go her letter to the Circle. She would have to add what Kettori had told her. What result would it bring? Jetta found that she was not sure she wanted to know.

The Ancient knew my name. Had Kettori meant that literally? What if she was not mad? It was true that fire had only come after the tremors here began. The quake that Anual's son had not been able to suppress—the quake that had killed him—had perhaps opened a door for The Ancient. But years had passed between the tremors and the appearance of flame. Or had they? How long had the Old Man raged in the tunnels under Wind Point before the Delvers had gone looking to reopen the old shafts? Weeks? Years? And was the tremor only a convenient key, or had The Ancient itself caused it?

Hair prickled up on her neck and arms. "That is not possible," she whispered to the fading night. "How could fire cause the tremors?" But if it were true that flame inevitably followed, then answers must be sought.

It came back to the timeless question of The Ancient. Was the Old Man intelligent or merely an opportunist? Jetta remembered the debates in class, the old masters wrangling amiably in the sun on the practice ground. Some, bearing the scars of too-close acquaintance with flame, argued passionately that the fire had outmaneuvered them, driven them, somehow outwitted them. Others insisted just as vehemently that only a Dancer's mistakes let The Ancient bring them to grief.

For the first time in over a year Jetta forced herself to think about that night in Setham: saying goodnight to Kori, going to bed in peaceful darkness, no hint in her mind of fire lurking anywhere within the village. Waking to screams and the awareness of fire beating at her mind, breaking through exhaustion and the leaden nausea brought on by the child in her womb. She remembered fright, the first she had ever known when facing fire, and confusion, for surprise was also new to her. And she remembered the fright changing to terror when she ran into the street and saw fire raging through the three new houses at the far end, the ones built of windstone that she had approved against all sense and custom. She remembered running, remembered people gathered in the street, faces staring, mouths shouting words she did not hear. All she heard were the screams, Kori's screams as the Old Man sprung its trap and caught a Firedancer in its claws. And when the screams abruptly fell silent, she remembered the voice, the roaring voice of The Ancient from the flames.

She stiffened, staring into the growing light over the ridge without seeing it. *Jetta ak'Kal.* She had thought it nightmare, fever dreams, perhaps the voice of the healer in that Water Clan hut above the sea. Even yet she was not sure, but the voice was there in her mind, deep, demanding, laden with wind and fire. *Jetta ak'Kal.*

She wrapped both arms around herself and stood shivering, heedless of the glory of color creeping into the eastern sky. "No," she whispered fiercely. "It can't be true! Fire is a mindless thing. Voiceless. Stupid. It's ruled by its hunger. It has no ability to plan."

But what if it does? A small voice in her head would not be convinced. *What if fire does think? Then what have the Fire Clans been fighting all these long ages since the Beginning? What have we been killing?*

Disturbed beyond measure, Jetta sank slowly onto her heels, her arms wrapped tight around her body in useless defense against the thoughts in her head. What was the enemy if not a thing to be fought and annihilated? Fire destroyed all it touched, and only the Dance allowed any other life to exist in the world. They could not co-exist, for each needed what the other must have to survive. Jetta thought of fire raging unchecked across the fields, the forests, blackening everything in its path. *Even if it won, it would die.* And yet the Old Man still fought to come to the surface, into the free air and the endless fuel it craved.

Mindless, indeed, she concluded, but still the doubt rode her. She thought of flame trapped in cookfire and torch and lantern, well-fed but unwilling, a slave to the needs of men, extinguished without a thought when it was no longer needed. Nausea coiled in her stomach; she swallowed hard, wondering if all this time they had been killing a living thing.

It has been killing us since the Beginning. The thought brought her no comfort. Legend spoke of the Beginning as a thing that could be measured; an event, as legends do when they cannot conceive the infinite. A story, yet founded in something like truth, for the Dance certainly existed, and it had held flame at bay for all of time. Legend said both Dancer and Ancient were bound to it, the single rule in a warfare otherwise waged without quarter. Dancers who failed died. Fire that could not break a Dancer's will did likewise. In that light, both sides had an even chance of victory. And yet, Jetta wondered. Could it be that the legends of the Beginning were only legends, and the Dance only a thing that had shaped itself over time, changing with every generation as The Ancient found new ways around it?

"No," she whispered. In such case every Dancer would know. Every Dancer would be aware that patterns changed, that the Dance they learned as children might not be the one they would dance in their prime. But neither did masters dance as beginners did, nor Fourth Rank the same as Third Rank. Jetta frowned, drawn to examine a thing she had never questioned. A child mastered the forms of First Rank and moved on to journeyman of the Second. First Rank knew the tricks of infant flame, how to call it, how to kill it, how to predict which way it would run. A First Rank never left the clan, for it would be murder to send one to face fire alone. A Second Rank journeyman must be able to stop a *hysth* from forming, but what happened after that was a master's business. She thought of Setti in a circle of fire that day in the storehouse, bravely inventing forms to quell a demon beyond his scope, and shuddered, appalled at how she had pushed him. *Hysths* were a master's business, for *hysths* were the children of The Ancient, cunning, malevolent, the gateway for the Old Man. A Second Rank master might tame them in their infant stage, but let them combine...

I am Third Rank because I vanquished a circle of hysths *that grew too quickly for Kori to control.* She remembered that day too well, when flame sprang up nearly under Kori's feet, leaping from a knob of windstone recently exposed by a farmer's plow. It had leaped into a farm cart and from there raged into the field, a wall of yellow flame running madly toward the village itself. Jetta recalled how it had fled from Kori, the scattered, wind-blown tufts of fire racing together into a circle, rearing high in the center of the field. While Kori chased the remnants, she had confronted the *hysth* soaring three times her height and turning white at its heart. White, the color of The Ancient.

It is for Fourth Rank to face The Ancient, she thought, chilled. *I should not have been able to subdue it that day.*

Had she danced a Fourth Rank dance that summer afternoon at Setham? She could not remember. Surely she had been studying them, but was it that which had driven the *hysth* to dust before the Old Man could fully form, or had she improvised as she had done here in Annam? It troubled her intensely that she could not remember what steps she had performed, lost as she had been in confronting the flame.

Disturbed, she shed her cloak and stood up, facing the band of color creeping over the eastern ridge. Shivering, she slowly lifted her arms. She raised herself onto her toes, found solid balance, and lifted her left knee. Immediately her right leg began to cramp; she ignored it, focused on the fingers of rose and orange reaching over the distant trees to grab the stars. She watched the light grow, forcing her mind to empty, to think of nothing at all but the dew-chilled grass under the ball of her foot, connecting her to the Mother that had spawned all things. Muscles protested; she forced them to relax, letting light fill her eyes, her mind, her soul. Light like fire, but harmless, beneficent, bringing illumination to the world. She forgot to blink, and then to breathe.

Bring your head back. Kettori's bitter advice leaped into her mind from nowhere. Slowly, because it felt as if any move would throw her straight to the ground, Jetta relaxed the muscles of her neck and let her head tip, just a little. And as though the movement had shifted something in her mind, without warning the tension setting mind and muscle and nerve at war melted into harmony. She gasped in the sudden, pounding rush of power blazing up through that slender connection of earth and flesh.

Stunned by having finally mastered this impossible position, she nearly lost it before she thought to close her eyes and simply bask in the cool sense of endless stone under her, the living fastness of forest breathing into her nostrils, the touch of wind on her face. Relaxed, centered, every nerve thrummed with quiet joy. Wrapped in the Mother's embrace, she felt an overpowering urge to stamp her foot down and call The Ancient. Let it challenge her; let it rage! The *Mother* knew her name!

And on that flash of arrogance she did lose her center. The connection snapped as suddenly as it came. Jetta gasped and hurriedly set her left foot down before she ended in a humiliating tumble straight down the hill.

She opened her eyes, staring into the sunrise. "Old Man Fire," she whispered, torn between conflicting winds of exultation and chagrin. No wonder Kettori had said the Mother's touch could burn as well as bless. How many Dancers had flung themselves into the face of The Ancient, certain of their own invincibility?

Yet she could not deny the tenfold increase in awareness, in sheer power and connection to the Mother and the Dance itself. Surely, connected to that, a Dancer could laugh in The Ancient's face.

"So if Fourth Rank is sufficient to subdue The Ancient," she muttered. "Then what is Fifth Rank for?"

"Fifth Rank *makes* the Dance," Sheshan's voice said behind her.

She spun around, startled as he had never startled her before. He took a step back, surprised in turn. "Forgive. I thought you knew I was here."

"Don't you *ever* sleep?"

He draped the red cloak around her shoulders. "I could ask the same of you. That was," he smiled, "incredible to watch. And very beautiful."

Jetta's face heated. She turned away, fumbling with the cloak pin. "What did you mean, Fifth Rank makes the Dance?"

She closed her eyes in relief when his voice came back, steady and neutral. "Did you never wonder how masters are chosen?"

She frowned and turned to look at him. He stood with the inner stillness that seemed a mark of a Rider, no longer in his shimmering finery. His feathery blue shirt fluttered in the dawn breeze lifting out of the Vale. Spider-silk hair glinted gold in the sunrise that made his eyes seem very blue, very intense, as he turned his head slightly to meet her gaze.

"I—no, not really. I presumed it was on merit."

"Then why do some stay Third Rank all their lives, even

though they are often capable of meeting challenges far greater?"

Jetta felt her brows pulling tighter, and consciously smoothed the frown away. "Some never study for Fourth Rank. Kori was content at Second."

"Contentment. Yes." Sheshan looked up into a sky still pale with the sun not yet clear of the ridge, fragile blue like fine, thin glass. "Some do not want to progress, for with greater rank comes greater danger. I was surprised to learn that you are Third Rank, not Fourth. I would have expected the Fire Clans to send someone of higher rank to Annam."

"I was all they had," Jetta said, trying to make light of it.

"Are you?" His wandering gaze returned to her, intent as a raptor's. "Were there no retired Fourth or even Fifth Rank Dancers available to come and see what lurked in Annam Vale?"

"Well yes, but..." Jetta floundered in confusion. "The Circle is all Fifth Rank, but they are the *Circle!* They don't go on assignment. They're too valuable to risk."

"And why are they valuable, they who have defeated even The Ancient and have seen all the Old Man's tricks? Why should they fear to go afield?"

Jetta blinked. "They're not afraid. Someone has to teach the First Ranks."

He smiled into her confusion. "Yes. But Fifth Rank rarely teaches, at least among Windriders. We seldom see Fifth Ranks except in the greatest storms. I saw three together once, two Windriders and a Firedancer, years ago when a great storm converged with an outbreak of fire in the south. I was only a boy then, and I was frightened of that Dancer. His eyes were entirely black, even more so than yours. As if fire had eaten them."

"Norlahk," Jetta said with certainty. "He is the greatest of us."

"Is he?" He smiled at her, warming away the chill in Jetta's gut. "I warrant he sits in the Circle, does he not? And decides who will be what rank?"

"Yes. But I don't see—"

"Think, Jetta." He unclasped his hands and leaned down toward her, his eyes intent. "The most successful make rank, but only the best of those make it to Fifth Rank. Why?

Because only the creative ones, the ones who don't acknowledge limitations, the ones who are not content with where they are, are worthy to advance that high. And when they arrive, do you suppose all they do is sit around and argue about who to promote?"

Jetta stared at him. "They create the Dance? That's mad."

"Is it? Yesterday I had no business playing the masters' game with Wyth. He is my superior in every way. But I remembered how you said you had improvised against The Ancient, that the old forms of the Dance were not enough. So I—experimented. There at the end, when I caught the balls—that was nothing I learned from my teachers. I might not have thought of it were it not for you, because you do not mindlessly bind yourself to tradition. And so I say that Fifth Rank makes the Dance, for who teaches Fourth Rank, which teaches Third, which teaches Second, which passes on those forms to First?"

Jetta froze, caught inward into a memory of Minna muttering and carping at her class as she drove them through the patterns of the Dance, cursing Norlahk for thinking he knew best.

"Then it's true," she murmured. "That the Beginning is only legend and the Dance evolves to check the Old Man as needed. So what is The Ancient, Sheshan? I have a terrible feeling."

"What?" he asked after a moment of lingering silence.

She hesitated, unwilling to say it aloud, and then blurted, "Fire is alive. I've always known that. But now I begin to believe it thinks."

She dared not look at him. The silence stretched, broken only by the snorting of cart beasts in the meadow. Sunlight kissed the rocks around them; she felt its warmth on her shoulders and neck, but inside she was cold, afraid.

Sheshan's hand on her hair startled her into lifting her head. He set both hands on her shoulders, his face grave, intent. "Come. I will show you a thing."

He turned her to face the broad sweep of mountains to the north. They gleamed like crystal in the clear light, jagged as fangs, as pitiless to travelers. "Look up there," he said quietly, standing behind her with his hands resting on her shoulders. "Up at the top of the highest peak."

She squinted at snow blowing across one of the glaciers, chewed off by a stiff wind raging at the summit. Jetta shivered, imagining what it must be like up there.

He lifted his right hand off her shoulder and reached toward the distant mountain. "Come," he whispered, but she knew he was not speaking to her.

And the wind came. Jetta watched it sway the tops of trees down the length of the valley, charging up the ridges toward them until it struck all at once in a blast of frigid air and a swirl of dust from the dance circle. It moaned around the warehouses and ruffled the grass, brushing a stray wisp of hair back from Jetta's forehead. Sheshan lifted his face into it and closed his eyes, breathing deep.

"Do you hear it?"

Jetta looked up into his somber face. "I hear the wind."

"It has a voice." A strange sadness touched his face. "Do you hear it?"

"It's wind," she said stubbornly.

"Has fire no voice, then?"

She stilled.

"Ah," he said. "Fire does speak. Maybe Firedancers don't hear the voice of the wind, as Windriders don't hear The Ancient. But the wind has a voice, and I have always known it is alive."

"Alive. But does it fight you, trap you, try to out-think you?"

His hands tightened on her shoulders. "Since that day on the cliffs—I have wondered."

She swallowed hard. "Then you know what I fear."

"You can't kill the wind, Jetta. However hard you try."

"Nor do you harness it, keep it like a pet neera, or smother it as casually as you would squash an insect stinging your arm. No wonder The Ancient hates us."

"The Ancient hates us because we deny it what it wants. Would you give in to the Old Man and let the world burn?"

"*No*," she whispered. "No. And yet—"

"And yet," he said softly. "Water and fire and air and earth. All these things serve as well as oppose. So long as we are master, we retain a standing place to live our lives. I for one am not ready to see the Hag scour the land clean of all life."

She craned her head to look up into his face. "Is that how you see wind? As the Hag?"

His eyes turned suddenly pale as rain. "Wind is a woman, fickle and fey, now here, now there, gentle as a caress, as unbending as a shrew."

"Thank you," she said dryly. "No wonder Windriders are so few."

He laughed, and suddenly his arms went around her, hugging her against him, his breath tickling her hair. Caught off-guard, she did not resist, leaning against him as she had once leaned into Kori's solid body, safe in the circle of his arms. For a moment it felt right, so pleasant she forgot it was a Windrider behind her, a man complicated enough to make Setti seem a child.

Setti.

She stiffened, suddenly anxious that he should not see her like this. Sheshan let her go and stepped back. Jetta moaned, feeling bereft and traitorous and thoroughly confused. She spun around and looked up at him as the wind he had summoned swirled away down the hill, plucking idly at tree branches and bushes on its way.

"I'm sorry," she stammered. "Please don't go—"

"I think it well if I do," he said, his face and voice alike without expression. "Good day."

"No, Sheshan—"

But he was already gone, slipping like smoke back up toward the village. Wretchedly Jetta watched him go. To save Setti's feelings she had dealt Sheshan hurt. This was impossible.

She started after him, determined to make amends, and ran straight into a Delver walking out from behind a storehouse, the firewatch, sleepy and awaiting his dawn relief. Jetta bounced off, staggered, and found his thick fingers clamped around her wrist.

"Jetta ak'Kal! Pardon! Is there fire?" Huge eyes got bigger and his shaggy head jerked around to stare across the meadow at the quiet camp.

"No—" Jetta tried to free herself as gracefully as she could manage.

The Delver blew a sigh of relief and withdrew his hand. "Glad I am to hear you say that. All these people." He spread his fingers, taking in the caravan and the wagons where no one had yet stirred, despite the coming day. "All night I have been imagining what it would be like if fire rose in the middle of the dance ground."

Hylli Fargoer's megrims are infecting the whole village, Jetta thought, doubly irritated because Sheshan was now almost out of sight among the first houses. Then the Delver's comment wound into her brain and shocked her to a dead halt. The dance ground.

The dust had been *warm* under her feet.

Without a word to the Delver she turned and ran, pounding up the newly-laid black stones of the road. They burned cold with the night's chill under her feet, as the bare dirt empty of dancers should have felt. Three heartstones had leaped from this ground two scant cycles of the greater moon ago; the dancers could very well have scraped bare the last remaining thin layer over another.

A few sleepy drovers were stirring among the wagons, yawning and stretching; Jetta wanted to shriek warning but that would only bring the whole train swarming out, a confusion of bodies she did not need in danger's path. She needed Fargoer, the one man least likely to believe her or cooperate, and the one man who might get those wagons moved without panic.

She darted across the meadow through a cluster of snorting cart beasts that blinked at her stupidly with great black eyes and then shied away, blatting in alarm. "Hai!" she called to the nearest drover as he stood stretching his back out, his face lifted to the morning breeze. "Where is Hylli's wagon?"

The man stared, taken aback by a Dancer running toward him shedding her cloak. His head swiveled in search of fire; Jetta cursed his slow brain as she pounded to a stop in front of him and let the red cloak fall in a swirl of cloth.

"Where?" she demanded.

Stiff with anxiety, the man pointed at a wagon across the dance ground. Jetta ran straight across it, her bare feet marking the warmth of the hard-packed dirt. Was it hotter? She could not tell, but it spurred her on. She pounded on the bright blue door of Fargoer's wagon, calling as loudly as she dared, "Hylli Fargoer, up! It's dawn, and there's need."

A heavy thump and a querulous voice inside answered. Fargoer stuck his tousled head out the door, glaring and red-eyed. Every line in his face pulled down at sight of Jetta.

"What do you want?" he said thickly.

"Is your head filled with drink?" she asked, matching him glare for glare. "How fast can you move this train? There is heat on the dance ground. Three heartstones rose under the road two moons gone; I think another is close, and I will not see innocents die running in panic where fire is coming."

Hylli blinked and jerked around to stare at the beaten circle of dirt. "Is that steam?" he croaked.

Jetta dared not look; she could hear other voices now, sense eyes turning toward them all over the camp. "How fast? At the least, get your people out. Sacrifice the wagons if you must—"

"No!" Home and livelihood for his whole train lay in those wagons.

"Then hook up and move, drover! Now!"

"I see nothing," he said, his eyes darting every which way around the quiet meadow, the camp, the storehouses hulking dark against the sunrise. "I'll not roust the whole camp on the word of a failed Dancer, Jetta ak'Kal."

"Will you cling to old stories and risk your whole train?"

Without warning heat flushed through her. Jetta gasped, staggering under an overwhelming sense of fire rising—somewhere. "It's coming," she gasped. "Close!" *Where?*

Fargoer ran a harried hand through his unkempt fair hair and stared at her in profound dislike. Jetta saw the memory of his humiliation yesterday in the thin set of his mouth, the flick of his eyes over the camp in search of a reason to refuse. She tried to snatch away from her pounding anxiety the sure connection to the Mother of so short a time ago, to reach consciously into the earth and discover where The Ancient lurked, but she could not think with his contemptuous eyes on her and her guts winding tight with fire sense.

"If I'm wrong, you'll be alive, and you can blacken my name from here to the Great Water to your heart's delight. If I'm right, you'll be dead. Choose, Drover!"

A black shadow darted past Jetta and swarmed to the top of the wagon box above Fargoer's head. Slink, the neera, sat up on his haunches and tilted his pointed muzzle at the sky, filling the dawn with his shrill, chittering cry. Fargoer stared, and then he drew a deep breath and yelled, "UP!" a stentorian boom equal to any Delver's. "Fire, flood and danger! Move!"

The wagons erupted as though someone had tossed a boulder into a pool. The bright, wheeled boxes spat out women in every stage of undress, men barefoot and shirtless, children tousled and sleepy and staring. But not one shouted a question; not one seemed confused as to what to do. Children ran to catch cart beasts; women threw pots and trade goods willy-nilly into wagons; men sorted out harness and flung it on the blatting, confused animals. Slink darted down into Fargoer's wagon and disappeared.

Jetta, too relieved to be insulted that Fargoer took a neera's word over hers, edged out of the way and watched the discipline of a lifetime lived at wits' edge at work. Fargoer brushed past her, barefoot but otherwise fully dressed in yesterday's finery. He gave her not a glance, but his face was set and hostile, unwilling to believe, not daring not to. Jetta shifted from foot to foot in the chill grass and watched the curl of steam from the dance ground, her stomach in knots.

The Delver on firewatch ran up. "Jetta ak'Kal, what—"

She rounded on him. "Go rouse Settak a'Kam and warn the village that fire's coming. Double the firewatch among the houses. Tell every household to be on watch. I think it will rise here, but I don't want an ugly surprise."

"Ak'Kal," he gulped, and ran.

The first wagon in line started to move. *Faster,* thought Jetta, shivering in the agonizing certainty of fire about to burst forth to ruin the summer dawn. The second wagon started, the cart beasts blatting and swinging their pendulous beards, as anxious as Slink now. Too slow, too slow! All at once Jetta felt the fire bursting toward her, hot, close, malevolent.

"Scatter!" she screamed. "Fargoer, scatter the wagons, it's here!"

Hylli Fargoer took one look at her and bellowed, "Outward wheel, *move!*"

Drivers wrenched teams around, even in their haste and confusion never fouling another, wheeling outward in a huge starburst away from the crowded and vulnerable center of what had been an orderly camp. And then with a cough and a roaring rush, fire broke from the ground in front of her. Malice struck her like a blow in the face; her head snapped back in realization that here was no heartstone heaved newborn to the surface, but an arm of The Ancient that had found its way into the free air. Not since Setham had she felt such malevolent greed from fire, or sensed such clear purpose below the hunger. Intelligent or not, it *wanted*, like an infant screaming for its dinner.

Jetta quailed, feeling naked and powerless and very much alone in the face of a menace already straining the limits of her knowledge. She hesitated, her insides wound into knots so tight she could scarcely breathe. And then a child shrieked in terror, breaking her paralysis.

She resisted the instinct to whirl into the arching spin of the first movement, that gathered energy even as it spun away fear, and lifted instead into the Fourth Rank control. She swept her arms up, poised on one foot, every nerve atwitch in agonized realization that the fire was gaining ground each second. Every instant crawled like years; she wanted—*needed*—to be moving, to dance, to drive the enemy out of this meadow. Grimly she held, shutting her ears to the screams and rumble of wheels and wild braying of cart beasts and the hot rush of the fire in front of her. Her name echoed across the meadow, an outraged roar demanding that she do *something*. But she could do nothing against this monster on willpower alone.

Eighteen
Dance for Life

I am master! she cried to the turmoil in heart and mind and spirit, and held on, clinging to the knowledge gained in the dawn. For a long, long slice of eternity she hung in a mindless frenzy of impatience and fear and guilt. And then the fire smashed heat into her face on a rush of malice that all but flattened her, but in its wake came anger of her own. Her eyes snapped open on a gasp that filled her lungs with wickedly hot air. It cooled instantly as the same rush brought a boiling, bubbling awareness of the Mother under her fire-tough feet. The air thickened as though it had frozen around her, chilling the fire's malice.

Jetta whooped in a great breath of relief and exhilaration and opened her eyes. The fire was roaring Delver height at the edge of the dance circle, spitting flame in every direction. She jerked her wrists apart, planted both feet, and brought her palms together, driving the fire in on itself, trying to stop its greedy reaching for the abandoned trestle tables and trampled grass beyond the beaten patch. Cart beasts blatted and fled with the wagons, thin tails flicking in panic. She glimpsed one with fire riding its shoulders, bucking and plunging in its harness, and winced, but she could not spare a thought for its pain or the danger to the wagon it pulled. The fire roared at her, defying the command in the Dance, and split itself in two. A second tall column reared up, red-yellow but paling rapidly, turning gold at its center. Grimly Jetta watched them both turn to *hysths*. She stamped a foot, experimenting. The first sank as if in obedience to the Dance; warily she pushed it toward the other, aware of shouting behind her, of fire starting to skip through the grass, a danger beyond the creature trying to birth itself in her front.

Without warning the first *hysth* exploded skyward and turned white. The abandoned dance ground began to cave inward; in horror Jetta realized the dirt was sloughing away, exposing pale stone that turned black in a breath. Heat scorched up, shocking her; with the Mother wrapping her in a cool, stone-scented shell she should not feel it. She hesitated, her left arm and leg feeding her memories of agony. The second *hysth* leaned toward her, reaching licking arms of flame down to engulf her.

"Jetta!" Setti's voice reached her over the roar. An instant later he appeared in the corner of her sight, clad in leathers, dwarfed by the first *hysth* towering above him.

Jetta flinched backward. "Get *out*, Setti!" she shouted back. "Get clear!" This was no place for a Second Rank, even Setti.

"No! I won't leave you to face—"

Fire flicked into the grass at his feet, leaped upward in his face. He cried out and stumbled back, his arms still reflexively shaping the first warding of the Dance. "No!" Jetta shrieked, and abandoned confrontation with the second *hysth* with the memory of Kori's screams suddenly filling her ears. *Not Setti, too. No.*

She leaped, twisted, kicked a bare foot into his shoulder, knocking him rolling in the yet-untouched grass behind him. Jetta landed lightly where he had been standing and whirled to face the flame that had attacked him. It crackled and spat, but she scorned its defiance and drove it ruthlessly back in upon itself. Too disorganized to form a *hysth*, it consumed the grass in a flash and then had nowhere to go, nothing to feed on. It sank and died into a blackened spot on the ground, its danger spent.

"Setti, are you—" She stretched a hand down to help him up.

"Jetta ak'Kal!" a voice bellowed, deep and terrified.

Jetta spun around and stared in horror. In just those few seconds the *hysths* had seized the advantage; one was burrowing in frenzy, the other was racing across the meadow, hunting a place to root and form a second doorway. The windstone under the first glowed redder than rockweed; the air above it boiled with heat. She stood there for an awful, endless second, transfixed between the twin spikes of fire raging in front of her and the power churning inside her. Setti drew a shocked breath beside her.

"The Ancient's coming," he said, his voice a strangled whisper.

Jetta launched herself impossibly high, over the vanquished ash, height born of the power thrusting up through her. Heat blasted at her; she spun it aside as she landed lightly on one foot and thrust off again, aiming for a tiny bare patch between two flames. She coiled her arms tightly around herself, drawing the scattering flames of the nearest *hysth* back together. Jetta advanced on it, driving it back in sudden confusion from the cratered dance circle. She swayed to the farthest stretch of her left leg, then to her right, palms flat toward the *hysth*, sweeping it away from that half-formed doorway, pouring the endless cool power soaring up through her out through her hands. Without warning the *hysth* abandoned the blackening vein; she heard a sound like a molten roar of fury as it retreated with The Ancient still trapped underground. It roared after its mate, tearing up the hill through wagons and loose cart beasts and fleeing people.

The *hysths* left blackened trails of destruction in their wake, scorching the summer-green meadow, snatching greedily at flotsam falling from wildly bouncing wagons. The lesser one, the one still yellow at its heart, ran toward the stream, yearning toward the teller trees nodding on the other side. But the water intimidated it and she saw it crawling restlessly up the bank, stretching long fingers toward the trees. Sparks hissed into the racing water. In despair Jetta guessed that in seconds the *hysth* would have grown enough to reach those beckoning branches, a disaster that could overtake the whole Vale.

Without warning it swirled into a column of fire four times her height. Jetta shied back, so stunned she could not move for a second of utter shock; no fire could grow like that, so fast, so hot. Nothing in the Dance she knew or imagined could stop a thing like that—and then she saw that the fire was raging within that spinning, impossible column, furious, but held tight on the blackened ground beside the stream. Wind streamed past her, buffeting her enough to make her step sideways to catch her balance. It swirled into a tight cage around the fire.

Impossible, her mind tried to tell her, but beyond the fire and smoke she saw four pale figures stark against the grass up the hill, spinning wind into a ball, holding fire and malice and all in a feast of air it nonetheless could do nothing with.

Jetta gasped in a sob of relief and rounded on the other *hysth,* the one with The Ancient at its heart, now trying to root itself in an outcrop of windstone halfway up the hill toward Annam.

Ah, no! Let it get in there and it can tunnel under the whole village!

The thought crashed into her head with the whole weight of imminent disaster on its heels. She could not outrun it. She stopped, remembering Sheshan calling the wind from the glacier two leagues from where he stood.

"If you know my name, Old Man, then hear me," she whispered, and gathered her will.

She clenched both fists and jerked them backward. With a roar the *hysth* reared straight up, the greedy fingers that had been reaching for the outcrop fingering the sky instead. A long tendril of flame shot toward her on the west wind streaming down from the ridge in answer to the Windriders' call. The *hysth* fell short and retreated into the main fire, harmless. Flame billowed and tore into fragments that landed all over the grass, driving toward the other *hysth.*

Ordinarily it would have frightened Jetta to her bones. With the raw power of Earth Mother thrumming through every nerve and bone and muscle, she laid her fists together and willed the heart of the fire in on itself. It roared at her, the deep coughing roar she remembered from Setham, from Firehome. She closed her ears to it, refusing to hear a voice under the snapping of the flames. She thrust her clenched fists out, holding them rigid though her shoulders began to tremble under the strain, spinning the fire in on itself.

The roar changed to a crackle. The white heat at the *hysth's* heart faded to gold. The flames sank. Jetta advanced a step. The fire writhed like a thing in torment, but it sank and sank toward the earth, consuming itself as it died. The core turned yellow, then red, and suddenly it was gone. Only a column of smoke rank with the bitter smell of burning grass remained, trailing up from the scorched earth.

Jetta looked only long enough to know it was dead before

whirling toward the other one, ignoring for the moment the scattered smaller fires smoking in the grass. And there was Setti, grimly dancing in front of that impossible column of flame, trying to tame a *hysth* with determination alone. Jetta ran toward him, trying to think how to use the unexpected advantage the Windriders had given them by penning the fire with the winds sweeping in from east and west, flattening the grass and whipping the trees across the stream to frenzy.

"Setti!" she shouted over the coughing roar of the flames. "Get back! We need to try something new!"

He spun, the beautiful, skyward-reaching spin of the eighth movement of the Third Rank master's dance. It had no effect on the *hysth*, though he performed it perfectly. She saw his face, sweaty and pale, set in a rictus of concentration, and screamed his name again, wondering if he had not heard, or thought he could tame this thing on will alone.

Two long tongues of flame escaped the winds to swat at him. Setti swayed aside, untouched, but he was stumbling, exhausted, overmatched. "Setti! Come! Now! I have an idea!"

She caught his shoulder, dragging him farther from the *hysth*. Wild-eyed, he staggered, caught himself, and stared at her as the fire writhed and roared and fought the winds. "What—"

"Watch for anything that escapes!" she shouted at him, and spun toward the Windriders. "Wyth! Drive it with the north wind only!" she yelled with all the force in her lungs, and hoped he understood.

"That's toward us!" Setti gasped, and then there was no time, for the winds around them died as though someone had dropped a wall to east and south and west. The column of flame writhed, staggered, and broke apart into a shower of fire, dropping into the grass in a raging yellow line.

Yellow! Jetta caught a breath in sheer relief and screamed at Setti to dance before it reformed into a new *hysth*.

She whirled away into a dance of her own, watching fire stream in golden trails down the wind that no longer fed its hunger but drove it along the scorched path it had already run. Jetta danced the edges to the west; Setti took the east, and once more they found a rhythm, mirroring each other as they had on the dance ground last night, so attuned to each other the fire could not find a clear space to run. Through flames trying to leap together into a new *hysth* Jetta saw Setti dancing like a master, laughing as he had laughed when the music held them both in thrall to a fall of silver notes.

We have it, Jetta thought, exulting in a rhythm unfelt since the last time she danced with Kori. And deeper in her mind, marveling, *The Windriders* held *it*. Possibilities broke open like a dam bursting even as she forced her tired legs into a combination of Fourth Rank spin and Third Rank leap, riding the Mother's strength high over a curl of flame spitting impotent heat at her. She saw the fire hesitate, shrink, and whooped an exuberant laugh of sheer relief.

Setti stumbled. Jetta's triumph turned to horror as the flame licked toward him, seizing like the opportunist it was on that instant's chink in the firewall they were weaving against it. Even as it flung itself at him it turned gold, forming another *hysth* in the flash of a thought; smaller, but no less malevolent. Setti flung up his left arm to catch his balance— and the *hysth* snatched at it, wrapping the flesh in a sleeve of flame. Even then his nerve held. He stripped the fire from his arm with his right hand and flung it back at the *hysth*, shouting something Jetta did not catch over the fire's roar.

Fear galvanized her. "*Go, Setti! Get back!*"

She leaped around the flames to dance between him and the fire, watching the *hysth*. It trembled and spat but did not spread, unable to move north, blocked in every other direction by Jetta darting to meet it. As she worked her way up the forms it began to cool, until an imperious step-step-spin, thrice repeated, set it shivering like a soul in pain, and then shattered it.

Tendrils of flame rained down around her. Jetta let them burn, for she stood in the blackened and cooling dirt at the edge of the dance ground with the crater smoking in front of her. Coldly she watched the remnants flicker and die. *You exist to destroy. Now be destroyed.*

Shouting behind her turned her about, weary and dreading to see what remained in the meadow. She expected to see fire spreading through the lush grass, perhaps running up the hill toward the village, but only blackened trails marked where the fire had run. A horde of Delvers with picks, shovels, and buckets stamped through the meadow, occasionally pausing to shovel dirt onto some struggling spark, smothering it before it could spread. Blowing cart beasts and a mass of wagons jammed the far end of the meadow, looking untouched save for one wagon sitting alone, blackened for half its length, and the clothseller's wagon overturned, trailing tongues of cloth in billowing streamers of red and gold and blue.

Between one breath and the next the soaring rush of the Mother's embrace abandoned her. A stink of charred wood and burned grass and smoke swooped in around her; the air turned hot with the fading heat from the dance ground. Jetta staggered and nearly fell, feeling bereft and so weary all she wanted to do was fling herself down and sleep. But Nuurn was running toward her, his face anxious, his huge eyes raking her head to foot.

"Are you hurt, Jetta ak'Kal? After Setti, we feared—"

"Setti?" She closed the distance between them with a rush. "Setti is hurt?"

"His arm—" Nuurn twisted a look over his shoulder.

"Where?" Jetta demanded, her heart thumping painfully. "Where is he?"

"Among the drovers. They have a fair healer—"

She ran where he pointed, haunted by the memory of Setti's arm clothed in flame. A *hysth* could strip flesh to bone in seconds; would he lose the arm? He would never dance again—

"Jetta ak'Kal! Here!"

She turned toward that imperative voice. Hylli Fargoer beckoned urgently from the steps of a wagon slewed sideways across the road. Jetta ran toward him as he jumped to the ground; he stopped her when she would have pushed past him.

"He'll live, Dancer," he said gruffly, catching her arm when she sagged in relief. "Come, sit. Narda said you were to drink this."

He plucked a mug from the driver's seat and thrust it at her. Jetta ignored it, craning past him for a glimpse inside the wagon. The green door was shut.

"How badly was he burned?"

"Drink first."

Fargoer was nothing if not a trader. Frustrated, Jetta took

the mug and drank, grimacing at the bitter aftertaste. "What is it?"

"Narda is good at awful-tasting remedies. But they work. This one's for strength." He eyed her, still cool, but the overt hostility had vanished. "Quite a feat, Dancer, to know fire is coming before it appears."

"Slink knew," she said coolly.

"But he can't dance it away." He sighed, looking at the ribbons of bright cloth painting the meadow. "I suppose I'll hear about that."

Don't argue with a Firedancer next time, Jetta thought tartly, but there was no point in saying it. "How is Setti?"

He grimaced. "His arm is badly burned but he won't die. Narda is trying to determine how deep the damage goes." His voice warmed. "The lad has courage. Even with the fire chewing him he still fought back."

"He did well." Jetta fought off a convulsive shudder, remembering him wrapped in fire. "Very well. So much flame." Visions of a bucking cart animal passed in her mind. "Was anyone else hurt?"

"No. We'll be picking up trade goods for two days, but-" He could not quite manage a nonchalant smile. "I never saw fire run so fast. Thought it was going to run right over you."

She remembered someone screaming at her to act, to move. "It didn't."

"Aye, we were lucky. Lucky there were Dancers here worth the name after all." He gave her a straight, level stare that Jetta guessed was as much apology as he knew how to give.

She could not return it. The black streaks in the meadow shouted livid accusations of divided loyalties. She remembered the sound of Kori's screams, remembered Setti surprised by fire, overmatched before he began, easy prey. And she remembered leaping to his side, risking hundreds to save one. If she had left Setti to dance his own dance, the *hysths* could not have split and run as they had, endangering the whole village. If she had driven them down to start with, he would not be lying hurt inside that wagon.

His life is equally worthy! love raged at her. But duty answered coolly, *Risk comes with the rank.*

Jetta swallowed a strangling tightness in her throat, for it was not Minna's voice in her head this time, but her own.

Am I so callous? I don't want to make such choices!

Setham had *never* been like this.

Heavy footsteps pounded up behind her, a lot of them. Jetta turned slowly to face half a hundred beaming Delvers with Huunall in the lead. He stopped in front of her. "Well done, Jetta! For all its ferocity, you kept it from doing real damage. Though it might be a job rounding up your loose beasts, Hylli."

Fargoer shrugged. "It won't be the first time. Most of them will come home when their fright wears off. I only hope none fall over a cliff and break their silly necks."

"We'll make good their price if they do," Nuurn said, walking up behind him.

Fargoer shook his head. "A hazard of the road. As is flame."

Huunall turned to Jetta. "You danced well, ak'Kal. How did you know the fire would come?"

"I suspected that the dancing last night had laid bare a heartstone. I didn't expect The Ancient itself to come bursting up." Her hand drifted out toward the smoking dance ground. "Dig there, ak'Kal. I believe you'll find a burned-out vein of windstone. The *hysths* were trying to hold it open for The Ancient. It's dead now and useless to the Old Man, but if it branches..."

The beaming smiles faded on every face. Nuurn said slowly, "Are you sure? If the meadow is not safe, what of the village?"

She shook her head wearily. "I don't know. This fire felt malicious. Like nothing I have fought before. The Ancient is growing bolder."

She turned to Fargoer. "I think your notion of taking your folk out of here might be a good one after all. Load your wagons and go. Set my letter on its way to the Circle with all speed, and get your folk out of danger's path."

"Where might that be, Dancer? The lowlands are full of flame, and I see now that it is not through failure of the Fire Clans. The world is changing. Where do you suggest we hide?"

The Delvers slid uneasy glances at one another. Nuurn raised thoughtful eyebrows; Huunall sighed.

The door of the wagon opened behind Jetta. She spun toward it as a serene-faced woman in sober brown to match her close-cropped hair stepped down beside Fargoer. "What news, my love?" he asked her.

She turned quiet eyes on Jetta. "He did more for himself than I can, ak'Kal. When he flung the fire from him he limited its grip, but the damage it did was grave. It will be many weeks before he uses his arm again. His right hand is burned as well."

Jetta closed her eyes on sick dread. "But he'll live?"

"Yes."

Jetta sagged against the wagon wheel in relief. "Can he travel? I'll send him to Firehome with my report, where he can heal in peace."

"I doubt that," Huunall said. "Suppose it was you leaving him to face The Ancient alone? Fret yourself gray, no doubt. You'll do him no favors by sending him away."

"You think he won't fret here?" Jetta could well imagine watching him dance while she stood by, useless and helpless to aid him.

"Don't shame him, ak'Kal." Wyth's cool voice startled Jetta upright. Fluttery movement caught her eye as Delvers moved aside in haste to let Wyth and three other Riders through. Sheshan gave Jetta a raking, intense look and stepped behind Ayesh, standing quietly beside Thess as Wyth stopped beside Huunall.

Jetta met Wyth's strange, pale eyes. For a moment no one else seemed present, though she could hear boys shouting as they tried to round up cart beasts, the low, rockfall sound of Delver voices, and the whisper of cloth as Hylli Fargoer turned to look at her. Wyth inclined his head a slow, deliberate fraction, respect offered master to master. Jetta nodded into his eyes, remembering the swirling, impotent column of flame.

"I think," she said slowly, groping through exhaustion, "that I need to think about what happened here this morning. I am," she paused in search of words. "I am awed, Wyth ak'Kal. To use the very air The Ancient craves against it. It was inspired, and so fitting. How long could you have held it?"

"Not much longer," Wyth said, surprising her with such

candor. "We hoped to hold it long enough for you to deal with it. You did."

"With Setti's help. There is no Dance so powerful as when Dancers are able to combine as Setti and I managed today. He is—erratic. I'm not sure we could do it again."

"It is an experiment worth waiting to try again," Wyth said. "But that is Dancer business, and I leave it to you."

He turned away as though suddenly bored with the conversation. "Wait!" Jetta said. "There are other experiments to be made, I'm thinking. Wind and fire might..."

Her voice trailed off as Wyth turned, his eyes cool and expressionless. "That is a discussion for another time. Ak'Kal." He seemed to include all twenty or so of the nearby folk entitled to that greeting in his farewell, walking away without another glance at any of them.

What ails *him?* Jetta wondered in pure frustration. She tried to catch Sheshan's eye, but he followed the other Windriders without looking at her.

Huunall shifted his broad bulk, a small, restless movement. Jetta looked at him, wondering what he thought of Wyth's manners, but his eyes were on the sad, burned swathes streaking the meadow, assessing damage inflicted by an enemy they could not prevent striking where it pleased. After a moment his eyes shifted to her, somber now.

"If you send Setti away, you will be alone in this fight, Jetta, unless your Circle sees fit to replace him. And it may be they haven't the numbers to spare."

"Not if it's as bad in the lowlands as Hylli says. But I'm not alone, am I? Your folk did a fine job on the lesser flame, and the Windriders still stand ready to protect the mines."

"Strange allies," Fargoer snorted, watching Wyth's stiff back departing up the hill.

"One takes them where one finds them," Jetta said wearily. "Now I would like to see Setti. Narda?"

"I would be grateful, ak'Kal," said the healer. "He is a bad patient."

Jetta climbed the wagon steps and pushed open the door, suddenly dreading what she would see. Merry Setti, laid low and in pain. Her fault. She had failed. Again.

Early sunlight poured in the single window, illuminating the low bed running the length of one wall. Setti lay on it under a pile of bright blankets, his right arm hidden under wet cloths. A sharp reek of herbs struck Jetta in the face, transporting her instantly back to awakening to that smell in a Water Clan hut. She crept closer, fearful of jarring him. His eyes were closed; he looked gray and spent, the gold of his skin turned a sallow bisque. Jetta stopped beside him, biting her lip to keep the tears from coming.

"Setti?"

He stirred and opened his eyes. "Jetta!" Even now, a wan, glad note warmed his voice at sight of her. She swallowed hard and dropped to one knee beside him.

"Don't talk. The healer says you must rest."

"Healers." But the scorn did not quite come off; pain twitched through his face and he caught his breath, let it out again slowly.

She laid her fingers against his cheek. "She knows what she's talking about. You must listen to her. She says your arm will heal, but you must rest. Perhaps it would be best if they took you to Firehome."

"No. You need me here."

"I need a Dancer who can dance, a'Kam. And I need you to get well."

"I can do that here," he said stubbornly. He tried to raise himself onto his good elbow, hissed and turned gray. Alarmed, Jetta reached to push him down again, but he sank back into the pillows without her urging, breathing hard.

"Setti, please, I can't—"

His eyes widened. "You're frightened."

"Yes! The thought of you not dancing again frightens me to my marrow. And if anything happens to you because you didn't go, I couldn't—"

His good hand wavered up to touch her face. "Tears for me, Jetta? I'm not Kori. I didn't die. I won't."

Jetta could not summon words. "I couldn't bear it. You are my dearest friend—"

Setti's hand fell away. "Friend," he said dully.

"Friend!" Jetta said, fierce and low. "A friend who danced far above his rank without regard for his own life, and kept his nerve when I most needed him to!"

He turned his face to the wall. "I froze like a First Rank faced with his first spark. If you hadn't pushed me out of the way, this would have happened much sooner, and much worse."

Jetta bit back guilty confessions. "Anyone can be surprised. I certainly was. I expected a heartstone, not The Ancient or an instant *hysth*, let alone two."

"Even so. But not everyone needs to be kicked out of the way to make space for the real Dancer to work."

"Setti!" She caught his face between her hands, trying to make him focus on her through the haze of whatever drug Narda had given him. "Setti, it is because I love you that I want you safe. Do you think I want to see you crippled? When I saw the *hysth* attack you, it was like watching Kori die all over again. Better that the Circle sends me some first-year journeyman I don't know. Or that I remain alone."

Setti jerked his head out of her grasp. "So you will never care for anyone again? That's stupid, Jetta!" He moaned and fell back into the pillows, his eyes screwed tight shut.

Jetta's heart all but stopped. *"Setti?"*

"I will not go," he said through his teeth. "I can still instruct the villagers and take charge of the firewatch. That much I can do."

"Setti..." Jetta fought for words. For mastery of her feelings. Wanting him clear of this place where the fire must surely have learned his name.

"Who else can confuse the Old Man better than I, remember?" He did not open his eyes, and his attempt at a smile died in a grimace of pain.

"Stubborn! You should have been born a Delver."

He chuckled, a breathy, painful sound. "I win," he breathed.

"Fool! Stay then, and learn the lessons of folly."

"Already have," he grunted, and sagged against the pillows, spent and so pale Jetta stepped to the door and beckoned to Narda. She swarmed up the steps with the speed of long practice and bent over Setti, her fingers curling around his wrist. Her lips thinned and dark eyes flicked toward Jetta.

"What have you done, Dancer? What did you say to him?"

"Promises I should not be making." Jetta sighed. "I should send him away, but I think that would kill him faster than if he stays."

Slowly Narda drew back her hand. "There are many ways to die, Dancer. If you value the spirit within him, don't shame him."

We would both be safer with him gone. The thought brought shame flooding up in a hot wave. Setti was no more a conduit for fire than she, who had also once been touched by flame. The only threat in him was to her peace of mind—and to his heart, which she knew now would be broken whether he stayed or not.

She leaned down past Narda to kiss his forehead. "Be well, Setti," she whispered in his ear. "I'll see you at Anual's."

His lips curved into the faintest of smiles. "Save me—a cookie."

"You'll be too fat to dance. Sleep, a'Kam."

"Yes, ak'Kal." His head lolled against the pillow.

Narda caught Jetta's arm as she turned toward the door. "He *will* mend, ak'Kal."

Jetta managed a smile. "He's too stubborn not to. Thank you for all you've done." She escaped out the door, bleakly aware that even with Setti still here, she was truly alone now, one Dancer against the menace determined to claim all of Annam Vale. A menace that knew her name.

Nineteen
New Ideas

The first of the drovers left the next day. Fargoer split his caravan for the first time in their history, sending Jetta's report to Firehome ahead with three wagons needing repair while the others worked day and night alongside the Delvers to load the heavy freight wagons with containment stone. They left the windstone on Jetta's advice, for in these times it was too uncertain a cargo. The Delvers agreed, though Burrood's voice complained loudly in council over the loss of profit.

"Would you rather the caravan burned and no one came again to take any stone?" Urrana asked him tartly, ending it, but the villagers' peace had died with the twin *hysths*. The scorch marks on the meadow remained a stark reminder to even the most skeptical that The Ancient was no longer a distant tale filled with other folk, but a real and vicious enemy battering at their own containment wall.

On the day the caravan left, Jetta stood with Rununn at the bridge, watching the wagons creak their slow way over the eastern ridge in the late afternoon. As the last one topped out and disappeared Rununn said softly, "I wonder if we'll see them again?"

"Of course!" Jetta said. "Fargoer didn't strike me as the sort to abandon a profitable trade route because of one scare." She dug a sly elbow into his hip. "Besides, he owes you those better tools you ordered. And you owe him more of your little people, remember?"

His face lit up; many a Fargoer wagon now sported a small Delver tucked up on a shelf above the driver's head, "to watch for stonefalls ahead" some wag had said, and they wanted Dancers, too. Then he sighed, his eyes troubled. "But what will they encounter down there in the lowlands? He spoke of fire springing up everywhere. It could strike them some night."

"So long as they escape with their lives they can start again. Wagons, a few cart beasts—even a village can be rebuilt, a'Kam."

"Well said, ak'Kal."

She turned and found Huunall at her elbow watching the dust settle on the ridge. "Though I should hate to rebuild Annam," he said. "The Circle desires your company, Jetta."

She searched his face, arrested by an odd note in his voice. "What's wrong?"

"Nothing yet. Will you come?"

"Of course." She touched Rununn's arm in reassurance and turned away with Huunall, feeling suddenly very small walking beside him. For all that Setti was noisily protesting Anual's fussing and confinement to his room, his absence at her shoulder seemed curiously permanent. She missed his laughter and his enthusiasm for all the small things of life, and his courage that would not let him back down even from The Ancient.

She walked up the road with Huunall, keeping her questions to herself; she guessed he would not answer any more than Wyth had responded to an invitation to discuss further cooperation against The Ancient. It rankled, but she could not force cooperation, and she had not dared seek Sheshan out to ask him to intercede. The memory of him walking away from her rebuff made her cringe.

The wind sweeping down the ridge filled her nearly to bursting with the scent of sun-warmed meadows. *So clean,* she thought, *the mountains must have breathed it out just now, new-made and ripe for sitting and breathing.* Jetta lifted her face into it, thinking of Ayesh, and quite suddenly she wanted to wrap all of Annam in her arms and hug it close, loving this place with a fierce protectiveness she had never felt even at Setham. The winding street with its looming stone houses, so out of scale with where she had been born, no longer seemed strange. Gently she touched the rough black wall of the nearest dwelling, so solid and yet so oddly fragile, like the Delvers themselves. She smiled, guessing Huunall had never in his life thought of himself as fragile. Oddly, the thought lent her hope.

Half the village seemed to be at the inn when they arrived, surprising her, for the sun would not set for another hour. Six Windriders made a pale knot among them, which surprised her more. Huunall had said this was a Circle meeting. Still, danger threatened the whole Vale. The Windriders had made themselves part of Annam's defense.

Her glance slid straight to Sheshan, and found his eyes already on her. Her face heated but she did not look away, too glad to see him to waste the opportunity. Six days now since the fire in the meadow, and he had somehow kept out of her sight. Avoiding her?

A deep murmur among the Delvers noted her arrival. Urrana said briskly, "Welcome, Jetta ak'Kal. You are well?"

"Very well," Jetta said, puzzled. Urrana knew she had taken no harm from the fire.

"That is good hearing," the innkeeper said formally. She gestured to Jetta's special bench beside the fire banked down on the hearth. Gingerly Jetta settled, eyeing the somber faces watching her.

"We meet today to discuss what must be done now to save Annam," Urrana said. "It is clear that the danger Jetta ak'Kal warned us about in the spring was no child's tale, as some maintained."

Burrood kept remarkably silent. Urrana swept the room with one forbidding glance and nodded at Jetta. "The Fire Clans chose well in the Dancer they sent to us, but she is now the only able Dancer in a village sorely beset. Jetta ak'Kal, what can we do to aid you?"

Jetta started. Of all questions, that was not the one she had expected to hear. She looked around that roomful of huge moon eyes, and not one blinked or shied away, no more than Annam's stolid houses had shied from her touch. After the shambles the *hysths* had made in the meadow, she would not have blamed them had they chosen to wall themselves up in their houses and left her to do her job alone. But they were Delvers, as tough as their mountains.

She drew a deep breath and stood up. "What can be done is being done, ak'Kal. I have sent for help and I trust my Circle to send what is needful. Meantime, double the firewatch. Keep buckets of dirt handy in your homes. Water scatters flame; heartfire will burn even atop a flood. Dirt will at least slow it down. Don't tarry to see if it's dead after you dump your bucket. Run, if there is even a hint of flame behind you."

"Scant comfort, Dancer," Nugurr muttered.

"Do you expect me to track The Ancient to its lair? Would that I could and be done. Our lore tells us the heart of the world is fire. Destroy it, and the oceans will freeze, and permanent winter will descend on the land. We need The Ancient as much as it needs the open air."

A gale of soft sighs swept the room. Jetta chuckled, and laughed out loud when a score of lambent eyes blinked in unison. A weird, fizzing confidence had hold of her, drawn from the solidity of Annam itself, and these people who dared chase fire with a bucket.

"What happened in the meadow cannot happen again," she said, drawing more startled blinks. "Not unless there is another vein that we have not found. The Ancient will have sucked all the air from the windstone this first time, and so it has lost its route to that spot. If—"

"The meadow is safe, but what about our homes?"

She looked at quiet Wuruun, whose brood of merry children occupied the house nearest the meadow. She saw six nights of haunted watchfulness in his face, and said gently, "While I live, no fire shall touch them."

She met Huunall's eyes. "The Circle of the Fire Clans will soon know what I surmise about The Ancient's behavior. I watched the *hysth* attack Settak a'Kam. It saw opportunity and it took it. We have long known that *hysths* are dangerous because they are cunning as well as hotter flame than any but The Ancient itself. Dancers debate whether The Ancient is intelligent or simply reacts, like any wild beast running on instinct." She drew a steadying breath and said, "*I* believe it thinks, ak'Kal. Perhaps not as we do, perhaps not well, but it thinks, and—it hates."

She turned her back on their puzzled murmurs and held out a hand to the banked fire. Instantly it flared. She drew her hand back before it could find her vulnerable sleeve and pressed her palm toward the floor. The fire sank, the coals glowing sullen red. She left it so, then turned her hand over. The fire revived, licking at the logs laid against the evening gathering outside the windows.

Absolute silence reigned in the inn when she turned to face the Delvers again. "This fire you think tame is only a half-trained beast. Feed it, and it cooperates. Give it the opportunity, and it will burn your house down around you. As would I, if someone kept me as a slave."

Urrana gasped. "What are you saying, ak'Kal?"

Jetta frowned at the fire. "I'm not sure. The Ancient is a puzzle for which there is no answer. We have taken and tamed small bits of it, but hearth flames are only pieces of the larger beast. If The Ancient lives, trapped in the heart of the world, then its incursions into the free air are struggles to survive, the right of all living things. Yet how can we let it run free? We would die, and we too—" Her voice lowered. "We too, have the right to live."

"You could always get Fargoer to negotiate with it," a deep voice said. Laughter rumbled through the inn, but it died too soon. Jetta guessed they found the concept too radical even to ridicule.

She smiled. "What would we offer it? To feed it continually at some carefully chosen spot? To toil our lives long at felling forests to appease its greed? We could strip the world bare and still it would not be enough. Our options are few, save to go on fighting."

"Fire that thinks," Huunall muttered. "Can't say it's a notion I favor."

"Nor I," Jetta said. "But Hylli Fargoer was right. The world is changing. And we must change, too, or lose everything we love."

A small ripple ran through the Windriders. Wyth raised his head. "We hear truth in that, Jetta ak'Kal. You have wrought change here already, since three clans stand together as allies. Yet the question remains. How do we prevent what happened in the meadow from happening in this room? With buckets of dirt?"

Jetta met his eyes, another long look that seemed to shut the world away. "The Dance is changing, Wyth ak'Kal. I'm willing to widen its scope to include whatever it takes to stop The Ancient. Wind, water, dirt—I would haul the moons from the sky if I thought their light could burn The Ancient in its lair. Will you help?"

"We are here," Wyth said simply.

Jetta could not tell if that meant wholehearted cooperation or just a willingness to listen. *I'll take it either way.* Her gaze slipped involuntarily to catch Sheshan's. The nightmare of fire leaping out to consume pale, silent figures set her skin creeping; grimly she forced it out of her mind. The only way forward was together.

She looked around at the Delvers. "I think the key lies at Wind Point."

Nuurn stirred in his seat. "Wind Point is sealed. What could we do there that has not already been done?"

Sheshan straightened from leaning against the wall behind Wyth. "You mean to try to block the Old Man's exits."

Jetta thought of tunnels filled with fire. "If it were possible, yes."

"How could it be possible?" Nuurn shook his head slowly, his gaze turned inward. "We barely approached the inner seal and fire from the lantern ran wild. What must it be like beyond the wall the Windriders built?"

"It's surely a place I have no wish to go," Jetta admitted. "Yet The Ancient rose there, and the maps say those veins are connected to the ones running under the village and the meadow. We can't predict where The Ancient will try next, or how close to the surface those veins may come. Our only way to carry the fight to The Ancient is at Wind Point."

"How?" Burrood askcd flatly.

Jetta sighed. "I don't know. Had I a speedier means of communicating with Firehome I might enlist the wisdom of Dancers far greater than I. Until then—"

Urrana fidgeted. Jetta turned to look at her. Uncharacteristically, the innkeeper would not meet her eye. "There might be a way, Jetta ak'Kal."

Jetta's eyes narrowed. "To speak to Firehome? What way?"

"Our way," Wyth answered. Was that amusement in his voice?

She frowned, watching as he held out one hand. An odd brownish cylinder lay on his palm, quivering in even the slight breeze of his breathing. It looked light and fragile as a dead leaf, yet when he stroked it with the forefinger of his other hand it took no damage.

Jetta eyed it. "What is it?"

For answer he tossed it in the air and gave a casual flick of his forefinger toward Jetta. The cylinder swooped toward her fast enough that she ducked. Wyth smiled a thin smile and crooked his finger. The cylinder stopped, quivering mid-air. Jetta felt the slightest brush of a breeze against her face, barely enough to stir her hair. Hesitantly she reached out and took the cylinder, not without an inquiring glance at Wyth.

He inclined his head a finger's width. "It is sturdier than it looks."

Gingerly she caught it between finger and thumb and found it solid to the touch, though thin as cobweb. "What is this?" Her exploring finger tapped one solid end; she almost dropped it when it popped open and a tiny roll of paper slid out.

"Oh!" she breathed. "For messages. But how are they delivered?"

Wyth crooked his finger again. The little tube tugged out of her hand and floated back to his. Jetta frowned. "That is well and good in this room where you can see it, ak'Kal, but it's a long way to Firehome."

"And such a messenger has traveled there thrice already this summer," Wyth said smugly, putting it away. "The last but five days ago."

Jetta blinked. "Five days—" Her temper snapped. "You let me send a letter by caravan that you could deliver the same day?"

Wyth shrugged. Ayesh threw a quick glance from one to the other and said quietly, "Messages sent in this manner must of necessity be short. Your letter will provide details to your Circle that could not be included in this."

Jetta fumed, betrayed from an unexpected direction. "This is how they knew of fire rising here since Setti and I came." She turned an accusing look on Urrana.

The innkeeper threw up her hands. "Forgive, Jetta ak'Kal, but the Circle here was divided after your coming. You seemed—" She blushed, a remarkable effect on a face so moonlike. "—less than we expected. We needed to know what the Fire Clans had sent us. We know now. There will be no more messages sent that you don't know about."

Jetta's anger cooled as she found herself forced to look at their side. "It was your right to question, ak'Kal," she said to the room at large. "But did no one think I might have need to ask advice while you were busy querying my clan?"

Guilty faces turned from hers; eyes dropped. Huunall chuckled. "You were doing fine on your own. Should we have eroded your confidence?"

Jetta drew a pinched breath, and finally snorted a laugh. "So now that you're satisfied I'm competent, will you share clan secrets, Wyth ak'Kal, and tell me how you can send this thing so far and expect it to land where you will it? And how one receives a reply?"

Wyth smiled his wintry smile. "We are Windriders. It's no trick to us to capture a zephyr and send it where we will, no more than it is for you to call sparks to your hand and banish them again at will."

"But—to go so far—"

He shrugged. "I don't pretend there is no skill involved. One must possess the will as well as the ability."

Her eyebrows shot up. That Wyth had been willing to expend so much effort on behalf of the Delvers told her a great deal about his desire to remain in Annam.

"And how do you know when it has arrived?" she asked, fascinated.

"How do you know when the fire has gone deep enough to no longer be a danger?"

"Hm." Jetta nodded slowly. "One just does."

"One just does."

She tried to imagine it, that tiny leaf of a thing riding the wind over ridge and forest, flung farther and farther afield by the will of a Windrider, until somehow at the other end of that tenuous thread he felt the touch of another's hand on it. Incredible.

Urrana brought her back to the inn and the subject at hand. "If Wyth ak'Kal agrees, we will send another message to Firehome that will get there faster than the one Fargoer carries."

"They haven't replied to the first one?"

Worry flashed into Urrana's face. "Not yet."

Jetta wondered what the Delvers hoped for from that message. Even the full Circle of the Fire Clans present here could not stop The Ancient from rising if it chose. She locked eyes with Wyth. "I have questions to ask before another message goes," she said slowly. "Of Kettori."

"Jetta, no!" Anual spoke up from the rear of the inn. "The woman has burdens enough—"

"She knows things she has not told me. She is a fully qualified Dancer and one who is not nursing wounds. If she wishes to live in this village, let her help to defend it."

The Windriders exchanged glances. Ayesh nodded. "Well said."

"And—" Jetta added. "I want to look at Wind Point again before I send to Firehome."

"Why?" Nuurn asked, his broad face troubled.

Jetta met his eyes. "I want to know if the seals are holding."

Stark dismay settled onto every face in the room. "As you wish," Nuurn said after a moment. "I'll accompany you."

"And I," Sheshan said softly.

"And I," Wyth said unexpectedly. Even Ayesh threw him a surprised glance. The senior Windrider ignored the sea of lambent eyes on him and met Jetta's. "We created the inner seal. If it fails, it is our failure to redeem."

"But—"

Cold eyes flicked to her face and away. The brief accord seemed over. She watched the chill descend into his face again and chewed the inside of her cheek in annoyance. Had he reached his quota of cooperation for the day?

"We will go tomorrow," Huunall said, sealing the matter. "It's too late to climb the ridge today. We don't want to lose our only Firedancer over the edge in the dark."

The low rumble of Delver laughter filled the room. Huunall grinned and Urrana gave Jetta a sly poke in the ribs. She blushed, hated herself for it, and blushed deeper when someone hooted, "A Windrider will catch her, eh, Sheshan?"

She could not look at Sheshan. What did the villagers think, and who had been telling tales? Then Sheshan said, his voice both deep and amused, "I will do my duty by Annam, good folk."

That time it sounded like an avalanche falling on the inn. Delvers chuckled and slapped their knees and bawled at Urrana for burli. The council broke up in a far happier mood than it had begun as Rinood and Mururrn hurried in from the kitchen, their hands full of stone mugs.

"And noë for you, Jetta ak'Kal," Urrana said firmly, bustling off herself to fetch it.

Jetta sank onto her bench, listening to the hopeful talk. The Delvers had seized upon the expedition to Wind Point as though it might actually solve something, spinning hope from the air itself. Fire at Wind Point would be only a little less of a disaster than fire rising here in the village itself, for it might run unchecked for leagues before anyone could stop it. She thought of all that greenery clothed in fire, and closed her eyes, willing herself not to lend The Ancient ideas.

"What troubles you?"

Sheshan's soft voice got her eyes open with speed. He stood beside her, too near the fire for her liking.

"Get back" she said in a weary voice. "That shirt of yours is an open invitation to flame, and I am tired."

He lifted an eyebrow and moved gracefully to sink onto the bench beside her. "I bend to your wisdom. Is this better?"

No! Still, no one seemed to be watching them. She managed a smile. "Yes. I doubt, dressed like that, that you would be as lucky as Setti." She could not suppress a shudder.

"You fear for him."

"Yes. He has never acknowledged limitations, and he is so anxious to help. And," she let a smile cross her face, I could not bear to lose him. He has been one of my dearest friends from childhood."

"Is that all?" The pale eyes watched her without distress or jealousy that she could see. Jetta relaxed.

"I will always love him, but I could not take him for lifemate."

"Because you love him, or because you do not?"

Jetta looked away. "Both," she whispered. The weight rising from her with the admission.

Sheshan looked over his shoulder at the Delvers noisily settling to their evening burli. No one seemed interested in them, but he lowered his voice anyway. "One thing I am cursed with is imagination. I watched the fire engulf Setti's arm, terrified that it would consume the living man. In that moment I knew what it was like for you when your lifemate died. I, at least, was spared seeing it happen. I could not face that memory, I think. Imagining is unbearable enough."

Jetta bit her lip, staring at the ground. "I didn't know my own heart until that moment. My first thought was not to stop the *hysths* but to save Setti, to not let him die," she closed her eyes against the vision. "Like Kori. I love him too much to lose him to fire. And not enough to risk it anyway." She bit her lip. "What sort of coward does that make me?"

His hand closed over hers, warm as a summer wind. "An honest one."

He smiled when her head jerked up. "Fear makes a poor bedfellow. He would hate it if you tried to shelter him. Let him discover what must be discovered on his own, and learn what wisdom he can from it."

"And who made you so wise, Windrider?"

"The Hag," he said flatly.

Mortified, Jetta could find no answer. She was never so grateful to anyone as when Urrana came back with two steaming mugs and a tray laden with a Delver-sized supper. She set it down on the nearest table and beamed at them both.

"That should give you reason to sit. Blessings of the day."

She hurried off before Jetta could get a word in. Jetta eyed the two scaled-down mugs, the two plates. "Well," she said.

"It would seem Urrana made our decision about dinner companions," Sheshan said. "If you will risk eating with a Windrider in such dangerous proximity to fire?"

Jetta snorted. "If I can't tame that little pot fire I'll give back my rank badge."

"Then let's eat." He reached for the bread and tore it in two, gravely offering her half. She took it, and grinned suddenly.

He smiled back with an inquiring tilt of his head. "Tell me the joke?"

"I was thinking of my mother. The last thing she said to me before I left Firehome was that the trick to dealing with Windriders was to always keep them in sight."

"Then she should be pleased that you heeded her advice."

Jetta coughed, tried to suppress a laugh, and failed. It pealed out before she could stop it, cutting through the low rumble of Delver voices like a firewatch bell.

Heads turned. Knowing smiles appeared. She snatched up her mug and buried her face in the steaming depths, fighting the heat creeping up to her hairline. Sheshan was laughing; she could see his shoulders quivering, cursed man. But it *was* funny; she could picture her mother's scandalized face if she knew that half the village assumed she had taken up with a Windrider.

And have I? What would be so wrong in it? And more weight lifted from her shoulders, flow away on the wings of honesty.

Surreptitiously she eyed him over the mug. He had sense she had not expected from the tales that spoke of conflagration at the merest proximity of Rider to Dancer. Or maybe it was Wyth they had in mind, for he was enough to strike sparks from ice. But Sheshan? How was it wrong to rejoice in his company? Here stood a man she need not fear to lose to The Ancient.

Fear is a poor bedfellow. She frowned into the cup. *I am not afraid!*

But if that were so, she would not be wasting time denying it.

"What do you expect to find at Wind Point?" Sheshan asked, pitching his voice over the din.

"Nothing, I hope. I will be best pleased to discover the scals holding and thc Old Man wcll containcd."

"Then why go there?" He ladled some stew onto her plate from a huge bowl.

"I'm not sure." She looked over her shoulder in the direction of that gale-swept ridge and said slowly, "Maybe it's the tug of fire. I think it's always with me, even when fire is not imminent. My thoughts—and nightmares—are drawn again and again to Wind Point."

"Maybe because it is the first place you encountered fire in Annam?"

She took a bite of bread and thought about that. "No. The fire in the meadow was far worse. I can't stop thinking about The Ancient creeping up through those tunnels, level by level."

"But there is nothing for it to feed on. Is there?" He stopped eating, watching her, his eyes steady, somber now.

"There shouldn't be, but the worked-out veins will retain some stone. Heat is a slow thing, but inexorable. It creeps through layers of stone and dirt, slowly chewing its way to the surface, winding here, there, wherever it can find a pocket of air to feed it long enough to creep on, always with The Ancient behind, breathing life into it. I have seen trees wither and die from the heat under their roots, the water in the boles boiling out in the space of a day. And then they burst into flame, and soon the whole forest is burning."

"And you think The Ancient has begun to plan its attacks." There was no mockery in his voice. Eyes that had looked into the feral face of the Hag flicked to the fire and back to her face.

"Perhaps. But it is still balked by its own limitations, and therein lies our hope."

"What will you ask of the Circle?"

She frowned, looking at him over her spoon. "Is that Sheshan asking, or Wyth?"

He shrugged. "If we are to work together, does it matter?"

"No. I suppose not. What will I ask? Nothing. Thanks to Wyth, they know already that Setti is hurt and I am alone. The Circle weighs, the Circle decides. If they decide the danger is great, they will send what help they feel is required."

"Another journeyman?"

"Setti was the best possible choice they could have made!" She reared up, angry until she saw the smile playing around his lips. "And well you know it, ak'Kal."

"I wanted to know if you did. Are there more such inspired failures as Setti at home?"

"They sent me, too," she reminded him sourly.

"But neither of you failed. Eat. Your food grows cold."

She toyed with the stew, wondering what the Circle *would* do. Would they think her mad, or frightened, to send such a report? They would regard claiming sure knowledge of The Ancient as arrogance, and she could guess how some would greet her assertion that The Ancient had begun to think. *I don't care, if the Circle will only consider the possibility.*

Norlahk might listen. Surely he, if any, had survived so much flame by keeping his mind open. Was it not he who had told her to look for a pattern? To show no fear? Above all, to show no fear. If she feared to report to the Circle, then she should not be here. Only in truth could change be born.

She frowned into her empty bowl. "How does the Circle reply without a Windrider to send the cylinder back?" She wanted to know her clan's thoughts now, not weeks from now when a courier had managed the whole dusty return.

Sheshan smiled. "There's a bit more to it than Wyth confessed. The cylinders are attuned to their maker. If someone touches mine, my hand tingles as though the cylinder lay nestled in my palm. A queer feeling, but effective."

"So the Circle could debate for days, and still send an answer." Her hope of a quick reply died along with the image of the Circle standing around a newly-arrived cylinder, writing a reply before the wind died.

"Yes. But do you think they will delay with such grave tidings in hand?"

"I don't know. At this moment I have no idea what they *can* do."

He gave her a sideways glance. "You present a good face to the village."

"Should I frighten them witless because I have no idea how to stop The Ancient?"

One pale eyebrow lifted. "Everyone in this village will follow where you lead. Give them a chance to help."

Jetta thought about children dancing up to give her flowers, so certain in her ability to keep them safe. Her wild, ridiculous hope suddenly faltered. She set the bowl down abruptly.

"I need to see Kettori." *And this time she'd best give me answers.*

"I will accompany you, if you like."

"No. Thank you. My encounters with her are difficult enough without witnesses."

"All right." His hand stayed her when she started to rise. "Will she dance?"

Jetta shook her head. "She's afraid. Not so much of The Ancient finding her, I think, as that through her The Ancient might find Annam."

He let her go and leaned back, his face thoughtful, sad. "I

think that she, too, needs a clean wind."

Jetta stared. "I—maybe we all do. Good night."

"Good night. Be gentle with Kettori."

"As gentle as I can. But she needs to choose between her life and the lives around her and her fear."

She slipped away out the front door, shutting it on the low murmur of voices and the busy clack of spoons and clink of mugs on stone tables. The night wind blew chill, belying the summer stars overhead; Jetta shivered and wondered what winters were like, guessing wryly that perhaps she did not want to know. Except she knew, to keep Annam standing, she would brave the worst snows.

Twenty
Allies and Enemies

She turned right, uphill toward the waterfall and home. At the top of the street the falls gleamed in the starlight, a race of white water breaking itself on the rocks and running madly away in its endless pursuit of the sea. She crossed the bridge and started toward the scatter of ruined houses beyond, winding through jumbled boulders lurking in the night like nesting raptors. Stars gleamed overhead, like chips of windstone glinting in the mine. The inky shoulders of the mountains crowded the sky, crowned with gleaming glaciers gathering faint pearl light to themselves. She paused to admire the view, breathing in the wind that never stopped out here on the exposed slope. Kettori at least had picked a magnificent place to retire.

"What brings you to my door, Jetta ak'Kal?"

For once the voice from the darkness failed to surprise her. Jetta turned her head and saw a dark shape sitting on a rock farther up the slope. "I came for answers, Dancer."

"Then you wasted the walk. I have none to give."

Jetta climbed swiftly up until she found a perch approximately level with Kettori's. She sat down facing that shapeless huddle of shawl and threw a hand out toward Annam. "You told me how to master the Fourth Rank control. I think you care a little bit."

"What I care about is none of your affair."

"Annam must not be among them. These people have been good to you. Will you turn your back on them, too?"

The robed shadow flinched. "If fire comes, what do you expect me to do?"

"At the least you can wield a shovel like everyone else."

Kettori snorted. "Against a *hysth* like you fought in the

meadow? Is that your great plan? Then you are madder than I."

"Madness seldom recognizes itself," Jetta said coolly. "I've thought about what you said. I want to know what you think I could not understand. I want to know why you came here to the place you knew The Ancient would come next. Why, if you fear it so?"

Silence. Jetta kept her eyes on that black and faceless shape, determined to pursue this time if she fled, but Kettori sat as if carved from black ice, the only movement around her rock the shifting of her unbound hair in the night wind. It snapped and rippled like a banner, an announcement to the Old Man that this Dancer would not fight. Jetta itched to pull it out by the roots and force her to stand to her fear.

"What do you want from me?" Kettori asked, the words pulled from her like petals from a flower.

"Truth, ak'Kal. Why did you come to Annam?"

"Atonement."

The word fell into the space between them like fire itself, so unexpected that Jetta stared. "How can you atone if you will not dance?"

"I came to warn—"

"But you didn't do that either! For half a year you lived here alone, and then the fire came, and caught the Delvers unawares."

"To my shame." Bitterness breathed into Kettori's voice, well mixed with regret. "When it came to it, pride held my tongue. And then you came, and I was no longer needed. The best I could do for Annam was to stay away from anything in it that the Old Man could destroy."

Jetta shook her head, her braid whipping back and forth. "I don't accept that. You hid from us, Setti and I. Yet you came ready to dance that night by the storehouses. Did you expect us to fail?"

"Yes." Such unequivocal honesty at least was refreshing. Jetta pressed her harder.

"Why?"

"Fresh from Firehome, what would you know of the Dance but what they taught you?"

Jetta sucked in a breath in outrage. "You knew the forms of the Dance no longer held true, but you didn't tell the

Circle?"

"I did tell the Circle," Kettori said bleakly. "But who listens to a Dancer who has betrayed her village?"

"Father Flame. When was that?"

"Nine years."

"Before ever I left Firehome the first time. And only now do they begin to acknowledge truth. They spoke of a pattern they could not see in The Ancient's attacks. Is that the same pattern you spoke of: the tremors, followed by The Ancient?"

Kettori's faceless head moved back and forth. "No. In my pride, I kept that knowledge to myself, basking in my uncanny reputation for predicting fire. And then it was too late. How many villages have died since, for my pride? Surely Setham was one."

Jetta's head jerked up. "*What?*"

"There was a tremor in Setham eleven moons before the fire, was there not?"

Her jaw dropped. "Yes, but—Fire and Flame! *Kori!*"

Anguish poured down the hill, a wail to rouse the rocks. Kettori bowed her head, becoming but a shapeless mass against the stars. "I am sorry, child. Perhaps if you had known, you might have been warier."

Hot tears streaked Jetta's face, blinding her to the night and the old Dancer sitting on her rock, vulnerable as a flower and yet untouchable in the irremediable quality of her crimcs. Kori! Dcad for an old woman's pridc.

Jetta's hands flexed into claws; she fought an unbearable urge to leap at Kettori and rend her, as her heart had been torn. But she did not; she sat on her rock and shook, long, uncontrollable spasms that gradually lessened and left her weak, empty, rudderless. Kori was dead, and nothing could ever change it.

After a time she could not begin to measure she raised her head. "There was fire in Setham before the tremor."

"But it was worse after, wasn't it?"

Jetta thought about it. She had never considered Setham's fate in that light. Fire had been all the same to her then, just a challenge she had never failed to master. Sometimes it put up a harder fight, but she had thought only that The Ancient had tried some new way, or that she had come late to the scene, or the flame had begun from a hotter flashpoint. She had not considered that the tremor had opened some new avenue for The Ancient.

"Perhaps. I—don't think the fire would have won had I not been with child."

Kettori sucked in a breath. "I had not heard."

Jetta sighed, looking down the dark sweep of the Vale. "It no longer matters. Past is past. It is the future that must concern us now."

"Us? You are the Dancer here, not I."

"Stop it! Setti cannot dance and I can't fight The Ancient alone. Will you let Annam burn while you watch and do nothing?"

"There is nothing I can do. I know only the forms of the Dance I was taught, and they are now useless to both of us."

"You can learn new forms."

Kettori stood up. "No. I've told you what you wanted to know. Go now and leave me in peace, Jetta ak'Kal."

"There will be no peace while The Ancient threatens us all, Dancer," Jetta snapped.

"Then drive The Ancient back to where it belongs."

"How?" Jetta leaped up on her rock, but only stars and mountains showed above the rock where Kettori had been. "Kettori! Flame find you, come back here!"

"Flame has already found me, girl," came the cold voice out of the night. "Go, and trouble me no more."

"Then burn!" Jetta shouted in utter frustration. "These people deserve better from you! You take their hospitality and return *nothing!*"

Silence. Jetta muttered a curse and turned away. Questions, always more questions.

Slowly she made her way home to change into leathers and go on patrol, her stomach in a knot of anguish too taut to let her sleep, though her bones ached to lie down. Without Setti she dared rest only a few hours at a time, reluctant to leave the burden to the firewatch, who could not stop any real incursion with buckets and shovels. At Nuurn's door she stopped and turned to look up. Only the stars and the dark swell of the ridge above Annam met her eye, no distant glow of fire running wild in the night. The seals still held at Wind Point.

Somehow it gave her little comfort.

She pushed open the door. Anual looked up from her chair by the fire in the front room and smiled. Yellow cloth filled her lap. Jetta recognized the material, amazed. With all of Annam threatened, still Anual carried on, making clothes for her guest as though through routine she could forge a weapon to beat off The Ancient.

Maybe she can, Jetta thought, appreciating the way the lamp glow lit the hangings covering the black stone of the walls and caressed the stone children on the bannister. A rich smell of bread and roasted meat wafted out of the kitchen, reminding her of the supper she had abandoned to hunt for Kettori. She sniffed appreciatively; instantly Anual leaped up, thrusting the half-finished shirt aside.

"Are you hungry? You left the inn so quickly you scarce had time to eat—"

Hastily Jetta shook her head. "I ate with Sheshan. I'm fine."

Anual cackled. "I saw. It was a good sight, I must say."

"It was a meal," Jetta said tartly, edging toward the stairs. "No more."

"Windrider and Firedancer eating together. Surely a first. Should we not mark the occasion?" Anual asked innocently.

"You are an incurable meddler, ak'Kal, do you know that?" Jetta started up the stairs.

Anual's laugh pealed out behind her. "And where would be the fun in life if we all kept our noses inside our own houses?" She lowered her voice, her eyes darting toward the stairs and Setti sleeping in his room at the end of the hall. "You could do far worse in a lifemate, child."

Now we're back to child, Jetta thought impishly. *I suppose the whole village will be trying to match Sheshan and me.*

"Pity the children, never knowing what color their eyes should be," she said, and fled, laughing, as Anual's eyes widened to blue saucers.

Children, Jetta thought, dismayed. How could any offspring of such a pair have a future, when a breath could call flame down upon them?

Or drive it away? Jetta paused halfway through changing into her leathers, frowning at nothing. Windriders could guide a wind across forty leagues and never let it go. Where else could they drive the wind? How strong a gale could they control? She had watched a storm wind smother an infant fire once, snuffing it as her breath could snuff a candle, but no Dancer she knew—herself included—would trust to such a solution.

Still, the idea intrigued her. She could not forget the winds swirling into a prison for an angry *hysth*, or Wyth's casual arrogance. He was a Fourth Rank master, doubtless with enough ability to rise to Fifth if he cared at all. What kind of unbending will did it take to bring a storm to heel? What would Wyth consider a challenge? For the first time she began to appreciate the other Windriders' respect for their prickly master.

Quietly she pushed open Setti's door and stood looking at him. For the tenth time she returned a quiet blessing to the Mother that this had happened while the drovers were present in Annam. Annam's healer could in no way match the vast experience of the lowlands with burns, nor did the healing herbs carried by the drovers grow in these highlands. The village healer learned quickly. Setti's left arm lay unbandaged atop a Delver-sized pillow, glistening in the light from the hall under a clear paste concocted from a drover remedy refined over untold years of experience with fire. His right hand, mittened in bandages against the shocks that came from every thoughtless move, lay atop the coverlet, lifting gently to the steady rise and fall of his easy breathing. Safe, mending as only Firedancers could, full to the eyebrows with a numbing tea of Anual's brewing.

And his eyes had turned the color of Annam's dirt: rich, brown, full of the memory of smoke and flame and victory. A master's color. Another victory, and a conundrum.

For the first time Jetta let herself think about that dance six days ago, the two of them melded in harmony any pair could wish for, step for step, beating back The Ancient while the Windriders drove it where it had no wish to go. *So close,* she thought, mourning a moment snatched away before it could shape itself into—perhaps—the solution Annam needed. Setti was unique, a talent so wild even The Ancient could not outguess him, and so willing to trust he could bend mind and soul to her lead. Of all the Dancers she knew, only he could have so quickly abandoned the forms that bound their lives. Yet she knew he had done it in large part because he loved her, and some part of him hoped for reward in the doing. And she could not forget that even their inspired victory had not been purely a thing of the Firedance. Somewhere in the pattern stood Sheshan, wrapping them both in wind that did no harm.

Three, not two. Three for victory. Three for heartbreak.

There must be a way!

Jetta wheeled away toward the stairs, frustrated anew. Wind and fire! She suspected it would take both to defeat The Ancient's grab for Annam. But even if she could induce Kettori to dance again, Kettori could not dance like Setti, giving all, opening herself to the rhythm as it needed to be, not as she felt it should be. And Jetta knew without asking that maybe no other Dancer could accept the feel of wind rushing past as an ally and not an enemy.

Anual was talking to Nuurn in the kitchen when she came back down the stairs, their voices a quiet rumble beyond the door. Quickly Jetta slipped out and turned left toward the inn. She had not taken three steps when Sheshan materialized out of the night beside her.

"You should be sleeping," she told him, unsurprised.

"So should you. Let the firewatch do their duty. You cannot be everywhere all the time."

"I have to try, until the Circle sends another Dancer, or the Old Man gives up."

"Kettori will not help you?"

"No." Jetta shied from the painful revelations that came with that refusal and looked up at him, a tall pale shadow in the night. "You knew she wouldn't."

"It seemed likely. She is badly hurt inside and, as yet, unhealed."

"It is possible to live with hurt," Jetta said tightly. "She nurses hers like a new rank badge."

"Perhaps she needs someone to send her forth to her duty again."

Jetta stopped dead. "As the Circle did to me, you mean."

His head turned but his face was lost in shadow. "I would not presume to guess your Circle's reasons for sending you here. But it seems to have been good for everyone concerned."

"Except Setti." Jetta started on, guilt gnawing her.

"He'll mend. What else is on your mind?"

She stopped, looking up at the ridge. "Wind Point."

"Why are you so certain the danger lies there?"

"I just am. I feel like there is some great raptor perched up there, awaiting its time until we've grown complacent."

"Then it will wait a long time."

She turned her head to look at him, caught by the flat promise in his voice. "You love this place, don't you?"

"It is the only home I have ever known," he said, his head turned away. "Windriders are wanderers, following the storms. Nowhere in my childhood was there a place we remained more than a season. The Hag is less determined, or more fickle, than The Ancient. She seldom troubles the same place often. Villages are unwilling to pay the upkeep of Windriders on a permanent basis." She heard no bitterness in his voice, only calm a shade too reasoned. That bitterness lay under it, she could not doubt.

"Annam seemed like a dream," he said. "Folk who did not judge or pry, or look askance at us when we passed. We were half afraid to breathe for fear we would wake."

"I'm sorry," Jetta said, knowing it was inadequate.

He shrugged, a ripple of feathery shirt fluttering in the darkness. "Annam is precious, and we will defend it."

They came to the first firewatch post at the fork in the street, greeted the young apprentice there and walked on down to the southern bridge arching black over the silver ripple of the racing water. The youngster stood leaning one hip against the stone railing, staring down the road toward the river far below. He jumped and spun around when Jetta greeted him.

"Eh? Oh, Jetta ak'Kal. And the evening's blessing to you too, Sheshan ak'Kal. Come to see if we're awake, Dancer?"

"I know you are. In that I trust."

"No fire will rise undetected on my watch," he said flatly.

"Nor mine." She touched his arm in reassurance and prowled on, wishing she believed that promise. With The Ancient rising directly under her she had still been unable to pinpoint its location, only feel its amorphous threat. Sheshan walked beside her, soundless as the night, and wordless until they had finished the whole round of the posts and started back up the hill from the storehouses. He glanced toward the burned meadow, then suddenly turned aside.

Jetta stopped, startled. "What do you see?"

"Here is where the fire rose," he said, standing beside the mound of dirt thrown up by Delvers hunting for the vein The Ancient had climbed. "Can you sense the Old Man still?"

Jetta came to stand beside him, looking down at the black depression amid the dance ground. Only a faint edge of ruined windstone caught the starlight; the fire's rise had cracked the stone apart and left it blackened and brittle and useless. She stooped to touch it, wrinkling her nose from the faint fire stink, and rose again rubbing ash off her fingers.

"No. When stone burns there is nothing left at the end to allow a second passage of fire."

"Then what if we drove fire into the stone from this end?" He knelt to finger the charred rubble. "Could we deny The Ancient entry by ruining his avenues? A different sort of windtrap."

Jetta caught her breath. "Release fire into the stone?" The thought took her aback with radical possibilities she had never considered. "Old Man Fire."

She sank onto her heels beside him, looking at the faint gleam of pale stone cracked from the vein. "I don't know if it could be done. Domestic fire is never as hot as what rises from the earth. I'm not sure we could heat the stone sufficiently, or keep driving it deeper into the vein."

"We would not have to drive it far from the surface to render the vein useless, surely?"

Jetta stared unseeingly across the Vale, prickling all over with sudden hope. A score of difficulties leaped to mind, balanced by a hundred benefits. "How would the Delvers feel about ruining so much windstone?"

Sheshan stood up, dusting his hands. "To save Annam? Huunall would light the fire himself."

She shuddered and stood up. "Unleashed fire hot enough to form a *hysth*. There's a notion to set the Circle stamping sparks." But excitement tickled the back of her brain. Possibilities chased each other through her mind, swarming into fantastic jumbles like clouds piling into thunderheads that somehow managed to produce rain. "I need to think about this."

He caught her hand. "Jetta—it is a notion born of ignorance. Even I can see the danger in it. Do nothing foolish."

"Such as?" She stared up at him, cursing the darkness that hid his face.

"Such as experimenting alone." His hand tightened, drawing her closer. "I would not wish to see you lying injured beside Setti."

She laughed away his concerns. "Setti would be thrilled to have me lying beside him."

"Not that way, he wouldn't. And I—could not bear it." He ducked his head suddenly, so that even the faint gleam of starlight on his pale forehead dimmed as his cobwebby hair shifted to hide his face.

"Sheshan—"

"Don't." His finger on her lips silenced her. "You are not ready, and this is not the time. Go and think about defeating the enemy. One new idea at a time."

"If you think that a Windrider-Firedancer match is a new idea, you haven't spoken to Anual lately," she said, and won a breathy laugh.

"Nonetheless. Go. Sleep. It is a long walk to Wind Point."

"For you, too."

"Ah, but don't you know that Windriders can fly?" Laughing, he turned and disappeared into the night as effortlessly as smoke on the wind.

Jetta stared. "Well, that would help!" she yelled after him. "Fly to Firehome and bring back the Circle!"

His laugh drifted back. Jetta grinned, but it lasted only until her foot encountered one of the mounds of dirt ruining the meadow. Grimly she kicked it apart, half expecting to bring The Ancient ravening up. But only the wind swirling down from Wind Point stirred the dust, patting her cheek with chill hands as though to catch her attention. She turned and looked up the long, long sweep of the ridge, thinking of fire running up the hidden veins under the mountain, sucking Annam's lifeblood, laying a trap to kill another village.

Not while I live. Never again.

But every nerve drew her toward that lonely door on Wind Point, and she dreamed that night of fire.

Twenty One
The Coming Storm

The Windriders walked with the rest of them up the steep trail in the bright dawn, disdaining to fly, if indeed they could. Wyth glided up the steep trail as though it were level ground, his eyes on the ridgeline, not speaking even to Sheshan, who once again planted himself behind Jetta. His footsteps made no sound even on the gritty black pebbles the Delvers had laid down in places to shore up soft spots, so that time and again she turned her head to see if he was still there. Sheshan smiled at her but said nothing, and after a while she stopped checking. Her mind skipped up the ridge to Wind Point, thinking of the entrance that Nuurn had sealed. Were there other exits from that mine, even cracks in the rock, air shafts where The Ancient might climb into the free air? They must find them all and stop them up, or risk waking some night to fire racing down the ridge.

What will I do if The Ancient breaks free? That thought haunted her now as it had haunted her dreams. *I cannot beat down a major conflagration alone. The Ancient take Kettori. The two of us might do some good, but if she will not dance, what chance have I alone?*

At least the Circle knew her problem, if not her guesses about the solution. For that she could forgive Urrana reporting behind her back, and Wyth's smug superiority. The question remained, however: would they believe her about The Ancient? They had ignored Kettori nine years ago. Was that only because they had believed her nerve had broken, and so anything she said was suspect? Or were they too steeped in tradition to welcome new thoughts? Jetta could not believe that of Norlahk, but he was only one of seven. Still, they *had* recognized something was wrong when they sent her out this spring in such ignorance, hoping for new ideas from the most unorthodox pair in the Fire Clans. Perhaps they would listen to the results, however farfetched.

The trail broke over the ridge. Nuurn stopped to let her catch her breath. It irked Jetta to discover that she was the only one who needed to. Huunall, the oldest of them all, prowled restlessly up and down while they waited, as energetic as a boy. The Windriders breathed as easily as if they had indeed flown up here. Wyth stood with his face into the south wind and his eyes closed; Sheshan turned toward the western mountains and raised his hands in a curious gesture almost of greeting.

"Why did you do that?" Jetta asked.

He lowered his hands and turned his head, his face still. "As you sense fire, I sense where the winds lie. This one will shift before midday."

"Yes," Wyth agreed without opening his eyes. "It will be a west wind then, and strong. Let us see what there is to see at Wind Point. The west wind is an uncertain ally at need."

Jetta's eyebrow shot up. Just what did he intend to do with any wind up here? But he had already started on, forcing Nuurn to hurry into the lead again. Huunall shortened his stride to fall in beside Jetta on the wider trail across the ridge, his boots puffing up floury dust at every stride.

"You still think there will be trouble up here," he said.

"I hope not. But I can't stop thinking about four levels of fire. It's finding fuel somewhere, and I would guess that air is leaking into the mine. Are there ventilation shafts sunk that deep?"

"We blocked them," Huunall said. "Long ago when the mines were closed, lest children fall to their deaths. But we did not block them against fire. How could we know there would be a need?"

Jetta's heart gave an anxious thump. "Can you find them again?"

He blew a thoughtful sigh. "Maybe. It was many years ago."

"We must, ak'Kal. It will take only one to give The Ancient the victory."

Huunall gave the ridgetop a slow, assessing glance.

Jumbled boulders, tough, scattered needle trees, scaly lichen clinging to the rocks and a little stunted grass made it seem a barren place. To their left the ridge lifted up and up to a snowfield clinging to the southern curve of a jagged peak, seeping gently into a little stream running down beside the trail, as the snows on the other side fed the stream cradling Annam itself. Jetta knew that to his eyes it would seem like precious little foothold for the Old Man. But too many of the rocks were white, and too many of the trees overhung the greener valley below. Flaming branches falling over the cliffs could spread havoc into places she could not reach before the fire had rooted itself. She pointed at a twisted old teller tree with its roots cracking the stone apart near the edge of the cliff.

"Look how the tree splits the stone. A pathway exists that didn't before. How deep does that crack run down the cliff, and what might it connect to, eh?"

Huunall turned troubled eyes on her. "You see enemies everywhere, Jetta."

"A Dancer must think like The Ancient. The Old Man seizes opportunities. The flame you ignore as too small in your fever to kill the larger *hysth* is too often the one that escapes into the rafters and burns the house down."

"Has that happened to you?" he asked gently.

"No. But it was drummed into us on the practice ground from our first day in First Rank, and too often I saw my classmates make that mistake."

She stiffened as fire sense rushed over her, a gut-level awareness of flame somewhere close. Jetta quelled it, knowing it was the fire deep inside the ridge calling to her. But she could not stop an anxious glance down the slope toward Wind Point itself, craning for a glimpse of the tall doors sealing the tunnels. She could not see them from this angle. No smoke curled up from that direction, no bright tongues of flame licked the sky. Yet she could not shake a mental image of the doors lying cracked and broken and fire shooting out in triumph.

She looked somberly at Huunall. "Flame is least dangerous while it is still hunting fuel. Let it once get rooted, and it becomes arrogant, vicious. Malicious fire will pause to lure a Dancer, spending infant flames to build itself into a *hysth* and call The Ancient. Let it chew awhile on the accumulation of dead needles at the bottom of a crack in the rock, and it will rise up in your face and eat you alive."

He nodded slowly. "Then we will find the old vents into the mine. Tell us what to do, ak'Kal, and we will do it."

The trail dropped over the ridge and started down. Jetta craned past Wyth for a first glimpse of Wind Point, and gulped down relief at sight of its pale stone standing undisturbed. So much for nerves and nightmares. Huunall dropped in behind her as the trail narrowed; she heard him talking to Sheshan but could not catch more than "the seals" over the moan of the wind blowing up out of the canyon. She hurried on, eager to check those seals for herself.

The doors looked just the same as they had when Nuurn sealed them. He stopped in front of them and smiled at Jetta. "You had me worried, Dancer. I dreamt all night of fire creeping through the seal."

He ran a caressing finger down the join between black doors and pale native stone—and jerked it back with a gasp. "It's hot!"

Huunall made an inarticulate noise and stepped up beside him. He laid his own hand on the windstone framing the entrance, and withdrew it with equal alacrity. Jetta met his wide frightened eyes, steeled herself, and touched a palm to the join.

Her tolerance for heat far exceeded theirs; she kept it there a moment, her jaw clenching on despair. Heat lay in the stone, not yet enough to explode into fire, but it could only be a matter of time. The Ancient had broken the inner seal, or crawled around it through the veins of windstone forming half the walls of the old shafts. Seven levels of fire lay beyond.

She drew her hand back, unconsciously clenching it into a fist. "The Old Man is on the other side of the door," she said, proud that her voice was so level as she pronounced imminent disaster. "How thick is this wall?"

"Delver-height or better," Huunall said when Nuurn seemed paralyzed. "And the vein behind it three times that. Look around."

Jetta assessed the great knob of windstone that formed Wind Point. To either side of the black doors it sprawled across the headland above the drop to the valley, shallowing on either side until it disappeared under the coarse grass. She could not guess how deep it went, but it was thick, the only thing in their favor.

She moved away toward the sheer drop, trailing one hand down the vein. The heat diminished with distance from the doors, until the pale stone lay cool under the blanket of grass. She tried the other way, toward the ridge, walking back past the Delvers watching her with huge troubled eyes. The Windriders stood in wary silence; even Wyth held his tongue in respect of knowledge beyond his ken.

The stone felt cooler on this side. She walked back slowly, her head down lest her expression frighten them all witless. The fire, when it came, would explode outward to the west, falling unhindered into the green and uninhabited valley on the opposite side of the ridge from Annam. A valley with no road, no easy access, and uncounted seasons' worth of dead timber, fallen needles, and drying summer grass to feed the greed of The Ancient. It would run the length and breadth of the valley and up the ridges to either side, climbing soon or late into Annam Vale, a full-grown monster no single Dancer could hope to stop.

"Jetta?"

Sheshan's soft voice forced her head up. Hurriedly she fought to put reassurance into her expression and turned to Nuurn and Huunall fretting in front of the door. "It's not running toward Annam yet," she said, and saw Nuurn gulp down a great breath in relief. Huunall only watched her steadily, and she knew that he, at least, had seen beyond her facade.

"What must we do?" he asked, his voice a low rumble as deep as the mountains.

She turned to Wyth. "The message must go to Firehome with all speed. I can't be here and in Annam at the same time. The breadth of the windstone here is slowing The Ancient's advance. I don't believe it can tunnel through only a small portion of the vein quickly. The heat has spread through all this stone, radiating outward from the tunnel. As yet it is nowhere near flash point, but it's only a matter of time. Unless we can think of a way to contain it, the fire will come through at some point around the doors. I need help, and soon."

Wyth inclined his pale head. "The message will go today. What else can be done?"

She turned to look at the doors again. "How quickly could you build an outer wall of containment stone, Huunall ak'Kal?"

Nuurn and Huunall exchanged a look. "Three days," Huunall said with certainty. "Covering this whole face?"

"Yes." It would not stop an upward spread into the grass, but it might prevent a disastrous burst through into open air above the valley. At the least it might buy them some time.

"Begin now, masters," she said soberly. "The quicker built, the better I will feel."

Without a word Nuurn turned and strode off up the trail toward Annam. Huunall looked after him a moment and then at the innocent white wall of stone as though it would bite. "That is a stopgap measure," he guessed. "Is it not?"

"Yes," Jetta said honestly. "There are too many other paths for it to take. But we can slow it down while we think of other ways to stop it. If it drops into the valley—" She made a small, forlorn gesture with one hand, taking in that green and untouched invitation to destruction.

A gust of wind against her cheek startled her into turning toward the west. Wyth and Sheshan were both looking up toward the mountains. Wyth raised a tentative hand, fingers spread as though to catch the wind in his palm. It gusted fitfully, fell away to nothing, and then returned, sweeping steadily across the point of rocks and on up the ridge.

Wyth dropped his hand. "If it blows like this when the fire escapes we will have a firestorm, Jetta ak'Kal."

When, not if. Wyth was nothing if not a realist. Jetta quailed from the vision conjured by such a terrible word as *firestorm*. "Then we will hope for a different wind in that hour, and better cage The Ancient in the meantime."

"Could we build a firetrap here?" Sheshan asked.

Huunall spun around and surveyed the mine entrance. "Perhaps," he said with renewed hope. "We dare not pierce the windstone now, but perhaps there is a way. I will think on it."

Jetta nodded at Sheshan. "If there were a way to cool the rock it would help, as well."

Sheshan glanced at Wyth. "Ak'Kal?"

Wyth glanced up at the cloudless summer sky. "There is nothing to work with. It would take a good hand of Fourth Ranks or a pair of Fifth Ranks together to pull a storm in off the sea this far inland. I would not care to try even then without one of the Water Clan masters to help."

Jetta's eyes widened. So casually they talked of changing the weather itself. Huunall glanced at Wyth and then up the ridge, his eyes narrowing. "We may not have rain, but what of water?" He pointed at the little stream trickling from the glacier above. "We could divert that."

Jetta looked up the long sweep of ridge between this spot and the stream, and winced from the sheer amount of labor it would take to build a flume. Huunall saw her face, and laughed, if not with humor.

"A little hard work, aye. What is sweat against a ruined village?"

"You're right, and I have never doubted your industry. But I cannot help feeling that time is not on our side."

"Then the sooner we begin, the sooner it will be finished."

He turned toward Annam. Wyth stopped him with a languid flick of one hand. "From now on a Windrider will be stationed on the ridge, Huunall ak'Kal. We will give warning should the seals fail, and do what we may after that."

His glance turned to Jetta, so neutral it irked her. Did he still doubt the one who would have to climb that terror of a trail in haste and dance at the end? "A good idea," she forced herself to say without rancor.

"Aye," Huunall said, and strode off, his impossibly long strides swallowing the trail at a rate Jetta could not match if she ran. Nuurn was already over the ridge and gone. Wyth glanced at Sheshan.

"Take the first watch. I'll send to Firehome. Jetta ak'Kal, is there anything I should include in the message that would impress your Circle to act?"

"Say that I think The Ancient has planned this. But say to Norlahk ak'Kal: 'My eyes will match yours if we do not stop what is coming'."

Sheshan's eyebrow shot up; Wyth only nodded and abandoned them as thoroughly as the Delvers had done, seeming to drift up the trail without touching the ground.

The hair lifted on Jetta's arms, for truly it looked as if he were flying.

She shivered. Instantly Sheshan said, "It's not that cold up here. Are you frightened? Of the beast trapped behind that door?"

"No. Yes. I fear what could happen. What it will do to this valley if we can't stop it."

He set an arm around her shoulders and drew her close. "You won't let that happen."

"I don't know how to prevent it!"

He wrapped both arms around her and simply held her in the quiet warmth of his embrace. "We *will* stop it, all of us together, Delver and Windrider and Dancer. You are not alone, Jetta."

She wrapped her own arms around his waist and burrowed against him, staring dry-eyed down into the green and verdant valley below. "If we fail-"

"We will not fail." His arms tightened around her. "Jetta, my Jetta. You have given even Wyth purpose again. Do you not see how you have given Huunall and Nuurn hope, how your ideas keep them from surrendering to despair? And they're good ideas, Jetta. Do *not* let the Old Man win before the fight is even joined."

"I know now why Kettori fled her village," Jetta whispered. "Not for fear of the fire, but for fear of failure."

"You are not Kettori. Look at me. *Look* at me."

He loosened his hold and drew back, forcing her to take her own weight. Slowly, ashamed of letting her nerves show, she looked up into his face, and only then realized how shamelessly she had wound herself against him.

Blushing hotter than the Old Man, she stepped back and wrapped her arms around herself, pretending the cool west wind troubled her. Somehow she met his eyes, hoping her face showed only bland inquiry and not how much she craved to step back into the warm circle of his strength. *It is not for him to hold me up, nor Setti either.*

His hands, too, seemed to not know exactly where to go; he toyed with the restless layers of his shirt, his face somber, his eyes intent on hers. "It's time to look forward, Jetta. Setham is past, and there is nothing you can do for that village or its people. Because you failed once does not mean you must inevitably fail again. Clear your mind of fears without meaning."

"Meaning it's all right to be heartily terrified of The Ancient?" she asked.

He threw back his head and laughed. "The Ancient should flee to its lair now and save itself a deal of humiliation."

She snorted, but the intense fear and the confusion passed and left her mind focused. What future there was for them, for Annam, for Setti or anyone here rested in her hands. The Ancient still raged behind the barrier of stone; Wind Point was still a worry. Nothing had changed.

Hasn't it? she wondered, suddenly terrified that Sheshan might be here when The Ancient broke through. "Where will you watch from?" she asked, prepared to argue some brave and foolhardy spot too close to the mine.

Sheshan turned and pointed at the top of the ridge. "There. We must devise a signal that can be seen easily in the village."

He moved one long-fingered hand, shooing her up the trail ahead of him; Jetta moved off, content in his presence a step behind her. They had barely reached the top when a score of Delvers topped out carrying picks and spades and buckets, each with a small block of containment stone strapped in a pack on his back. Jetta blinked, still astonished by how quickly the Delvers could organize themselves at need.

Each of them murmured greeting as they went by but did not linger to talk. Jetta watched them hurry down the trail to Wind Point, chewing her lip. "If the Circle of the Fire Clans fails to act, I will personally rip the rank pins from their shoulders if ever I see them again."

"They'll act. If Annam falls, The Ancient will turn its eye on other Delver villages, and then where will the world obtain containment stone?"

Such calm practicality restored her perspective. "True."

"Go now," he told her. "Go and show your face to the village, and let them take comfort from the confidence of their Dancer."

If she had any. "What signal will you give if The Ancient appears?"

Sheshan looked around, at a loss. "A good question. Ah."

He moved away a few paces and stopped at the edge of a barren patch where snow and wind had scoured most of the thin soil away, leaving only a few hardy tufts of grass clinging among the rocks. He moved his hands together in a graceful, twirling gesture like a spinner twisting yarn. Jetta recoiled as dirt and grass leaped into the air fifty paces away, a tall, tight-spun column whirling tightly in place at the top of the ridge. It was dense enough to spot from anywhere in the valley, clearly unnatural with its lack of sideways movement.

Jetta shook her head. "Dancers spend their lives banishing the object of our talent. You spend yours calling it. That is," she said, "unnatural."

Sheshan smiled at her over his shoulder. "Unnatural is being at the mercy of either." He dropped his hands. The column collapsed in a puff of dust and scattered grass. "That will serve by day. I'll think of something else for the night watch."

"Well, fire isn't an option."

He chuckled. "No. I had in mind a lantern or a torch."

Jetta thought of fire leaping from Nuurn's lantern, but could not readily think of anything else. "That will have to do."

"Go," he said gently. "I'll see you this evening."

Twenty Two
Plans

Jetta could not believe the depth of her reluctance to leave him, but she started down the steep trail as fast as she dared, not anxious to linger above some exposed drop to oblivion. Halfway down she met another group of Delvers and pressed herself to the cliff on the uphill side as they passed her. Nuurn, coming up behind them, stopped when he saw her.

"We are indebted to you, Jetta ak'Kal. I would not have thought of this."

"I just hope it's enough."

"It can do no harm."

True enough. Jetta felt a little better.

Annam looked like a fest without the finery when she came through the containment wall and crossed the footbridge above Annam. Every Delver was out of doors and even the smallest children were running with purpose. Huunall had called everyone out of the mines and set the cutters to the containment stone remaining in the storehouses, knocking the big blocks down to a size that could be carried up the ridge. A steady stream of apprentices packed them up to the bottom of the trail and piled them ready for transport up to Wind Point. Jetta set a pair of Delver children to keep watch for Sheshan's signal and went on to the inn, where Huunall had ensconced himself, the fifth rank delver sketching furiously at one of the tables. She leaned over his shoulder and saw a firetrap emerging, shaped to the face of Wind Point.

"That will take a lot of stone."

"We have it to spare," he said without looking up. "If we can cool the windstone, how much will it slow The Ancient?"

She thought about it, staring unseeingly at the coals sleeping on the hearth. "I don't know. I'll experiment if you have some windstone to spare."

"Rununn!" Huunall bellowed. Jetta jumped.

Rununn dashed in from the kitchen, hastily stuffing the end of a spice loaf into his mouth. "Ak'Kal?"

"Run and tell the cutters to shape three or four blocks of windstone for Jetta ak'Kal. Big ones. Bring them to wherever she wishes."

"Yes, ak'Kal!" Rununn leaned down to peer at Jetta, poised to run at her word.

"Uh—bring them to the waterfall," she said. "If something goes wrong we can cool them down that way."

"Yes, ak'Kal." He dashed off, slamming the inn door behind him.

That brought Urrana out in wrath, dusting flour from her hands. "Who is trying to knock down the inn?" she demanded, and then saw Jetta.

"Ah. You'll be wanting food." She disappeared again. Jetta, bemused, sat down on the settle by the fire, already forgotten by Huunall. Now that it came to it, she was half afraid to try Sheshan's idea. But what choice had The Ancient left them?

She remembered something. "Huunall, are your folk looking for the ventilation shafts?"

"Aye," he said absently without looking up. "They will build caps across all they can find."

"Good," Jetta murmured, but it was not enough. How could anyone spot all the natural cracks in the earth that might serve as chimneys for the Old Man to climb?

One worry at a time.

Rinood appeared with a laden tray, she set it down beside Jetta, and dove back into the kitchen without a word. *She at least will not be glad to hear that Sheshan and I are clinging like frightened children,* Jetta thought, and blushed, sitting all alone beside the hearth. *I must be mad. A Windrider?* Hylli Fargoer was right. The world was changing.

We must *change,* she thought, sobered. *We can no longer stand alone, each clan hoarding its secrets. We can no longer afford stupid myths and baseless prejudice. Where will we be if someday there are no Windriders left in the world?*

And where are they, anyway? Unwilling to disturb Huunall again, she caught Urrana's arm as she hurried by with a basket of bread, bound for the front door. "Oh," Urrana said. "Wyth is sending your message and the rest are helping to find the old vents. Excuse me, ak'Kal. I must get food to the meadow." She hurried out.

Jetta picked at the roast and the crisp vegetables doubtless gleaned from Wuruun's garden patch by the stream, where he kept his brood busy weeding and hoeing to keep them out of mischief. She realized she had not seen them there when she came down from the ridge, and guessed that, like the rest of the village, they had been set to work elsewhere, running errands, or carrying stone, enlisted into the war against The Ancient.

Sorrow closed her throat that danger had so encroached upon their innocence. She set down her fork and thrust herself up from the settle, startling Huunall into an unplanned stroke of the pen. He muttered and reached for the blotter, craning over his shoulder at Jetta.

"Something wrong?"

"No. I'm going to the waterfall. Tell the children to stay away, and let no one approach for the next little while."

His gaze sharpened. "What are you going to do?"

"Call fire," she said shortly. His eyes widened. "Finish your drawing, ak'Kal. I'll keep you informed."

He nodded slowly, his feathery eyebrows drawn into a thoughtful frown over his lucent eyes. She felt him watching her as she made her way out of the inn, but he kept his questions on his tongue. The weight of his trust lay on her like a physical thing.

I cannot fail. I must not fail.

Not a soul passed her on the street; Annam could have been deserted save that when she glanced between the houses toward the meadow and the storehouses she saw the whole area swarming with Delvers. Here and there a child ran errands or dashed off to carry a message. The women who normally leaned out their windows to greet her were down there too, turning hands long accustomed to shaping dough to shaping stone. The village felt abandoned, a notion that set her teeth on edge and drove her lagging feet on in a more determined rhythm.

I will not fail them.

"Jetta!"

Jetta stopped dead outside Nuurn's door and looked up. Setti stood in the open window of his room, a little pale but fully dressed in green breeches and a gray Delver shirt Anual must have cut down to size for him, as she had neatly removed the left sleeve. His wounded arm rested across his right wrist. Jetta winced from the raw, livid look to the burns and the deep lines around his mouth.

"You should be in bed!"

"I'll go mad if I spend another minute there. What's happening? Anual's gone and the kitchen fire is all but dead, with nary a cookie to be had. The whole village is down in the meadow. And why did Rununn trundle windstone across the bridge?"

"He didn't tell you?"

"He said only that Jetta ak'Kal needed it."

Jetta hesitated. Setti's lips tightened. "Don't treat me like a child, Jetta."

She met the steady eyes staring out of his face like two chips of muddy windstone. "Come then," she said. "Come tell me if I'm mad."

His eyebrow shot up, but he turned without a word and disappeared from the window. A much longer time than she expected later, he made his careful way out the door, clutching a pillow under his good arm. It hurt to watch him stepping so slowly, careful of jarring his arm, his left shoulder hunched against pain, destroying the Dancer's lines of his body and hobbling his lithe grace. But he managed a smile when he looked up and saw her watching.

"Give me a week, ak'Kal, and I'll dance with the Old Man until he screams for mercy."

"You are a fool," she said affectionately. "But I believe you."

He gave her a sharp, surprised look. Jetta touched his shoulder. "I'm recommending you for mastery, Setti. You earned it that day in the meadow. I don't think even Kori could have danced as well, and certainly not as creatively."

He stopped dead, wide-eyed, his jaw sagging in shock. "You mean that."

"Of course I mean it! Have I ever said anything to you I

don't mean?"

The shy smile beginning to tug at his mouth faded. "No," he said glumly, and turned away from her to stare across the bridge at the five blocks of gleaming white stone waiting in the center of the narrow track.

"What are you planning?"

"Come watch. I may need you to put out a fire or two."

He snorted, but walked on beside her to the end of the bridge. He stopped there without her bidding, settling himself on the wide coping with what looked like relief. The pillow ended in his lap, propping the sore arm.

Rununn had done well. Four fair-sized blocks of pale stone, as long as Jetta's arm and as broad as Setti, waited in a stack; a much larger block lay beyond them, placed thoughtfully where it could do least harm to the village.

Jetta stripped to Dance leathers and rolled one of the smaller blocks to the very edge of the stream where she could kick it in at need. With all of its air pockets drowned, even heartfire must die eventually, and she could not call that; only ordinary infant flame that might grow into something else only if she let it. She cleared the yellowing grass of midsummer back and stamped the earth down on either side of the hard-packed path, then spent a little time building a small pyre of dead sticks and grass on the stream side of the block. Finally, she paused for a long moment to find her center, working her toes into the cool, moist earth beside the stream, taking calm from the reassuring solidity underfoot. When she had run out of preparations, she faced the windstone grimly, come down to it at last.

She caressed the cool stone with a fingertip, mourning what she was about to do to it. Rununn would carve no merry Delvers from this piece; it would adorn no one's mantle. Cursing The Ancient and the necessity, she drew her hand back and closed her eyes.

Since her first day on the practice ground in First Rank she had been able to summon sparks into tinder. To command flame was a Firedancer's heritage. But this was different, against all the instincts that led her to banish open flame, diminish its heat, stop its eager spread. And while she hesitated, Setti said quietly, "Let me."

Jetta shot him a quick, assessing look. True, he was

much better at this than she was, but he looked like a Windrider sitting there, pale and wispy in the gray shirt. His unbound hair rippled like Kettori's in the wind off the water. Jetta hesitated, and then walked over and braided it back for him.

"Nothing extravagant, a'Kam, just a little flame, if you please."

Setti smiled and moved his bandaged right hand. And just that fast, fire appeared in the tinder, sparking with obscene eagerness. Infant yellow flame sprang instantly from a glow to a licking tongue. Jetta fought back bone-deep loathing and let it grow into the piled sticks, quelling a nervous twitch as the fire leaped up to knee height. A breeze twitched at it; belatedly Jetta realized she should have asked a Windrider to stand by for this, to divert the wind at need. *Too late,* she thought grimly, and held her palm out to the fire.

Flames leaped away from her toward the stone. Setti gasped. "What are you—"

"The Ancient cannot rise if there are no outlets near the surface."

His head turned sharply. "That's—maybe just mad enough to work."

Jetta forbore to tell him whose idea it was. Gently she kept pressure on the fire with one outstretched hand, driving it toward the stone, away from the stream and the temptation of the waving grass. A small popping began as flame explored the block, sucking air out of myriad tiny pockets and crevices. Fire began to crawl over the surface of the stone, footing in nothing, it looked like, but Jetta knew better. She piled more fuel on the fire and watched it turn from dull gold to bright yellow, the heat licking up in a hazy shimmer.

Setti drew back suddenly. Jetta looked at the tight look to his mouth and found herself edging backward as well, wiping sweat from her face. Without the protection of the Dance the heat explored her skin, drawing a nervous shiver from nerves conditioned from the cradle to step into the Dance and fight it.

The near side of the block began to blacken even as the fire turned pale at its heart. Jetta shuddered, watching a *hysth* form, the smallest she had ever seen, deadly even so.

It flicked tendrils of flame out, curling around the block, reaching toward her feet, seeking to expand its grasp beyond this desolation she had created around it. Finding nothing, the tendrils died or pulled back; frustrated, the fire coiled in on itself.

"Father Flame," Jetta muttered. The one time she wanted fire to burn, it sulked.

"You're mad, you know that?" Setti stood up, tottered, and did not protest when Jetta leaped to brace him around the waist. "Prop me up, ak'Kal. This at least I can do."

He leaned against her and stretched out his bandaged hand, making a barrier only fire could feel. The fire flared briefly, and then suddenly swayed and wrapped itself around the block, attacking it, driving itself deep into the stone, sucking the life from it.

The first blackened chip flaked from the block and fell to the ground, spent. Jetta watched the *hysth* engulf the rest, wrapping the stone in a wreath of fire, doubtless thinking the block was the opening of some deep vein that would lead to The Ancient.

"Just tease it up hot enough to keep the coals alive," she told Setti softly, edging him back to where he could lean against the solid buttress of the bridge. "I want to know how long it can sustain its attack into the heart of the stone, and how much it takes to keep a *hysth* alive."

"Of all the mad things we've done since we got here, this is without doubt the oddest," he said, but he kept up the attack. Jetta kept an eye out for opportunistic sparks.

More of the block cracked and sloughed away. The flames began to falter, seeking more fuel. Her mouth a thin line, Jetta fed the last of her gathered tinder to the *hysth* and stepped back, palms raised to keep the fire from trying to follow. Greedily the *hysth* consumed the fuel and writhed up, fighting The Ancient's stricture, it hadn't yet strength enough to break. It failed, and shrank again, curling sullenly around the block that was now its only sustenance. The popping from the stone merged into a continuous low crackle.

"So that's how The Ancient rises," Setti said softly. He glanced at her. "Good to know."

"If you like nightmares."

A smile flickered across his mouth before he returned his

attention to the block, watching it with a concentrated attention that drew the small hairs up on Jetta's neck under her braid.

Abruptly the stone shattered. The fire flared on a last gush of escaping air, licking up nearly waist-height. Jetta twitched but managed to keep from stamping into the first form to drive it back, and after a moment the flame sank, wrapping itself around the blackened remnants of the windstone. The hysth turned from pale gold to yellow to red, wavered, and sank to embers crawling frantically over the dead fragments. But it had eaten all there was to eat. A victim of its own success, it flickered and sank and finally died, leaving only a scatter of black ash in the path.

Setti sagged against the coping. Jetta glanced at him and set her free hand on his shoulder. "Well done, Setti. Thank you."

"I would stand here until the mountains fall if it defeats The Ancient in the end."

Jetta looked at the dead smear of fire in the track. How easy it was to play on flame's instincts, to let its own greed destroy it. Had it known a moment of rejoicing when it flared into the world, a moment when it glimpsed life, and hoped for more? Or was there only the basic instinct of any animal sensing food?

Troubled, she knelt to sweep away the stone fragments, and startled, rising to her feet, when a familiar voice said behind her, "I see that whatever troubles Annam Vale, it is not want of nerve on the part of its Firedancers."

She whirled in astonishment, and had to catch Setti when he stood up too fast and swayed as he turned, as startled as she. "Farahk ak'Kal! What? How?" Her composure fought back to the surface. "Uncle, what are you doing here?"

Farahk smiled, his black eyes traveling slowly from her to Setti to the ruined stone. His brown breeches and red shirt carried a white film of trail dust that lent a silver sheen to the black braid trailing over his shoulder to his knees. He looked like the end of a long journey in haste, but the winged dark brows, the intent, intelligent stare, were the same. Jetta looked at the long experience of fire written in his black eyes, abjectly glad to see him.

"We have had interesting reports from Annam this

summer," he said. *"Your* silence, however, could swallow the world, so the Circle decided to send someone to observe firsthand what there might be here to see." His eyes lingered on Setti. "I see the reports did not tell all. What has happened?"

Jetta flushed. "The Ancient happened. My report is even now on its way to Firehome, and another with more recent word is going today, by means I'm sure you know. Did the Circle have so little trust, after the elders of Annam questioned my abilities?"

Farahk's steady gaze settled on her face. "The Circle no longer knows what to think, daughter of my sister. When a Windrider troubles himself to send word to a Fire Clan, it is surely unusual enough to catch attention, regardless of the message."

"Which message?" Jetta asked, quelling Setti's frown with a look.

Farahk sighed. "That Jetta ak'Kal leaped into the heart of fire to stop The Ancient bursting from three heartstones at once, moves so bold even the Old Man hesitated. We knew from that two things: that you had met more trouble here than even we had feared, and that you had shifted the Dance to your advantage. For lack of a report as to exactly how, the Circle saw fit to send a master to learn what might be learned."

"That was weeks ago," Setti blurted.

Farahk blew a slow breath that chilled Jetta to the bone. "There were other stops to be made on the way."

"More dead Dancers?" Jetta asked bitterly.

"Not yet. But plenty of village elders requiring answers we don't have to give. I fear my instinct to diplomacy frayed a great deal on the journey."

"They're frightened," Setti said. "They should be."

Farahk looked at him. "And you should be in bed, a'Kam. You're paler than the snows on yon peaks. If you would dance again before year's end, go and rest."

Setti sighed. "I would argue, but I haven't the breath. Jetta—"

"Go. I'll tell you everything tonight."

He nodded and started home, feeling his way from bridge to sturdy tree and finally in at the door. Farahk looked after him, his face troubled. "Tell me how that happened."

Jetta told him, sitting on the coping staring down at the swarming activity in the meadow. Farahk gave the scorch marks and the mounds of exploration a long look when she had finished, his fire-blackened eyes resting on the busy Delvers.

"Glad I am I did not linger longer on the way. Another message has gone to the Circle?"

"Just today, with the news of what we discovered at Wind Point. But—I think our time is too short for any help from that quarter. Uncle, you have no idea how glad I am to see you. How did you find me?"

"The innkeeper was most well-informed."

Jetta's mouth quirked. "What Urrana ak'Kal does not know is not worth knowing. Are you hungry? She's also the best cook in the Vale."

He waved the notion off. "Later. Tell me what you were doing just now with the stone. It was nothing if not intriguing."

Twenty Three
Help

She hesitated. His voice softened. "Jetta, no one thinks you mad. If you are, then half the world has gone there with you. In the lowlands, fire has taken three villages this summer, killed Menara ak'Kal, and forced us to send masters where journeymen once kept watch. That you have kept this village standing is to your very great credit."

Tears blurred Jetta's sight. "Menara," she poured the word out from her soul. Sweet Menara. Always ready to laugh. Ready to compete.

Farahk sighed. "She was in First Rank with you, wasn't she?"

"Yes," Jetta whispered. "We were always rivals, but she was my friend also. She was such a talented Dancer."

"Yes. The Circle was greatly disturbed to hear of her fall. As at Setham, the Old Man trapped her, in the witness of half the village. Those who survived say they never saw fire spread so fast." Farahk got up to poke a booted toe into the black spot in the track. "This notion of yours?"

"Sheshan's. I would never have thought of such a thing."

His mouth quirked. "A Windrider giving guidance to a Dancer."

"Is the idea less because you disapprove the source?"

His dark eyebrow shot up. "Did I disparage the notion?"

Hurriedly Jetta ducked her head. "Forgive, ak'Kal," she mumbled, her face flaming.

"What did you learn by destroying the stone?" he asked, his voice neutral.

She took a steadying breath and lifted her head. "With nowhere else to go the fire will continue to attack the stone. It did not take as much heat as I thought it might."

"It was a small stone." Farahk leaned to one side to survey the remains, his eyes narrowed in thinking silence. Hope shot through Jetta. She respected her uncle's quick mind, his clear-eyed practicality, above all, his long survival against more flame than most Dancers could remember. She looked at the Fifth Rank badge on his shoulder and could not feel slighted that the Circle had sent him.

"Let us see what may be done with something larger," he said abruptly.

"Now?" Jetta blurted. "You've only just arrived—"

He threw a sardonic look over his shoulder. "You said you felt time was precious."

Jetta felt like a child in First Rank again, awkward and gauche. "I was thinking of you, Uncle. It's a long walk from Firehome."

"And I am not so old and frail that it was a hardship. Come, Jetta, are you frightened of this trial?"

She hesitated. His eyebrow soared. "You should be," he said flatly. "But I'm intrigued by this notion. It must be attempted."

"Then we should enlist a Windrider to help."

He turned around. "Why?"

She saw from the slight frown pulling his dark eyebrows together that the idea made him uncomfortable. He did not have a summer's close acquaintance with them. "Two reasons. It will be easier to sustain the fire with a wind behind it, and it will more closely mimic the conditions on Wind Point and elsewhere."

He considered it, his frown smoothing away only reluctantly. "There's sense in that," he admitted. "So, where might we find one of your allies without turning the village upside down looking?"

Belatedly Jetta realized that she had seen none of them, and really had no idea where they might be. "Wyth is likely at the inn," she said, hoping for once that it was so. "He is senior, and powerful. And difficult," she added after a moment, because she could guess Farahk's reaction to Wyth's usual manners, exposed to them all unawares.

Farahk gave her a slantwise look but said only, "Go and find him. I want to think about what you've told me."

Dismissed like an apprentice, Jetta left him frowning at

the largest block of windstone. In truth she welcomed the walk; it helped her adjust to the sudden appearance of a Fifth Rank Dancer in the village she was charged to protect. All the way down the winding, uneven street to the inn she fought a cowardly desire to dump the whole problem in Farahk's lap and simply follow his lead. His experience with fire was vast, but he had not seen what she had seen. She did not yet know what he thought of her assertion that The Ancient was intelligent, but until he saw for himself it was unlikely he would take it seriously. And in his failure to believe at gut-deep level would come Annam's fall, if anything. Jetta was prepared to try any measure against some unforeseen trick of the Old Man's; she was not sure that Farahk would. She could not abandon Annam to half measures.

Deep in worrisome thought, she pushed open the door to the inn and nearly ran into Nuurn coming out. He looked dusty and wind-blown and tired, as well he might from tramping up and down the trail to Wind Point all day. He peered past Jetta at the empty street.

"Did I hear that another Firedancer has come? A master? Where is he?"

"And the blessings of the day on you, too, Nuurn ak'Kal," Jetta said, jerking his gaze back with a snap.

"Forgive, Jetta. I don't mean to impugn your abilities. But a sccond Danccr is good ncws."

"It is. He's at the waterfall, waiting to set stone on fire to see how long we may have at Wind Point before The Ancient burns through. Have you seen any of the Windriders?"

"Wyth was just here. He went with Huunall to site the firetrap at Wind Point."

Jetta suppressed surprise that Wyth had been willing to climb the ridge twice in one day. "Then I'll look for someone else." She peered up at him. "Have you eaten today?"

"No, and don't tell Anual. If you see her, tell her I will be up on the ridge supervising the building. If I ate as often as she wished I would be too fat to climb up there."

Jetta laughed. "But she's right that you need to stop sometime."

He ran a hand through his shaggy brown hair, his great blue eyes solemn. "I'll not stop until Annam is safe."

Jetta sobered. "Nor I, ak'Kal. But spare yourself a little, eh? We need you."

"Not so much as we need you. Be careful in your experiments."

"I will."

She turned back through the door with him, since Wyth was not in the inn, and walked beside him toward the footbridge and the trail branching away up to Wind Point. Activity at the storehouses had lessened, though a few youngsters were still carrying blocks up the hill. She glanced to her right, up the ridge, and saw a long file of Delvers climbing the steep path, tiny in the distance. The sun slanting to the west picked gleams of light off picks and shovels and other tools slung across their backs.

Nuurn answered her unspoken question. "They go to help with the work. Some will be hunting cracks and shafts, as you wished."

"Good." Jetta turned away. "Have you seen any of the Windriders?"

"Most of them are standing firewatch in place of the apprentices. You might find Ayesh at the forge. The smith asked his help in speeding the making of reinforcement bars for the containment wall."

Jetta touched his arm in thanks and farewell and hurried up the hill. The smithy stood by itself beside the spill of the stream below the footbridge, where the Smith could quench the hot iron directly in the hurrying waters. She found Ayesh leaning against the door, out of the worst of the heat inside, seemingly doing nothing. But a steady wind fanned the forge fire and the great bellows stood idle, unmanned by the apprentice who usually kept the fire roaring while the smith worked. Jetta peered through the door and saw the smith working a length of hot metal into a half circle with two very long shafts.

"What is that?" she asked Ayesh.

"They call it a hasty anchor, for times when a wall must be built quickly, without proper preparation of the ground. They will pierce the bottom course and sink these deep into the earth, anchoring two blocks at a time."

Jetta pictured it and nodded. The whole of Wind Point would have to shift before the containment wall slipped or cracked under the assault of weather or time.

She looked up into the Windrider's face. "Are you free to assist me for a bit?"

Ayesh straightened. "Jetta ak'Kal has need of me. Are you at a place where I might be spared?"

The smith nodded without ceasing the steady swing of his hammer. "I have but one more of these to shape," he said, his deep voice carrying easily over the roar of the forge and the clang of the hammer. "The fire's hot enough and will remain so long enough. Go."

Ayesh stood away from the door with such vigor that Jetta guessed he had been heartily bored. He matched his long stride to hers as they started up the street toward the far end of the village. "What is it that Jetta ak'Kal cannot handle herself?" he asked, smiling down at her.

"Shall I give you a list?" she said wryly.

"I imagine it would be a short one. Did Wuruun's youngest child tell me true? Is there another Firedancer in Annam?"

"We're going to meet him now. My mother's brother, Farahk ak'Kal."

"Really?" The admiration in Ayesh's voice startled her. She looked up at him searching the street ahead and had to stretch her legs suddenly to keep up with him. "I saw him dance once, long ago. I was impressed."

Jetta tried to think where that might have been. It had been long since Firedancers had worked beside Windriders. Farahk would have been very young, Ayesh, too.

Farahk was sitting on the rock above the falls when they reached the top of the street. He stood up when he saw them coming and picked his way down to wait beside the blackened spot in the path. Jetta lengthened her stride to arrive a pace ahead of Ayesh, so that she, junior to both masters, could present them properly one to the other.

She heard Ayesh stop behind her. Farahk's eyes were on the Windrider, his face devoid of expression. *He thinks this is Wyth!* she realized and hastened to correct him.

"Farahk ak'Kal, this is Ayesh ak'Kal of the Fourth Rank. He has agreed to help us burn the stone. Ayesh ak'Kal, I am pleased to present you to my mother's brother, Farahk ak'Kal of the Fifth Rank. He taught me much of what I know of the

Dance."

"Only what you were not born knowing." Farahk turned a small smile on her and then waited in silence, watching Ayesh.

The Windrider made one of his graceful gestures. "You are most welcome to Annam, Farahk ak'Kal. I saw you dance at Ghesh long ago. You did what seemed impossible then, as Jetta has performed the impossible here all summer. It must be a family trait."

Farahk's eyebrow lifted. "Ghesh. You have a long memory, Rider. I don't recall you among the Windriders there."

"I was a journeyman of the Second Rank then. My poor skills were far outmatched by the masters who answered that call. They turned the storm before I was needed."

"And now you are master." Farahk eyed the rank pin on Ayesh's shoulder. "Do you think any storm that comes to Annam will be as bad as the one that struck Ghesh?"

Ayesh threw a somber glance up the ridge. "It will be far worse, ak'Kal. But for Jetta, it would already have struck."

"Then let us see what we can do together to prevent it." Briskly Farahk turned to slap the pale lump of windstone astride the path. "Jetta wants to know if it's possible for us to drive fire through stone, and how long it will take. The Ancient travels that way. If we can destroy its pathways, we can lock it in the tunnels at Wind Point until it exhausts itself and must retreat or die. This—" He gestured at the dark crumbled bits under his booted foot. "Proves that we can force the fire into the stone. But this was a small sample. To sustain fire for the time it would take to travel deep enough for safety—that is another thing altogether."

"Dangerous," Ayesh said at once. "But you give me hope, ak'Kal."

"It was Sheshan's idea," Jetta said.

Ayesh chuckled. "I should have known. You have corrupted him, Dancer. He was not so eager to experiment before you came."

Jetta ran one hand over the stone, eyeing the size of it. If they could not drive fire through a block half the size of a Delver, there was no hope of making Sheshan's idea work.

Farahk began clearing grass back from the track. Without

a word Ayesh bent to help, tearing at the long dead weeds by the stream and dumping them where Farahk indicated at one end of the sacrificial stone. Jetta busied herself clearing the other side, rolling small rocks away, piling dead sticks and grass to one side, until the stone stood alone beside the water in a circle devoid of ready fuel. She would have liked twice the clear space, but the afternoon was running away from them. Ayesh took himself up among the rocks out of the way; Farahk grunted approval and turned to Jetta.

"Call the fire. I will dance if things go badly."

She nodded and stepped to the end of the stone. Not without a qualm and a secret wish for Setti at her back, she cleared doubt from her mind, closed her eyes, and summoned the enemy.

The tinder caught with a whoosh that surprised her into a step backward. "Greed," Farahk said dispassionately behind her. His voice steadied her. Jetta confined the infant flame to the tinder laid ready for it, letting it grow into a sullen red pillar knee-high. Farahk fed it from the larger pile Jetta had made, and it began to reach small tendrils outward, seeking the source. Jetta drove them back, forcing the fire onto the stone once more. As it began to explore the pale surface, she looked up at Ayesh and nodded.

Instantly a small wind kissed her cheek and cooled her bare arms. The fire flared waist-high immediately, swirling up with a greedy roar. Jetta shoved both palms outward as the flames turned from red to gold and then paled almost to white at the core. All in an instant the *hysth* formed, soaring up on the wind's steady breath like the forge fire under the bellows. Jetta fought the urge to dance, to drive the fire down to coals before it found a way out of her control. Farahk stood beside her, as tense as an apprentice facing a test, his hands half-raised in the first instinctive thrust of the master's dance of Fifth Rank.

"Wait," she bade him, and shoved the fire toward the stone before it could try to delve into the track, hunting its ancient master.

Hissing in fury, it curled onto the pale surface, driven as much by the wind behind it as by her will. The stone began to crackle and snap, and slowly to turn red. The glow spread outward, creeping down the stone as the end nearest the flames withered and turned black. Jetta's arm began to tremble under the strain of keeping the fire focused, but she did not lower her hand. The *hysth* writhed across the stone, seeking escape into the tall grass nodding just out of its grasp. It crackled and snarled, but could not twist back into the wind and come at the Dancer driving it on.

Farahk flung the last of the dried grass onto the coals forming sullenly at the near end of the block. It flared and withered instantly, but the fire leaped up. Without warning it split itself in two, one half still exploring the stone, the other licking sideways. Farahk spun into the Dance, graceful as a raptor stooping on the wind. Jetta itched to do the same, but held to her post, forcing the *hysth* onward into the stone. And still the wind blew past her, as constant as the water leaping down the hill.

Farahk drove the fire back into a single mass, white hot at its core, palest gold at the edges. Heat shimmered in the afternoon air, blurring the village in Jetta's sight and bringing the sweat up on her face, her arms. Through the haze, movement caught her eye; her attention flicked past the stream toward a tall figure in a feathery white shirt striding toward them. Her attention faltered.

Instantly the *hysth* leaped skyward, abandoning the stone. In the space of a breath it stood higher than a Delver, and then it spread itself on the back of the wind. Ayesh leaped up with a slicing motion of one hand; the wind blowing onto the block swirled in confusion for a moment, fighting the natural breeze up the hill. Without hesitation the *hysth* leaped to the updraft and rode it toward Annam, spurning the stream. Jetta gasped and abandoned the stone, leaping without thought into the Dance.

She caught a glimpse of Farahk doing the same, facing a man-high column of flame on the uphill side of the path. Jetta saw only the gush of fire touching down on the Annam side of the stream, roaring into the narrow strip of grass and needle trees separating Nuurn's house from the water. Fire leaped up a tree like a candle flaring, poised to jump to the roof slates and from there into the rafters and onto Setti's sleeping form.

"*No!*" Jetta found herself on the Annam side of the stream with no memory of crossing the bridge. Through a blur of smoke and heat she saw the Windrider in the street fling up his hands. The fire soared up and curled back toward her, driven by opposing winds into a writhing column roaring in thwarted rage. Jetta danced without any knowledge of what patterns she formed, heart and mind filled with a single dreadful truth.

Fail, and Annam was gone.

Abruptly the wind behind her died. The *hysth* fell toward her in a shimmering cascade; she flung up her arms, palms out, feet braced wide, and let it drop around her, a hot rain of sparks and flame running to establish themselves in the grass. She stamped on the nearest and spun completely around on the ball of one foot, summoning the rest back with one imperious flick of her hand. And they came, swirling sullenly together into a single demon, not a hundred, a solitary foe that roared and snapped at her even as it tried in vain to break her hold. Dimly she sensed that the fire in the needle tree was out, the danger to the village diminished, but there remained the *hysth*, angry and deadly, its hunger beating at Jetta's will.

"Be—gone!" she bade it, panting, and stamped her foot down onto the beaten earth of the path to Nuurn's door. Strength flooded up through her, a blaze so intense she gasped. She tried Setti's trick, lowering her palms, every muscle straining to crush the flames against the anvil of earth. The *hysth* shrank, struggled upward again, shrank again as Jetta forced the Dance out of ancient patterns to counter the Old Man's newfound tricks. The fire sank and sank, turning from white to yellow to red. She brought both hands together in the age-old extinguishing motion. The next instant it was gone, and only blackened grass nodded beside the stream.

She slid to her knees, spent. Footsteps pattered up to her, arms went around her. She dropped her head against a broad shoulder and found the elusive feathers of a Windrider shirt against her cheek.

"It's gone," Sheshan's voice said in her ear. "Rest."

"No," Jetta croaked, and fought out of his hold. She struggled to her feet, anxious for what lay behind her across the stream. Relief set her staggering; only the hot glow of the stone block gleamed red in the path. Ayesh still stood above the falls, slowly lowering his hands, safe. Sheshan steadied her with one hand under her elbow, then stepped back with all his usual tact when she turned to face Farahk.

He stood at the near end of the bridge, arms folded, watching her out of unrevealing black eyes. Jetta forced her shaky legs to carry her the three steps between them and bowed her head.

"Forgive, ak'Kal. I let the fire escape."

"Yes." His tone was neither accusing nor forgiving. "It was instructive, to say the least."

She looked up in time to see his gaze flick past her to Sheshan. Jetta's face heated but she kept her head up. "As you see, ak'Kal, the Windriders have been of great help in keeping The Ancient from gaining a foothold in Annam."

"I would say the foothold established has been of a different kind." He dropped dark, considering eyes to her face. His neutral expression softened to a wry grimace. "Also instructive."

Ayesh, coming soft-footed up behind him, chuckled. Jetta knew her face was flaming but had no means to stop it. She settled for lifting her chin and meeting her uncle's sharp gaze.

Farahk's mouth quirked. "It seems to be effective, and that I cannot fault. Nor do I fault you for the fire's escape. It was hard—much harder than it should have been, to quell even the small *hysth* that remained on my side of the stream. What you did on this side? I watched, and I still have no idea what you did or how you did it."

"Nor I," Jetta admitted. "It has been like that since we came, and we've Settak a'Kam to thank that we can fight it at all. He found a new pattern at practice one day, when the old forms failed. I have learned not to depend on them, and I am putting his name forward for master."

Farahk nodded. "I see now what you were saying. Logically the flame should have run on the wind, straight out to the street, where it would have quickly died. It should not have been able to fling itself downhill in that manner, with the prevailing wind blowing it away." He turned his head. "That was well done with the wind, Ayesh ak'Kal, despite that the fire did not act as it should." He nodded at Sheshan. "And you, Rider. That was quick thinking, to drive it back upon itself in that way."

Sheshan came forward, stopping an arm's length away from Jetta. "I fear it was instinct more than inspiration, ak'Kal."

"Good instincts." Farahk turned to Jetta. "There's no harm done save to the needle tree. And we discovered what we wished to know."

He turned toward the still-glowing stone. "Fire could not escape in that manner from an underground vein. Once begun, we could drive the fire through the rock and back into The Ancient's face, though it might be a long and weary fight."

"To summon the wind in that fashion for days and nights together will stretch us thin," said Ayesh. "But I see no other way."

"Nor I," Farahk said, gazing at the scorched needle tree. "Thank you for your efforts. Both of you. Now, if I might speak to Jetta ak'Kal alone for a moment?"

"Of course." Ayesh made one of those movements of his hand that seemed to float like the wind and moved off with Sheshan.

Jetta steeled herself and turned to face Farahk. Anger and shame fought for supremacy, setting her hands trembling: shame for an unforgivable mistake, anger that she must stand while he pointed it out to her like a First Rank beginner.

He surprised her. "You already know your mistake, Dancer, so I'll say nothing save to tell you to take care. Ask Ayesh ak'Kal what happens when the heart must choose between love and duty."

He started away, leaving her with stark images of hair floating like seaweed in a cavern taken by the sea. "I'm hungry," he flung over his shoulder. "Meet me at the inn after you've quenched the block."

Jetta glared at his back, and then had to laugh, transported back to Firehome and the strictures of her childhood. He was Fifth Rank. She was Third. Whose job but hers to clean up the mess?

She started across the bridge and found Sheshan flanking her. Jetta glanced up, warmed by his quiet presence. "It *was* well done," she told him.

"I was terrified. Turning it back like that meant forcing it toward you."

"I'm a Dancer, well equipped to deal with it."

"It doesn't change how I feel."

"No," she said, thinking of Setti with the fire eating his arm. "It's over, and no harm done save to this poor stone."

She eyed it ruefully, half eaten with flame and glowing like a forge fire throughout, the cooler end black and flaking to ruin. It hissed with the steady escape of air sucked from its depths, dying as she watched. It was too big to move into the stream to let the water cool the fire inside; she sighed and brought her hands together.

Black spread across the face of the stone as the red began to disappear. Sheshan watched in interested silence until the whole thing had turned a smoky, brittle black. Jetta lowered her hands, exhausted. His arm went around her shoulders, steady as the mountain they stood on. She leaned against him, content to take what he offered.

"You should go and rest," he said after a while. "I'll stay and make sure this does not flare again."

"No. It's safe now. Even The Ancient could not set it alight again." She tilted her face up, smiling. "Your idea worked. Even Farahk agrees."

"A formidable Dancer," he said. "He may think the fire was too slow to die, but it vanished quickly enough before him."

"Formidable," Jetta snorted. "Yes. Short of Norlahk ak'Kal, the Circle could have sent no one better."

She drew out of his hold, vividly aware of the look on his face—grave, intent—and of how easy it would be to close the gap between them and seal this folly with a kiss. But the swift thumping of Delver feet and excited voices announced the arrival of children to gawk at the aftermath; she reached up and touched his face instead, vividly aware of the brush of his pale hair against the back of her hand. He turned his head and kissed her palm, his eyes intent on hers.

Jetta cupped that cloud pale cheek for a moment and withdrew her hand, slowly, so that he would not think it retreat. "I'm tired. I think I will go and sleep a while."

He glanced at the wide-eyed children and sighed. "Good idea. Likely the only reason half the village is not up here to view the wreckage is that they are all at the inn gawking at Farahk. Go and rest while you can."

She looked at the scorched needle tree, withered up one side clear to the top, and winced. "So close," she whispered. So close to disaster.

"Go. Or would you rather I fetched Anual to drag you home?"

"And have to explain to her what happened to her needle tree? No, thank you!" She shoved him toward the inn. "For that you can go and deal with Farahk in my stead."

"So. There *are* things you are afraid of. I'll remember."

"Sheshan!"

He laughed and faded away down the street. Smiling, Jetta turned toward the house, and stopped. Setti was watching her from his window.

Twenty Four
New Tactics

She found him in his room, sitting in a Delver-sized chair that made him look ridiculously young. He did not turn from his fixed contemplation of the scorched needle tree outside the window.

"Setti? We need to talk."

"No, we don't."

"Setti, please. It was nothing I wanted. Nothing I planned. It just is."

His jaw tightened. After an interminable moment he turned his head, summoning a brittle smile that made Jetta's throat ache. "Then I congratulate you. And him."

Jetta crossed the room in four long strides and stopped beside him. The chair brought them eye to eye; he looked away. She laid a quick hand against his cheek and forced him to look at her out of those fire-touched eyes.

"I don't know if there is any future for Sheshan and me, Setti. But I know that whatever future there is, I want you in it. Not as lifemates. As partners."

He closed his eyes. "No. Partnership is—no. How could I dance with you, knowing it is all there will ever be?"

She tightened the pressure against his cheek. "Don't pretend you never looked at another woman. Kori and I were gone five years. You had no reason to think about me. Did you intend to live your life alone?"

He jerked away. "No," he whispered, still with his eyes closed. "She wouldn't have me, either."

"Because she found you unworthy in the Dance?"

"Yes."

"Then won't she be surprised to learn Setti ak'Kal is the chosen partner of Jetta ak'Kal. No one, ever, found *me* unworthy in the Dance before Setham. And precious few may argue with me now that you and I have stopped The Ancient together twice. And we will do it again every time the Old Man pokes his head into this vale." She patted his cheek, trying to make him open his eyes, and then harder when he still refused. "Setti! You will never be second best. I could dance with anyone, and I choose you. No one else I know—not Kori, not my mother, not Farahk—can do what you do. Does it mean *nothing?*"

He snorted and opened his eyes. "There's conceit. Minna would have you dancing the forms for the next week."

"And nothing in them would help us one jot against The Ancient. What you and I together have created is what will stop it. Only that."

"Jetta, I'm not made of stone. How can I watch you with— him—and not feel it? If I partner with you, what Dancer would have me for mate?"

"Anyone with brains. And for every Dancer in the Fire Clans, there are two like Marra, who either failed it or chose never to brave the fire, and made contented lives bearing children who grow up to dance, or not, as their talent takes them."

He caught his breath. Jetta's eyes narrowed. "You never considered such a thing, did you? Settak a'Kam must marry a Dancer to prove himself worthy of the Dance. Oh, Setti, you are a fool."

"I love you," he whispered, staring rather grimly out the window.

"And I, you. But if I must, I'll drag every available female in the Fire Clans here to parade past you Setti ak'Kal. And trust me, only the worthiest will get past my inspection to prove themselves to you."

"You make free with my life, ak'Kal." But the deadness had lifted from his voice, though he still would not look at her.

Jetta leaned in to kiss his forehead. "I outrank you."

He sighed. "And always will, I've no doubt." His eyes lifted, ash-dark in silhouette against the window. "Go away, Jetta. I need to think."

About his obsessive quest for perfection, she hoped, and a host of girls who would happily throw themselves at him if he gave them even half a chance. Surely he knew that, in the part of himself that had never allowed him to notice things that might distract him from his goals.

She drew her hand back, heard him draw a soft, painful breath. Still, the grim set to his jaw had relaxed to something more contemplative, and he met her eyes squarely when she said, "Whatever you decide, Setti, I'll support. But consider what you can do that Sheshan cannot. And then consider what the three of us might do together."

His eyes flew wide. He gave her an open-mouthed, shocked look that would have set her laughing on any other day. "Think, Setti, about creating something new in the world, something you and I, the failures, will be teaching Fifth Rank Firedancers."

She made it to the door before his voice stopped her in her tracks. "You don't fight fair, ak'Kal."

Jetta grinned at him over her shoulder. "I think you taught me that, a'Kam."

His bellow followed her down the stairs. "A Windrider! Have you no taste, woman?"

The knot in Jetta's stomach eased. Hurt, yes. Angry, yes. It might be he would never accept Sheshan, never forgive her that choice, never stop brooding on his failure to win her, as he had brooded all his life on his seeming lack of talent. But, at the core of him lived the irrepressible spirit who stopped to marvel at neera as they scampered on the rocks and could not wait to greet a new day. She thought it would not be long before he began to look sidelong at drover girls and started thinking about the possibilities in Firehome. *Dance well, soon-to-be ak'Kal. And come back to us, for I was not lying when I said we need you.*

~ ~ ~

Wanting a bath even more than sleep, she immersed herself until sleep threatened to drown her, and came out, raking the snarls out of her hair, in time to meet Anual coming in the front door with Farahk. "What did you do to my tree, Jetta ak'Kal?" Anual squawked, looking grimy and exhausted, her springing hair escaping her forest-green scarf in every direction. She blew out a sigh. "Never mind. Show

Farahk ak'Kal to the back bedroom, will you? There's supper still to be made."

She left them both standing there and disappeared into the kitchen. Jetta stared after her, open-mouthed. Farahk touched her arm.

"There is no slight. She claimed host right first and loudest. She is weary, and heartsore, and afraid, like everyone else in Annam tonight."

Jetta closed her eyes. "It makes me so *angry* to know that The Ancient can turn their lives upside down for nothing but its own selfish greed."

"Focus, Dancer," Farahk said sharply. "Anger serves no one but The Ancient. And Jetta ak'Kal's fear will take the heart from these people in an instant."

"I know it," she muttered. For a moment she wished he had not come to weaken her resolve with the sly knowledge that someone with higher rank and greater experience could shoulder the burden at need. Like taking the test for any rank, knowing that a master stood by to rescue a candidate who failed. *And some fail because they know it*, Jetta recalled.

His expression softened. "Go and rest. You look almost as bad as Setti, and no wonder. Huunall has been telling me tales I can scarce believe, but looking at you, I see them all etched in your face. Tired Dancers make mistakes. We cannot afford mistakes."

"I should help Anual—"

"Anual is taking out her fear on the vegetables. Go. Rest. Tomorrow I will go up to Wind Point and see for myself what is being done, and then I will become an apprentice again, and learn new forms from a master who knows what she's about."

Jetta blinked. "Speaking of masters, she said. "Will you speak to Kettori?"

His mouth thinned. "Huunall and I looked for her. She's gone."

"Gone? But-"

The best I could do for Annam was to stay away.

Jetta drew a slow breath. "She knew fire would rise in Annam but could not find the courage to say so. Perhaps she has found courage enough to leave the one place that gave her a little peace. She is," she sought the right words. "She is very afraid. Afraid because the Old Man knows her name."

"The Old Man knows Annam's name, whether or not Kettori ak'Kal goes or stays. Flame take a Dancer who will not do her duty." Farahk shoved her, not gently, toward the stairs. "Go. I need to learn the village and the Vale. I daresay Anual can tell me as well as anyone."

"Oh, yes. Beware the cookies." She dragged herself up to bed and never woke until a yowling stomach and morning light falling in her eyes brought her straight upright in shock.

She forsook attempting any sort of control this morning, driven to know what was happening. Setti's room was empty, the house likewise, save for a covered pot on the hearth and a pair of muffins wrapped in a cloth on the table. Jetta's stomach demanded food; she snatched a muffin and stepped outside, shading her eyes to look up at the ridge, but saw nothing save a distant, tiny parade of Delvers winding up the trail to Wind Point. More stone for the wall, more hands for the flume.

The angle of the sun shocked her. Nearly midday. *So, she thought, my mind dumped everything on Farahk after all*, she thought, embarrassed to have slept so hard and so long, but she felt better this morning than she had since Setti was hurt, rested and free of the dragging weight of exhaustion in every muscle.

"Jetta!"

She turned. Setti was sitting cross-legged beside the stream, watching Farahk and Sheshan driving fire into the blocks again. Jetta ran toward them, her peace shattered. Farahk had no idea how to contain rogue fire.

Setti snorted at her expression. "Relax, ak'Kal. The Old Man is frustrated this morning."

A *hysth* writhed in pale fury above the last stone standing like a pillar in the middle of the glacial stream, crowned in fire and rooted in water. Jetta watched with the hair prickling on her scalp and fire sense rippling down her skin as the *hysth* fought to gain a foothold in the stone against a wind-frothed attack by the water burbling around its base. Farahk stood on the bank, relaxed in the way of top Dancers who could summon the Mother before fire took its first breath. Sheshan sat atop the waterfall, driving wind straight over the falls to curl in small waves against the upstream side of the block as the *hysth* writhed over the top, trying to burrow through it into the streambed and call The Ancient.

The block broke in half first, toppling sideways to submerge itself in the racing water. Instantly Sheshan let the wind go; it ruffled Jetta's hair and sped away as she watched the fire break apart into harmless fragments and die at the stamp of Farahk's foot.

Setti held up his good arm; Jetta pulled him to his feet, careful to avoid his gaze. He snorted. "I am not so fragile as all that, nor so stupid that I can't see possibilities in yon Windrider's gifts. But Father Flame, don't ask me to work with him."

Jetta bit down hard on disappointment. What had she expected? "Wyth, then," she said.

Setti coughed. "I like a man who knows how to hate," he said matter-of-factly, and turned toward Farahk as he glided up.

Farahk nodded at Jetta and gestured at the broken stone. "There is hope in the flume at Wind Point," he said. "Even with the wind driving it and all of Setti's encouragement and its own desperation to aid it, the *hysth* found it hard going to root itself."

Sheshan jumped down from the rocks and came to stand beside Jetta. "Wyth approves of this experiment," he said, drawing a faint snort from Setti. Sheshan ignored him, his eyes on Jetta, very blue this morning. "The sooner we try, the better, I think."

Jetta's nerves drew taut. "What news from Wind Point, Uncle? Did you go up this morning?"

His face tightened. "I could barely hold my hand against the seals, but the Delvers worked through the night. The wall is a third high, and the flume will be finished by sunset tomorrow. For now, the water will run over the face and down the back side of the ridge. When the wall is finished, it will trap it against the doors first, a constant inflow of cold water and outflow of warm."

"The raptors can wallow in hot water all winter," Setti said. "Bathing in the Old Man's pool."

"I would rejoice if it held so long," Farahk said. "I will settle for however long it takes the Circle to arrive."

Jetta looked at him sharply. "Will they come?"

"Oh, yes," he said simply. "Wyth left little doubt of the need in the message he sent yesterday." Dislike flashed through his face; Jetta could not wonder, if he had spent all morning in Wyth's surly company.

"Then, Uncle, I suggest we spend the time helping you to unlearn the Dance."

Farahk's eyebrows lifted, but all he said was, "I would give much to watch you and Setti dance together. Failing that, you and I will have to try."

"Pardon, Jetta, but this strays into Dancer business," Sheshan said. "If you have no more need of me, I'm going to help seal the vents into the tunnels."

"Be careful," she said, aware of Setti's eyes on them both.

"Always." He sketched a respectful farewell to Farahk, nodded at Setti, and left, cutting slantwise up the hill above Kettori's house.

"Interesting man," Farahk said.

Setti turned stiffly toward the charred spots in the track. "And better gone for this, I think. When Jetta and I first experimented, we did it with a lantern in the storehouses, surrounded by containment stone. Since the Delvers are frantically cutting stone down there, that's not a possibility. We'll have enough problems up here with vagrant breezes without any additional hazards."

Jetta sighed; Farahk said nothing, but his dark eyes watched Setti hunching away to kick at the debris in the track.

"Give him time, Uncle," Jetta said softly. "The Windriders kept fire off us both. He knows it. He just needs time to accept it."

"Time is the one thing we do not have. It may be well after all that he will not be facing The Ancient in this state of mind. So." He turned to her and placed his fists together at chest height like an apprentice greeting a master at the start of a lesson. "Shall we begin?"

~ ~ ~

For two days Farahk danced himself to exhaustion without quite grasping the trick of staying ahead of the fire, while the flume advanced and the wall rose and the seals grew too hot to touch. Jetta watched him, sitting side by side with Setti on the bridge, the both of them rigid with wanting to leap in and help, held back by the knowledge that only he could manage the breakthrough in his mind to shed the ingrained patterns of the Dance wound into his every muscle and nerve. Jetta had never seen a finer Dancer; his form was flawless, every position precisely formed, beautiful in its grace, heart-catching in its fluid passage from one movement to the next. She could not begin to mimic the effortless arch of his back or the spring he achieved in every leap; when they stood side by side at the beginning of each session, settling into the centering control positions of their respective ranks, she felt like a clumsily carved piece of stone next to his relaxed and perfect grace as he stood on one foot, unwavering. But still he faltered when the fire defied the patterns, unable quite to let go of expectations to force a different outcome. Quietly Jetta despaired, for if one of the greatest Dancers of his generation could not master this, then the arrival of the entire Circle could not help Annam.

On the third morning she woke to find a new blue shirt on the bedpost, soft as water ruffling over her hand, stitched with a running yellow pattern like flame up the tight sleeves. Jetta's eyes blurred. When had Anual found time to carry on her life in the face of The Ancient waiting to eat everything she knew? It shamed Jetta, who had dreamed all night of fire that still had her stomach in knots.

She pulled on the shirt over her leathers in bright defiance of the Old Man and went down to breakfast.

Farahk sat at the breakfast table, deep in conversation with Nuurn. He looked up when she came in, greeted her absently and went back to the discussion, looking as relaxed in the big Delver chair as ever he had at Firehome. Anual ladled porridge into a bowl and set it on the table for Jetta with a tired smile.

"A good color, Jetta ak'Kal," she said, eyeing Jetta up and down. "Matches Sheshan's eyes."

She cackled when Jetta's face heated to the roots of her hair. Hurriedly Jetta crawled up onto her chair and pretended great interest in her bowl until the discussion across the table caught her ear. She let the porridge cool, listening with rising hope.

"The flume is finished," Nuurn said. "Water is already sliding over the face of the stone. I'm surprised you cannot see the steam from here. By tomorrow night the wall will be done. Huunall wanted the firetrap finished first."

"Firetrap," Farahk repeated, savoring the word. "There is an idea I relish."

"It has yet to work in practice, only in trial," Nuurn reminded him.

"All things that slow The Ancient are worth the effort, even if it's only for a few seconds."

"Wyth ak'Kal hopes to do better than that." Nuurn reached for a muffin half the size of Jetta's head and munched it thoughtfully.

"The Ancient might do well to run from Wyth ak'Kal," Farahk said dryly.

Nuurn's laughter rumbled into the kitchen. Even Anual smiled. Then she tapped a pointed finger on Jetta's shoulder. "Eat, child, before the porridge grows cold."

Jetta dug in her spoon. "Say the same to Farahk ak'Kal," she said innocently, looking at the half of a muffin remaining on Farahk's plate. "Apprentices need their strength."

Farahk blew a snort and stood up. "Impudent child. No wonder the Old Man hates you." He looked out the window at the long swell of the ridge. "No dancing today. I want another look at the seals."

"I, too," Jetta said.

"Be sure to take a Windrider with you," Anual said sweetly.

"Good idea," Nuurn rumbled. "Sheshan might be free."

Anual cackled. Jetta slid off her chair and made for the door, aware of Nuurn grinning at Anual behind her back.

Setti stood at the foot of the stairs, dressed in leathers, his arm resting in a gauzy sling looped around his wrist, which had taken no damage when the fire enveloped his arm. Jetta stared at him grimly. With a Firedancer's peculiar ability to throw off the effects of flame, he had come far in half a moon, but his arm was far from healed and his right hand still looked raw and red.

"And just what were you planning to do?" she asked him.

He shrugged. "I can scream warning as well as the next person and stamp my little foot better than most. I can free up at least one journeyman from firewatch."

She ran an eye over him, noting how he still hunched inward on the left, though he no longer looked as if even the touch of a breeze hurt. Behind her, Farahk stood silent as the mountains. *Thank you, Uncle. Annam is my responsibility. My decision.*

"Until midday only, a'Kam," she said. "You are no use to me if you push too hard."

For the first time in days his smile crept out. "Don't fall off the trail, ak'Kal."

Jetta flushed. Setti laughed and sauntered out the door, leaving her under Farahk's interested eyes. Jetta brushed a minuscule bit of blue fluff from her sleeve. "Are you ready, Uncle?"

"Certainly. I am learning many new forms of the Dance here in Annam."

Jetta, hot all over now, brushed past him out the door. She heard a low rumbling chuckle, remembered Nuurn, and walked faster as Setti disappeared down a side street ahead of her. The whole village was out and about again, but their faces held a shy hope now instead of frantic worry. Jetta quailed from the unreserved smiles lighting those brown, honest faces when they caught sight of her. They had lost all their reservations about her abilities, trusting in Jetta ak'Kal to keep Annam safe. Every smile felt like stone falling on her shoulders.

A child's shriek pierced the morning. Jetta looked around, surprised but glad that the children, at least, could still find a moment for laughter. But Nuurn cried out beside her and flung up a huge arm to point. Jetta stopped, riveted to the black stone of the street at sight of Hannahth standing atop the square roof of one of the new woodsheds beside a Delver child of perhaps ten, the pair of them pointing up at the ridge. Hannahth looked like a drift of spider silk, her long pale hair afloat on the breeze, her gray dress rippling around thin ankles, her white arms raised as if to let the wind take her aloft. Belatedly Jetta realized these two were the lookouts for this little while, standing where village children had taken turns for days to watch for a fearful signal from the ridge.

Hannahth shouted again, her piping voice nearly lost in a rising rumble of Delver voices beating against the walls of

Annam like the quickening destruction of an avalanche breaking free. "Si'nal!" she cried, pointing at a tight, unnatural whirlwind atop the ridge.

Twenty Five
Firestorm

"How can that be?" a woman shrieked. "The flume has been cooling the face all night!"

"It doesn't matter," Farahk snapped. "Jetta, come!"

He set off at a run, instantly outpaced by Nuurn. Jetta fled with them though she felt all at once as she had the night Setham died, staggering and ill and terrified. All around her, people frozen in shock spun into motion. The youngest Windrider, a boy not yet ranked, leaped in one bound to the shed roof and snatched Hannahth to him, his face bleak. Anxious women bundled wailing, protesting children into the forlorn safety of black-walled houses. Men splashed straight across the stream to the foot of the Wind Point trail, catching up tools as they went, though what they hoped to achieve, Jetta did not know. Sheshan burst out of the inn as they came abreast and fell in beside her.

"Who's on the ridge?" she cried, hoping it was some journeyman prone to panic.

"Wyth."

They ran up that heart-bursting trail until Jetta could run no more and was forced to walk, her vision turned to darkness shot with sparks, her lungs burning. Farahk was in worse shape, fresh from the low hills of Firehome and still adjusting to the thinner air of the mountains. His breathing sounded painful to Jetta's ear, but neither of them stopped, staggering on up, passed by long-legged Delvers driven by anxious dread.

"Stay—clear!" Jetta panted at the first, catching a stark look in return that did not ease her fears. She struggled on faster, staggering until suddenly Sheshan's arm went around her. All at once she felt lighter, buoyed by a gentle pressure against her back that seemed to flatten the trail under her feet. She gasped and looked down to see if her feet were still on the ground.

Sheshan tightened his grip. "Relax. It is only wind."

She tried, able after a moment to feel the stony path crunching under her boots. It was easier then, and she consciously fought for control of her breathing, dragging in air in slower rhythm. The spinning darkness at the edge of her sight faded and the pounding in her head eased. Sheshan did not let her go. His arm braced her all the way to the top, the pair of them outpacing Farahk leaning now on Nuurn's arm, the Delver half-carrying him. Jetta stopped where the trail flattened, snatching a moment's rest as the Delvers hurried on by.

She heard Farahk and Nuurn coming, and straightened, fumbling with the buttons on her new shirt. Sheshan let her go and strode to the far side of the ridge, hunting Wyth. Hastily she shed the beautiful thing over a bush beside her pants and boots. Farahk, blowing like a winded cart beast, did the same, and started on, stripped to Dance leathers as she was, his skin gleaming golden with the sweat of the climb.

Smoke marred the flawless sky to the northwest, a thick black pillar boiling up from the fire she still could not see. The path broke over the ridge and started to drop, winding around the first outcrop. Farahk cleared the outcrop and halted so suddenly that Jetta nearly ran into him.

"Father Flame!" he breathed.

Jetta went up on her toes to look over his shoulder and gasped in dismay. "Ah, no!"

The old trickster had fooled them again. Fire crowned the ridge *above* Wind Point, roaring through the ancient teller trees, dancing obscenely on the jumbled rocks, creeping into the grass above the trail. The entrance to the mine still stood unbreached, the doors gleaming wet under the outfall of the flume spilling water across the whole face of the outcrop. The half-completed black wall looked like a hand across its mouth. Jetta hunted above the adit for the fire's flashpoint, thinking of infinitesimal cracks in the stone, hidden vents.

Instinct brought her up on her toes, arms raised to ward off fire, before her eyes could even assimilate the sight of a solid wall of flame sweeping up the ridge, borne on the back of the west wind blowing steadily up out of the valley below. Flame soared half again the height of the trees, raging toward the sky in great tongues and spires. As she watched, one flung itself onto the wind, whether in ecstasy of freedom or some notion of rooting itself farther up the ridge, she could not tell. The wind caught it, blew it to incandescence for a searing second, and then consumed it. But a score of *hysths* spawned still more, a hundred pale, wavering towers anchoring the advance of the fire. Already it had climbed halfway to the top of the ridge, a roaring, crackling inferno burning level with the spot where she stood, pouring gray-black smoke across the slope. The trees thinned up there, but enough remained to serve as anchor points for the Old Man's reaching fingers, allowing it passage over the ridge and down into Annam Vale itself. It was creeping north, aiming for the richer forest atop the lower hills bordering the Vale. Let it root itself there, and they might never stop it.

"Up," Farahk snapped. "We must get above it. Nuurn, find your people and get them clear. They can do nothing here. Beware even the fringes of this thing. The Ancient is loose."

Jetta turned and ran back up the trail, cold clear through. She was at the top before she realized that Sheshan was no longer in sight. She spun around, hunting his white shirt. All she saw was knots of frightened Delvers hovering at the break of the ridge, torn between fear of the fire and an itching need to do something to save their homes.

"Where's Sheshan?" she screamed at them.

"He went to help Wyth!" An arm lifted and pointed.

Jetta turned to look, and her breath stopped in her throat. On the peak of the ridge above the fire stood Wyth, facing the oncoming demon with both arms raised to chest height, palms out. Fire swirled and swayed farther down the slope, writhing in angry confusion in the face of a wind blasting down from behind him, whipping his fluttery shirt to rags. The fire could not advance into the teeth of it; it roared its defiance and spat flames skyward that blew back and disappeared into the inferno below. Jetta stared, awed.

Farahk's voice in her ear recalled her. "Hurry, Jetta! He cannot hold like that for long."

Numbly she followed him across the slope, angling for an

outcrop above the flames. Farahk stopped and began to dance amid a jumble of stone both white and black; Jetta climbed higher, her eye caught by a flash of white through the smoke wreathing the slope above. Sheshan, blocked from reaching Wyth by a finger of fire, stood midway between her and his mentor, facing the west wind with his pale hair streaming back from his forehead. Jetta's heart cramped in fear, not of The Ancient, but for him. Without conscious volition she began to dance.

First movement to fourth. Third to second. First Rank half steps to Third Rank leaps, arms now flung wide, now curled tight to stop fire's spread. Her feet moved lightly from stone to grass to needle-thick soil littered with charred remnants of grass and tree limbs raining from the sky around her. She felt them, warm underfoot as she ground them to ash, smearing them back into the skin of the Mother. But though fire trembled and swirled in front of her, confused by the pattern that was no pattern it knew how to evade, she did not feel the heady rush of the Mother's welcome wrapping her around. Cold and numb inside with fear for Annam, for Sheshan, for the Delvers swarming the slopes below her, Jetta danced on instinct and fought to clear away terror, to find her center even as flame made eager rushes at her, testing her resolve.

One bold *hysth* spawned a dozen smaller fires right in front of her; the largest charged at her, a bold challenge that abruptly focused Jetta's wandering wits. A flick of her hand sent it shying back. Wyth's east wind caught it, flinging it down the slope into the main body of the fire. Jetta could not look into the bleached heart of the flames, but she heard the coughing roar of the Old Man marshaling his forces to the attack. White heat boiled even from the dimmer *hysths*; raging alabaster worms of heartfire crawled across the slope, crusted with red, molten flame escaping the prison at the center of the world. Smoke billowed in the summer sky, eating the blue, announcing to any with eyes that a war raged here.

She glimpsed Farahk on his outcrop, making a move she did not recognize even from Fifth Level patterns. Pride flushed through her; somehow he had found the wild center they had tried to teach him and shifted a lifetime's knowledge to a new weave. A confused *hysth* flared and died in front of him, leaving a blackened spot avoided by its brethren.

Center, Dancer. Farahk's success only drove home her own haphazard efforts, unconnected to anything but raw talent. She could not see either Sheshan or Wyth now for smoke; why, oh why had Wyth refused to experiment with her, when at this moment a coordinated strategy might save his own life?

With a supreme effort Jetta turned her back on the higher ground, closed her eyes to the flames and planted both feet on the uneven stone of a black outcrop and willed her anxious muscles to relax, to stop their trembling in response to the driving anxiety pushing outward from belly muscles still clenched in fear for Sheshan. She clung to the feel of the earth underfoot even as the fire roared its triumph and withered living greenery to ash in front of her.

She heard deep Delver shouts laden with panic and fear. One clear voice shouted calm orders, bulling its way through the confusion. Jetta seized on it for hope, relaxing her spine, letting the weight of her braided hair pull her head back and her chin skyward toward the sun peering unconcerned through the boiling smoke. Sun to sky to earth, the unceasing, unchanging cycle of nature beyond the grasp of the ravening Old Man in his prison. No matter how high The Ancient reached, it could never eat the sun.

Nor utterly destroy the Mother without killing itself. Awareness of the absurdity of The Ancient's quest burst through Jetta. And all at once her center was *there* in a cool rush of strength smelling of riverbanks and sun-warmed grass and a sense of depths of stone underfoot, an ineffable connection to the one thing greater than the Old Man that lay within her reach.

In sheer, bone-deep relief she surrendered to the power bubbling up through her and began to dance again atop the outcrop, but this time not as a child danced, half in instinct, half in the carefully remembered movements drummed in by masters. This time she pulled each movement around her like a cloak, mining it for its power as Delvers mined the earth beneath her. Patterns. It was all about patterns, from the very Beginning of all things. Intent, she wrapped herself into the Dance, feeling her way toward new patterns, shaped from very old movements.

Down the slope, Farahk was methodically making more black spots from dead *hysths*. Grimly Jetta set out to widen that circle of victory. She killed a *hysth* in front of her with a spinning step into the fifth movement of the Second Rank master's dance, using the swirling vigor of it to spin fire back on itself. The imperious downward sweep of both arms from their highest skyward reach in the sixth movement of Third Rank pulled tongues of flame earthward, foiling their quest to snatch the wind; she built on that with the downward push of First Rank, eliciting a coughing roar of rage from The Ancient that set her smiling in grim satisfaction. Jetta advanced on another *hysth* and faltered as the east wind rose at her back, pushing past her. It drove the fire in on itself in swirling confusion, scattering *hysths* running backward away from the dual menace of Firedancer and Windrider. Exulting in its confusion, Jetta leaped to dance it still tighter, launching herself high over crawling flame, turning in the air, curling it back from its outward rush.

She came down from a series of leaps that carried her halfway across the slope toward the north, pulling fire inward as she went, and paused, panting, to squint through the smoke. For one instant she rejoiced, seeing a swathe of smoking ground in her wake, fire-free. And then she saw the danger of success, as *hysth* joined to *hysth*, building a wall of fire half as tall as the ridge itself, a column of seething flame towering up and up, caught in the maelstrom where west wind met east and neither could gain supremacy.

A deep, coughing roar shook the mountain. She saw the flames build themselves into a shape, a wavering, hulking thing of fire and smoke, reaching up the slope with an arm of flame to touch the ground beyond the barren space of withered greenery wrought by Jetta and Farahk. The wind fought it, shredding the arm into blazing trails, but still it reached inexorably against the power of the Windriders, caught a stray flicker of the west wind, and rode it into the trees at the top of the ridge.

Fire exploded in a circle of ruin around the slim, pale figures on their separate outcrops above her. Jetta screamed as nightmare became real and both disappeared behind a red wall that turned almost instantly to pale gold.

"Dance, Jetta!" Farahk roared behind her.

She danced, for Sheshan's life, for Wyth's, in anger and wild, driving fear. She spun recklessly across the blackened ground, screaming defiance into the Old Man's face. Dimly she became aware of another figure dancing above her, unbound hair swirling like a black curtain, but she had eyes only for the hand of the Old Man pressing in on the Windriders. A ragged chant formed itself in her head and shaped the rhythm of her steps. For Setham. For Annam. For Kori. Sheshan. For Setham. For Annam. For Kori. Sheshan!

For Setham, for Annam, for—

The east wind faltered and died. A scream reached her through the crackle of dying trees. The Old Man started to laugh, as she had heard it laugh at Setham, a deep, rising roar of triumph. Jetta saw fire leap onto the west wind unchecked and flung up her arms with a shriek of defiance and rage and grief.

"Sheshan!"

Fire fell and exploded around her. She gave it no chance to root itself. Anger killed it as it fell, but there was too much, spread too wide. The *hysths* up the slope ran to reinforce it, building new walls as quickly as she battered down the old. She glimpsed Farahk dancing beside her, his face running with sweat. Then the curtain of fire above her parted, and she saw a pale, tottering figure coming out of the flames, stumbling after another whose skin gleamed gold under a nightfall of dark hair.

Kettori stepped as lightly as a girl through the maze of small *hysths* shying back in front of her. Jetta recognized the dance, the Fourth Rank forms she had been studying for so long. *No*, she thought breathlessly. The Old Man knew those, knew how to counter them, knew the old forms.

Fire rippled down the wind. Kettori spun to face it, and froze when the movement failed to deflect it. Jetta watched her retreat a step, saw the Windrider behind her crumple to the ground.

Kettori stopped, staring into the face of the Old Man. Then all at once her chin lifted. She swept her hair back and raised her arms, screaming, "You know my name, Ancient! Here I am!"

The maelstrom of fire pulled itself into a tight column with two arms reaching toward the old Dancer. Almost gently they closed on her as Kettori stood with eyes fixed on the heart of doom. Her hair caught, a puff of yellow, and then she flung herself into the fire's embrace, dancing, as once she must have danced as a girl, dancing the Dance Jetta had dared her to dance for a village that had opened its doors to her, that had *not* surrendered to fire.

Horrified, Jetta flung out her arm—to stop Kettori, to help, she scarcely knew—but The Ancient roared and shied back, instinct maybe, fear, or perhaps bewilderment. Fire flattened and sucked back the smoke and flame all over the slope as though Kettori had, after all, found some form of the Dance the Old Man respected. For a breathless second Jetta hoped, and came up on her toes to broaden that retreat— and then the Old Man breathed out a wordless, consuming thunder of fury and snatched at Kettori with arms of white fire. She disappeared into the maw of flame, a living torch crumpling to ruin.

Something moved on Jetta's right; she tore her gaze from Kettori's end and spun toward the Windrider lying in the tiny clear space Kettori had made. He tried to crawl away, and collapsed onto his face, pale hair streaked with black trailing forlornly over the ashy ground. Jetta hurried to catch his shoulder. He rolled over, coughing fit to tear his lungs out, and Jetta's heart died within her.

Wyth.

Farahk loomed out of the smoke. Screaming in grief and rage, Jetta thrust the Windrider at him and turned back to face the Old Man. Above her on the left, Delvers fought with axe and shovel and bare hands to stop the smaller flames running up the slopes, a swarm of activity she only dimly saw through smoke that turned everything to shadows writhing in some obscene and futile dance. Below her, The Ancient burned in a column of pure, unadulterated white fire too hot even for smoke, for everything that might have protested its coming had vanished into its pitiless maw. Grimly Jetta walked toward the wavering, melting shimmer eating the whole slope, ignoring Farahk's "Jetta, no!" behind her and a confused tangle of shouting on her left. The Ancient had stolen her heart twice. All she had left was revenge.

Power thrummed up through her, setting every muscle, every hair, vibrating in time. Her hands lifted. Her arms bent into an arc that belonged to no form of the Dance she knew. Her feet began to move, finding footholds on the scorched and smoking earth and stone as easily as if she danced in the storehouse on level flagstones beside Setti. Setti! Jetta set his name from her mind, from her heart, lest the Old Man hear it, and began to chant again—low, furious, defiant.

"For Setham. For Annam. For Kori. *Sheshan!*" She screamed it and spun into the Dance, aware of white-hot, destructive arms shooting up the slope again, reaching to surround her impudence and crush it. She pulled the chant around her like an iron cloak, holding heat and fear at bay. "For Setham. For Annam. For *Kori.* Shesh-"

"JETTA!"

A Delver voice roared her name. Something huge and heavy crashed past her and fell sprawling on the hot ashes. Twin cries of pain shocked her to a standstill, one deep, one lighter, and so familiar her gut cramped. Rununn scrambled to his knees at her feet, coughing in desperate, racking heaves, half dead from smoke. Somehow, he heaved himself up, bouncing from foot to foot in pain, his boots smoking.

"I have brought help, Jetta ak'Kal!" he gasped, reaching to pull Setti to his feet.

"Fool!" Jetta yelled at him. She coughed, her lungs suddenly stinging with smoke, and shoved him away toward the cleaner air, out of the intense heat licking even at her now that the Dance no longer held it at bay. "Get *out!*" she screamed, reaching her hand down to Setti, but Setti only stumbled out of her grasp and started to dance, a clumsy, shambling thing with no hope of achieving anything but the Old Man's scorn. His sling was missing, his left arm clenched hard against his ribs, his gold skin streaked with dirt and sweat and smoke, but still he danced, and confused flame fled around him.

Rununn stumbled to his knees, coughing so hard it strangled his sharp cry of pain as his knees plunged onto fire-cracked windstone. He struggled to rise, tears streaming down his smoke-stained cheeks, his great moon eyes squinted to slits against the smoke and heat. Jetta faltered halfway through a turn, her vision filled with smoke and flame racing to form a circle around this blackening spot. Up the slope, a hundred Delvers scattered in panic from flames leaping up from nowhere, aiming to consume them as The Ancient had consumed Kettori. She saw Nuurn leap an outcrop and fall; Huunall trying to rally them; young Hunnood running with fire flapping from his shirt tail. Fire stalked them, gleeful and close.

Frantic, Jetta spun completely around, assessing the fire's reach nearer at hand. Only one tiny, shrinking gap in the circle of fire remained around Rununn—across the slope, on the opposite side of this small clear space from the endangered Delvers.

"*Run,* Rununn!" she screamed at him, whirling to shove her hands outward toward the flame trying to trap the panicking Delvers. She caught one glimpse of Rununn surging to his feet, his face turned toward her, grim, determined, *trusting* her to force the Old Man to bend to her will as she had in the meadow. *Run,* she bade him in agony, and spun away to drive the flames away from those hundred, a third of Annam's miners, a loss to make the Vale a place of mourning for decades, with uncounted ripples far into the lowlands if the flow of containment stone from these mines slowed to a trickle.

Setti, too, had seen the danger; he was trying one-handed to shove the flames away from the Delvers, down the slope into the argent fury of The Ancient. Jetta heard The Ancient roaring, laughing, and forgot everything in white fury to match the Old Man's contempt. She leaped in front of Setti as she had done twice before, and danced a slower Dance, matched to his rhythms, mirroring his one-handed reaches. With her left arm trapped against her she felt off-balance, awkward, slow, but still the Dance boiled and surged around her, a column of power to match The Ancient. She abandoned any attempt to form perfect movements and simply let it buoy her up like the waters in Anual's bath chamber, her eyes in constant movement from Setti to the flames to the Delvers. She stamped a foot, and a towering *hysth* died in front of her; Setti kicked into a leap, and fire died in a puff of ash and smoke on his right. She caught a glimpse of his face, set and grim and determined, as she had watched him dance on the hill above Firehome for all those years, refusing defeat.

Ah, Setti, they will sing your name to the end of time.

She wove a protective circle around him, the pair of them dancing closer and closer to the trapped Delvers, and everywhere the fire fled, except for the white arms of The Ancient closing the deadly ring around them both. Flame flattened and died on her right; Delvers hauled fallen comrades up and fled through the gap. Jetta threw back her head and laughed in the Old Man's face, shoving her right hand downward toward the hulking inferno above Wind Point. She caught a glimpse of Setti reaching too, but up the slope, his scarred palm upward as though taking the fire's febrile hand.

And wind curled over her fingers, ruffled loose hair around her face, cooled the ravening breath of the Old Man across her skin. A solid hand of air pushed past her down the slope, flattening the smoke, blowing ash and debris across the argent purity of the rings of molten heartfire. Flames blew back onto blackened ground where no more fuel remained to feed its greed. The Ancient's laughter changed to a roar of rage as the wind flung itself into the face of fire and swept all before it.

Jetta danced, cradled in wind, backed by Setti mirroring her moves, by Farahk creating his own deadly Dance farther down on her left, by Delvers defying The Ancient's advance up the slope behind her. Stepping from stone to withered grass to ash, stamping, spinning, weaving the intricate, floating steps of the Fourth Rank with movements snatched from every Dance she knew, she drove the ravening *hysths* ahead of her down the slope. They ran together; she broke them apart. They stood and hissed defiance; she forced them back. What pattern she danced she did not know, caught into a wild, unthinking rhythm born of flame itself. Where it flared, she quenched it, point counterpoint, driven by instinct that was the reason for her existence. And step for step, leap for leap, Setti mirrored her, seeming to pluck intention from her mind, imitating every move in his one-handed way, confusing the flame everywhere he turned.

The ring never closed. The reaching white destruction faltered, cooled, and died where it lay as Jetta advanced step by spinning step down the slope, not feeling the heat, not smelling the smoke, caught into the puissant magic of the Beginning, the only law The Ancient knew. The only law it must obey. The white column that had been the Old Man broke apart into a score of *hysths* running from a widening dark spot in the heart of the fire.

Still locked in mirror rhythm with Setti, she watched the remnant shrink and shrink amid a confused cracking and rumbling and thrashing roars, until all at once the mountain collapsed in front of her and Setti's hand snatched her back a step from falling with it.

They fled up the slope and stopped, clinging to each other, staring wide-eyed into the ruins of Wind Point. Below on the left, Farahk appeared, driving the remnants of flame toward the dark walls of Huunall's firetrap. Pitilessly he danced them into the embrace of containment stone, and finished them with a child's gesture, the very first movement of the Dance from First Rank long ago, a stamp and clap of his hands as though snuffing a candle. The last *hysth* wavered and puffed out, and only smoke still moved across the top of Wind Point.

Jetta stood, panting and spent, bracing Setti, or perhaps he was bracing her, the both of them shaking with exhaustion. Gradually the silence reached her, a hush comprised of the absence of flame and wind. An absence of life. A great racking sob broke from her on the knowledge that death had visited on her watch still again, that she had not saved what she had sworn to save, that Annam must mourn as Setham had.

As she must.

All at once Setti let her go, depriving her of support so unexpectedly she stumbled. Hands caught her shoulders, bracing her up. *Two* hands, unburned, long-fingered, pale as spider silk.

"Jetta! Hush now, oh, hush. I'm here."

Arms clad in soot-streaked white caught her close. Absurd cloth feathers waved in her face. A strong heartbeat pounded against one ear; in the other Sheshan's voice said, "Stubborn woman. Will you have me now?"

Twenty Six
Aftermath

For a time she could never afterward measure, she stood in the circle of Sheshan's arms trying to absorb his living presence, breathing in the smoke stink clinging to the layered cloth and listening to the impossible thunder of his heart. Gradually other noises intruded: deep Delver voices calling up and down the slope, the sad *ka-whump!* of a tree belatedly surrendering to the Old Man's livid touch, the sharp pop and crackle of windstone cooling. Somewhere a long moan began, low and mournful, building like the rising of a storm wind around the stony corners of Annam's houses.

"Ah, no," Sheshan whispered over her head.

Jetta stiffened in his arms and looked up at him. He looked exhausted, the pure alabaster of his skin tinged with gray under the smoke grime. Tears leaked from sky-colored eyes offended by smoke and soot, but the look on his face told her grit alone was not the reason. She remembered the trapped Delvers, and turned upslope, fearing what she might see, but it was not distant bodies that drew her eye, but Setti on his knees amid the blackened remnants of living forest, wreathed in thin curls of smoke, his good hand reaching toward a long, motionless lump half covered in ash.

A whimper forced its way up from Jetta's throat. "Rununn!" She tried to break away from Sheshan but he caught her back, turning her bodily away from the sight of moon eyes staring blankly from a young and bewildered face.

"No! NO!" Jetta's triumph crashed to grief, for the Old Man had won after all. "No, Sheshan, ah no oh no!"

He caught her close and bowed his head over hers, his lips against her hair. "Don't, my heart, oh don't. It was not your choice but his—"

She tried to draw back, her fists clenched in helpless fury that needed an outlet. The Ancient was gone, vanquished, turned to smoke and heat writhing up from a crater over seven collapsed levels of tunnels. But still it had won. "He *trusted* me!" she screamed at Sheshan. "He trusted me to keep him safe—"

"And so did they," he said gently, turning her bodily toward myriad tall figures drifting out of the smoke, coughing, black with soot, some nursing burns, broken limbs, bleeding heads, but alive. Scores of them, stumbling across the hot ground, dazed, unable to take in the fact of their survival. Alive.

Jetta stood in numb and helpless sorrow, unable to rejoice, not with Setti trying vainly to brush the marks of fire's victory from Rununn's face, his own streaked with tears and sweat. Mercifully, Sheshan stepped in front of her, blocking her view, and then simply folded his arms around her and cradled her close.

"This is not Setham, my heart," he whispered. "There was never any chance of saving them all from the time The Ancient burst into the open. Rununn—" He faltered. "Rununn *carried* Setti up that horrendous trail, because Setti would have killed himself trying to get up here alone, and because Rununn knew you needed help. Were it not for the pair of them, I would be dead."

Jetta stiffened in his arms, remembering Wyth stumbling alone out of the smoke behind Kettori. "Setti Danced you clear."

"Yes."

"No one ever entirely wins against The Ancient, daughter of my sister," Farahk said quietly beside her. "But you came closer than anyone ever has. Rejoice in what was saved. Rununn, too, wanted Annam to live."

She turned her head to look at his tired face, blackened with smoke, his skin dull with it. But his eyes, black and alert, watched her with the same steady, unflinching gaze she had associated with him from earliest childhood. The look of mastery, that gave nothing, not even sorrow, to the Old Man.

The sound of Delver grief, deep as the winter storm winds, throbbed in her ears. But mixed with it were quiet, joyful cries as fathers discovered sons alive, women found lifemates undamaged, brothers recognized living sisters under the grime. She heard Anual give a shrill yelp of joy, and Nuurn's gruff, "What, no cookies? What have you been doing all morning, woman?"

Jetta snorted despite the awful lump in her stomach. Sheshan's lips curved into a smile against her hair. "Look forward, my heart. The future is the legacy of the living, else what is all this for?"

She sighed and lifted her head; he seized the opportunity to kiss her, his lips warm against hers, tasting of salt and smoke. Jetta stiffened in surprise, and then melted against him in sudden hot confusion as Anual's clear cackle lifted behind her, a little shrill, slightly hysterical, but audible down the whole slope.

"And that's about time, Sheshan ak'Kal!"

~ ~ ~

Annam lost seven of its own and Kettori. Every one of them a great loss and a reason to grieve.

Jetta spent most of the first night sitting on the chill stone of her window sill, breathing the clean scent of the flowers nodding in the box and quietly fingering Rununn's little carved Dancer. Brave, loyal Rununn, who would never now use the tools he had bought with the earnings from his joyful little people. *Why him?* she mourned, watching the moons rise together over the eastern ridge, as brilliant as a young Delver's eyes peering at her from the dark that first night by the river. Of all the people on that slope, why her first friend in Annam, her sheltering mountain?

Why any of them? the cold and ruthless part of her wanted to know, the part that coldly made impossible choices, the part that looked back from the silver mirror behind her door. The Firedancer. The master. Even yet, sitting there, she could feel the slight tingle of *connection,* a faint, lingering sense of the Mother that refused to fade now that the immediate need was past. It surprised her even as its implications disquieted her. Like Setti, she had passed beyond some unseen barrier. And like Setti, she had paid in pain.

Wyth survived, as Wyth did, unsmiling and nursing a burn that would scar his face as a nameless village on the plain had scarred his heart. But Jetta, watching him coldly fending off Finnua's salves and sympathy, thought he would wear it like a rank badge, earned defending the one place that had ever accepted him without a second look.

And maybe, someday, he would learn to trust enough that his first instinct would not be to fight alone, risking no betrayals.

She sat between Sheshan and Setti on the north bank above the waterfall on the tenth day after Wind Point collapsed into a cauldron of smoke and flame, watching Farahk and the Circle dance fire into the veins of windstone that were Annam's death warrant should the Old Man try again. Below their feet the stream thundered over the drop, unchanging, soothing in its immutability. High above, a different waterfall from the flume the Delvers had shifted eastward poured the chill of melting glaciers into the pit above the untouched doors at Wind Point, drowning whatever remained of fire in the tunnels. Already the Delvers were cutting stone for a tall marker to stand above it, that would, Nuurn had assured her gravely, immortalize both Delver and Dancer. Jetta shivered, thinking of Kettori, whose bones lay somewhere in that crater, wrapped in the ashes of the ruined veins that could never again carry The Ancient up to threaten the far side of the ridge. Where had she found the courage to embrace the flames she feared?

Sheshan's arm went around her. "This will work," he said encouragingly.

"I know." She slid an arm around each lean waist and hugged them close. Sheshan kissed her hair; Setti sighed, watching Wyth and the other Windriders directing the steady south wind onto the fire as the seven masters of the Circle drove flame mercilessly into the stone. Watching them awed even Jetta. She had never seen the Circle Dance; at once she understood why these few had been chosen. The controlled grace in every position, arms arching as one, legs thrusting them skyward together in the flowing intricacies of Fifth Rank, not one an instant before or behind the beat, made them look as though they shared a single mind, a single body.

"Old Man Fire," Setti murmured. "In all my wildest imaginings I would never have thought to see wind aiding the Dance. Nor be glad to call it myself, either."

He looked over her head at Sheshan, who turned his head at the same instant. Jetta said nothing, thinking about Setti stretching out his hand as he danced his strange, inimitable dance above Wind Point. Neither of them would speak of what happened before that, when Setti plunged into fire on Kettori's heels and brought out the Windrider he could have left to die. Jetta guessed that courage, or stubbornness, or even pride had not been enough in that Dance; had Kettori not checked The Ancient for that one, crucial moment, they would have died together. Jetta had nightmares about it. Yet some thin but steel-strong chain of accord had been forged in those flames, maybe strengthened by shared grief for Rununn, who had made survival possible for so many.

Delvers crossed the bridge below them in a steady stream, many sporting bandages, all of them round-eyed and tense with grief and hope. Not one blinked at sight of the three of them sitting so closely entwined, as though such sights were only to be expected when The Ancient had turned all things upside down. Jetta no longer cared what anyone thought. The entire Circle had arrived, spoken with Farahk, and awarded her Fourth Rank on the spot. It meant nothing. How could rank change anything when the whole world was burning? Clan differences seemed equally trivial. She looked up at the calm, alabaster face above her, and no longer saw a Windrider but simply the man she loved.

Fire drove deep into the windstone, driven by a steady wind fanned by the Windriders standing in a half-circle well clear of the fire. Delvers sat or stood on the slopes, watching in stony silence as the beautiful pale stone withered and blackened, scarring the meadow for all time. No one had argued the need. Even Burrood's faction could not lay the deaths of seven Delvers at Jetta's feet. The blackened row of trees at the top of the ridge stood as a mute reminder of the disaster so narrowly prevented.

The sun slid overhead and balanced itself above Wind Point and still the wind blew and the Dance went on, the Circle taking turns now, driving the flames back from every darting attempt at escape, deeper and deeper into the stone.

Finally, as shadows began to merge in the Vale, it was over. A line of withered grass wandering across the meadow marked the heat rising from the dying vein of windstone below. No more could The Ancient follow it stealthily into the heart of Annam Vale; if fire rose again within the village, it would come from heartstones heaved from the depths, and those she could handle.

Sheshan's arm tightened around her. Jetta scrambled up at sight of Norlahk advancing on her, backed by Farahk and thin, fire-eyed Kekkali, eldest of the Fifth Rank masters of the Circle. Jetta envied Kekkali the weight of silvering hair tipping her head back toward the great knot of it at her neck, but nothing else. Whatever ambition she had once nursed had died on Wind Point.

Norlahk stopped in front of her as Sheshan and Setti stood up too. She felt an uneasy quiver go through Sheshan as the black on black eyes lifted toward them. Norlahk regarded them silently for a moment, and then bowed his head in a gesture that included them all.

"You have done well in Annam, Jetta ak'Kal, Settak ak'Kal. As we knew you would."

Setti straightened with a jerk. "Ak'Kal? Me?"

The midnight eyes seemed not to move, but Norlahk smiled. "One *does* attain rank for mastering the *Dance*, ak'Kal."

Setti stuttered something inarticulate and lapsed into quivering silence. Jetta hugged him and let him go, facing Norlahk with simmering anger bursting out on the only target she had left.

"Setti nearly died earning that rank, ak'Kal. Could you not have told us what danger lay here before you sent us in so unprepared?"

His black eyebrow drifted up. "Unprepared? You are Dancers. You knew there was fire here. What else can you prepare for?"

Anger blasted through Jetta. "You could have warned me the Old Man was behaving oddly!"

Kekkali said, "You already knew it, from the time it took Kori. If we had given you our suspicions, would you have seen the truth on your own? The truth that turned out to be different from what we thought it was? We guessed that The

Ancient's cage was weakening. Kettori ak'Kal's guesses nine years ago helped us to that conclusion. Your insistence that The Ancient had trapped Kori, an experienced Dancer, made us face the possibility that the strictures of the Dance were failing. How could we know what form the Dance should take, save to send the best of us out to face the Old Man with no preconceptions?"

Jetta glared at the three of them, so complacent in their decisions. "And what have you learned? I cannot tell what forms Setti and I danced, or in what combination. The pattern is no pattern. That is the only truth I have learned this summer."

Norlahk nodded sharply. "As have we all. We have become too rigid, too bound to the forms of Second Rank, or Fourth Rank—or Fifth. We had forgotten that change is the only constant in the world. Our carelessness let the Old Man learn too much, and we have paid in death and mourning. No more. The children will learn to dance fire as Jetta ak'Kal dances, as Setti ak'Kal will dance again—by opening their minds to the call of flame. We are bound to it; it is in our blood, and when we deny it we end like Kettori, fleeing truth."

"Oh, well done," Sheshan whispered beside her.

Norlahk tilted his head up again, his eerie eyes searching the Windrider's face. "This was unexpected," he said to no one in particular. "I await the outcome with interest."

Jetta lifted her chin, but Norlahk was already turning away, striding with his floating step down toward the bridge. Kekkali followed; Farahk lingered a moment longer.

"Well done, daughter of my sister." His eyes flicked to Sheshan and back to her face. "Settak ak'Kal, there are questions I would ask, if you've time."

Setti, still looking a bit stunned, leaned down and kissed Jetta's cheek. "Who am I to say no?" he said to Farahk, but his eyes were on hers, a clear and even brown now, and so steady that tears leaped to Jetta's eyes.

"Go and explain to them how a one-armed Dancer defeated The Ancient," she said. "I certainly can't."

Setti's face loosened into the merry grin of the boy who had walked with her from Annam. "If I figure it out, you'll be the first to know."

He walked away beside Farahk, his arm in a sling but his

stance no longer hunched, or deferent, or shy. Jetta smiled for the first time in days.

"Well," Sheshan said after a moment.

She looked up into his bemused face. "What?"

"Wind and Fire. Who could have imagined?"

Jetta's mouth quirked up. "Setti spent a good deal of time imagining it. He will always be ahead of me, I think. Will you mind?"

"You expect *me* to dance flame with you, Jetta ak'Kal?"

She chuckled and burrowed against him, listening to the quiet thunder of his heart under her ear. "No. I only expect you to stay with me."

"Setti stayed with you in the heart of flame. And he makes you laugh." A faint, faint question still rode his voice.

Jetta looked up at his lean face etched against the sky, framed in a cloud of bone-pale hair. "But *he* does not know when to be silent."

Something flickered in Sheshan's eyes. He nodded, slowly, his gaze turning inward. And just as slowly a smile spread from his lips to his eyes and warmed his whole face. He leaned down and kissed her, not with passion, but with infinite tenderness.

Jetta, breathless, drew back and stared at him through the rippling black wave of her hair winding around them both. "Will our children be Riders or Dancers?"

He looked down at her, his face suddenly so still it frightened her. Then his shy smile bloomed and lit the whole day. "I don't know, but I'm going to have Nuurn carve us a fireproof cradle. Just in case."

She chuckled, and heard it echoed deep in his chest. For one instant Kori's ghost rose up in a vivid memory of hearing his laughter rumbling against her ear like this; Jetta swallowed hard and banished it. Surreptitiously she slipped the silver bracelet from her wrist and slid it into the pocket of the yellow shirt Anual had made from drover cloth. *Goodbye, my love,* she thought in sorrow. A sorrow no longer sharp, but a deep and distant ache. She felt it like she felt The Ancient sleeping in his prison and lifted her face to the future.

The story continues in *Windrider,* coming from
B-Cubed Press Spring, 2019

ABOUT THE AUTHOR

S. A Bolich is a fulltime freelancer with a number of published fantasy stories as well as many nonfiction articles. A native of Washington state, she resides there again after serving six years in Germany as a regular army military intelligence officer. She graduated summa cum laude from college with a degree in history, which she confesses was greatly aided by devouring historical fiction of every era and kind through her formative years. Her first novel, *Firedancer*, is due out in September 2018. Her short fiction has appeared in *Beneath Ceaseless Skies, On Spec, Damnation Books*, and *Defending the Future IV: No Man's Land*, among others, and is upcoming in *Tales of Moreauvia* and *Witches and Pagans*. Currently she is working on *Windrider*, the sequel to *Firedancer*, as well as an alternate history series using an unexplored explanation of what really happened in Salem, Massachusetts in 1692.

S. A. Bolich was born and raised in Washington State, where she returned after many years traveling the U.S. and the world. As a regular Army military intelligence officer, she saw a great deal of Germany from the front seat of a jeep, back when the Iron Curtain still defined "East" and "West". Her favorite places remain, however, the high-up meadows of the Cascade Mountains where she has often traveled by horse. Over the years she has been a teacher, a project manager, a riding instructor, and a good many other things, but always a writer. A history major, much of her work is informed by the jaw-dropping details of real history (you really can't make that stuff up), bent in any number of creative ways, and a boundless love for the wild places of the world.

ABOUT THE ARTIST

Sara Codair, the cover designer, is also a talented writer. They live with a cat, Goose, who "edits" their work by deleting entire pages. They teach and tutor at a community college, write when they should be sleeping, and read every speculative novel they can get their hands on.

Sara's debut novel, *Power Surge*, will be published by NineStar Press on October 1, 2018.

Find Sara online at https://saracodair.com/ or @shatteredsmooth.